The Binding

Also by E.Z. Rinsky

Palindrome

The Binding

A Lamb and Lavagnino Mystery

E.Z. RINSKY

WITNESS
IMPULSE

An Imprint of HarperCollinsPublishers

Excerpt from *Palindrome* copyright © 2016 by Ephraim Rinsky.

THE BINDING. Copyright © 2017 by Ephraim Rinsky. All rights reserved. Printed in the United States of America. No part of this book may be used or reproduced in any manner whatsoever without written permission except in the case of brief quotations embodied in critical articles and reviews. For information, address HarperCollins Publishers, 195 Broadway, New York, NY 10007.

Digital Edition JULY 2017 ISBN: 978-0-06-249546-4

Print Edition ISBN: 978-0-06-249545-7

WITNESS logo and WITNESS IMPULSE are trademarks of HarperCollins Publishers in the United States of America.

HarperCollins is a registered trademark of HarperCollins Publishers in the United States of America and other countries.

FIRST EDITION

17 18 19 20 21 LSC 10 9 8 7 6 5 4 3 2 1

For Da,
Who's still teaching me about people.

Twenty Years Ago

BECKY WAS CROUCHING in the alley behind the Rocky Mountain Bar and Grill, smoking a cigarette next to the dumpster, when the back door creaked open and her manager Elaine stuck her head out.

"He's here again."

"Who?" Becky asked, shooting to her feet, already knowing the answer. She tossed her unfinished cigarette to the ground and smoothed out her apron.

"The creepy guy. And he just asked for you."

Becky's heart thumped hard beneath her dark green button-up.

"Creepy guy?" Becky instinctually feigned confusion. She hadn't told Elaine yet about what happened with Oliver last Friday night. How he met her as she was leaving the restaurant after her shift and tried to kiss her. She had instinctively flinched, backed away, and apologized. He'd just smiled and said he understood completely. No harm done. When she rejected boys in school they got angry at her. But Oliver had respected her decision, which made Becky feel guilty she'd said no.

If she mentioned what happened, Elaine would flip out and overreact. Probably ban him.

Becky didn't want him banned. She liked talking to him. The stuff he said made her think. Sometimes he was funny, sometimes he was serious, and sometimes Becky couldn't tell. A few nights before the Friday incident, she'd been sweeping the tile floor, and had maybe lingered a little longer than she'd had to by his table. He'd ignored her at first, focused on the page in front of him, but then had suddenly glanced up, locked his bright white eyes on her, and told her that there's a certain hell where you have to sweep a floor with a broom that loses a few of its bristles every time you use it. So you have to keep sweeping up the bristles that are falling off.

Sad story, she'd said, hoping she sounded clever.

Don't blame me. I didn't write it.

Oh?

God wrote it. I think it's his idea of a joke. Do you believe in God?

Yeah.

Do you believe that He can do anything?

I guess . . .

So answer me this: Can God create a rock so heavy that He can't lift it?

She'd thought about that question all night, and still wasn't sure if the question was supposed to be funny, serious or both.

Elaine folded her thick arms in front of her chest and said, "You know who I'm talking about."

"Oh, Oliver?" She ground out her cigarette with the toe of a Reebok sneaker as an excuse to avoid Elaine's wilting gaze. "He asked for me? What do you mean?"

"I asked him what he wanted, and he said he wasn't hungry. Just wanted to talk to Becky. He didn't even ask if you were working tonight. He already knew. Creepy, Becky. I'm gonna page Joe. This is a whole other level. I'm going to ban him."

Becky gathered her long brown hair and tied it back into a tight ponytail, per Rocky Mountain waitress regulations.

"He's actually really interesting once you start talking to him," she replied quietly. The ghostly falsetto of a Backstreet Boys tune hung in the alleyway. Becky's uniform—sticky from the pre-storm humidity—clung to her body. She didn't need a close inspection to know she had some pretty serious pit stain action happening. The uniforms were ugly, starchy, and the kind of cheap acrylic that didn't let your skin breathe, but at least they were dark.

"Becky," Elaine sighed. "You're young. You don't know about the line."

"Yes I do."

"Fine. You *know* about it, but you don't have the intuition for it. I've been in customer service for longer than you've been alive, and I know the difference between customers who are friendly, *really* friendly even, and the ones who are bad news. And this guy, the way he looks at you when you're walking back to the kitchen, you don't even understand."

Becky thought: *If Elaine knew about last Friday, she'd call the cops.*

"Relax," Becky said, squeezing past the much larger woman into the kitchen. She hardly smelled the sizzling onions and burning grease anymore; probably because the smells followed her home every day after her shift; nestling in her hair, clothes and skin like parasites.

She pulled her ponytail tighter, wiped some sweat off her brow with a paper towel. Breathed deep, then pushed through the cantina-style swinging wood doors. There was Oliver sitting in the same booth he had every single evening since Becky had been hired fourteen months ago. Every night he ordered the same thing from her: rib eye steak with fries, and an extra side of fries.

These greasy things will be the end of me, he said each time she brought him his food, but would dig in greedily all the same.

But tonight was different. And it wasn't just that he hadn't ordered any food, Becky realized. He wasn't writing.

For the first time she could remember, the book in front of him on the table was closed and his writing tools nowhere in sight. Every time previous he'd sat down and carefully prepared his protractor, ruler, drafting pencil, charcoal pencil, blue ink pen as if arranging a place setting, then immersed himself, losing all awareness of his surroundings, surfacing only for a bite of steak or fries.

She knew the tools well. He'd shown them to her on an evening a month or so ago, when it had just been the two of them in the restaurant for about twenty minutes.

Why don't you write with a plain pen like everyone else? Or on a typewriter?

These are the tools I'm used to. These are what every architect uses.

So that's your job? You're an architect?

I used to be.

Why did you stop? Did you not like it?

I loved it. But this book is more important.

Tonight, no tools. Just the book, closed, and him sitting expectantly.

He'd shaved off his beard. Without it, his smile felt unfiltered. He was handsome. She realized her thighs were trembling. His seat was beside the line of windows that looked out onto the mostly empty parking lot. An early moon hung over the mountains, and the Rocky Mountain Bar and Grill was glowing with soft red evening light. There was a family at the other end of the restaurant, near the door, and an older man at the bar. Elaine had followed Becky back inside, and was watching, concerned, from behind the bar.

"Hi Becky." Oliver grinned. "Take a seat."

He was staring at her more intensely than he ever had, the whites of his eyes so clear that they appeared translucent; two glowing jellyfish swimming in his skull. His small hands were clasped in the universal sign for both pleading and praying. It was hard to tell if his smile was a happy one.

"Becky, come on. We don't have long," he said, glancing at his watch. He said it playfully, but it was an order. Becky found herself obliging, butterflies in her stomach.

She thought: *Oh no. He wants to talk about what happened on Friday.*

"Hi," she managed weakly. "What's . . . Do you want to order . . ." She fumbled with her words.

Oliver laughed a little bit as she squirmed. In clear focus was the fact that, despite countless evening chats, she didn't really know anything about this man.

"I want to show you what I've been working on the last few years," he said.

"Um, okay," she said, relieved to be talking about anything besides the kiss that wasn't.

There were three identical volumes resting one atop the other on the greasy table, each without a proper binding, held together with twine. His slender fingers opened the top book to a page roughly in the middle and gestured for her to look inside. Becky stared into the book, for a moment, confused, then looked up at Oliver.

"I don't understand. It's nothing. It's not English. It's just shapes and lines . . ."

"You're right, it's not English." Oliver nodded. "It's written in the first language of men. It predates Arabic numerals by at least ten millennia. It's the language we wrote in before the Tower of Babel."

"You have three of them?"

"Yes. There will be twenty-four in the end."

"And this one . . ." Becky motioned to the top one, feeling stupid that she couldn't understand exactly what he was saying. "Is this the first one in the series?"

Oliver smiled.

"Wonderful question. No. The answer is that there is no first one in the series. When the twenty-four are complete, they will go in a circle. No beginning, no end."

What if Elaine is right . . . A cold started in Becky's toes and crept up her legs until she could barely feel anything below her waist. *It's nonsense. He's just drawing nonsense doodles all this time* . . . And yet, there was something so calm about his demeanor, so gentle and friendly in his gaze. He certainly didn't *act* like a crazy person.

"I—"

Elaine suddenly appeared beside the table.

"I'm going to page my husband." Elaine was leaning over the table, and the scowl on her huge face was more menacing than Becky would have believed her capable of.

"Elaine." Oliver grinned. "Relax. We're just talking."

"He's way bigger than you, and has a hell of a temper," Elaine snapped. "If you're still here by the time he gets here, he'll break you in half."

"I won't be."

"Get *out*."

Oliver cocked his head curiously at Elaine, as if struggling to comprehend the peculiar habits of this subhuman primate.

"Why don't you ask Becky what she'd like?" he suggested.

Elaine, face bright red, turned to Becky and gave her a look like *well?*

"Just . . . Elaine, we're just talking. It's okay."

Elaine took a deep breath through her nostrils. "*Alright* then," she said, and spun away toward the phone behind the bar. Oliver turned his attention back to Becky, apparently pleased by her loyalty.

"It's not nonsense," Oliver said, like he had read her mind. "You just don't read this language yet. But you will someday. This book is full of wonderful stories. You want to understand them, right?"

"I . . . guess. Yeah."

Oliver suddenly reached across the table. She stiffened as the tips of his fingers grazed her neck.

"Oliver," she whispered and tried to move away, but he was gripping the small silver crucifix she always wore around her neck. His smooth hands smelled strongly of anti-bacterial soap and something else . . . a salty smell she knew from the kitchen but couldn't place. Then he dropped the crucifix and sat back in the booth.

"You believe in God?" he asked, just as he had last week.

Unable to form words, she just nodded slightly. Somewhere far away Elaine was shouting into the phone.

"Me too." Oliver nodded quickly. "God, in his infinite kindness, created us. He did a very good job making this world. This city. This restaurant. You. Overall he did an excellent job. But not a *perfect* job." Oliver winked in the way that she usually found charming. But this time something indiscernible was happening to his face that was scaring Becky. His pupils were too dilated maybe? His nostrils flared open for deep, expectant breaths? "And that's what this book is. It's a way of taking advantage of God's little mistakes in order to subjugate him to my will. Do you understand?"

Becky nodded even though she didn't. Elaine returned, wielding a wooden broomstick.

"You need to leave," Elaine shouted at him, but her voice was wavering. The family at the other end of restaurant had gone quiet and was watching. The old man at the bar seemed disinterested.

"What happened to your man?" Oliver grinned. "What happened to being broken in half? Listen, I'm going soon. Relax, Elaine."

And then, when Elaine failed to relax, he pulled an eight-inch heavy-duty Phillips screwdriver from his bag and trained it on Elaine, the way a headmaster might aim his pointer at an unruly student.

"You need to leave us alone," he said sternly. "This evening has been meticulously planned. I only have a few more minutes before the police arrive. So you need to get back behind the bar."

Elaine backed away, perhaps noticing what Becky already had: The yellow handle of the screwdriver was flecked with fresh red specks. Not big drops, like from a bloody nose, but freckle-sized splatters that suggested a spewing fountain or high-pressured stream.

The family at the other end of the bar was silent. Oliver kept the screwdriver level with Elaine's chest.

"Go away," he said, his voice deep and resonant. And Elaine, whom Becky had never even considered capable of experiencing fear, slowly backed away.

Oliver turned back to Becky. Now white lights flashed in and out of her vision. Her whole body was trembling. Why was she still sitting here? Why hadn't she taken the opportunity, when he was distracted by Elaine, to shove out of the booth and run like hell?

"Moses, Jesus, Mohammed, and now me," he said. "But times have changed. And today, the difference is that we no longer need God. Unlike my predecessors, who spread his message, I have a message for him: Thank you for everything, but your services are no longer needed."

A wail in the distance. A siren. Becky's mind was near paralyzed with fear, unable to process what seemed to be meaningless syllables pouring from his mouth. But some part of her consciousness registered blinking blue and white lights approaching the restaurant.

Oliver slammed the book shut, and checked his watch.

"I'm going to prison now," he said, standing from the booth and gathering his three books and screwdriver into his bag. "It will take me some time to finish writing my books. But when I do, I will come for you and make you my queen and we'll read them together."

Warm tears streamed down Becky's cheeks. She couldn't speak.

Oliver looked out the window, as if to confirm that the police weren't running late. There were at least a dozen cars.

"Earlier this afternoon, I killed your family," he said, watching the police stream from their cars and point their weapons at the restaurant's facade. "Your parents and your brother. They would have just distracted you. You'll need to be alone—the lonely are the only ones who turn to prophets in their time. You'll understand this eventually."

Becky's vision went halfway dark. Elaine emitted a muffled scream from behind the counter. Becky managed to form only a gurgle.

"God created several rocks he can't lift. He can't lift them. But I can. I will," Oliver said, staring out the window at the dark mountains, face awash in the glow of blaring lights.

Amplified police voices outside. The restaurant filled with swirling primary colors. Under different circumstances, the normally dull interior of the Rocky Mountain Bar and Grill might have appeared unusually festive.

Oliver turned to Becky and looked at her with something like disappointment. "You shouldn't have said no to me, Becky."

Oliver raised his hands over his head and walked to the front door. Opened it with his hip, walked out, and smiled knowingly as he was tackled by four burly officers.

Part One

Sunday/Monday

Genesis 39: 20–23

Joseph's master took him and put him in prison, the place where the [Pharaoh's] prisoners were confined.

But while Joseph was there in the prison, the Lord was with him; he showed him kindness and granted him favor in the eyes of the prison warden. So the warden put Joseph in charge of all those held in the prison, and he was made responsible for all that was done there. The warden paid no attention to anything under Joseph's care, because the Lord was with Joseph and gave him success in whatever he did.

IT'S TWO THIRTY in the afternoon when I finally force myself from my bottom bunk. Feel gross from sleeping too much, as usual. Moths fluttering around in my skull.

The other seven bunks are empty. Bright-eyed kids backpacking through Europe, shooting out the front door with that miraculous optimism that accompanies waking up in a new city. They considerately left the shades drawn on the lone window in the dorm room; didn't want to disturb the token "guy who's way too old to be staying in a youth hostel."

I shuffle barefoot to the window and open the curtain. Rather than a full pane panorama of scenic Budapest, I'm treated only to the stuff that will never make the brochures: A decrepit prewar apartment building across the alley that looks like a clothing rack commercial—it's like air-drying rags is a passion project for these people. The fire escape that runs down the side of the building ends about twelve feet off the ground, and every morning (read: afternoon) that I see it I imagine a growing pile of broken-limbed lemmings fleeing a fire caused by spontaneously combusting piles of laundry.

On the ground level of the apartment is a closed metal grate covered in Hungarian graffiti and a spray-painted mural of Tupac. I can't read the faded letters above the grate, but after countless mornings of observation I've decided this shop used to be a bakery, based on what appears to be a cartoon muffin baked into an *e* on the defaced lettering over the entranceway.

Frank Lamb and the case of the abandoned store: solved.

Might not sound like much, but lately the old sense of deduction has been employed exclusively to decipher the alcohol content of foreign beers. In any case, this storefront now seems to be a favorite evening hangout for prostitutes.

I leave the window. Tread over bags spewing T-shirts and city maps. The walls in here are orange and brown with water damage. The wood of the bunk beds is warped and moldy. Faintly salty smell of urine and strong disinfectants.

This place is about as low as you can go, which makes it even more surprising that one of my bunk mates left his laptop case on his bed, concealed halfheartedly by a thin yellowing sheet. Does this kid think the simple fact that we're sharing a room in a hostel is enough to foster mutual trust? Does he not realize that the only requirement for a bed here is a face and the same quantity of Hungarian Monopoly money that buys two vacuum-packed cheese and eggplant sandwiches? Indeed, this kid would probably wet himself if he knew he was sharing a dorm room with me—a suspected murderer on Interpol's watch list. Based on the smell in here, maybe he was tipped off last night.

Nobody is in the hall. I enter the bathroom and flip on the lights. Take a deep breath of mildew. Sweet privacy in here, finally. Coed bathrooms, much like the fugitive life, aren't nearly as exciting as they sound. Freezing, cloudy water gurgles from the rusty spigot. I splash some water on my face. As has become a near daily ritual, I inspect my beard in the mirror and vow to buy a razor today on the way to *Voci*. It won't happen.

I steal a squeeze of toothpaste from someone else's tube, and am brushing my teeth halfheartedly when the best part of my day ends abruptly: The few moments before I start worrying about my daughter.

And now I'm back to thinking about how stilted our last phone call was; me consulting the notes I'd prepared, worried (justifiably it turns out) that another call might alienate her even further. Me refusing to tell her where I was—to protect her—then asking about school as if there's no outrageous subtext to this conversation. Hanging up after five minutes sweating and shivering. Sadie's getting old enough to question whether Dad is just a serious fuck-up; whether it might be in her best interests to cut her losses now and stop answering my monthly scripted calls.

That was three months ago, and I haven't dared call her since.

The toothbrush is dangling from my mouth, the head clenched between my teeth like leather during an old-time amputation. I spit a wad of toothpaste foam. Some gets caught in my beard.

My eyes feel droopy. I already want to go back to sleep. Sleep another few hours, pass another day. My brain again replays my conversation with Sadie, as it surely will dozens of times today, until I shut it up with booze. The last few years have been like sitting on a lounge chair that's resting on a tar pit. Can't feel the imperceptible changes day to day, but every time I bother to put down my Pilsner and look over the side I see I've sunk a little bit deeper.

That's the worst part. Being aware that my mind is fogging over, underperforming, and not doing anything about it. Used to be that picking up and moving hostels or cities would excite me a little bit, but now the routine is a well-worn groove. Still, assuming self-preservation remains a priority—that there's any self still worth preserving—I gotta force myself to move periodically. And I've already been in this hostel for six weeks, and Budapest for ten months, which is definitely too long.

I walk back to the dorm room, only now noticing how much

it absolutely reeks of unwashed man. I'm sure I deserve at least a little credit for that.

I pull my Velcro fanny pack out from under my pillow and count how much money I have left. Two thousand dollars, a little over a thousand Euros and about a hundred thousand in Hungarian funny money, which is only worth about three hundred bucks. Getting down there. I've probably got four more months before I have to do something drastic.

I pull on my only pair of jeans, a Pink Floyd T-shirt on its last legs and clip my money belt around my waist.

Voci for a few hours, then I'll come back here, pack and go to the train station.

The bunk across from mine has a few cans of cheap lager half hidden behind a suitcase. I grab two and head out.

PER ROUTINE, I stroll around the city for a few hours before *Voci*. I tell myself it's for exercise, but really it's because *Voci* doesn't open until six. I've already done all the museums; spent a few hours in each pretending like I was enjoying myself, picturing myself at some cocktail party a decade from now, recalling the entire Greta case and ensuing years for a rapt crowd of beautiful women. And when the women inevitably ask what Frank Lamb, professional hero, did in Europe, as he was hiding from the law, I'll casually explain that I actually took the time to really get to know art.

I'd divide my days between modern and classical, usually modern in the morning because it can be so stimulating that I find sleeping after it difficult. I guess I just figured . . . as long as I'm here in Europe, I should make the most of it, you know? Really be the best person I can be . . .

I descend the concrete steps on the Pest side of the Megyeri bridge, and find a shadowy place to add a few ounces of Lamb-processed lager to the great blue Danube.

The shallow climb back to the bridge leaves me embarrassingly out of breath. I pull my knockoff Ray-Bans down over my eyes and start the march over the bridge. A lot of families out; kids on summer break I guess. Some Scroogey part of me wishes for a spontaneous heavy rain, driving all these happy nuclear families indoors, where they can't remind me how far I am from being a healthy, productive member of society.

Instead the sun has no choice but to reluctantly bathe me in the warmth and light meant for everybody else. Parents chide kids spitting over the side of the bridge into the river. A young couple, of one mind, stops walking and embraces.

I wish I'd taken three beers.

I arrive at *Voci* ten minutes before it opens, and sit on a bench across the street. Someone left the sports page and I pick it up and pretend to read. I consider that since Hungarian uses more or less the same alphabet as English, I've always assumed that I knew how the words on the page sounded, even though I couldn't understand them. But what if a Hungarian *T* sounds like an English *B*? Or some sound that doesn't even exist in English? Hell, for all I know this newspaper is total gibberish, a joke that only locals are in on, and every time they see some schmuck pretending to read they elbow each other knowingly and snigger.

That's some seriously high level paranoia, Frank.

I wait another couple minutes, so I'm not the first one into *Voci*, and then drop the paper and cross the street. Spirits slightly aloft with the promise of distraction. Comfort washes over me as I push through the heavy oak doors. Return to the womb type sensation. Familiar musk of tobacco, old leather and spilled beer.

The gorgeous waitress who's here every day besides Saturday smiles at me.

"Hi Ben, welcome, yes," she says with a thick accent, the kind that used to make my heart flutter. Her hair is so black that it's almost tinged blue.

"Hi Ruth." I smile weakly, appreciating her pretending I don't smell awful from the walk over here.

"One here for you now," she says, pointing to a balding septuagenarian, head pecked with liver spots, sitting across from a backgammon board expectantly. I think we've played before, but I can't remember his name or his skill level.

"Thanks," I say, sitting down across from the man. He left me the booth, so I get to watch Ruth over his shoulder as we play.

"*Ötszáz frankot pontonként,*" the guy says, half to himself, as he arranges the pieces. He's got enough ear hair to knit a small blanket.

"*Angol?*" I reply. "English?"

He snorts and picks something out of his eye.

"One point five hundred forints," he says.

"Right, right. Sorry," I respond. Pretty standard stakes.

"Hmf."

He doesn't make eye contact with me once. Joylessly shakes his dice, rolls and moves. Collects his dice and readies himself for his next roll.

I move. Ruth brings me an espresso and double vodka without me asking, and grins in a way that's probably supposed to be flirtatious. Then swivels and retreats to the bar, hips seemingly swaying on their own accord, like they're their own distinct organism.

So why don't I feel anything?

This isn't the first time I've noticed this. If I'm being objective, she's absolutely gorgeous. Her blue eyes are the kind that inspire men to write symphonies. Her skin is like cream. But I only seem capable of appreciating her beauty in an abstract way. I feel nothing in my flesh, and this has increasingly concerned me.

"Eh?" my opponent grunts with impatience, as he studies his yellow fingernails.

"Sorry," I say, and roll.

We play for two hours or so. He's an automaton. Only time he betrays any emotional investment whatsoever is when I get outrageously lucky. He's up a few thousand francs when he looks at me for the first time. We're in the midgame, and he's slightly ahead. It's my turn to roll, and I'm shaking the dice, trying to think what roll I'm hoping for.

"*Zugzwang*," he says, smiling cruelly.

"Gesundheit," I respond.

"*Zugzwang*," he repeats. "You have *Zugzwang*."

I squint at him. "I don't understand."

"You also do chess?" he asks.

"No."

"*Zugzwang* . . . It mean every move you make . . ." He gesticulates moving pieces around. "Any move *fuck* you. Better not to move."

I stare at the board and suddenly understand what he's saying. My current position is decent. But any move I make will compromise it, leave me horribly vulnerable. My best strategy would be to pass—to not roll at all.

"Okay," I say, without rolling. "Your turn then. I pass."

He shakes his head slowly, a yellow-toothed grin.

"No, no. You *must*." He pantomimes rolling the dice.

I sigh, and oblige, ending up with a roll that's particularly bad. He takes an impish glee in my reluctant move.

"Every morning." He smiles to me. "Every morning, another *Zugzwang.*"

That's the last time he acknowledges that I'm anything other than a backgammon piñata filled with Hungarian currency. We play another half hour. Eventually, after handing me a particularly bad beat down, he wordlessly collects his cash and tobacco pouch, sidles out of the booth and out the door.

I linger in the warm depression in the booth my ass has been working on the last couple hours. I'm four vodkas and two espressos deep; about halfway toward a little fleeting bliss. I stare at Ruth, who's grinning and tossing her hair for another customer, and feel my forehead start to burn. Lower my gaze to my hands, shaking slightly from the caffeine.

I got exactly zero joy out of my backgammon session, and not just because I lost. Usually a game is accompanied by at least a little human interaction. But with this guy, I might as well have just played on the computer.

I sit up straight in my seat.

That kid's laptop. He left his laptop lying in the dorm room.

I haven't checked my legal status at the library for at least a month; started getting paranoid about someone looking over my shoulder. But if that laptop is still there, I could check in private.

I'll check, then pack and leave right away, just on the off chance it raises red flags on the hostel's IP address.

I pay, ignore Ruth's wave good-bye, and half jog past glitzy casinos, goulash depots, ads for bathhouses, currency exchanges . . . back over the bridge.

It's only eight thirty. The kids might still be out partying.

I force a smile to the pimply girl at the hostel's check-in desk, and in a frenzy I'm up the stairs and into the dorm room. Looks exactly as I left it this afternoon, including the carelessly concealed laptop. The door doesn't lock, so I throw a few of someone's bags in front of it, just to give me enough notice.

I pull the laptop out of its case and open it. I grin. Login doesn't require a password. Only bad news is everything is in French, but I find a browser easily enough. I lick my dry lips. This feels exactly like sitting down against a very good backgammon player, for very high stakes.

First I Google "Frank Lamb Interpol Wanted."

My heart sinks. I'm still there, one of about 300 American fugitives on the watch list. There's no good reason why that would change; no statute of limitations on shooting a woman to death in an NYC hotel room.

Even if she was a serial killer who kidnapped your daughter and—

I stop myself before running—for the thousandth time—through the events of that night five years ago. I know how that ends: Me pounding vodka until my eyes tear up, blacking out until I come to on the floor of the shower, some brave hostel employee kneeling beside my whimpering form, politely explaining that I'm going to have to check out.

My driver's license photo on the Interpol site looks as convincingly criminal as ever; easy to mistake that morning's fury at the incompetence of the Brooklyn DMV for murderous intent. Only good news is that the site still says that I'm thought to be in France.

I Google "NYC Murder Tower Hotel 32nd floor."

Old *NY Post* article I've read countless times. The details are correct, but taken—if I do say so myself—somewhat out of context. Yes, I shot Greta Kanter three times in the chest in a hotel room. They have a blurry picture of my face from the hotel hallway to prove it. And yes, I boarded a flight to Paris a few hours later with my daughter. But the *Post* gets the motive wrong. They speculate it was drug-related. In fact, Greta Kanter had hired me a few weeks before. Offered me 350k dollars to find a cassette tape for her. And when my partner and I weren't finding it fast enough, she decided to kidnap my daughter to speed things up. Throw in the fact that it seems pretty clear she murdered at least two people, and that she was practically pleading for me to pull a Kevorkian in that hotel room, and I think my actions are a little more understandable.

I briefly flirt with the idea of Googling Sadie's name, but refrain just in case these searches are enough to draw Budapest's finest to this room. I can't imagine they would be, but am not confident enough in my knowledge of Internet surveillance to draw even the slightest attention to my daughter.

I Google "Frank Lamb Cassette Tape." Want to know if anybody's figured out the true nature of that tape, or that it's in my possession.

I raise an eyebrow. Here's something new. I glance at the door then back to the laptop. It's a real amateurish site. *behindthecurtain.com*. A sidebar reveals that older articles are rather inconsistent in their reputability. It's some kind of public forum that allows anybody to upload their stuff. Earlier entries include an "exposé" on a military complex in Alaska that can control the weather, a detailed explanation of how 9/11 was both perpetrated by the Bush administration and predicted by the Bible, and several articles concerning extraterrestrial life. But there's also some stuff that sounds at least potentially plausible. Timothy McVeigh's ties to a well-respected Cardinal in the Catholic Church; a fuzzy video of what might be Vladimir Putin receiving fellatio; hacked email accounts of politicians.

The relevant entry was posted about four months ago (did I not Google "cassette tape" last time?), and was submitted by a journalist from a small-time online pub—the intro explains that his employer refused to print his "revelatory true crime piece" for fear of "ruffling feathers."

His investigation is the first to tie some things together about the tape. He figured out that I and an as-yet-unidentified partner were in Beulah, Colorado, just a few days before I killed Greta in New York. He speculated—correctly—that we were asking questions about the Beulah Twelve—the group that ritually sacrificed a kid and then disappeared. And he also caught up with enough people we'd badgered along the way to learn that we were after "some kind of tape that may explain why those twelve men became satanic murderers overnight."

But for every detail he nailed, he got at least three completely wrong. And then, to my great relief, the whole thing goes off the rails by the end as he tries to extrapolate meaning from various anagrams of "Beulah," "Satan" and "Tape" and combinations thereof.

I've been searching and reading for almost an hour. Pushing my luck. And now I'm locked into leaving tonight; if anybody out there still cares about finding me, this sequence of searches will surely raise some eyebrows.

I'm about to close the laptop when I remember there's one more place to check. I don't like to log into my old email account—it seems like a sure tip-off of my identity—but it's really the only way to get in touch with me. And lately I've been entertaining the wholly irrational fantasy of receiving an email from Helen Langdon, ex-flame and NYPD Detective, both offering me hope for exoneration and a couch to crash on.

And since I've decided to leave tonight anyway . . .

Before I can really think through the consequences, I log into my email for the first time since arriving in Budapest.

Fifteen new emails in ten months. I'd be depressed if I wasn't so nervous. They're all trash. Promotions. Except one. From Leonard Francis. The alias of Courtney Lavagnino, my partner from the Greta case.

Fingers trembling, I open it. It says simply:

> We're in the same city. I want to talk but can't find you. Nice work. Every night from 9–10 I'll be in the lobby of the hotel named after the spot where we once enjoyed some repulsive nachos. If you don't show by July 15 I'll try to find you wherever you go next.

My first thought is that I have no idea what month it is now. The French kid's laptop says it's July 11th.

My second thought is that this could quite conceivably be a trap. They found out that Courtney was an accomplice to the sundry crimes committed five years ago, but they'll let him walk if he delivers me.

My third thought is that Courtney figured out long ago that I have the tape, and a buyer contacted *him* because they couldn't find me.

I shut the laptop and put it back in its sleeve. It's nine fifteen. Within five minutes I'm out the front door of the hostel, duffel bag containing all my worldly possessions on my shoulder. I don't even have to rush to make it to the Ritz-Carlton Budapest before ten.

I SURVEY THE revolving doors of the hotel from behind the safety of a parked car across the street. Watch people walking in and out for five minutes before accepting that if this is a setup, there's really no way I'm going to be able to detect it beforehand. Muscle memory has me reaching for my Magnum in the back of my jeans, feeling naked at its absence. Not that it would be particularly helpful against an Interpol sting anyways.

I close my eyes and massage my temples. Try to think this through reasonably.

If it *is* a sting, I'll be extradited to the States and sit in jail for a year while they get the trial arranged. From there I'll have little more than a puncher's chance of proving who Greta Kanter really was, thanks to the lack of witnesses, and the fact that it went down five years ago. So, likely looking at something like twenty years in the slammer.

But if I just walk away I'm going to run out of money in a few months and more importantly, Sadie's boarding school is only paid for another year and a half. And the options for ameliorating that situation are pretty stark. I can't work here legally for obvious reasons, which leaves some unsavory prospects like armed robbery or running drugs.

And if I get myself killed in the process of either of those ventures I'll leave Sadie even more screwed.

I grab a handful of beard and tug on it urgently. It's strangely reassuring to think that no matter what I do here, I'll probably be filled with remorse and guilt in a few months.

Zugzwang.

Ultimately, it's curiosity that pushes me across the street, through the revolving door, and into the softly lit lobby of the Ritz-Carlton Budapest. Everything is white and gold, including the chandeliers, plush carpet and concierge uniforms. Someone is tickling a creamy grand piano behind a row of Roman columns.

Groups of business travelers, European tourists, people on laptops sit on broad white couches and around Parisian-style café tables. I feel horribly conspicuous. I'm underdressed, undergroomed, underarmed . . . equipped only with what little buzz remains from that double espresso.

I proceed warily across the ballroom-sized space. The light bouncing off every spotless polished surface makes me feel dizzy. I can't tell if I'm just imagining that every person I pass breaks away from their conversation for a moment to steal a glance at me. Are they all cops? Half expecting to be tackled and cuffed, read my rights in barked Hungarian, maybe kicked in the gut a few times . . . I'm breathing very hard.

Then I spot Courtney. He's sitting toward the far corner of the room, to the side of the reception desk, enveloped in a white armchair, reading a paperback. As soon as I see him something melts in my chest. I immediately feel guilty for even suspecting that he's here to turn me in. This is the guy who apologizes profusely when he accidentally grabs your water glass. He once chastised me for failing to tip a hotel maid. *These people live off of tips, Frank . . .* He cares about fruit being organic for philosophical reasons. He explained to me once that he doesn't drink coffee because he doesn't like to "lose control."

He'd never be able to live with the guilt of betraying me.

I can't help myself from grinning as I walk toward him. I wind around the lobby to approach him from behind, clamp a firm hand on his boney shoulder and grunt in his ear:

"You have the drugs?"

Instead of spazzing, flailing out of his seat, as I'd hoped, Courtney Lavagnino takes a half second to finish whatever he's reading, calmly lowers his paperback to his lap and looks up at me. Immediately his long face contorts in shock.

"Oh geez, Frank," he says in a low voice. "You look awful."

I snort and plop down into the chair across from him, trying desperately to stop myself from smiling; don't want to give him the satisfaction of knowing how glad I am to see him.

That's the first time anybody's used my real name in years.

But he's not smiling at me. His thin eyebrows are furrowed in concern, giving me the look you give a terminally ill kid who tells you he wants to be an astronaut when he grows up.

"Good to see you too."

"Have you been sleeping and exercising? You look exhausted."

"Yeah. I sleep plenty, and I've been jogging like twice a day. But actually you don't look so hot yourself," I lie. Or rather, he doesn't look any less hot than usual. He's always borne an uncanny resemblance to Morticia Addams, but five years have barely changed him: long, cruel chin; hollow cheeks; broad pale forehead. His hair is shorter, that's the big change. He used to have a ponytail— now he has a buzz cut; a sad dusting of grey and black pinpricks.

"I cut my own hair now," he says, noting my gaze. "I finally decided, why should I pay someone to do it? It's not sensible. I don't pay someone to cut my fingernails or brush my teeth."

"Cool," I say. "This is exactly how I always imagined an Interpol sting going down."

Courtney's eyebrows shoot up in disbelief, as the rest of his face crumples.

"Frank, I would never—"

"I know. I'm kidding. I'm here right?"

Courtney's skeletal shoulders relax beneath a wrinkly white

polo shirt that's way too big for him. A montage of him at some outlet mall flashes through my head, an upbeat pop song playing over his carefully calculated attempt to assemble a touristy, seasonally-appropriate wardrobe for his Eurotrip.

"So you're too cheap for a haircut, but you're shelling out for one of the nicest hotels in the city?"

"I'm not *staying* here, Frank." Courtney seems insulted by the suggestion of decadence. "Just costs me one tea to sit here in the evenings."

"And wait for me."

Courtney nods.

"You couldn't find me? Really?"

Courtney shrugs. Marks his page in his book and closes it, as if finally resigning himself to a long conversation.

"I probably could have, but thought it was better this way. Didn't want to see you if you didn't want to see me."

"How did you know I was in Budapest?"

He shakes his head at me, almost disapprovingly.

"You've been traveling on the same fake passport for years. You should change *at least* biannually."

"If I'm so incompetent, why am I still a free man, hotshot?"

Courtney claws his unshaved cheek.

"You're not a high priority obviously. Because, I stress, you've been *very* sloppy. You didn't change your appearance at all. If your picture had made it onto the news for five seconds it would have been over."

"I grew a beard."

"Right, the beard." Courtney nods to himself. "Brilliant. The beard has been confounding facial recognition software and law enforcement officials for decades. Perhaps someday technology will be able to simulate—"

"Alright, alright," I snap. "Fine. I look awful and I'm a terrible fugitive. Why did you want to talk?"

"Mmm." Courtney sits back in his chair and folds one boney leg over the other. "First, tell me about Sadie. Is she okay?"

"She's fine," I sigh. "In a fancy shmancy boarding school that's more like a country club. Called 'The Farm' or something, but they're not fooling anybody. Used a good chunk of the Greta money to set her up with phony papers, tuition and room and board."

Courtney frowns seriously—which usually means he's either happy or deep in thought. He only smiles when he's being a wiseass; when he's figured out something before I have.

"Good to hear, Frank."

"So?"

Courtney clears his throat. Glances quickly around the hotel, presumably to make sure nobody's eavesdropping. As if any of these put-together, purpose-driven-life, let's-meet-up-for-cocktails-and-catch-up people give a shit about us.

Satisfied, Courtney makes a steeple with his fingers and says:

"Somebody would like to hire us."

I narrow my eyes.

"Hire us? Don't they know that I'm wanted?"

Courtney nods slowly. He takes a sip of iced teas and stares at me seriously.

"He does. In fact, one part of our compensation package is fixing that for you. He had to, so you could come back to the States."

From the pocket of his faded blue jeans, Courtney removes an American passport and hands it to me. I bite my lip as I open it. It's my picture with a new name, new birthday, new everything. I leaf through, inspecting the watermarks, the edges . . .

I look back up at Courtney, heart fluttering.

"This is a hell of a forgery," I say.

"It's not a forgery," Courtney says. "It was printed in the American passport office. But the details belong to someone else. You have to burn it once we get through security, too risky to use it more than once. However, should we complete the job, the Senator has promised to get you a real one. New details in the database. A new *identity*. New Social Security number, new credit rating . . ."

I put the passport on the table between us, shaking my head.

"This is already too good to be true."

His eyes twinkle in amusement as he takes another long sip of tea, slurping up the bottom of it.

"It's not a hard job," he says softly. "And it pays quite well. But if your schedule is too full . . ."

I lower my head into my palms. Grind my eyelids until I see stars.

"Of course it's a hard job. They're all hard jobs."

"I did my due diligence. Followed up on all the odds and ends I could, didn't want to waste your time, and everything seems quite legitimate. Plus he's very impressed by us. He was initially referred by a woman I did an excellent, discreet job for some time ago who really talked me up. And of course I pulled some strings to arrange a stellar lineup of references for both of us—"

"Real ones?"

Courtney winces.

"I mean, we really did crack the Beulah Twelve case, succeeded where thousands failed. By all rights we *should* have amazing references. But of course I couldn't exactly mention anything related to the Greta case. Let's say, the references were real in spirit."

"Who is he?"

Courtney taps the rim of his glass with a spidery index finger.

"James Henry Sampson. Ring a bell?"

"Nope."

"He's a two-term Senator. Independently wealthy. Owns Sampson Dairy. It's huge in the Southwest. Or, used to. He sold it when he went into politics."

"So the passport—"

"He's a *Senator*. Connections out the wazoo. He got this thing printed and shipped to me in one afternoon."

"Wait," I say. "That name does sound familiar. Is that the guy with that crazy sex scandal? He was cheating on his wife with super young girls or something?"

Courtney clears his throat.

"They were all of age, but yes. That's him."

"And he's still a Senator?"

"Actually, he won his first election a few years *after* that story. But since being in office, his record has been astonishingly clean. Not a single blemish. I'm fairly certain that having this fake passport printed is the shadiest thing he's done in years."

I can't stop staring at the blue passport on the table between us. Once I'm in the States I could go see Sadie face-to-face. Hell, with a new identity maybe I could get a place close to her school in North Carolina so we could see each other regularly.

"What's the job, Court?" I grit my teeth. "What's this *easy* job?"

"I don't have all the details yet—"

"Oh great." I throw up my hands. "Everything's easy when you don't have all the details."

"Patience, Frank," says Courtney calmly. "I understand his thinking. He can't fill us in on all the details until we commit. But the bottom line is this: One of Sampson's ex-employees—a guy named Rico Suarez—stole some very valuable books from him four years ago. He's been patiently demanding ransom. And now, Sampson has finally agreed to pay."

"Why doesn't he call the cops, Court? He's a Senator and knows who the guy is—"

Courtney sighs. "Can you please let me explain, Frank?"

"Sorry."

"So the job is this: Rico wants an outrageous amount of money. Sampson has finally managed to gather the exorbitant sum. I think he's had to sell property and liquidate tons of assets. But he has the cash, and is ready to pay. Our job is to get in touch with Rico, tell him we have the money, and put an end to this. Swap the money for the books and put the fear of God into him to make sure he stays away from our client." Courtney coughs. "The only leverage Rico has over Sampson is the books. If it wasn't for the books, you're right, Sampson would have called the cops straight-away. But Sampson stressed to me: Nobody can find out that he has these books in his possession. Says it would ruin his reputation and political career. But that he *needs* these books back . . ."

I exhale through pursed lips.

"So let me get this straight: Sampson has the money and is ready to pay the ransom. All we have to do is call Rico and convince him we're serious about swapping and then maybe putting a tough face on while we do it?"

Courtney nods.

"Yes. The job itself might only take a few days. Arrange location and date, meet up, swap, collect three hundred grand."

My pulse jumps at the thought of my half of that money.

"Sounds like he's overpaying."

"Maybe. But you should read this guy's emails Frank. He's been destroyed by this ordeal. And he's wealthy. He'll pay what it takes

to make it end. Also, as I mentioned, he holds the arguably misguided belief that we're highly competent private investigators."

"You've only communicated with him by email?" I ask.

"Well, yes. You know . . ."

Courtney has never owned a telephone. If pressed, he'll explain that he doesn't like being traceable—the more he figures out
how easily a person can be tracked through technology, the more
frightened he becomes of being tracked himself. I tend to suspect
his reasons have more to do with either shyness, or paranoia that
the person on the other end is an impostor. Whatever the case,
as long as I've known him, he's only been reachable through one
of several heavily encrypted email accounts he maintains, and
checks a few times a week at Internet cafés or the library. It's a
neat system, because he can generally figure out where his refer-
rals are coming from, based on which email address he's contacted at. It also gives him an air of mystery, a sort of initial upper
hand with clients. But—most importantly—he avoids turning off
clients with that unsavory personality of his, that demeanor that's
somehow intertwined with the bitter sprigs of root vegetables and
flavorless vegan fig bars he's always eating. Those foul foods that
we generously refer to as "acquired tastes."

I think for a second.

"Well . . . Sounds like Rico's been pretty patient, eh? Stuck to
his guns for what, four years? Impressive."

"Oh yes." Courtney nods and waves his hand at the bar to
signal that he'd like another tea. "Very professional. Gave his price
and never budged. I admire his patience."

I rub my neck.

"This guy Rico is obviously pretty serious. This already sounds
like it could get ugly."

"Alright." Courtney reaches to take back the passport. "Sorry for wasting your time. You obviously have a lot on your plate."

I slam my hand down on top of his, pinning the passport to the tabletop. I glare at him, rage tickling some spot behind my eyes.

"Don't fuck with me," I growl, suddenly feeling stone cold sober. "I'll snap these little fingers off and make you swallow them."

To my increasing fury, he just cocks his head at me, like he's disappointed with the banality of my threat.

"So you'd like to hear more then?" he asks, as nonplussed as a waiter listing the evening's specials. His refusal to even acknowledge my threat badly makes me want to follow through on it.

He just smiles smugly at me until I have no choice but to withdraw my shaking hand, and take a few deep breaths.

"So." Courtney clears his throat. "What you're wondering, surely, is what are these books? Why does Sampson think it would ruin his reputation if this got out? We're obviously not talking about first edition Melville manuscripts or something."

"And," I add, "why is he willing to pay . . . How much is he giving Rico to return them?"

Courtney scratches a stubbly cheek.

"Forty million."

"*What?*" I jump in my seat. "How rich is this guy?"

"Rich," Courtney says. "But by my estimation, this is well over half of his total worth."

"I see."

A waiter with a towel draped over a cuffed wrist brings Courtney his tea on a tray.

"*Van egy barátom ma este.*" He smiles.

"*Igen,*" replies Courtney. "*Beszélnem helyett olvasni.*"

They both laugh.

"What the hell?" I ask as the waiter delicately accepts Courtney's payment and returns to the bar. "You speak Hungarian?"

"A bit," says Courtney. "I mean, I have been here over a month.
Couldn't help picking up a few words."

I decide not to admit that I've been here nearly a year and have
no idea what they just said. "So I guess the three hundred grand
makes sense now. It's a big deal, handling that much money."

"Yes." Courtney nods. "As a percentage of the total transaction,
it's obviously negligible."

"Paid up front?"

"Upon completion. Didn't push him on that yet. Maybe we can
negotiate."

Before drinking, he takes the glass of tea and holds it up the
light, swirling and squinting like it's a fine wine. Finally satisfied,
he lowers his glass to his lips and takes a tentative sip.

"I got one two weeks ago that tasted a little funny. Noticed a
little layer of film on the top. Means either it had been sitting for a
while or—more likely—somebody sneezed into it."

"You can't taste sneeze," I snort, as he continues to drink warily,
like the speed of germ intake will mitigate chances of infection.
"But Court. What are these books? Are they coated in platinum?"

Courtney shifts in his chair. Finally having made peace with
his tea, he squeezes his lemon slice into it and takes a healthy slurp.

"I won't lie to you Frank. I have no idea. I asked, obviously. He
refuses to tell us until we're there on his property, face-to-face.
He's—justifiably I suppose—rather paranoid these days. But of
course" —a little fire flashes in Courtney's eyes and for just a
second I catch sight of the insatiable curiosity that is ultimately
the only reason he's in this line of work, instead of teaching at a
university or writing long form journalism—"I'm sure we'd have

the opportunity to find out what makes these among the most valuable books in the world."

For a moment we just listen to the woman playing Chopin across the lobby, the clink and clatter of highballs and real silver, the thick soup of conversations in dozens of different languages.

"Why did you come here?" I ask. "Why not do the job yourself."

Courtney sniffs a little too quickly.

"I need your help."

"I thought it was an easy job." I flash my nastiest grin.

"It will be easy for two of us."

I smile to myself. It sounds like Courtney has finally discovered the gaping holes in his skill set, that have been obvious to me since we first met. He's quite possibly the smartest person I've ever met—speaks like eight languages; once wrote a paper on game theory just for kicks that was picked up by some renowned mathematics blog; somehow managed to hunt down a ninety-year-old Nazi hiding out in New Zealand, based only on a water-damaged black-and-white photo of him from the war—his ability to complete clearly defined cognitive tasks is unparalleled. But being a successful private investigator requires much more than solving abstract logic puzzles; there is, of course, the human element. And poor Courtney must just now be realizing that humans don't behave like the rational actors in his economics textbooks.

"Well, I'm flattered that you think I can help, Court."

Courtney attempts to compose himself. He bites down on a piece of ice and sucks it down.

"We would fly to Colorado tomorrow."

My stomach knots.

"Colorado?" I ask. "Shit. I hate that place."

Courtney nods knowingly. I'm sure he's thinking the same thing as me: Last time we were there five years ago we were looking at bloodstains on an altar, a woman who'd had her head bashed in, and sat in the front yard all day, mostly brain dead, tied to a post so she didn't wander off. I wonder if she's still alive. Don't exactly have fond associations with that particular flyover state. Reading my mind, Courtney says:

"It's nowhere close to Beulah really. He lives in Aspen. Very bougie. Plus we were there in winter last time. Colorado summers are supposed to be beautiful."

I clench my teeth.

"If we go check it out, he fills us in on the details, and we don't like it, can we still walk away? Realistically? I mean, where would I go from there? Back to Europe?"

"You could go visit Sadie in North Carolina," suggests Courtney. "I'd drive down with you."

I mull this.

Wait.

"When did I tell you she was in North Carolina?" I ask.

Courtney's face freezes. He clears his throat.

"I suppose I misled you a bit when I asked how she's doing," he says, and then lowers his voice. "I've actually visited her a few times."

"You what!?" I half shoot out of my seat.

"Frank, please. You emailed her school email address to yourself so you wouldn't forget it. You might as well have posted her Social Security number on a billboard. Don't worry, I deleted the email."

"Why the fuck would you go see my daughter?"

"To make sure she's okay. Figured she would be lonely without you. I was going to tell you, really."

I'm feigning anger, but actually feel mostly gratitude: that he's doing my job for me, that he cares enough about us to shlep all the way down there to check on her.

"And how long have you been checking my email?"

"Frank, you know I keep tabs on everyone I've ever worked with or for. It's just smart business."

I could milk this; twist the knife and earn some upper-hand morality points, but he's just too pathetic. I can tell he's in an even worse place than he's letting on. He needs to work, needs some purpose and focus. Probably as badly as I do.

"I was just trying to help, Frank, I swear."

I glare at him.

"If I say yes, there will be absolutely no more deceptions. Even if you think it's for my own good."

"Yeah." Courtney nods seriously. "Of course."

I take a few deep breaths.

"Bottom line Court: What does your gut tell you about Sampson? What are the odds this is some kind of a ruse?"

Courtney chews his lip. He feels awful about his minor betrayal of my trust.

"Nil," he says. "Seriously, Frank. He's a Senator who knows what bad press is like. He wouldn't risk getting a fake passport made unless he desperately needed help. I'll show you these emails where he's pleading for me to consider the job. And it's just a swap, Frank." He bites a few fingernails. "I'd be shocked if it takes more than a weekend."

"If you believe that, I know a Nigerian prince who needs some help making a bank transfer. Senators don't get passports forged for easy jobs."

I stand up and snatch the passport off the table, glaring at Courtney as he chugs the rest of his second tea.

"But, as you surely anticipated," I sigh, "I can't say no to this."

A wide, genuine grin spreads over Courtney's normally dour face. It's like watching the sun rising over the tundra.

"We'll fly tomorrow morning," Courtney says, instantly energized, rising to his feet, limbs unfolding like a spindly marionette being gently pulled from above. He stretches his thin arms toward the ceiling, pulling up his polo shirt to momentarily reveal his pale midriff—could belong to a teeny bopper were it not for the tufts of dark black hair emanating from his belly button. This guy—this spindly goblin—is the closest thing I have to either a work colleague, friend or, hell, spouse for that matter.

Now that's depressing.

"In the spirit of full disclosure, I think Sadie might have a boyfriend," Courtney says absently as we talk over marble floor, toward the front entrance. "I could smell aftershave."

"Appreciate your honesty, Court, but please don't—"

"Of course I have no reason to believe it was serious. Guess it could have just been a one time kind of thing . . ."

I SPEND THE entirety of the trans-Atlantic flight white-knuckled, waiting for a grinning sky marshal to pistol-whip me. It's only on the second leg of our trip, after passing through passport control at JFK without incident, that I settle down enough to get to work.

We spend the flight from New York to Aspen poring over news clippings about Sampson, as well as reviewing the insane nondisclosure agreement he emailed Courtney.

Sampson ran the family dairy business uneventfully, until about twenty years ago he started getting contracts with some big groceries—scaled up dramatically and within a year or two he was a multimillionaire running an enormous dairy operation. Ran for mayor of a nearby town, won handily, then sold the business to run for Senate. A few months into the campaign, his opponent uncovers a history of some serious floozing around; he's got a very bad habit of screwing girls young enough to be his daughter, visiting erotic massage parlors, posting lewd Craigslist personals and following through on them . . . This is political death, especially with a conservative constituency like his. His wife is too ashamed to be seen in public. He drops out of the race, a laughingstock.

But then the interesting part—after disappearing from the public eye for a year or so, he reemerges, claiming he's a "changed man." Well, maybe that's not so surprising. What's so surprising is that it *works*. He runs again and this time, he kills it. And now he's totally beloved—polls through the roof. When the sex scandals are occasionally mentioned, everyone talks about them like they were a sickness which infected poor James Henry Sampson, and now he's recovered, all the stronger for overcoming.

So I guess the contract he wants us to sign makes sense. He's been burned by his secrets getting out before. But some of these nonstandard terms seem a bit overboard, considering that the job could conceivably take us only a few days: For *twenty years* we basically can't mention his name to anyone in any context, zero photos of his property, he wants us to work without documenting anything in writing or taking any photos.

Hard to imagine what this guy is hiding . . . Has he fallen back onto the canoodling wagon? But Courtney and I finish poring over the contract and by the time we deplane, decide to just sign without fussing over any terms.

Five years of tension melts away as we make our way out of the terminal. I'm on the same continent as my daughter, and I can speak to the locals. Aspen-Pitkin County airport is a particularly welcoming environment. Unlike JFK, there are no drug dogs, or cops with machine guns. Seems to be an understanding between all the smiling travelers and airport staff: *We're all rich, and nothing bad ever happens here.*

I convince Courtney to split the cost of an iPhone and burner SIM card at a Verizon kiosk—we'll need a phone for the job, and it's not exactly professional to ask Sampson to borrow his. We snap pictures of every page of the contract and email it to Courtney's account.

Someone's at baggage claim holding a sign that says Courtney. The woman waiting for us is probably early thirties, and looks like she just rolled out of bed. Her brown hair—interspersed with strands of premature grey—is strewn like a pile of spilled spaghetti. Thick-rimmed black glasses, loose white wifebeater and red corduroy pants. Despite her best efforts, she's pretty. Has a cute kind of squirrely look.

"Hi, I'm Mindy Craxton," she says. She forces a smile, like introducing herself is some awful chore. She has an accent I can't place and a dead look in her almond eyes. She seems so exhausted, you'd think she's the one who just finished a double-legged transatlantic flight. "You two have bags?"

"This is it." I gesture to the duffel bag that I carried on. Courtney has only a black attaché that looks like it's been through a world war.

"Alright." Mindy throws the scribbled sign in the recycling bin, and plucks two bottles of water from a plastic bag.

"James asked me to give these to you. It's always important at this altitude, but the air is especially dry now—the whole state has been in borderline drought for months. This happens here every couple years. Make sure you drink copious amounts of water. James doesn't want you getting sick, yeah?"

"Thanks." I smile, taking the two bottles from her. We stand there for an awkward beat. She doesn't move.

"Well?" she says, agitated. I think her accent is blended British and South African. "Drink them."

Courtney and exchange a look, then open our bottles and chug while Mindy watches impatiently.

When we finish drinking she wordlessly turns, and we follow her out of the sliding glass doors, into the slightly brisk Colorado morning. She walks fast, with the frantic strides of a musical theater major who forgot her anxiety meds.

Courtney's eyes scan the panoramic view as we cross the parking lot, as if scoping out escape routes. He's frowning, perhaps wary of the foothills rising on either side of us; some primordial instincts telling him that the low ground is where you're vulnerable.

"The air is thin," he says to her corduroy-clad backside. "What exactly is the altitude here?"

She pretends not to hear the question. I try to decipher the frown of almost comic proportions creeping down Courtney's face as we follow Mindy in silence, her purposeful pace like she wants to get this over as soon as possible.

Who the hell is she? Sampson's employee?

I do already feel the thin air. I'm out of breath after our short walk to the car. A black Humvee. Mindy climbs into the front, and it seems implied that neither of us is meant to sit shotgun. The back seats are spotless, and the interior smells of leather and freshly printed money.

"So you work for the Senator?" I ask. The words feel dumb as soon as they leave my mouth. In fact, just being around her makes me feel dumb.

"Not really," Mindy responds.

"So . . . girlfriend?" I ask.

She doesn't respond.

"Mistress?" I joke.

She turns to glare at me from the driver's seat. I see that the hand she's perched on the upholstery is splotched with white eczema. "Cute. But don't say anything like that around James. He doesn't have much of a sense of humor."

Courtney fidgets, his tiny butt struggling to find a groove in the spacious seat.

"So you're just like his chauffeur?" I press.

The silence before she answers indicates that she's really losing her patience.

"I'm a postdoctoral student in linguistics," Mindy says slowly, the timbre of her voice shifted down an octave. I notice that her lips are badly chapped.

This stirs Courtney to speak.

"Linguistics? What's your area of specialization?"

She doesn't reply, turns back to start up the car.

I shoot Courtney a wide-eyed look: *She's a little loopy, eh?* He shrugs: *I've seen worse.*

"I'm just curious why the Senator would send a linguistics student to pick us up from the airport," Courtney says.

It's immediately clear Mindy's a terrible driver—the kind that's so bad she doesn't even *realize* she's bad, and probably wouldn't believe me if I mentioned it.

"I'm sure James will want to explain everything to you himself," she finally answers. "He's a *tad* anal sometimes. *Especially* when it comes to anything related to the books." There's an obvious twinge of resentment in her voice. Decide to follow it—I can tell she's a natural talker; *wants* to talk. Shouldn't be hard to coax a little more info out of her.

"Anal eh?"

"Yes . . . well I mean. It's an honor that he chose *me* to show them to. It's absolutely the opportunity of a lifetime, really—" She's suddenly speaking very rapidly, words gushing out before she can judge their prudence. "But now I have hundreds of pages of research that I can't show anyone—let alone publish—until James is out of office. Not to mention we could have had them back years ago if he wasn't so bloody *terrified*. Hardly leaves his property unless he absolutely has to fly to DC."

I kick Courtney in the shin, like to make sure he's getting all of this.

"Terrified?" I ask "Of Rico?"

"Among others."

"What do you mean?"

Mindy takes an exasperated breath, then jerks the Humvee over to the shoulder and puts the hazards on. Turns around and gives us an exhausted look—like a burned-out librarian who's about to confess that the Dewey Decimal system is all a scam.

"Listen, I know you two are curious. You seem like nice blokes, so I'll just tell you now. You're wasting your time here. There's not going to be a swap, yeah?"

Courtney chews on his pinky. Mindy continues:

"It's too much money. James has gotten close before, but couldn't pull the trigger. He couldn't bring himself to pay forty million three years ago, he'll back out of it again this time. James will cancel at the last minute, and that will be that. What's more,

Rico is doing just fine as is. Every couple months he calls up James and demands a couple hundred thousand immediately, or he'll burn the books. And of course James pays. Rico is in no hurry. James has horribly mishandled this from the start."

"But—" I start.

"It's better that way, trust me," she sighs. It's like she used up all her energy with her little rant about James, and the world is now just a series of obstacles preventing her from taking a nap. "You don't want to get involved in this. It's not worth whatever he's offered to pay you. And you *certainly* don't want to spend time in that house. I refuse to even go in there anymore."

I'm about to ask her to clarify, when she turns back around and revs the Hummer back onto the highway and turns the radio on loudly, precluding any follow-up questions.

I glance over at Courtney, whose brow is furrowed in deep concentration, as he stares at the back of the seat in front of him.

I close my eyes and try to sleep. But the jerky driving and excitement of being back in the States, having a job, prevents me from shutting off my brain. Not to mention the jam-band type music Mindy is blasting over the car's sound system.

I open my eyes as the car pulls to a stop, at the entrance to a driveway, blocked by a tall white gate. Mindy rolls down the window and buzzes in.

"It's me, James. I have them."

After a moment a baritone voice crackles back.

"Did they sign everything?"

Mindy looks back at us like *Told you he's anal.*

"Tell him we signed them."

She does, and the gate creaks open. Mindy eagerly gives us some gas, nearly clipping the retracting gate with the side mirror.

The estate is unbelievable. Set on some kind of plateau, above the valleys but below mountain peaks . . . I wonder if this whole property was terraformed in order to create a flat parcel of land. Granite statues of nude figures adorn the perfectly trimmed green grass on either side of the driveway.

Once a perv . . .

The lushness of the property seems especially decadent given what Mindy said about there being a drought. He must spend a fortune watering all of this.

She jerks the car forward, and then slams to a halt right at the front door.

I was so enraptured with the rows of flowers, rock sculptures and pine trees that I hadn't noticed the house. But when I first take it in through the tinted window I'm physically jarred.

"Wow," whispers Courtney.

To say that the Senator's house is beautiful would be both to undersell it, and to mistakenly describe it as pleasing to the senses. In fact, my first reaction to the house—despite some objectively phenomenal craftsmanship—is nausea. It's beautiful in the same way as a Magic Eye 3D picture—impossible to imagine how it was made, but the shock to your visual system makes you dizzy and want to throw up a little.

We exit the car and Courtney and I just stare at it for a moment.

From a bird's eye view, the house would appear as a giant *V*, and the front door is at the vertex. It feels as if we're standing in the gaping jaws of the house and are about to enter her throat.

It's three stories high, and the exterior is roughly half glass, half some kind of polished orange stone, all held in place by a slick steel exoskeleton. The roof is opaque, but through the glass you can see the beams and columns that support it. It's like seeing a house with half its skin pulled off. The effect of the half-transparency is that various rooms and objects inside appear to be suspended in midair.

It's phenomenal, but—like some kind of insane amusement park ride—I'm totally content just observing from the outside.

We see what must be the Senator on the first floor, through a transparent wall. He doesn't wave, even though it's obvious that we can all see each other. He opens the front door and steps outside. He approaches us, brown leather Oxfords clicking against flagstone. He walks like a politician; slowly, thoughtfully, erect. He's wearing khakis and a light wool sweater despite the heat. He's holding a can of Diet Pepsi.

"Hi Mindy," he says with a booming voice. "Could you please order groceries for all of us? What do you two like to eat?"

Courtney says: "I'm a vegan. So just stuff like fruit and vegetables for me please."

"Alright," Mindy says. "I'll see if I can find a place that delivers twigs and dirt. And you?" She turns to me.

"I don't mind vegan stuff," I say.

Courtney looks at me with wide wary eyes, as if suspecting me of ulterior motives.

"I eat less meat than I used to, champ," I explain, patting him on the boney shoulder and smiling. "You helped me see the light."

James Henry Sampson turns to us as Mindy disappears around one jutting wall of the house.

"Contracts, NDAs and the passport?"

I hand him the temporary passport, and Courtney removes what's practically a bound manuscript from his attaché and gives it to Sampson. He leafs through it, alternately sipping Pepsi through a straw and checking that every page is initialed. When he reaches the end and sees the date and signatures he can't contain a sigh of relief.

"Please excuse the legal formality. Courtney, good to finally meet you in person." He tucks the contract under his arm and gives my partner a well-practiced handshake. His voice is resonant, warm and reassuring. "And Frank Lamb"—he doesn't quite smile, but conveys pleasure with a slightly upturned lip, like we're sharing an inside joke—"I'm glad you decided to come. God bless."

He's about three inches taller than Courtney. Lean but with a wide chest, thin salt and pepper hair, round spectacles, slightly ruddy face, cheeks so smooth it's hard to believe he even needs to shave. It's tough to get a read on him based on this first impression—he's very reserved and has excellent control over his facial expressions; typical of someone who spends a lot of time on camera and in the public sphere. It's not hard to see why he's a successful politician; if there's one thing he conveys unequivocally it's competence. This is a man who'd surely be able to roll up his sleeves and change a flat tire in a cinch, help his son with his calculus homework, or whip up a killer lemon meringue pie in a jiffy. I remember that his origins were as a dairy farmer.

He's wearing just a bit of very tasteful cologne.

"Courtney explained the confusion which resulted in your current legal problems, and it sounds like you've been the victim of a terrible injustice," the Senator tells me. "I want you to know, it will be my sincere pleasure to right this egregious wrong. I've already requested your new documents, and they should be ready by the time you complete the job."

"I appreciate that," I say, wondering just how much Courtney bended the truth, and how much of it Sampson really believed.

Bottom line is, the Senator probably doesn't care what I've done, as long as Courtney and I get his books back for him.

Sampson picks up his empty soda can and says, "I'll show you fellas to your rooms so you can put your bags down, and then if it's alright with you I'd like to get started immediately."

"Do you think it would be possible to shower first?" I ask, a private shower in a clean proper bathroom suddenly all I can think of. I've been bathing in communal, grimy hostel bathrooms for years—the kind where you have to wash all of the crowd-sourced hairs off the bottom of your feet afterwards.

"Of course." Sampson again gives an almost smile. I think for a moment his face betrays signs of extreme fatigue. "I'm just very eager to have the matter settled. I'll show you to your rooms."

"Your house is very unusual," says Courtney, as we approach the front door, trying to match the Senator's brisk steps. "Beautiful, but unusual. I've never seen anything like this before."

"Thank you. I think you'll find the interior even more distinct than the exterior."

"I think I recognize this architecture from somewhere," Courtney says. "Is this an Oliver Vicks?"

We're on the cusp of the front door, but this innocuous observation stops Sampson in his tracks. When he turns to look at us, he's struggling to maintain his poise.

"I don't recall asking you to look into that," he says softly.

This is why Courtney and I work well together. In these critical moments, we're usually on the same page. In this case, where neither of us have any clue what the hell is going on, the clear dominant strategy is to remain silent, coax him into betraying more information.

We both meet the Senator's level gaze, trying to keep our faces totally neutral. Sampson's face doesn't reveal much, but you can tell there's something bubbling under the surface. A bit of a twitch in his left eyelid; totally involuntary.

His eyes dart between Courtney and I.

"How did you find out?" he asks.

"I read occasionally about modern architecture," Courtney replies coolly, obviously just as confused as I am as to why any of this is a big deal. "Just general interest. Thought this looked familiar."

Sampson taps two of his beaming white teeth with the tip of his index finger, like he's worried they've fallen out, and the fact that they're still there appears to comfort him somewhat. He takes a deep breath.

"Well, onwards and upwards," Sampson says and forces a smile. "All part of God's plan, I'm sure." He turns and leads us inside. I see that the empty Pepsi can in his hand has been crushed by his grip.

Courtney and I exchange a quick glance behind Sampson's back. I ask him with my eyes:

Do you know what the hell that was about?

Courtney shrugs.

No clue.

THE SHOWER IS better than I'd imagined. I spend twenty minutes in there, another ten shaving off my beard, and then a moment I wish could last forever just rubbing the soft towel against my cheeks.

My and Courtney's rooms are in the north wing of the house. I was wrong about the shape of it. It's actually a complete *X*; more or less symmetrical from the outside. From any given location out-side on the ground, it's only possible to see two of the wings.

My room is, mercifully, not transparent, and I have accom-modations that wouldn't be out of place in a five star bed and breakfast: sparkling clean surfaces, fresh linens, my own enor-mous bathroom with a Jacuzzi tub, entire thing paneled with dark stained oak, floored in polished yellow stone.

The pink-tinted window in my room looks out onto an outdoor tennis court and lap pool, with stadium lights for nighttime use. The house and sports complex are surrounded by rows of pine trees that seem deliberately arranged to maximize privacy. And the whole estate is bordered by a twelve-foot brick gate. Also visible is a guesthouse, which, if Mindy refuses to step foot in this main house, must be where she went off to.

I pull on a pair of ratty white Jockey shorts and my jeans. Would have loved to go shopping in town before stopping here; these rags have long since reached the point of permanent soiling. Also asking Sampson to borrow some underwear and pants is clearly out of the question. I'm about to attempt a nap when there's a knock on my door.

"Just a sec," I call, pull on the same T-shirt I was wearing before, and stride to the door, savoring the fluffy beige carpet on my bare feet. Courtney's standing there, on a floor of pink-tinted glass, frowning. He doesn't appear to have showered. Wordlessly, he pushes past me, and sits on my still made bed. I close the door.

"Nice digs, eh?" I say.

"Mmf," he mumbles. He's fidgeting with his long fingers.

"What?"

"It seems . . ." Courtney scratches his scalp and exhales loudly. "Wait."

Courtney removes a little box from his pocket that looks like a radio and places it on the nightstand.

"That will jam any recording devices," he explains.

"Oh come on." I roll my eyes. "Why not wear tin foil hats in case he has a brainwave monitor?"

Courtney brushes off my skepticism.

"Well. I know what was bothering the Senator. It seems this house was designed by a felon. A murderer."

I try to process this unexpected sentence.

"What are you talking about, Court?"

"The guy who designed this house—Oliver Vicks—he's a fairly well known architect. I remembered seeing pictures of one of his houses some time ago. But I just Googled him. And it turns out that, after designing a host of quite interesting buildings around Colorado he murdered a family. Quite odd circumstances, too, I might add."

Courtney hands me the phone. I scan the article. Oliver Vicks— prominent architect—killed two parents and their son. Five hours later he was arrested at the restaurant where the daughter of the family worked. He had called the cops on himself.

"Why did he turn himself in?" I furrow my brow.

"Well, it gets a bit more odd. I read a few other articles. The parents were shot in the head. But the *son*, fourteen years old, they think was killed with the screwdriver Oliver had on him at the café."

"They think? Couldn't they tell?"

"Right, well." Courtney clears his throat." They never found the son's body. His blood was *everywhere*. But no body. Like he'd been, *ahem*, drained."

"So he took him somewhere?"

Courtney presses the tips of his long fingers together.

"Apparently."

"Motive? Did he know them before?"

"Doesn't sound like it."

"Bizarre."

"I know," Courtney says. "If he had a gun on him already, switching to the screwdriver is a lot of extra, unnecessary work."

I raise an eyebrow at him, in disbelief.

"I meant it's *bizarre* that we're currently inside of a house that this guy designed. And that Sampson is keenly aware of it."

Courtney shrugs.

"I guess he just doesn't want his name in the same sentence as the guy who carried out a grisly murder. He is a politician, after all."

I hand the phone back to Courtney.

"But . . . how could Sampson be surprised that you knew? If this guy was really a famous architect, it must be well known that he designed this place."

Courtney picks something out of his eye.

"You'd think so. However there are no photos or mentions of this estate in connection with Oliver Vicks anywhere online, at least that I could find."

I look at Courtney.

"This is what I was trying to tell you in Budapest. There's something nasty going on here. Senators don't fly guys on the Interpol watch list in for holiday weekends—"

"Yeah. But listen Frank, I was thinking." The tips of Courtney's fingers start tapping the air, as if playing an invisible piano. "Mindy wouldn't tell us what's in the books, but she did mention she's a postdoc in *linguistics*. How could a linguistics student keep herself busy with a book for this long? There's only one possibility: They're not written in English. In fact, there's only one reason why Sampson would recruit a linguistics student as opposed to say, a Spanish student or something: They're not *written in any language we know.*"

"Fine, but—"

"So they're in an indecipherable, original language and worth forty million dollars to somebody. Think about that. What if—"

"Dude." I cut off his increasingly manic ranting. "I don't care about the books right now. Can we talk about the fact that we're staying in a house designed by a serial killer?"

Courtney frowns in confusion.

"Why?" he says. "It's a spooky bit of trivia. But if we're going to be rational about it, it's just really not a big deal. This architect designed dozens of buildings. There's an office park in Denver that thousands of people work in every day that he designed. The buildings aren't changed by the fact that he's currently serving three consecutive life sentences."

I snort.

"Well apparently *Sampson* thinks it's a big deal," I say. "He had all mentions of his home's architect purged to avoid any negative associations."

He shakes his head in that subtly demeaning way of his.

"Based on what we know about his political career, I find his paranoia somewhat justifiable."

I stare at this creature sprawled on my bed. Sometimes I wonder if I'll ever understand him. A knock on my door.

"Just a second!" I bellow, then whisper to Courtney: "Look, I know you're curious what the hell is in those forty-million-dollar books. I'd be lying if I said I wasn't also. But screw your head back on, and let's figure out what kind of mess we're in. I don't want to get caught in something ugly. I'm done getting played."

Courtney's grimace tells me I don't need to spell it out: *like we were five years ago.*

"If he lies to us once, I'm bailing. I swear," I say.

I shoot Courtney an *I'm not fucking around* look, and then walk to the heavy cherry door. Pull it open to reveal Sampson, sipping on a new can of Diet Pepsi.

"Enjoy the shower?" he asks.

"It was exquisite," I admit.

"Glad to hear it. Fellas, I'm sorry to rush, but I'm very eager to get you two started. Would you like to join me in my office?"

I look back over my shoulder at Courtney, who has switched on his poker face.

"Sure," I say.

"Okay. You'll want to follow me. This place can be a little confusing at first."

"I noticed," I say.

Our guest rooms are on the third—and uppermost—floor of the house. On our way up we took a side staircase that was enclosed in stone walls, so we didn't really get to see the second floor. But Sampson leads us down a different staircase into a second-floor hallway, which makes my head spin. The floors are the same pink-tinged glass, which is jarring to walk on—impossible not to imagine it cracking beneath your feet. Every couple meters there's a small white carpet, little islands of sanity. Looking through several transparent walls, across the yard, to the perpendicular wing of the house, certain rooms appear to be floating off the ground, suspended only by a few thin steel beams. Others are walled in stone—creating a sort of vertical chessboard of alternating polished stone and pink or totally transparent glass. It's not hard to imagine the same mind that conceived of this spatial madness suddenly burning a fuse and going postal.

Beside me, Courtney is also mesmerized by the view. I pat him on the shoulder and we tear ourselves away to catch up with Sampson. From behind him, half to get him to slow down, I ask:

"So you live here alone?"

"Yes. I'm divorced."

"Your wife used to live here with you though?" Courtney prods. Sampson sips loudly on his soda to avoid answering the question.

There seems to be more natural light inside this hallway than there is *outside,* like the walls are partial mirrors that reflect and magnify every ray of Colorado sunlight. But it's not dandy and breezy light—it's way too much. It's more like every wall is emitting the harsh glare of an interrogator's lamp, designed to half blind, half disorient.

How the hell could you live in a place like this?

I'm feeling dizzy. I want to go back to my opaque bathroom and close the door.

I realize there are no doors in this hallway. The rooms that open on its sides are totally visible. We pass eight, four on either side. Again Courtney and I stop to stare. Sampson will just have to wait.

Each room is identical to the last: They're all totally empty, and the floor is some kind of milky blue glass which gives the appearance of a lake surface on a windless day. But the ceiling of each room is lined with a maze of intricate transparent piping, all filled with streams of water. It's beautiful, in a way. It's like some kind of postmodern museum gallery, but without paintings. Just bare glass walls and a futuristic plumbing system.

"What do you use these rooms for?" I ask, as Sampson comes back to us, clearly impatient. He doesn't say anything. "Did Oliver design these rooms?" I ask—really asking *why* Oliver designed them.

Sampson doesn't respond immediately. Instead a powerful bicep raises his Pepsi to his lips and he turns and continues down the radiant corridor. I figure the question—like the one about his wife—is going to turn out to be rhetorical, but as we leave the hallway and start down a dizzying spiral staircase made of pink glass, Sampson surprises me with an explanation:

"It's concept architecture," he says over his shoulder, a hint of pride in his voice, as he bounds down the steps two at a time. "Inspired by a verse from Genesis which describes the creation of man. *'And the Lord breathed into his nostrils the breath of life, and Man became a living being.'*"

The bottom of the staircase leads into a half-opaque living room. The floor is covered in a real bearskin, which elicits a flinch from Courtney. A fireplace as big as a bathtub, red metal bookcase packed with all white-covered books, a long white leather couch. There is no clutter, I note. The few objects are either out of sight, or arranged on shelves in what looks like the place they've been since the dawn of time. But at least on the first floor there are places to sit.

"The four branches of the house represent the four limbs of the body," he continues. "And the pipes our veins and arteries. By shaping it like an inert man, the home draws in the holy breath of life. The layout creates a sacred space."

I raise an eyebrow at Courtney like *thanks for ending my Eurotrip for this.*

"How do you know that's what Oliver Vicks intended?" asks Courtney, failing to sound innocuous. Sampson doesn't respond.

Leads us through another mostly bare sitting room, and finally through a heavy oak door.

If the four wings of the house are limbs, then this must be either the brain or the spine. The center of the X is a kind of core, insulated from the insanity of the wings by the same orange stone some of the external walls are made of. If there were a war, you'd hang out in the Spine. The lack of glass walls initially sets you at ease, until you realize that there aren't even *windows* in here, only chandeliers emitting soft orange light.

"I value privacy in my office," says Sampson, outside a second smaller door that presumably opens to his office. "There are no windows, so God can't see what I'm doing."

Reflexively, I force a chuckle at this bizarre comment. But when I do, Sampson gives me a curious look.

Wait—was that not a joke . . . ?

Courtney and I enter the office first. It's dark and smells like potpourri and cigar smoke. Sampson enters behind us, letting the door slam shut. As soon as we're sealed off from the rest of the house, the Senator collapses on a brown leather couch and breaks into sobs.

TRADITIONAL PAINTINGS OF boats and men with swords drape the wood walls. A stuffed and mounted twelve point buck hangs over a fireplace. Phenomenally stocked liquor cabinet in one corner. A huge desk with several phones and a big laptop. Stacks of loose files as tall as me form a minimetropolis of paper in one corner of the room. A few dampened bulbs in the chandelier struggle to reach the dark corners.

Courtney and I sit down on the couch across from Sampson. Between us is a frosted glass table atop a dark Persian rug. For perhaps three *long* minutes, Sampson just cries into his palms. Chokes on his own phlegm. It's to the Senator's credit, I suppose, that he doesn't try to hide his tears from us. The display of raw agony certainly makes me uncomfortable, while Courtney seems more empathetic—just watches Sampson with wide sad eyes, chewing on his fingernails, like he's upset that this kind of unhappiness exists in the world.

When Sampson finally runs out of steam and looks up at us, he's a different person. There's little trace of the gregarious politician remaining. His blue eyes are wide and desperate. His thinning grey hair no longer appears regal, rather, malnourished and prematurely dead. He's a frightened little boy, quaking with post-sob hiccups.

"I need help," he says. "I need help so badly. Please."

I clear my throat.

"Of course," I say gently. "That's why we're here."

He nods.

"Help yourselves to a drink," he says, and gestures to the liquor cabinet. I shove off immediately from the couch, eager to ease the tension.

"What do you want, Senator?" I ask, pouring myself five fingers of the most expensive looking bottle of rum I can find.

"Grab me a soda from the minifridge, thanks," he says.

"I'll take a soda too, Frank," says Courtney.

The minifridge is stuffed exclusively with cans of Diet Pepsi. Probably 150 cans.

Guy knows what he likes.

I grab two of them and return to my seat. Place the cans and my lowball on the tabletop. Sampson snatches one of the Diet Pepsis, cracks it open, and takes a long desperate tug, like it's the elixir of life. When he places it back down on the glass tabletop he seems instantly refreshed—he should do commercials for this stuff.

Courtney already has his notepad and pen out, perched forward eagerly like a little kid watching the classroom clock.

"So Senator. You want us to get some books back for you?"

For some reason, this comment causes Sampson to break out into a booming, anguished laugh that's like Santa at a funeral.

"Yessirree," he says. "Get some books back for me. Sounds so simple doesn't it?" He gestures to Courtney's notepad. "No writing. It's in the contract."

Courtney frowns.

"I know, but . . . it's how I think best. You can keep the notes after I'm done."

Sampson shakes his head.

"No. I'm sorry. Writing things down, it makes them realer."

Frowning, probably as confounded by this comment as me, Courtney reluctantly slides his notepad back into the pocket of his jeans.

Sampson takes another long sip of soda, and stares at the nearly empty can, as if he's having second thoughts about this whole thing. I notice how small the soda can is in his hands—they're enormous but still dexterous. Farmer's hands. I'm already making excellent progress on the dark-sans-stormy.

"I'm in a bad way, fellas. A very bad way. And I need those books back from the bastard that stole them from me."

I nod, attempting to demonstrate sympathy.

"Tell us about the books," Courtney says a little too quickly. "What are they?"

Sampson looks momentarily taken aback. He blinks.

"Kinda figured we'd keep that on a need-to-know basis, if you gents don't mind."

Courtney and I exchange a quick, knowing look. I put my hand on my partner's knee to stop him from blurting out what we're both thinking and to let me put it a little more politically.

"With all due respect, James"—decide to use his first name as a little power play—"you asked us to work for you. *We'll* decide what we need to know and what we don't. Any information you withhold could put us in danger, or reduce our chances of success-fully executing the deal."

Sampson doesn't look up from his drink, but nods slowly.

"I get it. I do." He sets down his can, sits back in his chair and crosses one long leg over the other. "I apologize fellas. You just have to understand that this situation . . ." He gestures vaguely. "I've been guarding this information very closely for some time. It can't get out."

I feel for my beard, wanting to stroke it thoughtfully, and am disappointed to embrace only my clean cheek.

"You have to remember the bottom line here," I say. "We both want the same result. So help us help you."

Sampson chuckles mirthlessly.

"Don't try to out-politician me, Frank." Then he sighs, takes off his circular glasses and wipes them clean with a little cloth. "Well. The reason I hired you two is that if I don't get this situation taken care of I'll soon have nothing left to lose anyways. So here we go. All chips on the table. I'm counting on you boys."

He takes a deep breath.

"Where to begin. Eleven years ago? With a dream. I had a very vivid dream, and then it repeated itself. Again, and again. I was having it every night, but I couldn't figure it out. I spoke to few friends about it, an acquaintance who's a therapist but—"

"What was the dream?" Courtney asks.

Sampson's poreless cheeks flush.

"The dream was this: I was swimming in the open sea. I felt strong and confident. And then something grabbed my heel and prevented me from swimming forward. It wasn't scary, just frustrating. And when I glanced over my shoulder to see what it was on my heel, that was always just when I woke up. So, it wasn't too difficult to think maybe it was about something figuratively holding me back in life, in my career, etcetera, but in my heart I knew there was more to this dream that I wasn't understanding.

"I'd been having this dream for a month or so already when I happened to have an appointment at Saddleback Correctional Facility. It's one of the largest prisons in the state."

"Why were you visiting?" I ask.

"I don't remember exactly . . . I think it was to speak to the directors about budgets or something. Anyways, as I was being given a tour, we walked past one of the prison yards. One of the inmates approached me and handed me a note through the fence. On a whim I accepted it and put it in my pocket. Nobody else saw, I don't think. When I was alone in the restroom I read the note. It said simply:

"I can help you understand your dream. The one grasping your ankle is not who you think."

"And then it gave his inmate number, and name, so I could find him.

"Well, perhaps you'll think it was foolish of me, but I was so baffled about how some inmate knew about my dream, and of course, I was so desperately curious what he had to tell me . . . I had my secretary arrange some excuse to return to the prison the following week. And when I did, I mentioned that there was also a particular inmate I'd like to speak to."

Sampson again takes off his round glasses and wipes them with the edge of his sweater.

"That was my first meeting with the man who was known around the prison as *Sophnot*, the man who wrote the books which were stolen from me—"

"But his real name?" Courtney asks, though if I've already intuited the answer I'm sure he has as well.

Sampson seems to have a hard time forcing his mouth to reply. In fact, he makes a little sound, a fraction of a syllable, and can't continue. Instead he gestures to Courtney to hand him the pen and pad.

"The architect that you mentioned earlier. I'm not really comfortable . . ." he mutters to himself as he writes two words down on the pad, and then shows them to us.

Oliver Vicks

Sampson clears his throat, he looks ashamed—precisely why is not quite clear.

"And somehow . . ." I ask. "Somehow he knew what you'd been dreaming?"

Sampson clears his throat. "Yes. Including details that I myself hadn't remembered."

I narrow my eyes. Courtney asks, "How?"

"I believe God told him."

SAMPSON'S CELL PHONE rings. He answers quickly, maybe relieved by the interruption. Courtney and I exchange a look while he's preoccupied.

This doesn't smell good, I tell Courtney with a furrowed brow.

How was I supposed to know!? he responds with bewildered wide eyes.

"Hi Mindy," Sampson says into the phone. "Yes. Yes. I'm speaking with them now. Perfect."

He hangs up and gives us the tight-lipped apology face.

"Sorry for that. Mindy took off for a few hours. She'll be back around late tonight or tomorrow morning to answer any questions that I'm not able to."

"Does she live in the guesthouse?" asks Courtney. Sampson looks confused by this question. I quickly change the subject.

"So the dream?" I say. "What did Oliver say about the dream?"

"Oh." Sampson seems to wince slightly when I say's Oliver's Christian name.

"Well, Sophnot, unlike everyone else I spoke to about the dream, explained exactly what it was that was holding me back, and what it was holding me back from."

Courtney and I lean in expectantly.

"And?" I say.

Sampson mutters something to himself, maybe a silent prayer? Or no, it's as if he's having a quick argument with himself about something.

Is he nuts? Has he gone completely bonkers and is just a master at hiding it?

Finally Sampson says: "I'd just run for a Senate seat and lost. Badly. It was humiliating. There was a scandal which I'm sure you two are aware of. It wasn't hard to deduce the goal I was seeking for myself. But the hand on my heel—I remember within three minutes of sitting down across from him, through that bullet-proof Plexiglas—Sophnot calmly explained there were several factors holding me back from my professional ambitions. Many were counterintuitive. That to rid myself of them would not be easy, and would take time, but with his help, I would reach a level of career success and personal gratification that I never imagined possible."

Courtney is chewing on his pinky. I attempt to appear unfazed.

So your life coach is a convict in a maximum security prison. What could go wrong?

Sampson rises and grabs another Diet Pepsi from the mini-fridge. The terrified little boy that overcame him the second he entered this office still hasn't left. He brings Courtney a new can as well, plus the bottle of the rum I'd been drinking.

"But this man was a convict," I say slowly, as Sampson sits back down. "He murdered three people. And you–"

"I didn't bring you here to question my life decisions," he says as he returns to his seat. Not angry, just matter-of-fact. "I understand why you'd be skeptical of my decision to listen to him at all. To not just stand up and leave immediately. But what can I say? Despite his crimes . . . something about him just drew me in. And as I came to learn, my initial instincts were correct. He is . . . brilliant. He understands things about the world, about God, that I'm not sure anyone else does. He truly, seriously helped me, fellas."

It takes a lot of willpower to suppress an eye roll.

"So you returned to visit him after that first time?" Courtney asks.

"Many times."

"How many times?" Courtney asks.

Sampson scratches his neck.

"Twice a week, whenever I wasn't in Washington. For seven years. In secret, of course. The official story was that I was volunteering there in their civics education program. The warden was happy to go along with that story: It was easy enough letting me meet with a prisoner, and he probably figured I'd protect his state funding."

I see Courtney's eyebrows raise in my peripheral vision.

The Senator hastily adds: "I never promised him anything explicitly of course."

This guy just can't stay out of trouble.

"So—you took Sophnot's advice?" I ask.

"Not right away, but eventually, slowly, I started trying out some of his suggestions."

"What were his suggestions?" Courtney asks. "Is that what the books are? Suggestions?"

Sampson shakes his head slowly.

"I simply can't tell you those things. And besides, they have no relevance to your task. They're in the past. Done. What's done is done is done, right?" He tries to smile like this is a joke, but none of us are fooled.

"Well, he instructed you to move into this house which he designed," says Courtney slowly. "I assume that was one of them."

Sampson is silent. Courtney either isn't aware he's treading on sensitive ground, or doesn't care.

"And your divorce, I'm supposing that was also a result— though perhaps indirect—of Oliver's advice—"

"Don't try." Sampson shakes his head. "Please, Courtney . . . don't make me . . ."

"I'm simply trying to elucidate—"

"It's not that I don't trust you two with the information, it's that you won't understand."

"My partner and I are simply—we're just kinda sticklers about getting all the details is all," I say. "Been burned before, you know. I urge you not to hold anything back. We need to know everything that Rico does."

Silent, Sampson gazes long and hard at us.

"You're correct," he says quietly. "About the house . . ."

"And the divorce."

Sampson's eyes are wet again. He blinks back tears.

"I had a problem with women," he says. "It was uncontrollable. Sophnot helped me . . ."

He trails off, shaking his head slowly.

"So?" Courtney tries to prod gently.

Sampson's face is like a stone. He clears his throat and lifts his chin in the air.

"The biblical prohibition is against *coveting* your neighbor's wife. That you shouldn't even *desire* her. In order for me to fully repent for my sins, I had to embrace this stricture to the fullest."

Wordlessly, Sampson stands up and unbuckles his belt.

My heart does a somersault. Courtney's whole body flinches as the Senator lowers first his khakis to his ankles, and then his flannel boxers.

Bile rises in my throat, brain screams.

There's nothing there but a mutilated nub. The room spins a bit. To avoid losing my airplane breakfast, I have to look away.

Sampson pulls his pants back and buckles the belt. Sits back down.

Courtney looks close to actual shell-shock. Hands shaking furiously on his lap. I'm gnashing my teeth together.

Oh my god. Oh. My. God.

"I'm cured," says Sampson softly. "Sophnot, in his infinite wisdom, gave me the cure. I no longer desire the flesh of any woman, nor am I capable of causing *her* to sin. Perhaps you think me a naive fool. Worse, perhaps. But I swear: I would not be where I am today without him. My desire for sin was grasping my heel, holding me back."

I think I'd rather just cut off my heel . . .

"Does Rico," I ask weakly, "the guy who stole the books, know about this?"

Sampson nods slowly.

"And that's why you can't go to the cops? Worried this would get out?"

"It's one reason," Sampson says, composing himself. "But by no means the only one. Let me explain about the books."

"Wonderful," I gasp. Courtney is breathing fast. I myself am a little light-headed. I find the lack of windows more troubling after finding out that the guy sitting across from us is a self-made eunuch. Sampson, however, is acting like everything is more or less business as usual.

"Sophnot's life's work is a collection of twenty-four books. He showed me one after we'd been learning together for a year. He translated parts for me—" Sampson takes a deep breath. "It was exhilarating. It was like the rush on election day, as you're watching yourself win, hearing your name on every channel . . . No, even that undersells it. Imagine that you're the size of an ant, and your whole life you've been running around on this rug here." Sampson gestures to the colorful tapestry underfoot.

"You understand only that sometimes the colors shift beneath your feet. And then suddenly you are lifted a foot off the ground, and you can see the pattern for the first time . . ." Sampson's huge hand squeezes his soda can tightly, and he's growing flushed. This topic excites him. "And after he read for me, he told me he wanted me to take and guard the books. Imagine! He had several books now complete, but was growing worried about keeping them in his cell. There's a volume limit for inmate's personal items. He said he trusted nobody more than me. That I was his loyal disciple, and when he left prison we would sit and read the books together . . ."

I find that my legs are shaking.

Okay. So he's a nut. Doesn't mean we can't still make the swap for him and get paid, right? Ideally we can do this without ever having to confront him with the truth—that he's been brainwashed by a murderer.

That's what I'm thinking, but apparently this obvious path of least resistance is less self-evident to certain dour-faced autistics.

"Did Oliver ever ask you for money?" Courtney asks.

I almost smack him. I'm sure we're about to be shown the door; replaced by PI's who aren't going to question the legitimacy of this wacko's incarcerated guru.

I butt in.

"What Courtney is asking is, did he ask for some sort of collateral for these books? It would seem reasonable—"

"No Frank." Courtney shakes his head at me, even as I try to shoot him the most obvious *shut the fuck up* look in my arsenal. I'd forgotten this guy is illiterate in subtext. "That's not what I'm asking. I was wondering—"

"You were wondering if I was being taken advantage of." Sampson nods. "Naturally. I don't blame you for being skeptical, Courtney. That's your job. But I'll tell you right now, in seven years of meetings, Sophnot didn't once ask me for a *cent*. Which is especially remarkable considering that his guidance helped me to quadruple my net worth, thanks to speaking fees and very wise investment advice."

Silence hangs in the air. I keep trying to reconcile our new-found info re: what's not dangling between Sampson's legs, with his all-American public persona.

"I'm not mad at you for the implication," Sampson says. "How could someone who's never met Sophnot, or peered into his master-work, understand? I'd probably be thinking the same as you."

Courtney fiddles anxiously with what could only be called a beard in the loosest sense. I tap my toe against the carpet.

"Sophnot gave me the books, one by one, as they were completed. Eventually I had all twenty-four here, in the secure room right beneath our feet. The only times they left that room were when I took one volume with me to the prison to read it along with him. The only people who ever went in that room were me and Mindy. But then, just a few months after I'd received the final one, they were stolen from me. The culprit was Rico—my trusted live-in chauffeur, bodyguard and personal assistant. It was my fault, in a way. I trusted him too much. Apparently I badly mis-judged his character. That his soul is certainly damned eternally for this is of little consolation. For four years he's been demanding a fortune for the books.

"You are to give Rico forty million dollars in the untraceable bearer bonds he's asking for. It's an exorbitant sum of money, you don't have to tell me. Just do it. I need this to be over. Rico has pro-vided a phone number to call when I'm ready. I can't take another second of this hell. Imagine again, to be the ant, lifted above, and then to come *crashing down*—denied the view of the tapestry you now know to exist. For years it's been hell. Hell."

Sampson's lip quivers; there's another dam of tears threatening to burst forth.

"So Mindy . . ." I ask. "Do you trust her?"

Sampson appears grateful for the topic shift.

"What do you mean?" he asks. "Of course. Mindy is like family."

The only family he has left?

"Well, if I understand correctly, her role here was to study the books. So what's she been doing since the books were stolen? Why is she still living in your guesthouse?"

"She has partial copies of the books to use in her research," Sampson says. "She's made a lot of progress. Once you get them back from Rico, once she has the whole set in front of her, she'll hopefully be able to read them pretty seamlessly."

"I'm just trying to get the whole picture," I say. "You brought Mindy on to study the books, so you could understand them without having to go visit Oliver in prison, is that right?"

"No, no," Sampson says. "No, no, no. Nothing could be further from the truth. I wanted to study at home to *supplement* my sessions with Sophnot. So that when I went to the prison to learn, we could make the most of our time together. He was so generous with his time, I wanted to show him I was really making an effort. But I just couldn't grasp the nuance of the language on my own. I needed an expert."

"Does Oliver know you hired someone to study them while you held them for him?" Courtney presses. "That doesn't really sound like it was in the spirit of him entrusting them to you."

Sampson's grip tightens on his Pepsi can.

"I'm sure my teacher would admire my intentions," Sampson replies weakly. "We're all perfect in the eyes of God."

"But just for argument's sake," Courtney says. "Is it possible

Mindy was a little lax with security, and that allowed Rico to steal them more easily?"

Sampson's right eye twitches.

"We're all perfect in the eyes of God," he repeats.

I sense we've exhausted this avenue of inquiry.

"What was your relationship with Rico like when he worked for you?" I ask.

The Senator shoots up and walks to his desk. Pulls a manila envelope out of one of the drawers and sets it on the glass tabletop.

"Here's everything I've gathered about Rico. From the background checks I ran before hiring him, to the text message records between us over his entire employment."

I frown at the bulky file.

"We'll read this, obviously, but your own words would be helpful. Do you think this is only about money?"

Sampson thinks for a second.

"Our relationship was fine. Really. I think about that a lot: if I was upsetting him somehow without realizing it. But as far as I could tell, he was content. *Professional.* That's how I'd describe him. He was in the Boston PD for fifteen years before I hired him, and as far as I could see he was thrilled with the cushiness of the job. Driving me around, maintaining the estate security systems, accompanying me on Washington trips . . . I treated him well. Really."

"If he was your driver . . ." Courtney says. "He was driving you to the prison? To visit Oliver?"

Sampson nods slowly.

I say: "He must have known something secret and important to you was going on there, and that you were leaving with books."

"Yes," Sampson replies softly.

"And so, it wouldn't have been hard for him to intuit their immense value to you," I say. "You gave them their own room, and hired Mindy just to review them."

Sampson nods slightly. I think about what Mindy said in the car: *He's badly mishandled this from the start.*

"Have you given Rico any money already?" I ask, to confirm what Mindy told us in the car.

The Senator sips on his Diet Pepsi. "A couple times, yes. I had to," he says. "Just to make sure he didn't destroy them."

I grimace. Rico has all the leverage here. This explains our hiring: Besides Sampson presumably not wanting to execute the physical handoff himself, he just doesn't trust himself to negotiate with this guy any more.

"Okay then," I sigh, snatching up the Rico file and grimacing at its weight. "I think Courtney and I understand the scope of the job. Let us discuss it, and tomorrow morning we'll let you know if we're prepared to proceed—"

"What do you mean, 'prepared to proceed'?" Sampson suddenly jerks up from his soda, his voice deep and stony. He leans across the table and rips off his little round glasses. Fixes his bright blue eyes on me with the stillness and intensity of lasers. "I got the passport for you—at great risk to myself—and flew you out here. You signed my contracts, I shared everything with you . . ." He turns to my partner. "Courtney—I thought it was agreed that if I brought your partner here you two would begin immediately."

I turn slowly to Courtney and glare at him, swallowing about a quart of concentrated rage: *I don't remember you mentioning that.*

He avoids my stare.

"Of course, Senator," Courtney says. "Obviously we'll proceed as discussed. Frank just meant we would need the evening to discuss strategy with each other, figure out timing—"

"Tomorrow! You swap with him *tomorrow*." Again, Sampson breaks into an inexplicable laugh. "I'm not sure you fully grasp the situation. I am trapped from every side. Sophnot is devastated— his life's work is gone. He's been in mourning for years, since I confessed they were stolen from me. Dressed in rags, sleeping on the cold floor. He's forbidden me from visiting him in prison until I have the books back. He *trusted* me, and I lost what might be the most important work of religious scholarship since the Old Testament."

Sampson shakes his head; he's gasping for air.

"He calls me every Friday evening before the Sabbath. Asks me if I've gotten the books back. He never raises his voice . . . he's so calm, understanding, even in this time of crisis. And every week, when I have to tell him no, I still don't have them, he comforts me. Reminds me that everything is for the best, and wishes me a restful and pleasant Sabbath."

Sampson's voice is a whine now. His limbs are constricted horribly; this physically imposing, powerful member of Senate now resembling some kind of asphyxiating fetus fighting for life.

"But every night I see him in my dreams. Every night the exact same dream as before: I'm swimming in the sea when my heel is grasped. Except now when I look back I see Sophnot, my teacher, and I understand that if I don't retrieve the books it will all come undone, everything we've made together . . . I love him so much. With all my heart and with all my soul. And there's nothing more painful than failing him. Admitting my failure to him week after week, after all he's done for me . . . no amount of money is worth this burden. I just can't take it anymore. I just want things to be back like they used to. The two of us learning together."

All three of us are silent for a moment. My mind is spinning frantically, trying to decide which part of this clusterfuck most urgently needs to be addressed. I settle for an extremely long sip of rum. Courtney is chewing on the tip of his pen with horrible urgency.

I clear my throat. I'm dying to get out of this room.

"The job is easy," Sampson says. "You're being overpaid because Courtney has a reputation for discretion. Call Rico, arrange a swap, bring Mindy with you to verify the books are real, and execute. That's all."

I stand up, and am relieved when Courtney and James follow.

"Alright Senator," I say. "We'll get some sleep and speak in the morning."

He extends his smooth right hand. Squeezes Courtney's limp fish, then takes mine, his smile suddenly the regal one we saw on his front porch.

"Thanks fellas. We're counting on you."

Wait.

"We?" I say, mouth dry. "You mean you and Mindy?"

Sampson looks confused.

"And Sophnot, of course," he replies. "I asked his permission to bring in outside help, and you'll be pleased to know you have his blessing. Once you retrieve the books from Rico, he'd even like to meet you in the prison, to thank you for your help in person."

I SLAM THE door to my bathroom, and don't even give Courtney time to set up his stupid jamming device before letting it rip.

"You did *not* tell me that you committed to this job before even getting all the facts."

"Keep your voice down!" Courtney hisses, on his knees fumbling with his paranoia pacifier. I rip the machine out of his hands, toss it in the bathtub and turn on the cold water.

Courtney dashes past me to fish it out. Tenderly dries it with one of Sampson's fluffy towels. Looks up at me.

"Well that was just plain stupid, Frank. These are not easy to find."

I jab his boney chest with my index finger.

"You very much implied that we were flying to Colorado to find out more about the job," I growl. "That if we didn't like how things shook out we could bail."

"Come on, Frank. Did I need to spell it out for you? You think the Senator is going to get a fake passport just to bring someone in for a *consultation?* Besides, I knew you'd say yes. So what's the difference?"

"I still haven't said yes!" I shriek. "This guy is totally off his rocker! At the suggestion of a *murderer,* he cured his libido with a hacksaw."

"Have some sympathy." Courtney scratches his nose. "The poor man is in an awful situation."

I sit down on the lip of the magnificent bathtub.

"I really can't believe you," I say.

Courtney slowly sits down next to me, clasps his hands and stares at the stone floor. He's quiet for a moment, and when he finally speaks his voice is pained.

"I'd planned on explaining in Budapest, but at the hotel I got scared you'd walk away and I'd have to do the job alone. I couldn't risk messing this up. These last five years Frank . . ." I watch his thumbs twitch wildly in his lap, little hatchlings anticipating their worms. "I haven't worked. I mean, I was hired for two or three jobs, but butchered them. Screwed up really badly, word got out, and I stopped getting offers. The woman who referred Sampson to me was my client almost a decade ago." Courtney takes a deep breath. "When I got the email from Sampson I was working in the kitchen at Long John Silver's. Defrosting and deep frying seafood all day. It was all I could get. I had no real work experience and no usable connections . . ."

I wouldn't let him work the register either.

"I thought I was doing you a favor!" he pleads. "I got you a passport. And look—if we do this right, we'll be set! A hundred-fifty grand each and a new identity for you! He wanted me to commit fast. I was scared if I turned him down I'd lose the job. I told him if he could get you a passport and Social Security number we'd do it."

"He wanted you to commit *fast*? Christ, it sounds like he was trying to sell you a used car."

"Look—" Courtney returns the finger jab. "I *saved* you, Frank. If I hadn't done this, you'd be on the run for the rest of your life. Who knows when you'd get to see Sadie again. I could have just tried to do this myself, but instead I risked losing the whole contract, *and* I'm splitting the money with you."

I breathe out slowly through my nose. He's not angry. Closer to the effect of an economics professor passionately expounding on the merits of fiscal responsibility. He always seems to make such perfect sense. I hate it.

"You want out?" he asks with infuriating calm. "If you really do, I could talk to Sampson. Take less money, and just put you on a plane back to—"

"Shut up," I snap. "I'm already here. Obviously we're just going to swap for these stupid books. But I'm still upset you lied to me."

"Lied? Maybe I *misled* you . . ." Courtney trails off, fiddling with his still waterlogged jamming device. Mutters something under his breath about *delicate circuitry, unsalvageable.*

I'm suddenly aware of how exhausted I am. Can't wait to go to sleep—haven't had a private bed for years. This whole thing might be worth it just for the warm shave and one night in a king-size bed.

I stand up and yawn.

"I'm gonna crash. Go fiddle with that thing in your own room."

Courtney drops the defunct device at his feet.

"Not yet Frank. We still have a lot to discuss."

"Oh right," I say. "So I'm pretty sure that Sampson's not *shtupping* Mindy.*"

"Frank, for heaven's sakes. Please don't be lewd." He points at the manila envelope—the Rico file—resting on the vanity. "We have to know who we're negotiating with tomorrow."

I snatch the heavy folder, and reluctantly rejoin him on the edge of the tub. I open it up. It's at least 200 pages.

"Let's just split it up," I say. "I'll read my half in bed."

One of Courtney's wary eyes lingers on me.

"Fine. But read carefully. This is important."

I hand him about two thirds of the pages.

"Okay?" I say. "Are we done here?"

In response, Courtney cracks his knuckles one by one. It's horrible to listen to.

"Aren't you curious what's in those books?" Courtney asks. "Those books that Oliver wrote. A book is—fundamentally—information. What kind of information is worth forty million dollars?"

"It's only worth that to Sampson, because he's brainwashed. They can't be worth forty million on the open market, or else Rico would have just found another buyer. This guy Oliver is clearly nuts. They're probably twenty-four volumes of some kind of manic or schizophrenic raving."

"Well, we'll have to ask Mindy tomorrow. She's been studying them for years."

I yawn again. I don't know if I'm going to be able to make it through more than a few pages of that file.

"I wonder about your premise," I say. "That books are intrinsically just information."

Courtney's eyes sharpen.

"What do you mean?"

"I mean like . . . to people that believe the Bible was written by God, that book contains a lot more than just . . ." I trail off, as the glow in Courtney's small black eyes suddenly intensifies. I know what's coming. He's been waiting for an opening since the Ritz in Budapest.

"What happened in that hotel room with Greta? Before you killed her? Did she play the tape?"

I breathe out slowly. Fortunately I've rehearsed this:

"I told you," I say carefully. "I didn't hear it all."

Courtney arches one eyebrow so high it almost brushes his hairline.

"You don't have to lie to me," he says, his tone clinically neutral. "If you don't want to tell me what you heard, just say so."

I scratch the back of my neck.

"I'm not lying to you," I lie. "I heard some stuff, but I don't really understand what it meant."

Courtney is quiet for a moment. Then, like a Jenga player surgically plucking out one more piece: "But was it what we thought? Did it tell you about what happens after we die?"

I stand up from the tub again and take my portion of the papers.

"Has it occurred to you that I'm not telling you everything to protect you?" I say.

Courtney stares up at me evenly.

"There's no need to protect me."

I bend over until my gaze is even with his. Shoot him a look that I hope conveys that he is not to raise this topic again. I say: "There is. You can't unhear these things, Court."

I let that hang for a second in the air, then straighten up. "I'm going to bed," I say. "Happy reading."

"So then . . ." Courtney starts.

"So tomorrow morning we'll call this guy Rico and take it from there. Swap and get paid."

Courtney frowns for a moment, clearly still processing the details of that exchange. He rubs a long index finger along his bottom lip.

"Yes," he says. "Should be fairly straightforward."

Part Two

Tuesday

Exodus 33:20
And [The Lord] said, Thou canst not see my face; for man shall not see me and live.

IF THIS IS typical, then Colorado summer mornings are amazing: dry, crisp and cloudless. Sky is a robin's-egg blue. I guess most Coloradans would prefer storm clouds—water is apparently outrageously expensive now because of the drought—but the fresh morning has me upbeat and optimistic as Courtney and I walk to Mindy's guesthouse.

Maybe this could all go smoothly.

Courtney made a pathetic effort to clean himself up before breakfast, and he looks all the worse for his failed attempt: His polo shirt is half-ironed, he missed a big spot shaving his chin, and the left corner of his mouth is blemished by a white splotch of dried toothpaste.

"So what about Rico? Did you read your half?" he asks.

"Yeah. I mean, skimmed a lot obviously, but I got the idea."

"And?"

"I don't think we're dealing with a criminal mastermind here. I mean, the guy worked at a processing center for junkies for ten years without a promotion. The best I can tell, Sampson mainly hired him because he's huge, and didn't ask too many questions. I figure he saw the same Sampson we did yesterday, realized how desperate he'd be to get the books back and took advantage."

Courtney frowns.

"But he's patient."

I snort. The highest praise Courtney can give someone is calling them "patient" or "thoughtful."

"There's a fine line between patient and stubborn," I say.

"Wouldn't take a penny less than forty. But guess it's about to pay off."

With five pages left in the Rico file I'd slipped into a series of horrible dreams: rabid dogs lunging for my throat, angelic faces crying tears of blood, a man who had an extra pair of limbs that he used to climb up walls. But out here in the sunny yard, surrounded by an Edenic scene of grass, flowers and topiaries, the images feel distant and silly.

In fact, it's not hard to imagine that *all* the unpleasantness of yesterday was an overreaction. For instance, it sure seems likely that Sampson's missing Erector Set was some sort of optical illusion or a bad dream, because as he greets us outside the guesthouse door, shakes my hand firmly, locks his eyes onto mine, grins and asks how I slept, I find it near impossible to picture that awful stump. He looks composed, confident and healthy—in short, like a United States Senator.

Sampson then takes Courtney's hand and gives him a hearty smack on the shoulder.

"Ready to see some action?" he teases, a far cry from the desperation he showed yesterday.

Courtney smiles weakly and manages something resembling a yes.

"Then let's get to it."

It's immediately obvious that the guesthouse is solely Mindy's domain. The cottage is packed with books. Like her strands of hair, there seems to have once been an effort to subjugate them, that's long since been abandoned. Only about half the books are shelved, the rest lie open on the floor or coffee tables, pages dogeared, some books serving as bookmarks for others. The walls are covered in posters for once-upcoming Phish concerts, and blown-up, framed French cartoons. I wonder if she's really working as hard as Sampson thinks, or just taking advantage of the room and board. An argument for the latter is a large bong made of green glass sitting in the center of the kitchen table, its prominence suggesting it's the primary reason for this home and its occupant's existence. She's poking at her oatmeal when we walk in, and barely acknowledges us, either lost in thought or just grumpy.

Sampson snatches the bong off the table and puts it in a cupboard.

"For heaven's sakes," he says. "Wouldn't kill you to at least be *discreet*."

Mindy just shrugs. She's wearing pajama bottoms with ducks on them, and a baggy button-down shirt that I'm sure she slept in. Her hair has a little bit of an Einstein thing going on. Yesterday she was wearing a little eyeliner, not today.

"Good morning, Mindy," says Courtney.

"Oh, hi," she says. "How did you two sleep?" Her intonation is like she's asking where we keep the horse tranquilizers, in case this day needs to be put out of its misery. I imagine that she wishes her cheeks weren't so round and pink; they could give you the mistaken impression that she's cheery.

"Fine, thanks," I say.

"Help yourselves to some breakfast," says Sampson, in a booming voice.

There's a big fruit arrangement that looks catered, some boxes of cereal and a bottle of rice milk. Courtney eagerly sits down across from Mindy and fills a plate with cantaloupe. Between bites he steals glances at her. When she catches him he squints and pretends to be studying whatever is over her shoulder. She couldn't care less. Just keeps joylessly shoveling spoonfuls of oats into her mouth, like sustaining herself is a minimum wage job she'd quit in a heartbeat if an alternative presented itself.

Sampson sits down at the head of the table, seems uninterested in the food, just watches us expectantly. I've hardly had a chance to start eating when Sampson says: "I have a conference call in a half hour—maybe you fellas could just go ahead and call Rico now?"

"Now?" I say, spearing a cantaloupe chunk. "I kinda figured Courtney and I would talk to you two a bit more about Rico, and take some time to strategize."

Sampson looks strained.

"I'd prefer if you called now," he says, his solemn tone conveying that this is more than just a strong preference.

Courtney fidgets in his seat.

"Surely a few hours of planning—" he starts.

"It will be fine," Sampson says. "Call on speaker, alright?"

Courtney is frowning intensely. But I don't think Sampson is open to debate on this.

"His number is 303-742-1829," Sampson says, from memory.

I slide him the phone so he can just enter it himself. He types the numbers with great gravity, like he's entering a nuclear launch code. When he returns the phone his enormous hand is trembling slightly.

"Okay." I address the Senator and Mindy. Try to recall my mannerisms from years ago, when I used to regularly instruct grateful clients on details of my MO, mostly just to convince them that I knew what I was doing. "Nobody talks but me. We don't want to spook him. Make him think we're with the feds or something. And once we call, we have to be ready to go right away. He used to be a cop. He knows that the longer he gives us, the better our chance of setting up a sting."

Sampson nods dutifully. I'm sure he's both nervous and excited, but unlike last night in his office, he's dignified enough to maintain a solemn air of nonchalance. Mindy keeps mirthlessly swallowing oatmeal, apparently still unwilling to take this whole thing seriously.

"Alright," sighs Mindy, pushing her now empty bowl away and sitting back in her chair. "Go ahead then."

"Don't worry," Courtney says to Mindy. "We have a lot of experience with this sort of thing."

"Oh do you now?" she retorts dryly.

I roll my eyes. Watching Courtney talk to women makes me feel like I'm in a *National Geographic* documentary on failed mating tactics.

"Okay," I say. "Quiet please."

I hit call and put the phone in front of me on the tabletop. Nine long rings on speaker. Pulse jumps as someone answers abruptly. Courtney jerks to attention. Sampson is staring intently at the phone, perhaps with loathing at the source of the voice.

"*Yes.*"

He's using one of those machines that makes your voice sound like Darth Vader, which immediately strikes me as odd for two reasons: One, does he always answer the phone with that thing? And two, we already know who he is.

"Is this Rico?"

"*Yes.*"

"Hi Rico," I say. "My name is Ben Donovan. I'm a private investigator sitting here with Senator Sampson. He's asked me to contact you on his behalf. And . . . we have the amount you asked for. We would like to set up an exchange."

Heavy modified breathing.

"Are you with the police?"

"No. I'm a private investigator. I have no affiliation with the police."

"Forty in bonds?" the voice says quickly.

"Yes."

Heavier breathing.

"I'll call back."

Click as he hangs up.

Sampson wrings his hands.

"What's going on?" he asks, voice trembling.

I shrug. "Could be anything. Maybe he's at work and needs to step outside the office."

"I doubt he has to work these days." Mindy purses her lips. "The Senator has already paid him what, two million since this whole thing started?"

I jump in my seat as the phone starts ringing. I answer quickly on speaker.

"Hello?"

"Price has gone up." He's trying to sound intimidating I think, and the pitch shifter is helping. *"Waited too long. Forty-eight now. Two per book."*

Every feature on Sampson's face falls toward the floor. He goes pale and grips two handfuls of hair. Mindy shakes her head like *what did you expect*? Courtney is totally focused, staring at the phone, an impartial data processing machine.

I lick my lips.

"I'll call right back, okay Rico?"

"As you like."

He hangs up.

Sampson lays his glasses on the table and groans.

"Every time you gave in to him it just emboldened him," Mindy mutters, ostensibly to herself, but loud enough for all of us to hear. "He knows he can do whatever he likes—"

"Enough." Sampson writhes in his seat. He's close to tears again. "I can do forty-eight," he says softly. "I can get another eight by tomorrow—I know somewhere I can get the money."

I shift uncomfortably in my chair.

"Listen, Senator, as much as I'd love to get the books back and collect the commission, I'm not sure it's wise . . ."

"Something is weird," says Courtney half to himself. "I need to hear him talk more."

"I'll do it," Sampson repeats. "Tell him I can get him the other eight in unregistered stock certificates. They also don't have the owner's name on them. They're nearly as anonymous as bearer bonds."

I hesitate. Look at Mindy—her eyes are widening, like she's starting to allow for the possibility of the Senator actually going through with this.

I look at Courtney, who's deep in thought. "I want to hear him talk more. That voice alternator is removing most of the tells."

"Call him," says Sampson, quietly but forcefully. "Tell him I can give him forty-eight by tomorrow. You are working for me. I am *telling* you to arrange a swap for forty-eight."

"Okay." I half laugh nervously. "You're the boss."

I hit dial. Rico picks up instantly.

"*Yes.*"

"Rico?" I say.

"*Yes.*" The voice sounds surprisingly calm.

"We can get forty-eight by tomorrow. The last eight will be in unregistered stock certificates."

Long, long pause. I think he's hung up, but a little scratching says he's just put his hand over the receiver for a second.

"You have the bonds now?"

"Yes."

"Lay them out on a table. Cut up the front page of today's Denver Post and put a piece on top of each bond. Take a high res picture and fax it to the following number: 303-555-4213. If I'm satisfied I'll call back."

It takes me a second.

"Fax? We don't have a fax—"

He hangs up. Mindy scrunches her eyebrows in confusion. Sampson is confounded, terrified, but obviously excited.

Courtney's eyes are glowing. I can tell he's secretly thrilled that Rico is proving to be at least a nominally worthy intellectual adversary.

"Why does he want it faxed?" I ask Courtney. "Why the hell can't we text it to him?"

Courtney shakes his head.

"I really have no idea."

"Senator, do you have a fax machine?" I ask.

Courtney preempts me.

"There are cell phone apps that let you send faxes. That won't be a problem." He turns to Sampson. "The paper is to make sure the picture was taken today, *and* that we didn't just Photoshop the bonds in," he explains, wiggling his tongue inside his mouth with excitement. "I assume you have the *Post,* Senator?"

Sampson nods, exhales. "Yes. I read it every morning. Rico knows that."

"Go get the bonds," orders Courtney, all business. "Frank, find a fax app."

Sampson runs out of the guesthouse doors. Mindy brings scissors in from the kitchen, and Courtney carefully cuts up the front page of the paper into chunks large enough to be recognizable.

"I'm not sure we should let him do this," I say.

"Not our place to say," Courtney says, embroiled in cutting. "He hired us."

We turn our eyes to Mindy, asking for her tie-breaker vote. She's on her feet, suddenly alert and on edge, shaking her head and staring at the table, as if in disbelief.

"Of course," she says softly. "Of course we'll let him do it. Don't you two want to get paid?"

Sampson returns with a brown leather suitcase, flushed in the face.

Wordlessly, Courtney snatches the case, unzips it, and pulls out a bond at random to inspect it. It looks like a college diploma. Each one is for a hundred thousand Euros, redeemable only at such and such bank in Switzerland. No ID required.

So . . . there's 400 sheets of paper in there? Or a bit less, I guess— Euro is what, $1.10?

I clear the fruit and cereal off the table while Courtney covers it in bonds, then find an app to send faxes from the smartphone. Courtney lays flat about thirty of the bonds, and stacks the rest in a pile in the middle. Places a newspaper clipping in the center of each face that's exposed.

"Take a picture with the phone Frank," he orders me.

"Good thinking Courtney," I say.

I was just going to take a mental picture and send it by telepathy.

I take a few photos of the bond-covered table from different angles.

"303-555-4213," says Courtney.

"I remember," I lie.

I fax the photos, then set the phone on top of one of the bonds and sit down.

"What do you think fellas?" asks Sampson, face pink. "Is he going to go through with it?"

Mindy bites her thumbnail.

I shrug.

"That's a hell of lot of money. If he doesn't call back I'll be shocked. Courtney, you think we can trace that fax number?"

Courtney smiles.

"He'd have to be pretty stupid to use a listed fax number. I think he's sharper than that. But I'll try."

The phone vibrates. I pick it up.

"Take the one in the lower left hand corner of the table, hold it up to the light and take a close-up of the watermark. Then fax it."

Rico hangs up.

I pick up the bond and hold it so that the morning sun seeps through it. Snap a few pics and fax them. Set the phone back down and cross my hands on the table. Sampson is breathing fast. Courtney is just frowning, staring at the idle phone, as if trying to intuit the thoughts of the man on the other end. Mindy's eyes are darting rapidly around the room. She's having a lot of thoughts that she doesn't feel like sharing.

Phone rings. Sampson's eyes go wide. Courtney just frowns. He's in information gathering mode—his memory of this phone call will be as reliable as a tape recording. He'll note phrasing, tone, breathing patterns . . .

"Hi Rico," I say.

A long pause. Then:

"Who are you?" Do I detect a slightly higher tone in his voice? Is he pleased with the picture?

"As I said, my name is Ben Donovan. I was hired by James Sampson to facilitate this exchange. So—do you want to go ahead with this, or you just wasting my time with games?"

Courtney nods slightly in approval of my mild strong-arming. Rico's response to some light pushback will betray a lot about what's going through his head. Sampson looks petrified that I've just challenged his tormentor, probably worried that I've displeased him and he'll renege.

"Yes. I would like to," he says. A quick flicker of a grin escapes from Courtney's face, but he instantly suppresses it, reverting to his default dour frown.

Sampson looks half ecstatic, half mortified at this news. Mindy's chest is rising and falling rapidly.

"Wonderful," I say. "Maybe you'd like to meet somewhere public next week once we've secured the last eight? A movie theater lobby?"

A sound sort of like a grunt. Long hiss.

"I want to meet today. Today or the price goes up."

"Rico . . ." I say. "Be reasonable. Nobody can summon eight million dollars on a day's notice."

A long pause. Sampson is close to tearing out his hair.

"Tomorrow," he says.

"Tomorrow?" I say, and look to Sampson, who quickly nods: *Yes, I can get it by tomorrow.* "Okay. Tomorrow. Where should we meet? Maybe a mall?"

"No . . ." He trails off for a second. *"It will be a restaurant in downtown Denver. I'll tell you the exact one at five. You'll wear bright yellow raincoats. Bring the money in a pink gym bag."*

"Raincoats?" I ask. "It hasn't rained here in weeks."

A modified chuckle. This is a first from Rico.

"I'm aware. Don't bring weapons. If I see weapons, it's over."

"Okay, listen, Rico, I want to tell you in advance there's going to be three of us alright? Me, my partner, and Mindy—who you know. She's just coming to make sure you give us the real thing okay?"

A long pause. Sampson wrings his massive hands. Crackly breathing.

"No. Three is too many. One of you and the girl. If I see three of you I'll burn the books, and send some photos of Sampson to the Denver Post. I have a few that capture some rather unflattering angles."

The Senator's left eye twitches.

"We're not going to try any shit, but there's going to be three of us."

I look up at Courtney, who nods in understanding. Having three would be nice, but more important is pushing him slightly—the way he reacts will tell us a lot about his intentions here.

"No. One of you and the girl."

Sampson spreads his hands, his face like: *Give him what he wants!*

I await a hand gesture from Courtney to tell me whether to push again. I'm sure he's already calculating the risks of this operation. He holds up two fingers: *Two is okay.*

"Fine. Two."

He hangs up. The four of us stare at the phone for a long silent moment.

"Well," Courtney finally says. "The good news is I'm pretty sure he's serious. If you can get the money Senator, I'm quite confident he'll go through with the swap."

COURTNEY AND I take Sampson's second car, a Lexus, into down-town Aspen to shop with Sampson's credit card. We buy canary-yellow raincoats from a sporting goods store (pretty sure this demand of Rico's is just for humiliation purposes), and a pair of sleek walkie-talkies. We find a flamingo-pink tennis bag at a golf and tennis shop, but Courtney isn't satisfied with the material.

"It's too thin," he says. "I want one with thick fabric, so I can sew in a GPS chip."

It takes me a second to understand his angle.

"You sly dog!" I smack him on the back. "You want to track down the money for ourselves once we're done with Sampson?"

He shrugs.

"Might as well keep our options open."

I grin.

"Now you're talking."

We have to leave Aspen to find a suitably robust pink gym bag. And then with our own dwindling supply of cash we buy the items we don't want Sampson to know about. Rico said no weap-ons, but everyone says no weapons. There's no way we're going to meet with this guy unarmed.

Courtney has permits for New York, Florida and California, which satisfies the fifth store we try. We both get small-frame Smith and Wesson .22 Magnums. They're a little dainty, and don't have great range, but are small enough to strap to our ankles or thighs. I also get a half-serrated ceramic hunting knife.

Once that's over we realize there's frustratingly little more to prepare for the following evening—especially because we don't even know the exact place we're meeting him. Besides, seems likely the first restaurant will just be to scope us out, then he'll call us and tell us to go somewhere else. That's what I'd do, anyways.

We come back to the estate in the early evening. Lights are on in Mindy's guesthouse. Sampson's Hummer isn't in the driveway. Guess he's out getting eight million dollars. Not asking how. Less I know the better. I keep reminding myself his long-term well-being is not my problem—we'll make this swap and be out of here in two days. Don't owe Sampson anything once the job is done. If he wants to liquidate some holdings to buy back some crazy ass books, fine.

"Court, come to the guesthouse with me," I say. "I want to talk to Mindy."

"Why?" he asks.

"This morning during the phone call with Rico . . ." I shake my head. "She's not telling us everything."

I rap on the door of the guesthouse. Nothing, but the lights are on, so I knock hard. Finally she turns the lock and pulls the door in. She stands in the entranceway, very much not inviting us in.

"What?" she asks. She's a wreck. Eczema-pocked hands jittery like she's over-caffeinated. Glasses smudged with what might well be peanut butter. Over her shoulder I see her open laptop on her dining room table, and a small forest's worth of scattered papers.

"We just want to talk," I say. Courtney opens his mouth, looks apologetic, as if to say *well,* he *wants to talk.*

"I don't have time now," she says.

"What are you working on?" I ask.

She squints at me like I'm crazy to ask that.

"I said I'm *busy.* I'm sorry. We can talk tomorrow morning." She starts to shut the door, but I catch it with my hand.

"What's going on with you?" I say. "Do you even want these books back? Have you been in touch with Rico yourself?"

Her face instantly goes pink with rage.

"I'm sorry," Courtney says. "We didn't mean—"

"Of course I haven't been in touch with Rico!" she shrieks, at a pitch that feels like it's splitting my skull in half. Her shrill cry hangs in the dry air for a moment. Then she narrows her eyes. "Listen, you two have been in town what, two days? You think you have everything figured out?"

"No, of course not," mumbles Courtney.

"We know Sampson cut off something near and dear to him," I retort. "If that's what you're referring to."

Her face darkens.

"Yes." She nods. "And that's just the beginning. What did I tell you? You two don't want to get involved in this. And you're both probably *still* too stubborn to take my advice, but here it is: Don't ask any more questions. Just do your job tomorrow and then get as far away from this house as you can. I sure as hell wish someone had told that to me eight years ago."

Courtney and I stare blankly at her. She takes a step back, and slams the door shut. We stand in the darkness for a moment, then turn and head back to the main house.

"What a peach," I mutter.

Courtney doesn't respond.

We enter the main house through the front door. It's the first time we've been in the main body—outside our guest rooms— after the sun's gone down. Courtney turns on the flashlight on his phone and we probe the glass walls in the foyer for light switches.

"Wait," I say, after a few fruitless minutes. "Is it possible there just aren't any lights in here?"

Courtney explores the pink-tinted ceiling—the floor of the second level—with his light.

"You may just be right," he says.

"Christ," I say. "Not exactly user friendly."

In the glow of Courtney's phone, we make our way to the side stairwell, neither of us particularly enthusiastic about walking down the second-floor hallway again. It takes us about ten minutes to get to our rooms.

I look at Courtney before retreating into my room.

"Do you trust Sampson?" I ask. "Just your gut."

Courtney hesitates for a moment.

"I do, actually. I believe his desperation, and that he wouldn't dare risk endangering the swap by not telling us everything." He pauses. "What do you think about Mindy?" he asks.

I chuckle.

"Well, she just basically admitted that she's holding out on us. So no, I don't trust her."

"No I mean, like, what do you *think* of her? Like . . ." Courtney clears his throat. "As a woman."

An involuntary snort escapes my nose.

"Courtney, as your friend, I sincerely urge you to steer clear of that train wreck," I say. "But more importantly, you need to stay focused. This job should be over tomorrow, then we're out of here. Keep your feet on the ground."

"Right, right." Courtney nods quickly, abashedly. "Of course. Thanks, Frank. Good night."

Sweet relief as I enter my opaque, illuminated room. Realize I'm too wired to just read and conk out. I'm excited about getting paid, and a new Social Security number.

I pull out the iPhone, and quickly enter Sadie's number. Don't allow myself to agonize over it, just grit my teeth and call my daughter for the first time in months. Two rings.

"Hello?"

My heart leaps at the smallness of her voice.

"Hey Sadie. This . . . hey, it's Dad."

I wish I didn't notice the brief silence before she responds.

"Oh. Hey Dad. How are you?"

"I'm great. I mean, fine. But working. Courtney and I, we have another big job. It could be huge for us. I don't want to get into details but I'm hoping I'll be able to come visit you at school pretty soon."

"Oh wow."

"Yeah! It's really quite a funny situation, I can't wait to tell you all about it. But what about you? How are you? How's school and everything?"

"It's good. Fine. I'm actually about to crash. Have a big test in the morning, so."

"Oh, sure sure. But listen, sweetie, really great to hear your voice. I'll call you back soon, okay?"

"Sure. Sounds good. 'Bye."

"I love you."

"You too."

I drop the phone on the bed. I'm sweating heavily, and breathing so hard I'm practically wheezing.

"Big test in the morning?" "You too?"

Disaster. Total disaster.

To calm down I draw a warm bath and float for about a half hour. Close my eyes and try not to think about that call. Instead run through the call with Rico. The extra eight he demanded.

He probably never meant for this to drag on so long. But once he realized the extent of Sampson's desperation . . .

I dry myself off and check my watch. Ten at night.

I'm still shaken from that call with Sadie. What if I get my money and identity, fly down to see her and she doesn't want to see me?

Better sleep before I slip too far down that rabbit hole.

I pop a Benadryl, wash it down with a couple swigs from a twenty-year-old scotch I found in Sampson's kitchen. If he's a recovering alcoholic, it's almost like I'm doing him a favor.

I stare out the window at the tennis court, savoring the feeling of my brain winding down, eyes getting droopy . . .

. . . My eyes snap open. It's still dark outside. Watch says three twenty in the morning. Don't know how I'm this wide awake after my Benadryl cocktail. I was having a dream similar to last night's: A creature with extra limbs scaling a wall, except this time it was Sadie's head atop that twisted body, horrible extra arms protruding from between its shoulder blades.

I get out of bed and look out the window. I'm as alert as if somebody splashed cold water on my face.

Nearly pitch black; Sampson doesn't keep any perimeter lights on at night.

There's a sick kind of feeling in my chest. It's the sort of queasy discomfort I remember feeling once sitting in the doctor's examination room, waiting for him to come back and tell me some test results. I turn on the bedside lamp, hoping it will calm me down, but it doesn't. Forehead damp with sweat. Am I having a panic attack?

That's when I realize there's been a sound this whole time. Maybe that's what woke me up? It's faint, but undeniable: some kind of smacking sound coming from outside my bedroom door, one crack every thirty seconds or so.

I wouldn't be much of a detective if I just let this go . . .

I grab the flashlight out of my bag and pad out into the hall barefoot. The sound is much more distinct out here. Coming from inside the house. I rap lightly on Courtney's door, honestly because I'm a little creeped out. Nothing. Flirt with the idea of really banging on his door, but some primordial part of my brain doesn't want to make any noise now, in case the sound is a predator— don't want to rouse its attention.

As soon as I turn my flashlight away from Courtney's door, to the rest of the house, it's like someone shined a floodlight on it. The walls magnify the weak beam like mirrors. Quickly I wrap the flashlight in my shirt, putting several layers over the glow until there's just barely enough for me to see my way.

But there's another light source. It's in the wing adjacent to mine, across the yard. I squint. It's not strong, but it's there, flickering. I think it's a candle.

I take a deep breath and start walking. To reach the light source I'll have to go to the Spine, then turn left into the other wing.

The glass is cool on my feet. I find the transparent floors are less dizzying at night, because you can't really see so much stuff below you.

The cracking becomes more distinct as I near the Spine. It's consistent. One every half minute. With each crack I feel a slight reverberation in the glass under my feet. This house is like an echo chamber.

I turn left into the other wing, and look at the glowing disc of light which defines the candle. It's below my feet, and perhaps fifteen meters in front of me. It's in the second-floor hallway— the "limb" hallway, and I'm still on the top floor. I find a spiral staircase and delicately feel my way down, until I'm level with the light source. The crack is definitely coming from the source of the light, but I can't see anything because of the glare on the several panes of glass between us. There's another sound intermingled with the cracking. A low wail. A kind of ghostly moan.

I switch off the flashlight now. There's enough light from the candle a few rooms away to make my way forward. I put a hand against the cold glass wall of the hallway to steady myself. The cracking and wailing grow louder. I drop to my stomach so I won't be seen. Finally, when I'm about a meter away, I can clearly make out the source of the sound.

It's one of the identical rooms with the blue glass floor, and intricate pipe arrangement hanging from the ceiling. Sampson is on his knees, totally naked, facing away from me. His back is pecked with a hundred red spots. Tiny lacerations. The glass immediately behind him is cloudy with bloody dots. He raises a hand to the ceiling and I see it's grasping a kind of multi-tailed whip. He flicks his wrist, and the tendrils of the whip smack into his back, opening a host of new wounds, and sending flecks of blood shooting backwards onto the glass wall behind him.

The whole time he's moaning softly, a mantra. It takes me some time to discern it as: "*Sophnot, for my father, my king . . .*" And with each flick of his wrist he gasps a number. "*twenty-seven, Sophnot, for my father my king, twenty-eight . . .*"

I stay flat on my stomach, observing in horror, numbers twenty-seven through thirty-two, and then retreat backwards, get back to my room as quickly as I can and lock the door.

I DON'T SLEEP another second that night. Just stare at the ceiling until Courtney timidly knocks on my door a few minutes after nine.

I roll out of bed, pull on an old Dark Side of the Moon T-shirt, and a baggy pair of jeans I treated myself to with Sampson's card; baggy enough that I can strap the Magnum to my left calf, and the ceramic knife on my right, without attracting attention. I must be wearing last night's Sampson sighting on my face, because Courtney says:

"You need to stop taking sleeping aids, Frank. It's not real sleep when you drug yourself."

Courtney doesn't look so well rested himself: dark purple bags under his eyes, high forehead more crinkled with worry than usual.

"Someday I hope to talk you into self-medicating. It will really change your life."

"I always sleep well," he says. "It's because of all the greens in my diet. I just stayed up late reviewing the Rico file. Then had to sew the GPS chip in the lining." He nods to the empty pink bag slung over his shoulder. "Was like a little surgery."

"I guarantee I had a worse night than you," I say, image of bloodstained glass suddenly vivid in my mind's eye. I pull Courtney into the stone-enclosed side stairwell.

"You know what you asked, about trusting Sampson?" I ask him. His eyes narrow.

"Yes."

As I describe what I saw the night before, Courtney's face contorts like he's sucking on a lime.

"Well," he sighs, shaking his head. "Unsettling. But is it really that surprising?" he asks. "As you put it, he's been brainwashed. This just confirms it's not an act."

I rub my eyes.

"Guess you're right. Someday it would be nice to get hired by someone with their head screwed on a little straighter."

Courtney grins.

"They don't pay nearly as well."

In the guesthouse, Sampson is wearing blue slacks, a white button-down and a generic red striped tie. He's not eating, just sipping on a Diet Pepsi, and his forehead is creased with worry. He looks exhausted, and I wish I didn't know why.

Across the table from him, Mindy is munching on honeydew, taken from a brand-new fruit plate. Today she's wearing a red tank top which isn't doing much to hide the surprisingly dramatic contours of her upper body from the two undersexed private investigators sitting down across the breakfast table from her.

Maybe all this time around de-libidoed Sampson has made her forget the lurid gaze of men. Or maybe she just doesn't give a shit. She's perky this morning; seems surprisingly refreshed.

I shoot her a look like *I don't trust you, you know.*

She half shrugs, half ignores me.

Courtney and I sit down, and he heaps a bunch of fruit onto a plate for me.

"Morning, Senator," I say, struggling to meet Sampson's eyes.

"I have a bunch of meetings today," says Sampson, as if I'd asked why he's dressed up. "Might have to fly to DC tomorrow, but hoping I can get out of it."

Yeah, that back's not gonna self-flagellate itself . . .

I take a few bites of slimy mango before I realize Sampson is staring at me.

"So," he asks. "Leaving soon? Denver is a three-hour drive, but there can be traffic."

Jesus. This guy . . .

"You think I could get some coffee?" I ask. "I don't think you want me handling forty-eight million dollars before I have coffee."

"Of course, of course," Sampson says, and shoots up from his stool. "Apologies. I don't drink coffee anymore. Anything in particular? We have a Nespresso in here—does that work?"

"Doesn't matter. Just defibrillate me."

Sampson walks briskly into the adjacent kitchen.

"Finish all your 'work' Mindy?" I ask.

"I did, thank you for asking."

Courtney observes Mindy eating for a moment, opens his mouth to speak a few times but nothing comes out. Finally musters a stilted "So how did you sleep. Sleep alright?"

Mindy frowns in confusion.

"Sure," she replies.

"Good," says Courtney mechanically. "Me too."

Watching Courtney trying to act smooth is making me physically uncomfortable.

"Alright then," she says. "So we all slept well."

Sampson storms back into the dining room and plops what looks like a quadruple espresso in front of me. Bless his heart.

"So you got the eight million?" I ask Sampson, after slurping down my first dose. He nods almost imperceptibly. "And . . ." I eye him dubiously. "You definitely still want to go through with this."

"Yes," he says.

Courtney's skinny hands coil into tight fists. Mindy appears to have expected this.

"You're the boss," I say.

"And make sure you do whatever he tells you." Sampson is slightly frantic. "Whatever it takes. Maybe get going now? There can be accidents on the highway you know."

With a mouthful of pineapple, Courtney says: "Ten minutes to eat."

"Of course."

I take a bite of fruit. "Sometimes, Senator, pushing back is the best way to make sure the deal goes through," I say. "Make *him* scared that we'll back out."

Sampson takes a desperate gulp of soda.

"Don't do that," he says.

While we fill up on fruits and berries, he cracks open a second Pepsi, takes off his glasses and rubs them with his napkin. Checks his watch every ten seconds. When he can take it no more he pulls the leather suitcase containing the bonds up and plunks it on the table. While we're still eating, he hurriedly pulls the papers out and crams them into the pink duffel bag. "That's it. Forty in bonds plus eight from yesterday."

His hands are shaking. Eyeballs pulsing like I've seen before with meth heads. Checks his watch again. "Yeah, you three should really get a move on."

Content, I wipe my lips with a napkin and say "Okay. Let's hit the road."

Courtney stands up off his stool and stretches for the ceiling. Mindy wolfs down another few strawberries. Her sudden zen is disquieting, calm before the storm vibes.

"Fellas." Sampson stands up with us, looks at us seriously through his round glasses. His eyes are pleading. Then he approaches us and lays one massive hand on my head, one on Courtney's.

Sampson closes his eyes and says aloud: "May the God who blessed Abraham, Isaac, Jacob, Moses, Mohammed, Jesus Christ and the latter day saint, my teacher Sophnot, bless these men on their holy mission."

Heads stooped, Courtney and I exchange a quick glance of

discomfort. The name of his tutor immediately evokes the image of him last night.

"Guide them and protect them. Grant them the wisdom to discern between good and evil, and guide their hands to slay evil where it lies. Let them return to me with the holy writings of Sophnot, so they, with me, may dwell in the peace of his wisdom all the days of their lives. Amen."

Courtney and I both mumble an obligatory amen. I turn and lock eyes with Mindy for a second; hard to get a good read on what she thinks of all this nonsense.

And then Sampson removes his hands from our heads and motions to the door. He's near tears.

"Please bring them back to me," he gasps.

We nod silently. I sling the pink bag over my shoulder. It's heavy. Fifteen or twenty pounds' worth of very dense paper.

We leave the guesthouse and climb into the Humvee. Courtney hops into the front passenger seat. I get in the back next to enough money to make God jealous. As we pull out of the estate, Sampson watches from the front porch like an abandoned puppy. It's a relief to get away from him.

"That was sure a beautiful, um, blessing by the Senator, eh?" I say to Mindy, keeping sarcasm levels vague.

"Mmhmm," she replies and reaches for the radio. Rather terrifying to watch her momentarily steer this tank down the mountainside one-handed. Some shitty country music comes on. A woman crooning about love lost.

I start dozing off, but come to about twenty-five minutes into our drive. The car is stopped. Mindy has pulled over at a rest stop and turned off the ignition.

"Let's talk," says Mindy.

"Shouldn't we talk while we drive to Denver?" I ask.

"We have at least an extra hour," Mindy says. Then looks seriously at me and then at Courtney.

"Well," she says. "If you were planning on taking the money and skipping town, you might as well do it now, yeah?"

Courtney looks horrified at the insinuation.

"Mindy, we would *never*—"

She holds up a thin hand to stop him.

"You don't have to play this game. You want it, you can fucking well take it. I obviously can't stop you."

Courtney looks back at me, fear in his eyes, like he's worried I'm going to take her up on the offer and he's going to have to question all the trust he's ever put in me.

"Tempting," I say. "But honestly, the money isn't of much use to me without that new identity and a clean record. And I'm fairly sure Sampson has enough resources to hunt us down pretty quickly."

"Okay." Mindy closes her eyes for a second, chews on one of her knuckles. "Well then, you need to understand these books—"

"They're not written in English are they?" Courtney interrupts. "You're trying to *translate* them! Aren't you? What is it, some kind of ancient Egyptian? Is it like a *new* New Testament?"

Mindy looks at him for a moment. I think she's impressed with him. I'm weirdly proud of my partner for intuiting what—based on her tense shoulder—is close to the truth.

She rubs a hand through her speckled brown hair. When she speaks her voice is strained.

"Let me explain, because it appears this may actually happen." She takes a deep breath. "So, it's not *precisely* clear what the books are." There's already obvious relief in her voice. A steam valve being released. How frustrating it must be to only be able to speak about her work with an ungenitaled religious nut job. "You're correct. I'm translating it, from what appears to be a wholly original, largely pictorial language—the characters are closer to drawings than English letters, and to my knowledge, have no sounds associated with them. They are only meant to be read silently.

"Many sections are stories, some original, some from the Old Testament, with minor changes. There are aphorisms, passages that I think are detailed instructions for types of rituals, but I can't be sure. Can't be sure about much at all, is the truth. But what I'm definite on is the structure of the books, which is astonishing. There is an order to them, but no beginning and no end. Rather, each book is a sort of commentary on the previous one. So they go in a circle, each commentating on the previous one, until you're back at the start. If you could read the books perfectly—and I'm nowhere close—you would just dive in at any point and start reading, following the circle around and around again, and each time you'd read a passage the second time you'd have a much deeper insight because of the layers of commentary and explanation that came before . . . It's a work of almost impossible scholarship. Every page assumes you've *already* read every page prior. The cross-references are mind boggling. I really—what's most incredible is that in years of study I've only scratched the surface. As I said—I've extracted certain interesting pieces, but still have no real concept of what the work—as a whole—entails."

Courtney quickly looks at me in the backseat, eyes wide. He loves this shit.

I look back at him like: *Don't just believe everything she says.*

"So, maybe I just don't get it," I say. "But if I understand what you're saying, you don't even know the language these books are written in. So are you sure it's not just really intricate nonsense? And that's why it's so hard to understand?"

"*No*," she says, perhaps more vehemently than she intended. "It's definitely a language of sorts. And I know enough that I can extract meaning from the books. I'm doing it. It just takes an extremely long time."

"Why? If you can read it?"

"Because both the content and the language itself are complex. Each character has a meaning that is dependent on context—and so I need to cross-reference tons of other pages to make sure I'm reading it right. Just an example: There's one pictograph that usually means *hunter*—but if the symbol for *woman* is in the same phrase, it means *lioness*. But after about a year, I realized that if the character which, loosely translated, is an adverb meaning *carefully*, is within a five-centimeter radius of *hunter* on the page, that original *hunter* character is devoid of intrinsic meaning, and only serves as an allusion to a story on page seventy-seven of a different volume."

Courtney is leaning in so close to her that he's straining his passenger side seat belt. He's like an addict who's just had his first hit. He just wants to open his brain and let her pour all the facts in.

"The language they are written in is, unbelievably, far more rich even than present-day English," Mindy continues, "which shouldn't be possible. Nearly all linguists agree that complete, functional languages can only be formed organically, developing to accommodate the needs of a culture over the spans of hundreds or thousands of years. If this was written by a single person over the span of a few decades—the implications are staggering. Do you follow?"

Courtney nods slowly, practically drooling.

"I guess," I lie.

"The bottom line is, they need to be studied. I have dedicated my life to the study of language, and finding these books is the equivalent of a poet stumbling upon the previously unpublished collected works of Shakespeare. It's not about personal glory. It's about potentially understanding the origins of language, and humanity. Which is why we can't bring them back to James."

I furrow my brow.

"Why?"

She hesitates for a moment.

"What do you think will happen once James gets the books back?"

I scratch my neck.

"He'll bring them to Oliver Vicks in prison."

"Right. And then they're lost from me, from the scholarly community, forever."

"So what are you suggesting, Mindy?" I ask.

"You help me do the swap, and then the three of us will bring the books to one of my connections at a university in London. I spoke to him last night, and believe me, when we show up with these we'll be *very* well taken care of."

Courtney is frowning intensely, a sort of panic in his eyes while his brain works furiously to analyze our situation, given this new information.

"What you're proposing, Mindy," I say, "is, in effect, stealing forty-eight million dollars of merchandise from the man who hired us. Who also happens to be a US Senator."

"That's right," she says.

I shake my head.

"Even if I was willing to screw Sampson over, and *even* if I thought we had a chance of outrunning him . . . He's my only chance to get off the Interpol list. I could never come back to the States, and my daughter is here."

Her almond eyes blaze.

"You've been in this two days, Frank," she says. "Two bloody days. If Sampson had never contacted you two, you'd still be romping around Europe. This is the last seven years of my life. This is so much bigger than—"

"I don't care," I say. "Getting these books back to Sampson means I get to see my daughter."

"Courtney," she says, exasperated. "Explain to him what I'm saying."

"I . . ." Courtney swivels his face between us like a captured fly, as spiders approach from opposite directions. "I mean, I suppose you both make a certain amount of sense . . ."

I gape at him.

"Why would you believe a word she says?" I say, voice cracking. "She probably just has another buyer lined up overseas!"

"That doesn't make any sense! If I wanted the money, I'd suggest taking the massive amount of *money* beside you in the seat."

"We're not *stealing* these things from a United-States-Fucking-Senator," I yell, jabbing a finger at her. "You want your made-up language? I'll make one up for you. *Quap.* That means turn the fucking car back on."

Her jaw drops in righteous indignation.

"You *buffoon,*" she shrieks. "You think you're qualified to—"

"Quap," I say. "Quap, quap."

"Guys, please. Guys—" I realize that Courtney has been attempting to intervene for some time. Finally Mindy and I go quiet.

"Please," he says, eyes wet. "There's nothing to even argue about yet. We're counting our eggs. We all agree on the first step, which is retrieving the books from Rico. So can we please cooperate?"

I glare at him. Using the royal goddamn *we* like a kindergarten teacher. Our eyes are locked. My look saying *I can't believe you're taking her side.*

His clenched lips and pleading eyes respond: *Please. We need her help right now.*

"Alright Mindy." The words are physically difficult for me to form. "Let's get the books back, then figure out what to do with them. Deal?"

She stares me down for a moment, like from across a poker table. "Fine."

She starts the car back up, and merges onto a highway with no regard for the flow of traffic.

I rub my eyes wearily. Those sleepless hours from last night are finally hitting me. I lean my head back and try to sleep, but am assailed by images of blood droplets smacking against clear glass . . .

Sophnot. My father, my king.

WE PARK OUTSIDE a Barnes and Noble for a few hours, until we get the message from Rico at exactly five. It's a prerecorded voice message, with him talking through that filter:

"*Trattoria Marcos at six. Sit in a booth and wait. Don't forget the raincoats.*"

We drive to a downtown Denver short-term parking garage, about a three-minute walk from the Trattoria. We have forty-five minutes to spare.

I step out and stretch, fill my lungs with hot, dry air. Then I climb back into the backseat to wait.

"Should we call him back, just to confirm we're coming?" Mindy asks Courtney.

"This isn't junior prom," I say. "No need to make ourselves look desperate."

Courtney cracks his knuckles one by one. He's frowning and scanning the rows of parked cars which we, in our Humvee, mostly tower over.

"Are you sure the bonds are real?" he asks, glancing at the duffel bag beside me in the backseat.

"Court, relax," I say. This always happens. The closer we get to the moment of truth, the more doomsday scenarios start materializing somewhere behind the pale-moon forehead.

"Alright," Courtney says, taking off his jacket, leaving only a very unassuming plain grey T-shirt draped over his bones. "It's 5:15. I'm going to go scope the area around the restaurant, then want to sit down at least twenty minutes before you two. See you in there."

"Review your hand signals," he says to me. I'm supposed to subtly pass on whatever Rico tells me on the phone.

"I got it, champ."

"Good luck," Mindy says, and pats his shoulder. It's pretty platonic, but Courtney blushes, and because he can't force himself to respond, quickly opens the passenger side door and slides out. He opens the trunk to get his red acrylic bag full of tools that he never goes into the field without. Contains things like lock picks, latex gloves, binoculars, a makeup kit, colored contacts, and sunglasses. Then he slams the trunk closed and Mindy and I watch his hunched shoulders and tiny ass recede into the labyrinth of parked cars.

As soon as Courtney leaves a near-palpable tension descends on us. He was the buffer between us, and now her proposed grand larceny is back front and center.

I can hear her breathing from the backseat, and her small shoulders are tense under her tank top. She's nervous.

We need to be on the same page when we go to meet Rico.

"Maybe I overreacted back there," I say. "Sorry. I'm exhausted."

She responds with a sound like *mmm*—the bare minimum expenditure of air to acknowledge that I spoke. What a ray of sunshine.

"What's Rico like?" I push. "Did you two get along?"

This at least elicits a response.

"That's like asking if I was friends with a brick wall," she says.

"What do you mean?"

She cranes her head to the side to crack her neck, but doesn't turn around to face me.

"We didn't have much to talk about. He's a meathead. Frankly, even this whole scheme surprises me. I never thought he had ambitions beyond watching American Football and doing push-ups."

How is Courtney attracted to this crabby woman?

"Gotcha."

A few minutes of silence. I'm a little worried about Courtney, but probably shouldn't be. In my experience, he just doesn't commit mental errors in the heat of battle. Especially when he doesn't have to talk to anyone. For probably the twentieth time since getting in the car, I check that my knife and Magnum are still strapped around my ankles. Mindy checks her watch for the fiftieth time since we parked. She can't stop fidgeting.

"So . . . you've been working from photocopies since the books were stolen?" I ask.

"No," she answers immediately. She likes talking about the books. "All I have are about twenty pages I meticulously hand-copied. It can't be photocopied."

"You mean Sampson wouldn't let you?"

"No, no. It quite literally cannot be photocopied faithfully. It's written partially in shades of near-white ink which are visible only from certain angles. Some backgrounds are filled in with tight multicolored patterns. It's a technique called prismatic coloring, which makes documents difficult to forge. When a machine tries to photocopy them it blotches the shapes and colors. It's used when printing things like passports or driver's licenses, but to my knowledge these books are the only known example of such a sample being produced by hand. Of course, my hand copies aren't perfect, but they're good enough to try to decipher."

"So," I say, "how do you account for one guy, a guy in prison no less, being able to create something like this? In a made-up language? He's just some kind of freak uber-genius?"

Mindy rubs a hand through her hair, rustling up the scent of lemony shampoo.

"I've given a lot of thought to it, and my personal belief isn't totally scientific. Essentially, it *can't* have been written by just him. The sheer scale is simply inconceivable. The layers of even a single page are like an hour-long orchestral score. And the language itself—as I explained most linguist theorists agree that even a team of a hundred academics, working for a hundred years, wouldn't be able to compose a language as wholly original as this."

"So—he must have some pretty brilliant colleagues in Saddle-back Correctional Facility, eh?"

Mindy is silent.

I prod: "I suppose Sampson would say that it all came from a higher power or something."

Mindy doesn't respond.

"Do *you* believe that?" I ask. After a long pause she says:

"Let's just say, I haven't ruled it out." Mindy finally turns around to look at me with suddenly soft brown eyes. "I suppose you think that makes me a fool?"

"Actually no," I sigh. "I kinda get it."

She narrows her eyes, surprised.

"Oh?"

"Yeah." I shift in my seat. "Courtney and I had a case together. About five years ago. Made me reconsider some of these things myself."

She raises an eyebrow.

"What happened?"

I bite my lower lip. Would certainly like to get some of that off my chest. But I should probably wait for a conversational partner who's bound by doctor/patient confidentiality.

"Some other time. We have to go," I say.

We put on our yellow raincoats, lock up the Humvee and proceed out of the garage. We're in what seems to be an upscale shopping/touristy district. Light foot traffic—although ever since I left New York five years ago, anything less than a total mob on the pavement feels light.

I use the phone to guide us toward the Trattoria, passing retro furniture stores, craft beer pubs, Starbucks. Almost everyone is white. Most of the men have facial hair. The women don't wear heels. A lot of people are smoking pot in the street.

The pink duffel packed with money is strapped over my shoulder. I grip it like it's a small child, not wanting to even think about scenarios where we get mugged.

The air is hot and dry on my tongue, and I'm already sweating inside my raincoat. Just a few blocks away from the restaurant, I pull the photo of Rico that Sampson provided from my pocket and refresh my memory for a few seconds.

"I'll recognize him," says Mindy.

I glare at her.

"Let me do my job," I say.

She seems to consider a retort, but swallows it.

I'd underestimated how visible the pink bag and yellow rain-coats would be, and I'm definitely feeling exposed. If Rico has a pal here reconnoitering, we've been spotted already. I grip the duffel tighter to my chest. Six minutes till we're supposed to meet, and nothing else from Rico. Guess that means we're on for the Trattoria.

My adrenaline finally fires up. I'm nervous. Haven't done anything like this for five years.

"Make sure you don't give him the money until you have the books," she says.

"Wow. Good thing we have a PhD here."

She wrings her eczema-pocked hands.

"I'm just saying, don't fuck this up."

"I'm not trying to be an ass," I say in a low voice. "But please stay out of my way and let me do this. That's what I was hired for. All you have to do is tell me if they're the real books. That's your only job. Don't say anything to him."

She mutters something unintelligible under her breath. She's breathing fast, and trying hard to hide her anxiety.

We turn onto the busy outdoor mall that contains the Trattoria. I hug the bag to my chest as we navigate past shoppers and families. Two kids with ice cream all over their faces sit on benches and cry, a street performer plays guitar, singing so softly that he's nearly inaudible.

Trattoria de Marcos is nestled between a trendy bookstore and an expensive-looking macaron boutique. The Trattoria has a green awning and well-groomed waitstaff. A family of four is eating outside, and that's it. Not dinnertime yet.

I can't decide whether I want more people around or fewer . . . depends how likely Rico is to just whip out a gun in broad daylight, I suppose. We approach the maître d', a young man with greasy hair.

"Two for inside, please," I say, and try to smile.

"This way," he says. Leads us into an interior kept dark by heavily stained windows. "Booth or table?" he asks.

"Booth," I say, quickly scanning our surroundings. There's an elderly couple silently picking at what looks like tiramisu; a pair of blonde girls speaking what I think is Dutch and looking at a street map; a family comprised of two parents, an infant and toddler sharing a pizza; and Courtney, with an untouched espresso, absorbed with a crossword. I don't think he's going to sound any alarm bells with Rico.

Maître d' leaves and a high-school-aged girl approaches our booth and brings us water glasses.

"You can still order off our lunch menu," she explains, as Mindy and I sit down across from each other. "Dinner doesn't start until six. Would you like to hear our specials?"

"No," Mindy snaps.

"You sure? We have a great duck lasagna—"

"No, *we're fine*," says Mindy, gripping a handful of hair and pulling so hard that her eyes tear up.

The waitress takes a step back.

"So," she says weakly. "Anything to drink to besides the water?"

"We'll just take a moment with the menus," I say. "Sorry about my girlfriend. She's hungry, but also just a generally unpleasant person."

The waitress smiles uncomfortably, then rushes away. Mindy's hands are shaking.

"It's okay," I say. "Take deep breaths. Have some water."

She's shaking so badly she struggles to bring the cup to her lips.

I check my phone. It's three minutes after six and no missed calls. Mindy unzips the chest of her yellow slicker to let herself get some air.

"Are these really necessary?" she asks, looking around the restaurant. "He's not bloody here. I know what he looks like."

"He could have a pal here doing reconnaissance. We want to look cooperative."

Mindy peers at me over the top of her black rims like I'm an idiot, then makes a show of looking around at our fellow diners.

A different waiter comes to our table and tops off our ice water, glances at our yellow coats, but doesn't comment. I stare at the phone, unsure if I'm hoping it rings or not. Three minutes pass. I'm just starting to feel that this has been nothing but an exercise in humiliation, when the phone buzzes. Not a call, a text. From a different number.

aquarium. Come str8 here. Confrm.

I show it to Mindy.

"There's an aquarium in Denver?" I ask.

"One of the biggest in the country," she says. "About a seven-minute walk away."

I'll be there right away.

I shoot to my feet and make a quick hand gesture on my cheek for Courtney: *Second location.* I'll call him in a few minutes and he'll follow. He's probably being paranoid, I could probably just show him the text. But once in a while, Courtney's paranoia turns out to be founded.

The maître d' tries to ask what's wrong, as I brush past him.

"You know where the aquarium is?" I ask Mindy, outside the restaurant.

In response, she just leads the way. We cross the walking mall, turn right onto a street that's busy, but in a quaint flyover state kind of way. I keep the pink bag squeezed into my armpit. Mindy chews on an already badly mauled thumbnail as we walk.

"It will be fine," I say.

She doesn't respond.

I check the phone. No new calls or texts. I badly want to reach down to touch my weapons, but resist. I plug in the earbuds attached to the walkie-talkie in my pocket and buzz him.

"Court, we're headed to the aquarium."

"Okay. I'm a few minutes behind," he says.

We rush across the street, take a left, and what must be the aquarium comes into view. It's a giant building the size of an enclosed sports stadium. Denver Ocean Journey, proclaims enormous lettering. We stride across acres of parking lot. I'm sweating heavily from the baking sun on my raincoat. We're in serious field trip territory here—a fleet of yellow school buses is clustered near the front entrance. Little kids in double-file buddy-system being led in and out of the hive by exasperated, hoarse teachers. There's an all-American eatery clumped onto the complex, and pasty families in baseball hats are enthusiastically streaming from the aquarium exit into the restaurant.

The line to buy tickets isn't too long; probably because it's already late in the day. I buy us two all-access passes with Sampson's credit card, which come in the form of orange paper brace-lets. Then I grab Mindy's arm and pull her behind me through the entrance.

Shit.

There's security.

Probably why Rico picked this place. Let someone else make sure we're unarmed.

We'll have to put the bag through a conveyor belt x-ray ma-chine, and also step through a metal detector.

"Go ahead and wait for me," I instruct Mindy. "Take the bag as soon as it comes out of the machine."

I watch her walk through the metal detector without issue.

I fight the tide of kids and tourists back to the front entrance, and step back outside. Pretend to tie my shoe and pull my Magnum out of my ankle holster, then drop it in a blue recycling bin near the entrance. I buzz Courtney.

"There's security," I say. "Maybe I could get the gun in, but don't want to risk it."

"Crap."

"I dropped it in the blue bin next to the entrance. Don't come in. Stay outside with the guns. You can listen in. If anything goes bad you can catch them on the way out."

"I don't like that."

"I'll still have my knife. That's why you get ceramic. And we have the tracer in the bag. How far away are you?"

"I'm across the parking lot. Don't want to get too close to you."

"I'm going."

I rejoin the steady flow of eager fish-watchers inching their way forward. Mindy is on the other side of the x-ray machine waiting for the bag. I wave to her to make sure she's ready, and put the pink bag on the belt. My chest tightens as I let it go. I consider the possibility that this has all been an elaborate ruse by *Mindy*, and she's just going to snatch it up and disappear.

I watch the machine attendant's eyes as the bag glides through. I doubt the bonds will be a problem—just paper—but the tiny GPS tracker might look weird on there.

No issues. Mindy grabs the bag on the other side. I rush through the metal detector to join her. It's a relief to take the bag back from her.

"What were you doing outside?" she asks.

I pretend I didn't hear her. Check the phone. A new text:

Come to Otters. Text when ur there.

Ok

I scan our surroundings. Signs indicate different walking paths: You choose to follow the path of a river, and get to see all the wildlife and fish that occupy their ecosystems. Choices are Colorado River, Kampar River, or African and South American freshwater creatures.

"Where are otters from?" I ask Mindy. "Africa?"

"You can't be serious. God, American schools are terrible," she says, and points to the Colorado River path. We enter into a narrow hallway. Walls and the arched ceiling are all glass, behind which swim what I guess are Colorado fish immersed in grainy, yellow river water: something that looks like bass, maybe a salmon? Walking through a parted sea. The water that surrounds

us is not still, rushes like a river, sweeping the googly-eyed creatures first up over our heads, then back down. Kids have their
palms and faces pressed hard against the glass.

Air is damp and smells like seaweed. The stone under our
shoes is slippery, and I nearly stumble as Mindy and I wind our
way through the aqua-tunnel. We rush past an animal-free exhibit
that illustrates the phenomenon of flash floods—a huge spout of
white water gushes into a rocky crevice and fills it in an instant.

An interactive station where you can actually touch real
crabs . . .

Can't believe that's a draw.

And finally, the otters. Their habitat is amphibious: half rocky
shore on which to flop around on their leathery stomachs, half
yellow-colored pool. It's structured so you can watch the otters both
while they're on land, and while they're swimming around; they're
infinitely more graceful when they're underwater. I look around,
probing the crowd for Rico. There are only around thirty in this
otter-viewing space, and he's tall enough that he should stick out. I
think I spot him from behind for an instant—recognize the buzzed
head—but the guy turns around and is about seventeen. I pretend
to tie my shoe again, and this time unstrap my sheathed ceramic
knife. Tuck it next to my butt, under the elastic band of my decaying
jockey shorts, then pull the back of my shirt over it.

I pull out the phone. Nothing new.

We're at the otters

My stomach clenches, waiting for a response. It comes quickly.

Trn around and come through ylw tape.

"What did he say?" asks Mindy. I ignore her, and search for yellow tape. It takes me a moment to realize what he's talking about. There's another hallway that branches off the otter exhibit, but is cordoned off with yellow "under construction" tape.

To buy thirty seconds, I text back:

What tape?

Then plug my headphones into the walkie-talkie in my pocket and buzz Courtney.

"Meeting him now. I'll keep the walkie on so you can hear what's going on."

Courtney's voice is solemn:

"Make sure you don't go anywhere private, Frank."

My phone buzzes.

Yelow tape across frm otters

I approach the temporary plaque beside the taped-up entrance-way explaining come fall, this will be a beaver sanctuary. Behind the tape is a narrow, cavelike tunnel.

I call Rico.

"Where are you?" he answers instantly. It's the first time I've heard his voice unfiltered. It's strained, desperate.

"I'm not going in that tunnel," I say. Beside me Mindy gapes in disbelief. "The whole point was to meet somewhere public. We'll be next to the otters. You have five minutes to come out and meet us, or else we're leaving."

I hang up before he can reply.

Mindy is staring at me, flushed from exertion and nerves.

"What the *fuck* are you doing?"

"He wants this deal to happen as much as we do," I say. "He's the one getting forty-eight million. He'll come out."

I lead Mindy to a bench beside the otter exhibit. A gaggle of ten-year-old kids laugh as one of the animals flops around on his stomach. The glass doesn't extend to the ceiling, so we can clearly hear them barking and splashing. Bright red signs dissuade aquarium-goers from tossing food or anything else over the wall, threaten violators with prosecution.

"What if he doesn't come?" Mindy mutters. "Sampson will *not* be happy."

"Then we'll pick a different location for tomorrow. Sometimes it happens like that."

It's pretty crowded in here. I scan the faces around us for Rico, squeezing the pink duffel against my side. Mostly kindergarten age kids, here on field trips. Tourist families, quickly snapping pics of the exhibit then moving on, as if their role here is strictly documentary.

There are self-guided tours, the ones where you rent headphones and follow them through the aquarium. A couple families are doing that. There are also real tours. A group of five men who look like they're in a Gap commercial—short-sleeve button-downs, khakis—are listening raptly to a college-aged girl explain how smart otters are. Weird choice of corporate team-building activity.

"It's been four minutes," Mindy snaps. "Just do what he says."

I grab her wrist. Rico just poked his head out of the yellow tape, and is looking for us.

"There he is," I say without taking my eyes off of him. "Just relax. This shouldn't take long."

Rico spots us and makes his way through the crowd. He has a

green duffel bag slung around his shoulder. He's wearing a high black turtleneck and winter jacket, despite the weather.

"Oh my god," Mindy whispers to me. "He looks horrible."

It's true. In the photos he had an athletic build. But his once round, steely face is withered and gaunt. His cheeks sag. His legs are terribly skinny, and he's favoring one knee.

He quickly sits down next to me, and I nearly gag at his odor. It smells like he lives in that coat. Up close I can see he's so pale that his acne-tinged face has an almost blue pallor.

He's sick or something.

His eyes are glazed over like he's stoned, and he's blinking fast. Nervous.

"Hi Rico," Mindy says. "Congrats. You're getting what you want."

Rico glances at her for a moment, eyes empty. I'm not sure he recognizes her.

"What I want doesn't matter," he says, his voice weak and strained. He unslings the bag quickly and unzips it. "Here, they're all there."

He's holding the bag open, offering them with a weird kind of eagerness.

He wants to get this over with.

Mindy pulls on a pair of latex gloves, removes a penlight from her purse, then reaches over my lap, into the bag and plucks one out.

The book is bound in yellowish leather, which she caresses with a gloved hand as one might a baby's face. The front is unmarked, although on the back I see some black etchings which roughly approximate a face: two eyes, nostrils, mouth. I look over her shoulder as she opens to the first page.

No letters of any kind. Only lines, pictures, shapes, etchings—pale blue lines and twisted marks of dark red. Some pieces are raised, like Braille—maybe these are the parts that Mindy said couldn't be copied. After a few seconds of staring I start to get a headache, like I'm at the eye doctor.

"Is it real?" I ask Mindy.

"Of course it's real," says Rico. His expression is pained. He's having a hard time breathing, I think, like that turtleneck is cutting off his air.

"Hold on . . ." Mindy mutters to me. "This looks real but . . . the twenty-four I had, only seven were already bound in leather. And this is bound now, but it's not one of the seven that was before. If he undid the binding he easily could have removed pages."

"Did you mess with some of them?" I ask Rico.

He flinches.

"Some . . . were bound," he replies. "But they're all there. I'm not trying to trick you," he pleads. His knees are shaking, like he has to pee. "Now put it back. They belong together."

"I need to check that each volume is complete and authentic," she says. "A single removed page would be enough for you to force us to go through all of this again. You know that."

He holds the bag open, stares at Mindy insistently, as she takes her time turning from page to page, inspecting the twine binding under her penlight, perhaps counting the number of pages as well.

"Rico, don't you want to check the bonds?" I ask, nodding to the pink duffel under my arm. He's staring into space, panting heavily.

"Yes, yes." Rico comes back to earth, coughs into the elbow of his puffy jacket. "Of course."

I open the pink duffel so Rico can see all the bonds, but don't let it out of my grip.

"You can reach in and select a few at random," I say.

Rico gropes around in the bag, and pulls out a few papers. His fingernails are yellow, his hands are peeling and dry. I watch his eyes while he examines the bonds. He feels the weight of the paper, quickly inspects the watermarks on the lower right hand corner.

He's in a hurry. Something's wrong.

"Okay, yeah," he says, putting them back in the pink bag. "Fine, fine. Let's trade."

"What? I need to look through all of the books," says Mindy, pointing to the green bag on Rico's lap. This suggestion makes him recoil.

"What! They're all there," he rasps. "I'm not trying to trick you. Let's do this and be done."

"Rico," I say gently. "We're giving you forty-eight million dollars. We can't trade until we know they're all there. I'll keep the money right here between us."

He bites his lip, and looks like he's about to cry with frustration.

"Of course," he whimpers.

I take the green bag from him and hand it to Mindy. She eagerly opens it and starts stacking them on the bench. Opening each one and flipping through the pages, really taking her time.

Something catches my eye.

Across the room, someone's looking at me. It's one of the Gap guys on the aquarium tour. He's staring at Mindy with some kind of disgust, as if she's handling not some books, but an urn containing his grandmother's ashes. When he notices me looking at him he quickly looks back to the tour guide. In fact, the tour guide is trying to move on to another room, but one of them is keeping her here, pointing at the otters and asking questions.

My stomach clenches. I knew something was off with their outfits. Their shirts should be tucked in. And I'm pretty sure I spot bulges on two of their hips.

"Are those guys with you, Rico?" I ask. "That was not part of the deal."

He hesitates.

"They're just checking that everything goes smoothly," he says.

I swallow and turn slowly to Mindy.

"Mindy," I whisper in her ear, with as much calm as I can muster. "Put the books back in the bag. We need to swap and get out of here."

"What do you mean?" Mindy looks at me. "I haven't gone through them all yet."

"There's twenty-four books there, right?" I'm trying to make sure Rico can't hear me, but the truth is he doesn't seem interested in our conversation. He's struggling with his breathing. "That's good enough for me."

Mindy shakes her head, whispers back, exasperated. "No, no, no. There's twenty-four volumes. But like I said, he easily could have pulled a page out."

"I don't give a shit about one page." My voice cracks. "Let's get the books and leave before these guys lose their patience."

Her brown eyes widen.

"You don't understand," she hisses in my ear. "These aren't normal books. Each page references hundreds of others. It's a complete set, and if one piece is missing the whole thing is incomplete. If we were missing a square centimeter of the Mona Lisa, would that be *close enough*? He already undid the binding on some of these. I have to check."

"How long do you need?"

"Forty-five minutes," she says. "At least."

I take a deep breath. If what she's saying about one missing page is true, and Rico knows that . . .

Is that why Rico's trying to rush us? And these guys are here to make sure she doesn't have enough time to check all of them?

"Put the books back in the bag," I whisper to Mindy. "We're going to reschedule for tomorrow. On our terms."

"No, no." She shakes her head. "We're not walking away without the books. I'll just look them over and confirm—"

I snatch the book she's holding from her hands and throw it back into the green duffel. Then quickly scoop up the ones on the bench and toss them in as well. The look she gives me has enough venom to kill an elephant.

"What in God's name are you doing?" she snaps.

"What if you find a missing page?" I say. "You think these guys are just going to apologize for the misunderstanding?"

I turn back to Rico, hand him the bag of books and smile. "I need to go speak to Sampson in private before we finalize the swap," I say. "Mindy and I will be back in a second."

Before I can stand up, Rico puts a yellow hand on my knee. He leans in a little closer. I can smell whatever fungal colony is thriving under that coat.

"Don't stand up, and don't look at them again," he whispers. "They'll kill you if you try to leave with the money."

My chest constricts and I feel my pulse pound in my neck. Two of the Gap guys are looking at us.

"Don't be a fool. You have no idea the horrors I've seen. They won't hurt us if this goes smoothly," he mutters lowly. "Take the books and go, like you're supposed to."

My mind races.

"This wasn't part of the arrangement. You were supposed to come alone."

He raises his eyebrows in disbelief.

"Do you not understand what's happening here?"

I don't like any of this. We need to get the hell out of here with the money and meet again tomorrow, where he doesn't have armed backup and Mindy won't be rushed.

"We just need to speak to Sampson," I say, standing up, squeezing the bag of money like it's a life preserver. "We'll be back in a few minutes. Mindy?"

She's still sitting on the bench. I grab her by the elbow and jerk her to her feet. She doesn't fight me, but her eyes stay glued to the green bag of books I handed back to Rico.

Rico remains seated. Looks up at us. His voice is bitter, and he's choking back tears.

"Pray that Sophnot kills us quickly."

Mindy stiffens. I'd love to ask a follow-up question, but one of the khaki-clad guys leaves the group, starts making his way toward us. I lower my right hand to my waist and grip the hilt of my knife, then tug Mindy briskly toward the walkway that leads to the front entrance. Her body is half-limp, like she's in shock at what just happened.

We make it only a few steps before the guy steps out to block our path. He's a bit shorter than me, but with a wrestler's build. It's hard to imagine the bulge at his hip, beneath his untucked shirt, being anything other than a gun he slipped past security.

"Something unsatisfactory, friend?" he asks.

"Everything's fine," I say. I look over my shoulder. Rico is sitting on the bench with the green bag on his lap, head in his hands. "I just want to speak with my employer for a moment to confirm he wants to go through with this."

The wrestler smiles strangely.

"Of course he does," he says. "He's purchasing something with value beyond measure."

"Not questioning that." I try to return the smile, but my adrenaline is through the roof. "Just doing the job I was hired for."

He reaches out and puts one hand on the pink bag.

"Why don't you leave this here with me?"

"That doesn't sound super prudent," I say. "Excuse us."

I take a half step away from him. His hand moves to his waist.

My reflexes take over. Whip my sheathed knife from my waist and slam the hilt into his left temple. He drops to one of his knees, dazed. I whack him again hard in the same spot, and this one puts him sprawled flat on the ground. Somebody behind me screams, and suddenly the hundred-odd people viewing the otter exhibit are in bedlam.

"Run!" I order Mindy, pushing her away from me. The other four khaki-clad men shove their way through the chaos toward me. Rico has left his bench, along with the green bag. I catch a flash of him dashing through the once taped up tunnel leading to the beavers. Two of the men in khaki follow him.

I whip out my headphones.

"Courtney, Rico's wearing a puffy coat and turtleneck. The books are in a green bag. Keep on the perimeter—I think he's headed for a side exit."

Mindy is headed for the pathway back toward the main entrance. I take the other, upstream on the Colorado River. Past the otters is some kind of swamp exhibit. A tank that just looks like a neglected swimming pool. Two security guards rush past me toward the otters. I hear someone behind me scream something about a pink bag and yellow raincoat. I don't slow to look behind me; I'm sure the khaki guys are close.

The Colorado River path winds uphill, spiraling upwards. The bag is really heavy. My legs are screaming as the path opens into a huge circular room with a pit in the center: a penguin exhibit.

I'm almost jerked backwards. Someone behind me got a handful of bag. I stop, whip around and crack the goon's jaw with my elbow. He stumbles, but doesn't release his grip until I stomp on his wrist.

The other three burst into the room. One is holding a gun low at his side.

Shit, shit.

Security has now successfully identified me, and the men pursuing me, as the source of the disturbance. But Colorado aquarium guards aren't really accustomed to action, and the two I spot are just providing color commentary into their walkie-talkies as I scramble across the room. Chest feels like it's going to explode. Someone screams, "He has a gun!" And the hysteria hits a new pitch. A bunch of people drop to their stomachs. I dash ahead, heading for the walkway opposite where we entered, then stop in my tracks. There's another khaki-clad guy there, blocking my exit. He's holding his hand under the fold of his button-up shirt; he also has a gun.

I look over my shoulder. One of the three goons has his pistol raised, trying to get a clear shot on me. The other two also are reaching for guns. Twist back around. The lone gunman just spotted me and is patiently holding his ground, well aware that he's obstructing my only way out.

I'm at the lip of the penguin pit. About ten feet below, a couple dozen knee-height penguins flop and waddle around, unfazed by the action above.

The shoulder of the guy aiming at me twitches. I see the steely determination in his eyes and realize he's hesitating only because I'm holding the bag of money against my chest, and he doesn't want to damage any bonds. He fully intends to kill me.

I suddenly remember Courtney's foresight: *We can track this bag.*

I heave it overhead and throw it down into the middle of the penguins. It narrowly misses one of their shallow pools. Smacks down beside one of the birds, who jumps in surprise, and then tenuously approaches the bright pink addition to her habitat.

I lock eyes with the guy who was about to shoot me. He doesn't seem to find this development amusing. He lowers his gun and the three of them dash to the edge of the exhibit—now totally disinterested in me. All three leap over the edge without hesitation. I hear a scream—a couple broken feet probably—but I'm already shaking out of my raincoat, heading back down the Colorado River toward the front entrance, walking slowly, trying to blend in with the rest of the evacuating crowd.

"We had them . . ." Mindy says, for what must be the fiftieth time since the three of us regrouped. We're on park benches, back on the walking mall. The GPS isn't working. Courtney is staring rapt at the tracker, as if willing the chip to reveal itself. Mindy sits beside him, the two of them opposite me. I hope this doesn't symbolize anything.

"I had them in my *hands*," she says, growing more unhinged with every repetition. She's tugging at a clump of her curly hair so hard that I can see a sliver of pale scalp. "Why would you throw the money in the *water*? Of all the boneheaded—"

"The chip is supposed to be waterproof. I read the user manual," I lie.

"Water *resistant*," mumbles Courtney. "It might just be water-logged, and will show up once it dries out a bit."

We spent the last hour combing the streets around the aquarium hoping to spot Rico or the guys in khaki. Nothing. They must have had well planned getaways, and I doubt aquarium security did much to slow them down. Sampson calls again, I hit ignore. Thirty-seven missed calls from him in the last ninety minutes. Each time his name pops up onscreen it's like a vise clamped around my chest tightens a little bit. Don't want to even imagine how he'd react to me explaining that not only do we not have the books, but that his forty-eight million dollars hinges on the water resistance of a thumbnail-sized GPS chip.

Forget the passport, he might just turn me in.

"I was holding the books. . . In my hands," Mindy says, then shoots me a look that could wither a whole field of daisies. "And *you* gave them back."

"There was nothing else to do," I say, hoping desperately that it's true. "Rico was trying to rush us. Get us to swap before you checked them all. Like you said, they were tampered with. Why *wouldn't* he have taken a few pages out? If you think they were just going to let you sit there for an hour and comb through them until you figured that out . . . The guy was going to shoot me in public!"

"And now you've lost *both* bags," she says, voice drenched in bile. "Good work."

"It will dry out," says Courtney, focused on the GPS tracker. He's desperately clawing at his cheek, like there's gold buried under his skin. "I trust this brand. Very durable."

"It will all be fine," I tell Mindy, forcing a smile. Not admitting, of course, that if those guys simply decide to transfer the money to a new bag, our plan is pretty cooked. And with every passing moment, my bag toss is looking more and more dubious. But I don't see any upside to admitting that at the moment.

Mindy pulls a little metal case out of her pocket and opens it to reveal several pre-rolled joints. The Zippo shakes in her hand as she lights it, and sucks greedily. Doesn't offer us any.

"You better hope it will be fine," Mindy says, exhaling a cloud of pungent smoke. "Because as it currently stands, my career is ruined, and you've just lost a United States Senator forty-eight million dollars. I don't think you even comprehend the *shit* you're in."

"Instead of blaming me, you should be *thanking* me for saving your skin." I jab a finger at her. "The situation was screwed from the start. Rico brought *seven* armed pals with him."

"I don't think they were his pals," says Courtney softly, looking up from the GPS, his forehead creased with worry. "Didn't you say Rico and two of those men ran away after you took one down?"

"Yeah."

Courtney slowly rises from the bench, unfolding his spindly legs like a spider doing a sun salutation. There's a look in his little eyes, like he's staring at looming black clouds on the horizon. He hands me the GPS, apparently trusting me now that it's worthless. He paces in a little circle between the benches.

"Who were they running from? Not from you and Mindy, certainly. I suspect *Rico* was running, with the books, and those two men were chasing him."

I mull this. The Colorado dusk above us glows purple and orange. Under different circumstances I might find it soothing. Can feel the dry air on my tongue and fingertips.

Not dry enough, apparently.

"You think Rico was these guys' stooge?"

"Well it sure seems he wasn't too enthusiastic about doing any of this."

"Or he's just a great actor," I say.

Mindy shakes her head and ashes her joint.

"They're *all* stooges. Sophnot's stooges."

I frown.

"What do you mean? He's in prison."

"That didn't stop James from drinking his Kool-Aid," Mindy says.

"C'mon," I say. "You think he 'tutored' all those guys too?"

Mindy licks her lips.

"If they have nothing to do with Sophnot, then someone is really good at imitating his leatherworking and binding style."

I stiffen.

"What?"

"I can't be sure," she says, "everything happened so quickly, so I can't be positive. But it sure looked the same as the others."

Courtney draws in a long breath through his thin nose.

"Well, that's a rather unsettling observation. But no reason to cause ourselves any additional angst by speculating." He smiles tightly, in a way I find a little frightening.

"James keeps calling me," Mindy says, displaying her own iPhone, flashing "James" on the screen. "Shall I tell him how badly you two performed?"

"I don't see how this is on me," I say. "You're the one who said we couldn't swap until you spent an hour with them. *You* said if they pulled out even one page—"

"Are you kidding me?" She drops the nub of her joint and grinds it beneath her heel. "Am I the one who threw forty-eight million dollars into a penguin pond?"

"It's an amphibious environment."

"If you don't make this right," she says, "the only person protecting you from the law is going to become your worst nightmare. And believe me, I won't be defending you to him when—"

"Enough," I growl. I felt queasy before, but now I'm getting truly light-headed as the implications of this afternoon sink in.

"I need to talk to James," she mutters, half to herself. "Maybe I can save myself."

"You can't tell Sampson yet," I say. "He'll do something crazy. Just give us a chance. A little time."

Mindy squints at me like I'm some sort of inferior life form she's having trouble understanding.

"Even if you find them, you think those men are just going to politely return them to you?" She laughs. "Oh, terribly sorry. Here's your forty-eight million dollars back. Perhaps now we can try swapping again?"

My vision goes red.

"Listen, you ungrateful shithead." I shoot off the bench and stick my face so close to hers that I can smell her weed-breath and all-natural body wash. "If I hadn't done what I'd done when I did it, we might be *dead*."

"That doesn't make this okay!" she cries. "Those books are the last seven years of my life."

"You think *I* don't want to get them back?"

I sit back down and check the GPS tracker again. Slide it into my back pocket.

"Courtney and I are gonna go see if we can get security camera footage of the aquarium parking lot, and surrounding areas. Maybe we can see them leaving and get a license plate or something."

Courtney frowns at me like *we are*?

Mindy snorts.

"It's come to that, yeah? Fine. Let me know when you give up. I'm taking the Hummer."

"You're not going back to Aspen are you?" I say. "Honestly, if we don't get those bags back, and Sampson goes ape, I don't think you'll want to be anywhere near him. I suggest you check into a hotel."

She frowns, and looks at Courtney for his opinion. He nods.

"I agree with Frank. Buy food, text only us where you are, and don't open the door for anyone."

She raises an eyebrow.

"I don't think James would—"

"I'm not just worried about the Senator," Courtney says. "Whether they've spoken to Sophnot or not, it's a good bet those men are interested in what's written in those books. They've been holding onto them for four years, and maybe have even been able to extract a little meaning from them. But they're not linguists. You're the *expert* we brought along. I'll bet they'd like a word with you."

She mulls this for a second.

"You'll call me immediately if you have anything, right?" she asks Courtney.

"Of course," he says, looking her square in the eyes. That look could sell snow to an Eskimo.

"Fine. Good luck," she says, and walks off toward the parking garage.

Courtney turns to me.

"It's going to be tough to get security footage, Frank. And even then, you've only got a prayer of being able to catch a license plate."

"I know." I grin and pull the GPS tracker out of my pocket.

"And tedious and hopeless enough that Mindy wouldn't feel compelled to join." I show him the dropped pin on the screen. "The chip showed up five minutes ago. The bags aren't moving. They're forty-five minutes east of here."

He blinks at me. He's about to say something—about Mindy I'm sure—but swallows it.

"Alright," he says. "Let's go."

WE RUSH TO hail a taxi, take it to the closest rent-a-car, and are in a Honda Accord, heading east by eight thirty. The beacon hasn't moved. It's in a rural area called Deer Trail.

I drive while the GPS navigates. Courtney is silent in the passenger seat, hands folded in his lap.

The phone is in the cup holder. Sampson has changed tack, and is now texting us:

Where are you!????

What's going on???

How dare u ignore me!!

The phone is on silent, but illuminated by a string of perpetual, increasingly unhinged messages. I can't even look at it.

I take us from the western edge of Denver to the eastern city limits in near silence, interrupted only by the robot instructions from the GPS. As night descends, my shoulders and neck tighten in anticipation.

Is this a trap?

"You shouldn't have lied to her," Courtney finally says.

"I don't trust her, and I didn't want her around," I respond. "Don't forget, by her own admission she wants to take the books to London."

"So we should have discussed that with her."

I tighten my grip on the steering wheel.

"Dude. I'm your partner. You didn't even back me up back there about what I did in the aquarium. You're acting like Mindy is on our side. She's not. She doesn't give a shit about us, and she has her own agenda. We took her with us to identify the books, and after the aquarium I'm confident enough I know what they look like. So that's it. We're done with her."

"I just don't like that kind of deception."

"Let's just call a spade a spade, Court. You wanted to preserve the possibility of you getting into her kidney pie, eh? Or so you figure. Well let me save you some time, champ: She's never gonna fuck you."

"Frank, please don't be crude."

"Maybe if you were fifteen years younger, and somebody completely different. But I'd say your chances of getting in her pants are like, subatomic level. Like the odds of a mouse surviving on the surface of the sun long enough to play a complete game of solitaire."

"You're being really abhorrent."

"Three-card draw."

We lapse back into a silence punctuated only the automated directions: "In 500 feet, take exit 328."

I direct the Accord onto a two-lane rural highway. No street lights now. The roadside landscape could just be a loop of drainage ditch, green mile markers, and wood fences. I listen to Courtney's fast breathing.

"Sorry, Court," I say. "I'm nervous."

"It's alright," he says. He's way too sensible to let something as silly as feelings distract him for too long. "Me too."

"You don't think they found the chip do you?" I ask. "And are waiting for us?"

"It's possible. But I don't plan on just rushing in, guns blazing."

I rub the bridge of my nose between my thumb and forefinger. "Rico mentioned Oliver Vicks. Well, 'Sophnot.'"

"I know," Courtney says quietly, staring through the windshield at the King Soopers truck ahead of us, like it's some work of art. "And I know he's in prison. But what if he's orchestrated all of this. Converted Sampson, trusted him with the books, and then manipulated Rico into stealing them. Then for years he keeps asking Sampson to bring the books back to him, while upping the pressure on the other side . . ."

I little shiver runs down my spine.

"That's a pretty clever way to make forty-eight million dollars."

I turn right off the highway, and we drive five minutes on a bumpy dirt road. Courtney's slight form bounces up and down in the passenger seat like popcorn in the pan. 9:25.

"Stop here," Courtney says. "Quarter mile away."

I pull over and turn the car off.

"Hardly anything out here," I say.

"Maybe it's buried?" Courtney says hopefully.

"The dot hasn't budged right?"

"Right."

Courtney walks first, following the GPS. I'm right behind him, Magnum drawn. We walk slowly, the only light some faint stars, not daring to give ourselves away with flashlights.

The landscape here is flat, and we see the two-story house from 300 yards away. Lights are on upstairs.

"That's it right?" I ask.

Courtney nods, and swaps the GPS out for his Magnum.

There's a driveway leading up to the house, which we give a wide berth. Crouch as we stumble blindly over rocks and high grass.

The air is crisp and dry. Mostly just follow Courtney's lanky silhouette, Magnum in one hand, red acrylic satchel in the other.

Courtney stops about a hundred yards from the house. We stand side by side.

"What is this place?" I whisper. The building is a dome. It's half a sphere, like the earth started blowing a bubble. By the dim light coming through a few portholes near the top, we can see that the exterior is thousands of rusty red metal shingles. They remind me of dead red leaves, trampled and flattened. "Is this a house?" I ask.

"If I'm not mistaken," Courtney whispers back somberly, "I saw a picture of this place when I was browsing Oliver Vicks designs."

My insides twist into a knot.

We continue slowly toward the dome until, about twenty meters away, I halt and show Courtney my palm. There's a guy sitting outside the front door. Big baby kind of look, wearing a leather jacket, smoking, sitting in a plastic chair, looking at his phone. Hasn't noticed us yet. I think I hear faint music reverberating inside the dome behind him.

"That guy's a bouncer," I say softly.

"A bouncer?" Courtney frowns.

"Yeah. And that must be one hell of a party, to have it all the way out here."

I point to our left: a row of parked cars. Shitty, most of them. A gold Ford Bronco, a beat--up Volvo station wagon . . . this is no cotillion. I wonder if any of them is Rico's car . . . which would mean him and both bags are still inside. I allow myself to fantasize about bringing Sampson back the books *and* the money. There's no way he wouldn't give us a million-dollar bonus. And if we *don't* get them . . . if we don't get at least one of those bags before Sampson figures out what happened, we might as well go down a few Drano and tonics.

I had the bags in my lap . . .

Again the events of this afternoon play, projected on my mind's eye, and each time it looks more and more like a blooper reel.

Courtney brings me back to earth.

"Let's scope it out," he says.

We wade through a field of burrs and brambles to approach the building on the far side, opposite the bouncer. As we near the house, I realize it's much larger than I'd thought—equivalent of maybe four stories tall, and at least the circumference of a baseball diamond. All the windows are small and round, like portholes on a ship. Pockmarks on the otherwise smooth red face of this dome. The glass is too thick to really make anything out besides some flickering lights and muddy shapes. There's noise though. The whole dome seems to act like a subwoofer, amplifying a booming high BPM bass line. At some point we hear something that's the muffled wail of either a human or cat.

"What's going on in there?" asks Courtney.

"Rave maybe?"

"What's a rave exactly?" he asks. "Like a party with loud music right?"

I stare at him.

"Didn't you used to work for the DEA?"

We continue around the perimeter of the house. When we're

halfway around, Courtney stops and squints through the darkness at the building, hands on his hips like a prospector.

"We could try to quietly break a window," he says. "Though it would be a tight fit."

"I'm not sure that's a very strong plan," I respond, imagining his tiny butt squirming as he tries to squeeze his lanky body through one of those portholes.

"Do you have a better idea?" Courtney asks.

I lick my lips.

"Yes, the obvious one. Go in the front door."

Courtney frowns.

"Fine. Let's go."

"Well . . ." I cough. "Let's say it *is* a trap . . . That they found the chip and they're waiting for us . . ." Courtney's face contorts into anguish as he deduces my meaning. I spell it out anyways: "Rico and those men know what I look like. But not you."

"You want me to go in alone?"

"Just for five minutes," I say. "Scope it out. Then I'll join."

Courtney's lips writhe like little worms, pale pink under the light from the dome.

"Fine. Keep your walkie-talkie on."

We retrace our steps, back around to the front of the house, but taking a wide angle of approach. Feet crunching over dry grass, each snap sounds like the earth crying out for water. I crouch down on my stomach about ten yards from the entrance.

"Give me your gun," I tell him. "In case the bouncer frisks you."

Courtney looks like he might protest, but relents and unholsters his weapon. Hands it to me.

I watch him trudge to the front door, like a man headed for the gallows. He looks over his shoulder at me, shakes his head like *this is a terrible idea*, then engages the bouncer. I bite my lip and flatten myself against the dirt. Maybe it is a terrible idea, but it's really the only choice.

The bouncer is immediately on his feet, his body language saying something to the effect of *who the fuck are you?*

Courtney extends an awkward hand in introduction like this is a networking event.

Oh boy.

The bouncer stares at Courtney's outstretched hand with confused disgust, like he's just been offered a cup of rancid milk.

Courtney then puts the hand on the shoulder of the guy's jacket, like to inspire camaraderie. The bouncer stares at the hand until Courtney removes it.

This isn't going well.

Courtney gesticulates like *can I come in?* Bouncer takes out a clipboard and asks Courtney's name.

Invitation only.

I see Courtney rubbing his scalp with anxiety. Now he's trying to sweet talk the guy ... *maybe I can just poke my head in* ... Oh no. Courtney's taking out his wallet, offering the guy a few flimsy bills. Bouncer laughs, and his body language pretty clearly indicates that, as far as he's concerned, this conversation is now over. Can't say I blame him; I wouldn't let Courtney into my party either.

Court awkwardly tries to peek into the ajar door behind the guy's shoulder.

The bouncer stands up and puts his hands on his hips. Shakes his head in a pretty definitive *you're not getting in here.*

Courtney holds up two fingers like *let me just come in for two minutes.* Bouncer points back into the night, shouts something whose import doesn't require much guesswork.

And then another guy slips out the front door, maybe he heard the disturbance. He's wearing only a pair of red boxer shorts. Must have heard the yelling. In his right hand is what appears to be a machete.

Oh boy.

Red Boxers immediately escalates, waving his blade in Courtney's face. He's obviously drunk. Courtney puts his palms up like *okay, you win.* But Red Boxers takes another step toward him, and the bouncer doesn't seem like he's in any hurry to help.

I'm on my feet, and close the distance between me and the action in seconds. I lower my shoulder and blindside Red Boxers like a linebacker. We crash to the ground, and I've got one hand on the machete hilt, tearing it away from him, the other on the back of his head, pushing it into the dirt.

I vaguely perceive the bouncer in my periphery milliseconds before I get decked in the jaw. I fall backwards, tasting blood. The world is momentarily an assortment of blurry shapes, one of them I think is the bouncer, closing in on me. Instinctually I roll away, which lets me recover long enough to rise to one knee. The bouncer is rushing at me. I can't dodge him, and I'm immediately in his grip, head and neck being maneuvered into a well-practiced chokehold.

Maybe he's not an amateur.

I try reaching for my gun, but my arm is trapped behind my back. I'm powerless. He has his bicep wrapped around my neck, about to start squeezing, when I hear a smack and his grip goes slack. He falls away from me, collapses backwards onto the damp earth with a thud. Totally unconscious.

Courtney is holding the machete like it's a baseball bat, breathing hard. The bouncer is bleeding a bit from the top of his head, where Courtney hit him. Courtney's hands are shaking.

"Nice swing," I say.

"Did I kill him?" Courtney asks, horrified.

I kneel besides the bouncer's limp form. Feel his pulse, look at his head wound, open one of his eyes. He stirs slightly.

"No, you didn't kill him."

Red Boxers squirms on the ground, groans in anguish. I kick him again in the gut, which shuts him up.

I take the machete from Courtney's trembling grip, toss it as hard as I can into the darkness, then hand him his pistol. Courtney's eyes are wide and he's breathing too fast. He's not as solid as he was last time we worked together. He's having a little freak-out. Can't make him go in alone.

"Let's go in," I say.

I put my shoulder into the cracked front door, pistol drawn, and it opens into a narrow hallway. Both walls and the ceiling are draped in red velvet. The floor is some kind of tile that's as black as tar. The hallway is lit with red bulbs. There's a naked guy sitting on the floor, a few feet from the door. He has a shock of sunflower-blond hair, and doesn't seem to notice us. Next to him is a woman with a ton of eyeshadow, wearing only lace panties.

I bend over and shove the picture of Rico in front of the blond guy's face.

"You seen this guy? Or a bunch of dudes wearing khaki?" I ask. He seems to be taking a while to process our presence, the photo . . . struggling to fit these different pieces into a coherent narrative. I ask the woman, who looks at me like I'm speaking Mandarin. Between them is an Advil bottle filled with what I'm guessing isn't Advil. I snatch the bottle from the dude, unscrew the cap to confirm: It's filled with some sort of toxic looking blue pills. I shove it in my pocket; maybe just saved their lives.

"Check the GPS," I tell Courtney.

Courtney pulls it from his pocket. "We're like thirty feet away, but it could be above or below us."

We continue down the hallway, pass a few more people, most wearing nothing but blank, slightly bummed-out expressions. Most look young. High school young. Some awful Marvin Gaye remix is pounding through speakers mounted on the ceiling. Despite it being the middle of the summer, there's hot air blasting from central heating. The air tastes stale and recycled. We pass two hairless naked forms of indeterminate gender intertwined in a sophisticated knot, one of the party's flabby buttocks rising and falling in sync with the music.

"I think this is some kind of sex party," whispers Courtney.

"Your powers of observation are unparalleled," I say, then prod a butt cheek with my shoe. "Hey, excuse me."

A girl looks up at me. Her eyes are vacant, and there's dried blood caked around her nostrils. I show her the picture of Rico. "You seen this guy?" I demand. When she doesn't respond, I waggle my Magnum and ask again.

The girl studies the picture for way too long before saying "Yeah." She licks her lips slowly like rediscovering their taste. "I saw him."

"How long ago? Was he with some other men all dressed the same?" I say.

She shrugs, as her partner continues probing her torso with his mouth.

"I dunno."

"Is there someone in charge here?" asks Courtney.

I glare at him: *Does it look like someone's in charge here?*

The woman blinks at us. "Y'all cops?"

Courtney shakes his head adamantly. "No, no. Nothing like that—"

"Then fuck off."

I could force the issue, but she doesn't seem to have much left to offer.

The hallway doesn't end, just curves around and around until we end up back at the entrance. We start around again, but this time we try one of the curtained doorways leading off the hallway. Courtney pulls the drapes back and I grip my gun tightly, but there's no room behind it—just a velvet-draped ascending stairwell, the same width as the hallway. We climb the steps, which lead into another identical hallway, also smattered with orgiasts. Most are too busy to notice us, the few that do glare at us like we're aliens. Rico is not among them.

The hallway smells of incense, vanilla, opium smoke, and a pastiche of sex-related fluids. Only furniture is an occasional velvet-upholstered ottoman. A girl of probably seventeen is unconscious, strewn awkwardly across one of the ottomans. Another man who looks nearly limp is propped up by his partner against a flannel wall, and being treated like a piece of meat. There's a woman on the cold black floor wearing a dopey grin as she touches herself.

Courtney is way past mortified. He has his hands deep in his pockets, like to avoid contamination. His face has taken on the corpselike green of a seasick sailor, and each new sight seems to jar him like a wave ramming the hull.

We turn through countless hallways, draped entryways, all

basically the same, only some contain ascending stairs, some descending. At one point the GPS says we're right on top of the bag, but the room is empty. It isn't long before I have no idea if we're above ground or below, or which direction I'd go if I wanted to leave. Check my watch. Only twenty minutes have passed but it feels like we've been in here for hours already.

Every corridor has the heat blasting—I guess it might be comfortable in here if you're naked, but my T-shirt is drenched in sweat and I'd kill for a glass of ice water.

We wander through hallway after hallway, getting more and more anxious that the GPS misled us, or they found the chip and buried it in one of these walls to throw us off their trail. Keep passing the same places over and over, or at least it feels like that. I have this uneasy thought that we'll keep wandering through these halls for years without making progress. Or that we've already been doing this for years, but can only remember the last few minutes, like two goldfish. So we keep thinking the next bend will hold what we're looking for, even though we've walked each of these corridors thousands of times already.

Finally, we encounter a change in the uniformity. A series of descending, curved stairways lead to the first true door we've seen here. It's a simple wood door made of unfinished pine. Reminds me of a pauper's coffin. At this point, I'm pretty sure we're well below ground level.

Courtney and I exchange a look, and then, keeping the pistol aimed straight ahead, I pull on the handle with my off hand. Another fucking hallway. This one has a mattress on the ground though. Two men and two women are—surprise—naked; limbs, mouths, phalluses entangled in an arrangement that it's hard to imagine is giving anybody pleasure. A third guy is naked and watching, and by all physiological indications, enjoying himself. Rico is not among them.

They're either so into it, or so fucked up, that they don't even care when we barge in.

"Hey, excuse me," I say. One woman half glances at me, but then returns to the task at hand. "Anybody here seen a bunch of dudes wearing khaki, with a pink duffel bag?"

Nobody answers.

Courtney is still standing in the doorway, gazing at the ongoing spectacle with morbid curiosity, like it's some horrible deformity.

"What about this guy?" I demand. I grab the shoulder of the voyeur and put the picture of Rico in front of his face. He's more coherent than the others, but also not so keen on the interruption. But he can't contain a flicker of recognition as I give him no choice but to absorb the image of Rico's face.

He's seen him.

"What did you see?" I ask. The participants on the mattress either don't notice or care that they're no longer being observed.

"Fuck off," he whines. I'm hungry, thirsty, exhausted and sweaty—patience is an increasingly scarce resource on planet Frank.

I grab his shoulder and ram him against the velvet wall. "Dude, what are you doing?" he shrieks and he spits in my face. My face must betray something, because he instantly apologizes.

But the damage has been done. My vision is red and sideways, and I think I can hear my neurons holding a memorial service for whatever was left of my patience. He's not entirely in the wrong: Some corner of my psyche is aware of that even as I switch my grip to his neck and knock the back of his head against the wall.

"I've had a pretty shitty evening," I growl, squeezing the air out of him. "If you don't tell me what you saw, I'm going to take it all out on your face."

"Frank." Courtney is behind me, trying to peel my hands off his neck, but I box him out. Courtney must give this guy a pretty convincing *he's out of control* look, because his resolve dissolves like warm butter.

"He went in there," he gasps, nodding to the end of this hallway, which terminates in another door.

"Did he come out?" I ask, squeezing harder.

"Don't remember."

"He went in alone?"

"No . . ."

"Who did he go in with?"

"A guy in a mask," he squeaks. "Wearing white."

I look over my shoulder at Courtney and we exchange a look.

"Did they leave?"

"The one in the mask. He left."

"When."

"Get *off* me man!"

I slam the back of his head against the wall, as if to jog his memory.

"Maybe an hour ago."

"Thanks," I say, releasing my grip. He drops to the floor and coughs.

I turn, and Courtney and I pass through the writhing mounds on the floor, like Moses parting a swamp of flesh, until arriving at the second door. This one is thick steel, practically a blast door.

I look at Courtney, then try knocking. Ready my pistol in case someone opens. Try again. Nothing.

"GPS says it's in on the other side. Twenty feet straight ahead."

Courtney sinks to his knees to inspect the lock.

"What is it?" I ask. "Can you get in?"

"It's a very heavy lock, but no magnets," he says. "Industrial make. Not custom. I can do it."

While Courtney fishes his tools from his red acrylic bag, I shoo the fornicators out of the hallway, then sink to the black floor. God I'm hungry. Have I really not eaten since leaving Sampson's this morning? That feels like another life.

Courtney is deep in concentration, working on the lock. Stethoscope chest piece on cool metal, eyes half closed.

A man in white, wearing a mask . . .

I lean back against the velvet wall. The floor is rock hard, but the walls are pretty comfy, padded like a loony bin. I shift around to get comfortable and doze off.

Courtney taps my shoulder. I was out cold despite the cocktail of adrenaline and dread swishing in my head.

"I opened it, Frank." Courtney also looks exhausted.

I wince as I stand up, my right butt cheek adamantly informing me that it didn't appreciate that angle.

I hold my Magnum out in front of me, and push the door in with my heel.

Before I can see anything I'm hit with a wave of scent. Some kind of incense that's so pungent and spicy that I feel a heaviness in my lungs when I breathe it in. It's not unpleasant—reminiscent of freshly cut wood—but the potency is overwhelming.

We both just stand there for a moment, looking into the darkness, waiting for someone to jump out of nowhere and attack us. When nobody does, I ease my way in, and some lights in the ceiling pop on automatically. Courtney steps in to join me, and the spring loaded door swings closed behind us.

The small room bears little relation to the red curtained hallways. The floor is spotless polished bronze. Beside the doorway, on the floor, is a gold-gilded basin underneath a sink—a place to wash your feet as soon as you enter. The walls are all covered in an ornate series of etched symbols, behind them inked veins of blue and red.

"Looks the same as the lines in the book," I say.

Courtney nods.

The incense smell is coming from a smoldering pile of ash in the middle of the floor, set on a small stone.

Courtney kneels beside it, inspects the potpourri. Inhales deeply.

"Frankincense, myrrh . . ." he says.

"What?" I ask.

"I used to work in a spice shop," Courtney says. "These are resins that are rarely used today. They were very common in the ancient Mediterranean. The Israelites burned these in their holy temple in Jerusalem. Incense offerings to God."

"It's still smoldering. Must be recent."

"The guy in the hall said the guy in the mask rushed out . . ." muses Courtney.

There are two metal chains on the ground to my left, fastened to the wall. The chains end in what look like elaborate dog collars, made of leather and intricate metalwork.

"Court, come look at these," I say.

He abandons the spices and joins me. Slips two pairs of latex gloves from his satchel and hands one to me. I know what the gloves mean.

He thinks this is a crime scene.

He picks up one of the collars and inspects it for a few moments. Tugs on the chain connected to it, first gently, then hard. It's definitely bolted into the wall.

"Tell me these were for someone's pet pit bulls," I say.

"I'm afraid not," he says, suddenly dropping the collar and approaching the wall at the point where the chain is fused in. He drops to his knees, squints at something, then turns to me looking unsettled. "There's an indentation in the wall around the welding," he says. "Looks like someone tried to scrape out the wall using a link from the chain itself. If I had to guess, this is at least a couple months' worth of scraping."

I grimace.

He returns to examine the collars, while I make my way to the far wall. I'd initially thought it was as solid as the others, but as I near I see it's in fact a hanging curtain. I pull it back, and from the light behind me I see it's a second room of at least equal size.

Please let the money be in here . . .

"Just like the tabernacle," I hear Courtney say behind me. "Two rooms—the antechamber . . ."

The lights click on in the second room and I stop hearing anything Courtney's saying.

To my right is a stone worktable, cluttered with tools. On my left is a sort of drafting table, beside which is a massive cubic filing cabinet—the kind an artist might use to store thin photos or drawing paper.

But the main event is between them, suspended from a wire clothing line. It's Rico hanging upside down, naked, fingertips grazing the floor. I only recognize it as Rico because of the cracked, yellow hands and acne on the cheeks. But the form is loose and empty. It's only his skin. Beneath him is a basin, like the one in the other room, filled with what must be his entrails. Around the basin radiates a gradient of freshly dried drops of blood. Nearest Rico, the floor is almost entirely dark maroon.

Courtney is at my side, breathing heavily.

"Oh my god. Is this—"

"Yes." I swallow. "Rico."

I tear my eyes from Rico, to the stone worktable. On a wooden shelf above it are an X-acto knife, a long butcher's blade, a chain mail glove—the kind butchers use, rubber gloves—still wet—and a blue-handled Phillips-head screwdriver. There's a corkboard mounted over the worktable with pins hammered into it. Hanging off the board are several collars of leather interwoven with metal—all variants on the ones in the other room.

On the table is a single object, a waxy mask the color of milk. Sunken cheeks and fat chin . . . It's a mask of Rico's face.

My legs feel wobbly. I've seen my share of crime scenes, but this is a different animal entirely.

It's so deliberate . . .

I put my hands on the worktable to steady myself.

"Frank!" Courtney is beside me. "Put your gloves on!"

I slowly pull them on, while he takes a pack of antibacterial hand wipes from his bag and carefully rubs down the stone counter.

I stare at the stone surface and take several deep breaths. Swallow the revulsion in my chest.

"Okay, okay, okay," Courtney is saying, mostly to himself. "We have a lot of data here Frank. Let's be methodical. Gather data now, analyze it later. TSP. Thoughtfulness, subtlety, patience. TSP."

He mutters this mantra to himself as he puts the tube of wipes back in his bag and removes his notepad and spy camera. While he snaps photos of Rico, of the tools, of the mask, I force myself to look around the rest of the room.

Gather data. Dispassionate. Just pretend you're a robot.

There's another mural on the ceiling. Blue and red stripes, symbols that look like hieroglyphics. My eyes trace the dizzying lines on the ceiling. Each square inch is unbelievably detailed: dots the size of pinpricks. I have to look away—feels like a quick-onset migraine—similar to the feeling I had earlier when I looked in the book.

Just like Oliver Vicks's writing. Did he make this before he went to prison?

This is some kind of workshop. But to what end?

Stone worktable, drafting table, file cabinet . . .

Behind Rico's hanging form there are more basins on the gold floor, filled with a clear fluid that smells vaguely reminiscent of the aquarium. Saltwater? Brine?

"Courtney, what is this place? What happened here?"

"I don't know," Courtney mumbles. "Torture?"

"Why would he *torture* Rico after he brought him back everything he asked for?" I do a 360 of the chamber, trying to straighten out some objective facts about this scene, pretend the flayed carcass belongs to some kind of animal.

Pray that Sophnot kills us quickly.

"Could Oliver Vicks have done this?" I mutter, feeling some pieces of this afternoon starting to slide into place. I force my brain to replay all the details of the botched exchange, now able to reframe them with more confidence that Rico was telling the truth. His fear was authentic.

I approach the drafting table on the far side of the room, behind

Rico's form. The birch tabletop has built-in straightedges, and the angle can be adjusted with a series of knobs which connect it to the base. It's a sturdy, professional piece of equipment.

I'll bet you find something like this in every architecture firm.

I turn to the filing cabinet. Each sliding drawer is exceedingly narrow—this is probably meant to hold photographs or documents. With a latex-gloved hand, I pull a shelf from the middle open. Inside is a folded piece of yellow-orange leather, the kind the books were bound in. I remove it from the drawer and unfold it. It's an uneven blobby shape, about a square meter of material. A large rectangle has been cut out from the center. A piece of paper clipped to one of the corners is a passport-sized photo of a young man and a little tag with a number.

My attempt at dispassion crumbles. I feel like I've been kicked in the nuts. Stomach goes numb, knees quiver like a pair of yolks frying in oil.

"Oh Christ," I whisper. "Courtney . . ."

"What?" he says, preoccupied with snapping pictures of the flaccid sac that was once Rico from every angle.

"Stop that a second."

He obliges, lowers the camera.

"Mindy was confused today, in the aquarium," I say, trying to keep my voice even, but I'm feeling the beginning of a dry heave. "Because the book she had was newly bound. In leather."

Courtney cocks his head, sees the hide I'm displaying, and then the implications of it seep down his face: His high forehead crinkles first, his eyes go wide, his lips pucker into a grimace of the most profound sort of disgust. The hanging skin, the basins of fluids . . .

"This is a tannery," he whispers in horror.

"And look," I say, pulling the shelves open one by one. Each contains a similar sample, with a different photo and number attached. There are twenty-four shelves. All occupied except the top three. The three from the top holds only a passport-sized photo of Rico, and the square for today's date ripped out of a calendar.

Courtney's hands are trembling. He frowns, opens the fourth drawer down, that contains the first skin. He stares at the picture of the boy for a second. Tears are welling in his eyes.

He swallows his emotion, and gets to work. Jerks open each drawer in turn, snaps a picture of each passport-sized photo. The numbers are squares cut from a calendar. Courtney kneels to open the lower drawers. He works through them methodically until the very bottom drawer. A little hiss of air leaks from his nostrils.

"Look, Frank," he whispers.

The picture paperclipped is of a young boy, along with a little square that says twenty-four in big letters, October in small ones. 1997. Twenty years ago.

"This is the first one," Courtney says. "The brother of the waitress that Oliver killed. His body was never found."

I have to look away. Take a step back and survey the whole grisly scene. Courtney closes the last drawer and turns his back on the cabinet, crouching. His skin is ashen. He looks like he's going to be sick.

"So Oliver Vicks isn't in prison?" I say, half to myself.

"I . . ." Courtney trails off, shakes his head helplessly. "It sure seems like he was here. But I don't see how he would have gotten out of prison without us knowing."

I grit my teeth.

"Say he's not in prison," I say. "Would he do this to Rico just because he needed number twenty-two?"

"I don't know," Courtney says.

I approach Rico's hanging skin. Force myself to get close, look down at the neck and chest area. As I'd expected, there's a ring of raw pink skin around his neck. He'd been locked up in the other room a while.

And that explains the turtleneck—

"Frank! Here's the bag!"

I jerk up. I rush to join Courtney at the back of the room. The pink duffel is tucked between a couple closed barrels of what might be brine.

I grab the straps and my heart sinks immediately.

"Too light," I say. "Money's not in there."

I open the zipper, and recognize Rico's puffy black parka. Pull it out and set it on the ground.

Indeed, there are no bonds. Just the rest of Rico's possessions: The blue jeans he was wearing, the turtleneck, both *folded*. Turn the bag upside down and shake. Wallet and keys clatter to the bronze floor and that's it.

"Shit," I say. "Shit, shit, shit."

I drop my head into my hands. The room is spinning. I feel like I'm in a nightmare.

No money. No books.

Courtney stares at turtleneck and jeans and wrings his hands, as if he still can't believe there's no money.

"We need to get out of here," I whisper, taking another look around. The hanging carcass, the brine, the file cabinet, the workbench, the nauseating pattern on the ceiling. "We can't be found here. With this body . . ."

"Agreed," he said. "Although . . ."

He picks up the pink bag, and probes through the stitching until finding the GPS chip he embedded yesterday.

"Oliver will come back for this skin," he says. "And he'll probably take it to wherever he has the books stashed."

I can't even watch as Courtney sews the tiny chip into some unspeakable part of what used to be Rico.

"Done."

Courtney snatches one of the collars off the corkboard and follows me back through the tapestry into the first chamber.

Something doesn't make sense. Rico brought back Oliver the books and *the money, and this is his reward?*

And it sounded like Rico was worried this would happen, so why didn't he ask for help on the phone?

If that was even Rico on the phone . . .

"Where was his phone?" I ask Courtney, as he pulls open the blast door leading back into the red hallway. "His wallet and keys were there, but not his phone."

Courtney stops.

"You're right. And we know he had a phone, because he was texting you."

I pull the iPhone out of my pocket. 142 missed calls from Sampson, and text messages scrolling down the locked screen forever.

I unlock the phone and go to text messages. 219 text messages from Sampson, two from the same number that texted me in the aquarium, sent at 8:02 pm. Around the time we were renting the car.

left Boks wher they belong, where Soph never goes. Ya

Dstry them b4 he finds them. God hlp us.

COURTNEY HAS BEEN very still since we got back in the Accord. I drove for just a few minutes, then had to pull over onto the shoulder, my hands were shaking so badly. Courtney's eyes are black and wet. He's usually got a pretty good stomach for crime scenes and, more importantly, doesn't dwell on them. What's done is done—all that matters are how the details can help him figure out what happened. When he worked for the DEA, overdoses and butchered drug mules were pretty much par for the course.

But he's obviously bothered now.

"Twenty-two people . . ." he says softly. "How could that have happened? He's supposed to be in prison."

I don't respond. Outside the car, fields of grain extend forever. The air is so clean, the earth so flat, that the moon and stars really light everything up.

"How could a person do that to a *kid*?" Courtney says, almost pleading, like he wants me to reassure him in some way. To tell him that what we saw was some kind of mistake. "He was fourteen."

"He's an animal," I say, although really that's being a bit hard on animals; creatures of all kinds kill each other. That's natural. But *mutilation*, playing with the bodies long after any rage has worn off, treating them like toys . . .

"It seems likely that *somehow* Oliver Vicks is slaughtering people," Courtney says slowly, gaze hardened with a sort of rage I'm not sure I've ever seen on him before. "And getting away with it because everybody thinks he's in prison."

"If he escaped why wasn't it in the papers?" I ask.

"It's been twenty years . . . I guess it's possible he got parole a few years ago and nobody cared enough to write about it."

I pinch my nose. Trying to get my brain to think clearly is like trying to start a fire by snapping your fingers.

"God man," I say. "I'm so drained."

Courtney winces.

Bad choice of words.

"A boy . . ." I massage my temples. "Why is he doing this? Just for binding material?"

"I don't know."

"Okay, let's just think this through," I say, speaking softly. "Rico had been chained up there for a while. Then he was released to do the swap with us. When he saw it wasn't going to go through, when those guys were distracted, he made a run for it, along with the books."

Courtney cocks his head and purses his lips, grants me the slightest nod of agreement without looking in my direction.

"So . . ." I continue. "He knew if he was caught with the books he was as good as dead. So he outran them enough to hide the books somewhere, presumably to use as leverage, to barter his freedom."

Courtney's head rocks side to side, as he weighs my logic.

"Okay. I'm with you," he says. "But apparently that negotiation didn't go well."

I scratch my cheek.

"I think Rico realized the situation was hopeless at some point. If I'm Oliver, I would chain him up until he told me where they are, then kill him. So he texted us, ditched his phone so nobody could see the text, then decided he might as well get it over with." I exhale slowly. "If we don't get those books for Sampson, fast . . . I mean forget about canceling my passport. The guy is a US Senator. He could make our lives really bad."

Courtney finally turns to me. There's a faint glow in his eyes. I know there's a part of him that, despite the horrid things we've seen tonight, craves this intellectual exercise.

"So where will Sophnot never go?" he asks.

I shake my head slowly.

"We need to first see what the deal is at the prison. He's *probably* still there, right? And people are just doing crazy things in a house he designed."

"Mmmhmm," Courtney says, a nice selection from his menu of patronizing sounds. "But it seems more likely that he got parole and Sampson didn't know about it. And that's why those men—*his men*–wanted the swap to go through, with us thinking we were just dealing with Rico. Sampson gives him back the books, and bam. Oliver Vicks steals forty-eight million dollars, and Sampson *doesn't even know he's been robbed.*"

I chew on that for a second. My stomach gurgles, but I can't tell if it's from hunger or nausea.

"You know," Courtney says. "This is not the first documented case of anthropodermic bibliology."

"Huh?"

"Anthropodermic bibliology is the medieval 'art' of binding books with—" Courtney coughs. "Human skin."

"I can't believe a term for that already exists."

Courtney gives me a courtesy nod. He's thinking hard, lips moving slightly like he's mumbling incantations to himself.

"What's he been doing, Frank?" Courtney mutters, mostly to himself. "What does Oliver Vicks *want*? Why did he turn himself in and go to prison? Why does he want all this money? Why did he write these books? Why does he have things like *this*?"

Courtney digs something out from the glove compartment with a hand still gloved in latex. It's the collar he took. It's like the two in the antechamber, except mounted on the front of this one is a double-pronged fork.

"What is that?" I ask.

"It's called a heretic's fork," says Courtney, holding the device by the tips of his fingers like it's radioactive. "I saw one in a museum once. It's a medieval torture device. Two prongs point upwards to rest upon the sinner's jugular, two against the sternum. If the victim lets his chin drop, he bleeds out in minutes. Most prisoners make it two days before succumbing to exhaustion."

"Heretic's fork? So they put that on nonbelievers?"

Courtney puts it back in the glove compartment.

"Yes. And I think this is handmade, Frank. Someone—perhaps Oliver Vicks–put an outrageous amount of time into making these things."

"Because he's crazy. And had a shitload of time on his hands in prison."

"No, no no." Courtney shakes his head seriously. The little fire burns stronger in his eyes. The fire of the hunt. "No, he's not crazy at all. If this is Oliver Vicks, well. Megalomaniacal, delusional perhaps, but he's methodical. I think he planned this all *twenty years in advance*. And it worked. He has just stolen forty-eight million dollars, and gotten away with yet another murder. He's—I hate to say it—but he might be a genius."

I start up the car. I think I'm ravenously hungry, but can't be sure. Toward the extremes, hunger and nausea can become indistinguishable.

"What was it you said?" I say. "'Come with me to Colorado, Frank. Got an easy job. Should only take a day or two . . .'"

Courtney's face wilts like a flower in vinegar.

"Frank, I'm so—"

"I was kidding, sorry. Don't feel bad about it," I say. "It's my own fucking fault. I should have stuck with law school."

Two in the morning. Four hours and change since leaving the red house. We're in a booth at a Wendy's in Denver proper, been sitting here for at least an hour. Only other customers are some drunk high school kids. I really am starving—haven't eaten anything since fruit at Sampson's guesthouse, but have long since given up trying to force down my salad of sour iceberg lettuce and beefsteak tomato. What a cruel trick that anxiety is linked to your digestive system . . . I'd take a headache over a stomachache anyways.

Just wait. That comes later.

The iPhone is between us on the table. I texted Mindy at eleven on the dot:

Nothing. Talk in the AM.

That initially provoked a flurry of responses demanding clarification, but she seems to have finally fizzled out. Anyways, Sampson is doing more than enough to keep the phone busy. Every couple minutes it buzzes again with his number. Eighty-three more missed calls since we left the red house.

Court is zoned out. His eyes keep swiveling back and forth, like he's mentally popping back into that grisly chamber to check if we missed anything.

I sip on my third Wendy's coffee of the evening, which I generously infused with a bottle of Jack I bought across the street. This combo is the only thing I've been able to get down the gullet. Not sure what I expect it to be doing—soothing me? I've never been so simultaneously wired and fatigued in my life. I can feel my pulse pounding behind my eyes, and my stomach feels like it's filled with fighting fish. Haven't slept since three in the morning, after walking in on Sampson.

"What do we do?" I say to the tabletop. "We can't keep ignoring Sampson."

I look out the window. Colfax Boulevard is pretty dead this time of night. Across the street glows an empty 7-Eleven. A juvenile delinquenty-looking crew sits on a curb laughing and smoking cigarettes. Envision myself storming over to them, plucking the cigs from their mouths, stamping them out, and telling them it's a fucking school night.

Courtney's eyes are droopy, and his pale face looks ghostly under the harsh light. He keeps blinking in confusion at his own untouched salad, as if the limp lettuce holds the power to clarify everything we've seen tonight. As the shock from the chamber fades slightly, the grim reality of our current situation takes its place. No books. No money. In just two days here we've spiraled down and crash landed in the middle of an incomprehensible swamp of shit, and it's not going to be easy to climb out.

"The way I see it, the job we were hired for is over," I say.

"In a sense." Courtney chews on his thumbnail. "Failed, but over."

The phone buzzes again. Courtney and I lock eyes.

"Maybe I should pick up and tell Sampson the truth," I say. "We fucked up. Forget our fee, sorry it didn't work out, but thanks very much for the opportunity. And if there's any way he could still give me that passport, that would be lovely."

Courtney prods his dead salad with his plastic fork. The phone keeps insistently buzzing, like an angry bee.

"That sounds foolproof," he says, despite his exhaustion, managing to summon enough strength for a snotty little smirk.

"What else can we do?" I say. Phone goes silent for the moment. "Huh? What's your genius idea?"

"Call the authorities. Show them the chamber, explain everything."

I actually laugh.

"First of all, I'm on the Interpol list. Second, you're suggesting that we bring the cops to a murder scene and tell them that Oliver Vicks did it. Well, what if they go to prison, and somehow he's still there, Court? You think about that? Then who's the prime suspect? Probably the last people who ever spoke to Rico—with hundreds of aquarium goers to testify to that."

The phone starts ringing again. Can almost hear the frustration in every desperate vibration.

"We'll ignore it," he says. "Until we decide what we're going to say."

Courtney reaches for the phone to silence it, and his eyebrows shoot to the ceiling.

"Frank," he says, almost choking. "It's not Sampson. It's the number we spoke to before . . . at the guesthouse. What we thought was Rico."

I snatch it from him. My throat tightens. There's no mistaking that string of digits.

"Should I answer?" I ask.

"No!" squeaks Courtney. "Er. Actually. I don't know. Wait."

He strokes his cheeks furiously.

"Answer or not?" I demand.

"I'm thinking!"

And then the call stops. We both stare at the now silent phone. For just a moment I understand what Courtney hates about these things: the cold inhumanity, the flashing lights which only represent—but are not truly–other people.

It starts buzzing again. Same number.

"I think we gotta answer," Courtney whispers. "It's worse if we don't."

I plug my headphones into the phone, and we each stick in one earbud. I close my eyes, think a silent, wordless prayer: just an ethereal wish to keep Courtney and I alive.

"Hello?" I say, as innocuously as I can manage. But my heart is in my throat, and knees shaking frantically under the booth.

"*I'd like my books.*"

It's the Darth Vader voice again. I feel like the booth just disappeared from underneath me, and I'm suddenly accelerating downward. The head of my plastic fork snaps off; apparently I'd been squeezing it for quite a while.

Before I can think, I say: "I'm sorry, you must have the wrong number."

Courtney attempts to fit an entire fist in his mouth. The robot voice laughs.

"*No, I'm quite sure this is the right number. Is this Frank Lamb? Or Courtney Lavagnino?*"

Courtney looks back at me with the frozen eyes of a cow discovering for the first time what hamburgers are made of. His fingers dig into the table like he's scared of falling off.

"Where did you get that information?" I ask.

"*James told me.*"

One of Courtney's eyes shoots up, the other down, like they're trying to escape his face in different directions. He might actually pass out.

"What—" I gasp.

"*I'd like my books back.*"

Courtney and I have a long conversation with our eyes which as far as I can tell is just variations on *This is fucking bad*. He grabs a Wendy's napkin and scribbles a note to me: *He thinks we have them.*

I hold out my hands helplessly. *Okay. So what?*

He writes: *Go with it.*

Courtney clears his throat, and manages to say: "Why would we give them back to you? We had a deal. You got the money, and we got the books."

.A long pause.

"So you'll be bringing them back to James?"

"So that he'll bring them right to you?" I say. "And then you'll have both? That works out nicely."

A staticky sound that might be a modified guffaw.

"I'm not sure why you think what happens between James and me is any of your business. Bring them back to James as you promised him you would. He's expecting them."

"Maybe I'll just call James and tell him you're extorting him," I say, trying to sound forceful. "That *you're* the one who has the money, not Rico."

A metal-coated laugh.

"You're welcome to tell James whatever you like. I don't think he's going to be very receptive."

"Listen . . . the thing is" —I'm so tired that without really thinking, I'm about to just tell the truth, mention the text from Rico, but Courtney realizes this and lunges across the table to smack me on the cheek. Shakes his head frantically. Instead I say, voice wavering: "We can bring the cops to the red house. Show them Rico, show them everything."

A metallic clang that might be him clearing his throat.

"This must be Frank. The boneheaded one—James's words. Frank, I suggest you defer to your wiser partner and exercise some

restraint. *Once you speak to James, I believe your only possible course of action will become clear. You have stumbled into something much larger than yourself. Something you cannot control. You are standing at the mouth of a cave that not even God himself dares to enter. Don't be a fool."*

"I'm not—"

"You just invaded one of my private residences. Few things upset me more than that. So it may be prudent to ask yourselves why you're still alive. The answer is: Because I'm a patient person. But James, decidedly, is not."

He hangs up.

Courtney's eyes are bulging. His face is the same pale white as the tile tabletop.

"Frank . . ." he says.

"Yeah?"

"Give me some alcohol, please."

"Congrats," I say and slide the liter of Jack across the table to him. "You've just been accepted to the prestigious Frank Lamb school of self-medication."

He takes a little sip straight from the bottle and doubles over coughing. I doubt he's had a drink since he last worked with me. Hands me back the bottle.

The phone starts buzzing again. This time it's Sampson. I close my eyes, hoping when I open them everything will be different. Nope. Still sitting across the table from what looks like a scarecrow who just accidentally saw himself in the mirror and freaked out. We each still have one headphone in. I take a long pull of whiskey—half hoping one of these Wendy's employees says something and gives me an excuse to go ballistic—and hit answer.

"Hi, Senator," I answer softly. "Sorry about the—"

"Where the heck are you?" Sampson's voice is throaty and raw in my ear. "How dare you ignore me! *Bring them to me!*"

"Senator, we—" I cling to the bottle, hoping to absorb a little more booze through osmosis. "We just experienced a little setback is all."

"You . . ." The Senator's voice has gone horrible. Soft, weak, cracked with pain. "What . . . ?"

"James. Listen, Rico is dead," I say. "Oliver Vicks killed him. I know he already spoke to you, but he's messing with you."

"What? *What?*" he flips out again. "How dare you besmirch his holy name! Where is the money? *Where are the books?!*"

"Senator, listen carefully to me," Courtney says, his tone pleading. "This won't be easy to hear. But you've been had. It seems clear that this has been an elaborate con by Oliver Vicks to extort money from you. We can prove it to you—we can be at your house in a few hours to show you pictures. He's not in prison. Must have been paroled or something. The authorities need to know about this. We need helicopters and German Shepherds. I'm going to call the police, and they'll get you your money back."

I hear the shrill crinkle of what I'm guessing is a Diet Pepsi can being manually crushed.

"Sophnot told me you'd say something like that."

I close my eyes and see bright lights. Listen to the buzz of the air-conditioning, the ding of the cash register.

"James," I reply, as calmly as I can. "He's a monster. He's manipulating you in a million different ways. Courtney and I are trying to help you."

My heart flutters in the silence that follows. The longer it goes, the more terrible it is to imagine the man on the other end . . . His mouth open, trying to scream but unable to. Is he actually struggling to breathe? It's impossible to tell how long the moment lasts. Time is stretched out like a man on the rack.

But when Sampson talks again, his voice is surprisingly calm, as if he didn't hear anything I just said. His politician voice.

"You stole the books from me," he says. "But I can forgive you if you make things right. Bring them back to me by Friday. Sophnot needs them by sundown on Friday. That's when the holy Sabbath begins."

"James," I say, ignoring the seismic event unfolding in my stomach. "It's more complex . . ." I trail off, lacking the strength or will to finish that sentence. My molars are gnashing together so forcefully I worry they're just gonna pop out, or erode into nubs. In my earbud pounds Sampson's frantic, impossibly fast breathing. Panting, almost. It's like we're listening to a man who is literally in the process of going insane.

"You think you can do this?" Sampson hisses. "You think I won't move heaven and earth, to retrieve my teacher's books? To *punish you?*" He trails off, whimpering, then starts up again, his voice again reverting to something resembling reasonable. "If you think you can simply flee with my property, you have badly underestimated the capabilities of my office. You think," Sampson gasps, "you can *hide from my wrath?!*"

Courtney is breathing and blinking at hummingbird speed.

"Now let's just back up—"

"Bring me my books. And if you dare, foolishly, to make this public, I'll drag you down with me. I'll clutch at your ankles and drag you down with me into hell."

"Please, James, if we could just be reasonable—"

"I would prefer to resolve this quietly. But if I don't get them by Friday you'll leave me no choice. Can you imagine what happens when a United States Senator tells the FBI that he's had very valuable property stolen from his house? You think you'd last a day with them looking for you?"

"James . . ." I lock eyes with Courtney, begging him for advice. *What do I do?*

I'm a fish flopping around on the sand, just looking to get back in the water even for a few moments. Have to avoid him calling in the infantry before then. Give us time to think. What's today, Tuesday early morning? I can't even remember.

"Okay. Friday," I say, dread washing over my body. "We'll bring them to your house."

"By four," he says. "Sophnot needs them before sundown."

I hang up.

Courtney's hands are trembling. Beads of sweat creeping from the creases on his forehead.

"This is . . ." He gasps, "Frank, I think I'm having a panic attack."

"I would have had one hours ago, but I'm too tired," I say, shooting to my feet, and retrieving a paper bag from the Wendy's staff for Courtney to breathe into. I retake my seat.

"Why does Oliver think we have the books?" I ask.

"I don't know," he says. "Maybe that's what Rico told him. But the irony is, that's better than him and Sampson thinking we *don't* have them. I guess."

"Yeah Court, everything's rosy," I say. "At least the ten-inch metal rod being shoved up our asses isn't eleven inches."

Courtney responds with a few rapid exhalations into the paper bag.

"We need to get the fuck out of here . . ." I say. "Out of this state. This country."

Courtney puts down the bag.

"We can't," he says. "Sampson will come after us."

I blink at him.

"So . . ." I say. "I guess we better figure out where Sophnot will never go. Before Friday."

Courtney puts down his bag, presses his palms on the table, and pushes himself up slightly out of his seat, so he's leaning over me like some kind of perched bird of prey. The tips of his fingers are vibrating like an electric current is running through them.

"And then what?" he says. "We just leave this serial killer on the loose? We can't, Frank. He . . ."

Courtney trails off, unable or unwilling to vocalize the atrocities we now know Oliver has been performing regularly.

I drain what's left of my spiked coffee, pathetically hoping this final caffeine surge will suddenly render everything a difficult yet manageable challenge that I can't wait to get to work on.

"Okay . . ." I say, trying to think out loud. "Right. Oliver. So then . . . we'll bring back the books, then call the cops on Oliver."

Courtney emits something between a laugh and a cry.

"No . . . making this public will bring down Sampson. And if he goes down, I guarantee you he was telling the truth about bringing us down with him."

"Well, then what the hell do you suggest?" I snap. Feels like my brain has run out of gas and is now just lurching spastically toward the garage.

Courtney sinks back into his chair.

"Let me think," he says, and he sits back in the booth and goes silent. I consider calling Sadie again. Trying to explain . . . what exactly?

It would be a selfish call. I just want to hear her voice. That will settle me down.

But she wouldn't pick up. It's two hours later on the East Coast.

I toy with the empty coffee cup.

What if Courtney had never found me in Budapest? Or if I hadn't gone to the hotel? Or if I'd said no to him?

There's a reasonable case for being upset at him for dragging me into this, but I don't feel that way. Instead I feel that this case, this whole state—fucking Colorado—is some kind of black hole that dragged me back from across the globe.

Why? Why does this place want Frank Lamb and Courtney Lavagnino?

I smirk to myself at the ludicrousness of the first answer that pops into my head.

What if we're the only ones who can fix this mess?

"Oliver is in a pretty spot . . . He's not particularly worried," Courtney finally says. "He's thinking: Either we'll deliver the books to him ourselves, via Sampson, or, worst case, Sampson will deploy the cavalry to get them back for him. And meanwhile, he already has his forty-eight million."

I bite my lip.

"He seems to have a knack for setting up situations in which he can't lose."

We sit for a moment in silence.

"What if we told Oliver the truth? That we don't have the books, but here's Rico's text? Maybe he would know what Rico meant, and he'd just go get the books himself."

"No, no . . ." says Courtney. "He knows who we are. And he's not going to just let us walk away knowing what we know. He'd either kill us or have Sampson report us."

"So what do we do?" I ask.

We sit in silence for a moment

"Option one: If we get the books by Friday then I can get my passport, and our salary, from Sampson. Then when Sampson brings the books to Oliver we can follow, and tell the cops where he is—I'd say skinning people probably violates his probation terms."

"And if we can't find the books?" Courtney says.

"Then our second best option is to just track down Oliver Vicks directly. To at least protect ourselves, stop him from killing anyone else, and get Sampson's money back."

Courtney purses his lips and taps his fingers on the table, and for maybe the twentieth time in the last couple hours, nods.

"Okay. I'm with you. Best case, get the books. And barring that, at least try to figure out where Oliver Vicks is and—hopefully— prove that he's on the loose killing people. So. Where will Sophnot never go?"

I scratch my head.

"Back to prison maybe? I don't know how the hell Rico would get in there to drop the books off, but if Oliver got out on parole, I mean, back to prison is probably the last place he'd ever want to go."

Courtney shrugs helplessly.

"Could be. Let's go tomorrow morning and figure out what the hell happened there."

Part Three

Wednesday/Thursday

Genesis 41: 41–45

So Pharaoh said to Joseph, "I hereby put you in charge of the whole land of Egypt." Then Pharaoh took his signet ring from his finger and put it on Joseph's finger. He dressed him in robes of fine linen and put a gold chain around his neck. He had him ride in a chariot as his second-in-command and people shouted before him, "Make way!" Thus he put him in charge of the whole land of Egypt.

Then Pharaoh said to Joseph, "I am Pharaoh, but without your word no one will lift hand or foot in all Egypt." Pharaoh gave Joseph the name Saphnat-Paneah and gave him Asenath, daughter of Potiphar, priest of Ond to be his wife. And Joseph went throughout the land of Egypt.

SADDLEBACK CORRECTIONAL FACILITY is in the foothills, near Golden, Colorado, about a half-hour drive outside Boulder. Much like it often was in Budapest, my mood is way out of sync with the scenery. Oceans of grain waving in the sparkling morning sun. Crisp blue sky. I see what might be an honest to goodness eagle riding the wind off to my right.

The star-spangled scenery does little to lift my spirits. Only serves as a reminder that, were I somebody different in a much better situation, I might currently be enjoying my stay on earth. I'd rather we were driving through a dark swamp in the dead of winter, occupied exclusively by crows and maggots.

We drive with the windows down, letting the warm wind whip against our ears. My right hip is killing me from the few hours of attempted sleep, contorted in the backseat of the Honda. Even four Tylenol PMs couldn't put me down. Just lay still, listening to Courtney's light snoring.

We picked up some oranges, apples and dry granola from a grocery store on the way out. I peel an orange and hand some slices to Courtney, who wordlessly swallows, keeping his eyes on the narrow highway.

The phone rings. Mindy, calling for the tenth time this morning.

"You wanna talk to her?" I say.

"I'm driving," Courtney responds.

"I'm not going to tell her exactly what Rico said," I say. "Can't risk her finding the books on her own."

"Fine. But have to make sure she doesn't leak to the Senator that we don't even have them."

Courtney obviously has more credibility with her, but this is a nightmare scenario for his technophobia: speaking to a girl he's crushing on, over the phone.

I hit call and she picks up almost immediately. I'm anticipating a screeching British earful, chewing me out for all but ignoring her calls and texts until now, but she seems to realize that she's going to have to play nice.

"Where are you?" she says. "Did you find anything?"

"Colorado. And no."

"Oh," she says, voice souring. "This is Frank."

"Courtney's driving."

He glances at me, dying to ask what she said about him.

"Speaker," he whispers.

I put my hand over the mouthpiece.

"Don't want to disrupt your concentration. While you're *driving*."

"Why didn't you respond last night? Did you find anything on the security footage?"

"We might have something," I say. "Actually wanted to ask you some questions. About Sophnot."

"What are you talking about. What did you find?"

"It's complicated, don't want to get into it now."

"*Complicated*? Please don't patronize me."

"Well, Courtney and I were wondering . . . well for one thing, if there's a significance to the binding itself. If it's more than just a cover."

"Let's meet and discuss this," she says.

"Look, if you don't want to answer my questions, that's fine. I'll call you later," I say, about to just hang up on her when she says:

"Let me guess: You discovered what kind of leather he's using."

I grit my teeth. Courtney looks at me, eyes wide.

"You knew?" I hiss.

"Of course," she says. "Do you know how many hours I worked with those things?"

"Then why didn't you tell us?" I yell into the phone. Courtney is so distracted he nearly veers into a drainage ditch.

"Didn't seem pertinent to you two."

"Pertinent!? He's been killing people to do this!" I shriek.

Mindy laughs dryly.

"Yes. It's *complicated* isn't it?"

I slap my palm over the receiver, emit a stream of curses, and try to control the anger in my voice.

"What else are you holding out on us?"

"About a decade's worth of research, Frank. I apologize for not compacting everything into an executive summary of quick-hitting sound bites."

"You didn't think the fact that the books are bound in *human skin* was worth mentioning? What else do you know? What about a mask? Do the books say anything about a wax mask?"

I hear the sharp breath on her end.

"You have a lead about where they are don't you?" she says. "Don't lie to me. I'm not stupid."

I don't respond.

"I can help you find them," she says carefully. "I know more about them than anyone on Earth besides the author."

My shoulders tighten.

"Okay," I say. "We're running around town, looking into a few possible leads. But we'll meet up tonight, alright?"

She takes a moment, considering whether these terms are acceptable.

"Wonderful," she says.

"Can't wait," I growl, and hang up.

Courtney opens his mouth to speak, I preempt him.

"We're not meeting up with her, and we're not telling her a thing," I say. "She'd sell us down the river in a heartbeat if it suited her needs."

Courtney frowns.

"Like her or not," he says. "In the end we might need her help to figure out Rico's text message."

I cross my arms.

"We're not going to work with someone who keeps lying to us."

I wait for Courtney to point out my hypocrisy. Instead he takes a gentler approach.

"You'd do the same thing in her shoes, Frank. You wouldn't have told us everything you know."

"We'll keep stalling her until we find the books ourselves."

"I'm not sure where your inherent distrust of women comes from," says Courtney. "Did you have a good relationship with your mother growing up?"

I gawk at him. What makes him so utterly infuriating sometimes is the earnestness with which he says this shit.

"You're a real piece of work," I mutter.

"I'm just trying to help," he says. His authenticity makes my forehead burn.

"I'll make sure to bring it up in group therapy in prison," I say, as SCF rises on the horizon. "Enjoy yourself today, champ. Will probably be the last time we're in jail on the right side of the fence."

As Saddleback appears on the horizon, I flip through the fake FBI IDs Courtney made for us five years ago during the Kanter case. We have no choice but to use them again, given the tight time line. I run over our story again in my head. The only reason they might take us seriously is that we're coming to them with the truth: Oliver Vicks doesn't seem to be in their prison.

Most prisons are content with two enclosure fences. Usually galvanized steel garnished on top with razor wire. But as the Honda nears the facility, I see that SCF has a super-max-type perimeter: There are the usual two outer fences, then a narrow strip of sand, then *another* thirty-foot wall lined with razor wire. And then the *interior* side of the inner wall is lined with huge coils of more razor wire, so inmates can't even get anywhere close to the fence. The guard towers are imposing concrete spires that look built to withstand hurricanes. The ground around the outside of the prison looks like it's been tilled, there's a kind of featureless moat of uniform grey. Even if you *somehow* tunneled under all three walls, you'd be totally out in the open—easy pickings for the snipers in the guard towers.

This is not a prison built for rehabilitation, it's a cage for monsters.

"Wow," I say.

"Second-highest security in Colorado," says Courtney. "Among the top twenty in the country, I read. 450 guards for 3,000 prisoners. Very high ratio."

"So I guess we can rule out the possibility that Oliver escaped, eh?"

Courtney nods almost imperceptibly.

There's only one entrance. One place where there's a break in the outer two fences, and the interior one slides open. But if I was an aspiring escapee, I think I'd rather take my chances with the fences. Six booths windowed with what I'm sure is bulletproof glass house a dozen guards. As we roll up, three officers in grey uniforms with rifles strapped to their backs burst from a booth, hold up their palms, indicating for us to stop well short of the first line of defense. Then they trot out to the car.

An officer motions for us to step out of the car. He has a formless face and lumpy body—a dirty potato in polarized Ray-Bans. The two behind him have hands on the butts of their side arms, but don't draw them.

"Visiting hours are Monday afternoons only," Potato states, breathing heavily just from his little trot over.

"We're from the FBI," Courtney says. "We need to speak to someone in administration about a prisoner you have incarcerated."

Potato seems momentarily paralyzed by this news.

"IDs are in the glove compartment," I say.

He finally nods slowly, then gestures for two subordinates to confirm this.

My heart thuds as the other two officers advance to the car, pass within inches of me, and pluck our paper from the glove compartment. One of them inspects them seriously, as if he has a lot of experience examining FBI IDs—you don't become a prison corrections officer because you're good with nuance.

"Looks good," one of them shouts to Potato. He seems slightly disappointed by this news.

"Hold tight," he says, then retreats out of earshot and summons someone on his walkie-talkie. Has a brief back and forth, nods, then returns.

"Step out of the car. Leave the keys in the ignition. We'll park it for you," Potato says, pointing to a lot obscured by steel and wire.

"We'll check you, then take you to admin. Do you have weapons with you?"

"In the trunk," I say, as we climb out of the car. "Two Magnums."

A guard with a deep scar on his cheek joins the party, walks slowly over to the car and starts combing through our bags with infuriating deliberation, confiscating anything that could conceivably be used as a weapon, and placing it in a transparent plastic bag.

He takes particularly long going through Courtney's red acrylic bag, the one that holds his tools. I can tell it's killing Court to watch this guard paw his beloved implements—he's really anal about his tools, to the point that he tries to fix them himself instead of replacing them, when possible, and doesn't even like to let *me* touch them. But he just stares at his shoes and does what looks like a calming breathing exercise.

In the passenger seat, Scar finds what's left of my Jack Daniel's from last night. He unscrews the top and pours it out into the dust.

"Hey!" I say. "Look, I know it's no McClelland, but I was still gonna drink that."

"Sorry," Scar replies joylessly. "No contraband gets in."

He screws the cap back onto the now empty bottle and tosses it back into the rear seat. We wait while this lone officer concludes his ludicrously inefficient search—*Why can't this stuff even be in our parked car?*—and then another CO climbs into the driver's seat and pulls our rental through the gauntlet of security checkpoints. Gate creaks open, they wave the vehicle through, then close it.

Potato motions for us to follow him. The COs stare at us as we pass them in their booths, same dead look in their eyes I've seen in postal workers who do the same route for decades.

He takes us to a walkway to the side of the gate. We walk

through a metal detector, and then are clinically and holistically frisked by a sad man wearing powdered latex gloves.

He must be a real bummer at his kid's career days.

The only holdup is the iPhone in my pocket.

"No phones. Can't have pictures or video," he says. "I'll put it in with your other stuff."

A no-phone rule for visitors seems a bit over the top for ostensible FBI agents. But they have the guns, and I'm pleasantly surprised someone has agreed to speak to us. Potato leads us through the walkway—the only way in besides the vehicle gate.

I catch Courtney's eye as we follow Potato: *So far, so good right?*

He replies with a raised eyebrow: *Stay vigilant.*

Waiting for us outside the tunnel is a stooped CO the same color as the asphalt he's standing on. He can't be much younger than sixty. He's shorter and skinnier than me, but he's rolled up his khaki sleeves to reveal sinewy biceps. Potato clasps his hands behind his back as we approach the man.

"Sir," Potato says timidly. "These are—"

"I know." The dark man nods and smiles at Courtney and I. "You two are from the FBI." His voice is high and crackly, filled with humor.

Beside me I notice Potato shift his weight uneasily.

"Yeah." I extend a hand. "I'm Ben Donovan and this is Leonard Francis. Are you an administrator? We had some questions we need answered."

In response to this, the old CO breaks into a huge grin and takes my hand in both of his. He's wearing a lot of very strong cologne, and there's something vaguely effeminate about his tender grip.

"I'm Sergeant Don," he says, eyes twinkling. "I deal primarily with overseeing our security team. You're going to need to speak with the warden."

"Perfect," I say. "Glad he could make time for us."

Sergeant Don cocks his head.

"Only the Lord makes time," he says.

Then, ignoring Courtney's outstretched hand, Sergeant Don simply turns and starts walking, stooped over, hands clasped behind his back. Potato rushes to follow the Sergeant, seemingly forgetting about us.

We jog across the hot asphalt to keep up with the two of them.

The scale of the prison complex is staggering. Three thousand prisoners is a lot. The buildings that must be the cell blocks are ten-story monstrosities of whitewashed concrete, pocked with hundreds of tiny reinforced windows. The five cell blocks I see are spaced out around a central yard the size of two or three football fields.

And I guess prison business is booming, because there's a construction site on the west side of the yard. A new wing, presumably. Workers—whom I think might be inmates—in hard hats and bright orange vests are mostly congregated on a floor around the middle, about nine stories up. The finished floors beneath them are all shrouded in white tarps, like to protect them from rain or dust. The tower is even taller than the rest of the buildings—it will end up looking like a high-rise apartment. A crane lifts I-beams as thick as a man a hundred feet in the air. Sounds of shouting, clanging of metal on metal, drilling fill the air.

"Are those all prisoners doing the construction?" I ask Potato and Don's backsides as they lead us along the yard's south border fence. Nothing.

I try again: "Guess it's good to have real work for them, eh?"

They ignore me.

I'm struck by the lack of greenery. This complex must be at least five square miles, and there's not a single tree in sight.

Courtney gives it a swing: "How long you two been working here?" he asks their uniformed backs.

No response.

"You know anything about an inmate named Oliver Vicks?" I ask.

This question, finally, gets a reaction. Stops them both dead in their tracks. They turn around. Potato grimaces like *why did you have to go there?* Sergeant Don's face tightens into a scowl.

"What?" he asks sharply.

"Oliver Vicks. Do you think we'll be able to speak to him?" asks Courtney.

Potato's face curls inward like he's constipated.

The folds of Don's already wrinkled forehead furrow even deeper in consternation. His little bald head is wet with sweat. Like a shiny eight ball. He scans my face slowly, as if he's looking for something very specific.

"Be careful," Sergeant Don says slowly. He looks like he'd like to say more, but the two of them turn and resume walking, perhaps slightly more quickly now.

Guess we hit a nerve.

They lead us to what must be the admin building and in through a side door, into an air-conditioned lobby that looks like a hospital waiting room. We follow them through a door, down a windowless hallway of white plaster that smells like Lysol. A few closed offices. One open, we see a man in a suit on a phone. We pass a few other grey-and khaki-clad guards in the corridor, who nod at our guides and eye us with curiosity.

Potato seems relieved to leave us at the elevator. Avoids our eyes and rushes away down the hall.

Courtney and I join Don in a cramped cage that creaks as it tugs us skyward, me pressing my back against the wall in a fruitless attempt to escape the cloud of patchouli fragrance emanating from some unspeakable crevice beneath Don's uniform.

The doors open onto a small waiting room. With a jab of his chin, Don indicates that we're to sit down in two puke-yellow chairs. He sits across from us and stares at the wall over our heads.

A receptionist behind a desk pays us no heed.

Across from us, Sergeant Don pretends we're not there. His demeanor has definitely soured since we mentioned Oliver.

"The warden will be with you two in just a second," the receptionist finally says, then returns to his computer. This prompts Sergeant Don to stand up and wordlessly exit the waiting room. I hear the ding as he enters the elevator.

I look at Courtney.

"Something happened to these officers," I whisper. "They're rattled."

Courtney sticks his tongue in his cheek and nods in assent.

"Weird vibe here, for sure."

We wait for only three minutes before the secretary says, "You two can go in now."

He hits a button under the desk which buzzes the lock on the door. We open and walk through, only to find ourselves in a vestibule facing a second identical door.

"Security," says the secretary from behind us. "Let the first one close and I'll open the second."

Courtney releases the first door, and for just a moment we're squished together in a room the size of a phone booth. Then another buzz and the second door swings inwards.

Waiting for us is a stout man wearing a bright blue Hawaiian shirt. He's probably early sixties, with a trimmed grey beard and very thick bifocals. He's lost a lot of hair, and his face is wrapped in an endearing layer of grandfatherly fat.

"Nathan Heald," he says, and smiles to us, extending a surprisingly delicate, smooth hand. His voice and demeanor are gentle—not what you expect from the warden of a maximum security prison. I shake his hand first, then Courtney.

"I'm Leonard Francis," Courtney says, per our fake IDs. "And this is Ben Donovan."

"Pleasure," he says. His glasses are so thick that they blur his eyes pretty severely. He must have a prescription like a fishbowl. "Come sit down and let's see if I can help you out."

His office is a stark contrast to the sterile waiting room. Burgundy bookcases hold hundreds of volumes on prison management, most bound in grey or dark blue. The curtains, spread to look out onto the complex, are a preposterous lime green. He has some very cool artwork: aborigine figurines on top of the bookcase, cubist paintings on the walls. I spot expensive-looking chess and backgammon sets nestled between an ivory statuette of a dove and a heavy Monet book, and suffer a brief moment of nostalgia for *Voci*.

"You play?" I ask, gesturing to the set.

"When I can find a decent opponent." Heald smiles. "Chess is like sex. Every man thinks he understands it, because he knows how the pieces move."

I grin.

"I would never claim to be competent at either. I meant backgammon."

"Ah, a backgammon player," Heald says, and cocks his head at me as if to study me more closely. "I prefer backgammon too. I like the element of chance. We'll have to play sometime."

"Sure," I say, though unless I'm incarcerated sometime soon it's hard to conceive of a situation where that would happen.

The floor is a lush blue oriental carpet that matches his shirt. For a second I think of the oriental carpet in Sampson's office, and cringe.

The warden sits in a swiveling office chair behind a metal desk and gestures for us to sit down across from him.

"So, the local constabulary!" he chuckles to himself.

Nervous?

He looks past us, out the window for a moment, Colorado sun reflecting in his bifocals. "What brings you gentlemen here?"

Courtney and I exchange a look. He nods almost imperceptibly to me like *go ahead.*

I say, "We have some questions about a prisoner here. Oliver Vicks."

Heald's face tightens ever so slightly.

"Sure," he says, forcing out the syllable.

"Can we speak to him?" I ask neutrally.

Heald doesn't respond immediately, just keeps staring wistfully out the window over my shoulder, like he's recalling a poignant moment from his childhood.

Or maybe he's been waiting for this visit for a while, and he knows the gig is up.

"Mr. Heald?" Courtney prods. "Would that be possible? To speak to Oliver?"

He clenches his jaw.

"No," he says, still avoiding our eyes. "That won't be possible."

"Because he's not here?" Courtney says.

He purses his lips and finally meets Courtney's gaze.

"I don't follow," he says.

"Was it an administrative error?" I say. "Did you grant him parole and then realize you weren't supposed to?"

Heald doesn't budge, holds a pretty impressive poker face.

"Whatever it was," Courtney says. "We know that Oliver Vicks is supposed to be here, and he's not."

The warden exhales slowly and lays his palms flat on the desk.

"Why are you here? What do you want from me?" he asks.

Courtney folds his hands in his lap and keeps his mouth shut. I do the same. Not exactly sure what's going on here. Hopefully the silence will push Heald into throwing us a bone. Indeed, after an awkward silence that feels interminable, Heald says:

"He's done something awful, hasn't he?"

Bingo. He's gone.

I nod slowly.

"Quite."

"Murder?"

"It's still an ongoing investigation," Courtney says. Bad cop.

"But . . ." I grimace. "Between us . . ." Good cop.

Heald rubs his temples and shakes his head slowly. "God have mercy . . ." He brushes a grey eyebrow, seems to deliberate with himself for a moment. "You two have no idea what you're dealing with here," he says softly.

"So tell us," says Courtney. "What are we dealing with?"

The warden rubs the tips of his fingers together. I notice the tight muscles on his forearms. He also looks like he has broad shoulders under that shirt. He's one of those guys who gets stronger as he gets older. I can picture him at the gym out-benching all the young punks.

"You two want a drink?" he asks, and before we can respond, he's on his feet pulling two books off his shelf to reveal a hidden bottle of Glenfidditch. "It's contraband," he says, pouring three very healthy servings, "but my post has a few advantages."

Courtney shoots me a look of disgust: *It's eleven a.m.*

Heald takes two of the lowballs and hands them to us. I accept mine and take a sip. Nice and oaky.

"No thanks." Courtney smiles. "I'm not a big drinker."

"That's fifteen-year scotch," Heald says. "I'm not pouring it back in the bottle."

The label is facing me pretty clearly reads 12-year, but I keep my mouth shut.

Heald shoots down what's at least a triple shot. His face flushes and he collapses back into his chair.

"I didn't ask for this," he says, strain in his voice. "Any of this." He takes a deep breath. His affect reminds me of a coach at a press conference, helpless after a bad loss.

We just didn't play as well as them, what do you want me to say?

"What happened, Nathan?" I ask.

He twirls his empty glass, like he's ready for another one.

"Oliver Vicks was sentenced to life roughly twenty years ago, and SCF was his first stop, with no plans to transfer. This was just before my time, actually. I was hired about a year after his incarceration. For the first ten-plus years or so of his sentence, Mr. Vicks was—to the administration's knowledge—a model prisoner.

"Not only did he not get into any fights, he helped break them up. He quickly developed a reputation as a dependable ally. A lot of inmates confided in him. He had no enemies, even though he'd commune with members of rival gangs simultaneously. This is almost unheard of, to be well liked by Hispanics, Blacks and Whites . . . it was most unusual. I even asked him for help on one occasion—an inmate had a horrible psychotic episode, and we asked Oliver if he could speak to the man. He did, and from what I understand, he even helped a bit."

The warden trails off for a moment. Just as I'm about to prod him to continue, he does on his own.

"But after a few years the administration finally began learning more about the nature of the inmates' respect for Oliver. How he'd managed to make so many friends. He had a sort of ideology that he'd started preaching, and apparently it had gained a lot of traction. By the time we found out about it, there were a few dozen prisoners who were, I suppose you could say, his followers. Converted, in a sense."

"What was his ideology?" I ask.

Heald grips his empty tumbler.

"I'm no expert," he replies. "But a few things are pretty clear: One is that he claimed to be a sort of prophet. He had some ideas about the changing tide in the relationship between God and man, that man had finally taken the upper hand, and that he knew how to exploit this."

"Did you ever hear the name *Sophnot?*" I ask.

Heald flinches.

"Yes. All his followers called him that. I don't suppose you know the meaning?"

We both shake our heads.

"It's from the Old Testament. A word found only once or

twice. It's in the book of Genesis. Do you two know the story of Joseph?"

Courtney nods yes, I shake my head no. I'm considering trying to get him back on topic, but I figure all information is good.

"The quick and dirty: Joseph was sold by his brothers into slavery, taken down to Egypt and thrown in jail. He rotted there for years, until one day Pharaoh, the king, had a dream that nobody could interpret to his satisfaction. Joseph had previously interpreted a fellow prisoner's dream correctly, and so eventually Joseph was brought to the Pharaoh. He correctly interpreted the dream, and Pharaoh was so impressed, saw the wisdom of this young Hebrew, that not only did he release him from jail, he made him second in command over all of Egypt. And there is one verse where the name *Sophnot* is mentioned. Pharaoh uses it as a nickname for Joseph, *Sophnot Paneah*, something like 'he who solves riddles.'"

I glance quickly at Courtney and it's clear he's thinking the same thing, *Oliver interpreted Sampson's dream . . . that's how it all started.*

"So, I suppose that's why he called himself that," continues Heald. "He was also imprisoned, only to slowly rise in the ranks. As I was explaining, he was gaining more and more followers. He began holding what he called 'demonstrations' during meals. We let them happen at first, since they weren't strictly speaking against the rules, but we quickly saw where this could lead—"

"What do you mean 'demonstrations'?" I ask.

Heald shakes his head slowly, as if still in disbelief of everything that unfolded. "The first time, this one I only heard second-hand, he stood up in the middle of the cafeteria and declared that, with the help of God, he would turn a cup of steaming coffee into a block of black ice."

Courtney raises an eyebrow.

"And?"

Heald shrugs. "Apparently he did it. Some sort of sleight of hand, I suppose. Others are harder to explain away so easily. The last one we allowed to take place, I was there. I saw it with my own eyes. He stabbed himself in the throat with a fork. One officer who was nearby, swore to me that he saw it pierce the skin. Oliver stuck it in, and blood poured out, drenching the lunch table beneath him. Then he pulled the fork out and there was no wound. The blood puddle remained, but Oliver was totally fine. We shut it down immediately, but it was too late. By that point he had so many admirers that all he had to do was utter the word *riot* and we'd have a total disaster on our hands. We put him in solitary. It was my say and I take full responsibility. But it was a horrible mistake. If he was a leader *before*, this punishment made him a martyr. His support grew exponentially. He was all the inmates talked about. The rumors spread . . . they said when he was released his next demonstration would be to resuscitate the dead. During his daily hour of freedom, he'd smuggle notes out to someone, and they'd be read aloud at meals. They were types of sermons. Again, nothing promoting violence, so it was hard to say whether or not to crack down even further. But when someone read a note from Oliver, you could hear a pin drop in the cafeteria. And perhaps you can imagine, that's not exactly a common occurrence around here."

Heald's hands are locked tight on the table.

"What happened next happened too quickly . . . there was nothing I could do, short of call in the National Guard. Unbeknownst to me, two of our corrections officers became smitten with Oliver. They were stopping by his solitary cell to ask him advice, perhaps to ask him to 'demonstrate' again. Who knows. They weren't exactly forthcoming about all of this when I grilled them later. But what seems clear . . . Four years ago, one of these two officers opened Oliver's cell for him. Oliver walked out to the inner gate, and asked the guard there to open it. He did. Everyone in the watchtowers was looking. But nobody dared fire. There was total silence as he strode across the courtyard. Some inmates were on recess then— broad daylight—and they just stopped and watched—"

"Wait," I interrupt. "Oliver Vicks told the corrections officers to let him out, and they *did*?"

Heald bares his teeth.

"You don't understand. I spoke later to the one who opened the inner gate for him. The poor man was in tears. Offered me his resignation. But told me at the moment all he could think of was his wife, his two kids. He was terrified of what the prisoners would do to him if he refused. If he'd refused him or laid a hand on him . . . Oliver had only to snap his fingers to instigate a full-blown riot. Usually we can put a riot down with rubber bullets and gas, but this was different. Four out of five of these prisoners would have given his life to defend Oliver. Officers would have died. So Oliver walked to that front checkpoint. There were perhaps fifteen guards with rifles. They let him walk out. And that was that."

Courtney is frowning intensely. I wonder how much of this he believes. I'm certainly skeptical myself, but it's hard to conceive of why Heald would make something like this up.

"But after," I say. "You didn't tell anyone? Instead of a manhunt, you're telling us you just kind of . . . pretended it never happened?"

Heald looks like he could use another couple drinks.

"What would you have me do?" he stays softly. "Implicate

myself and my entire staff? And, anyways, I have to admit, ever since he left, things have been running very smoothly."

Heald beckons us to the lime-green draped window. He points to the construction site. There are hundreds of prisoners at work on the scaffolded structure, all wearing hard hats and bright orange vests.

"Our new addition. A state-of-the-art facility that will house fifteen hundred inmates and allow us to expand our operation big-time. And the labor costs are dirt cheap because the prisoners are doing most of the work, with just a bit of supervision from outside professionals. Few prisons ever bother trying to get their inmates to do any sort of serious work, because it's inefficient, and they don't cooperate. But here, these guys work harder than anyone. It's like a lingering effect of Oliver—camaraderie or common purpose, perhaps. But anyways, it wasn't as if we were having *problems* afterwards . . ." Heald trails off.

I watch the prisoners at work. Wonder how many of them are still Oliver Vicks enthusiasts.

"What about the officers who let him walk?" I ask. "Do they still work here?"

"I conducted months of interviews, and ended up transferring a lot of our staff," Heald says. "But at least they still have jobs. And aren't being court-martialed. It wasn't their fault. I really believe that. I would have done the same. I think you two would have as well. I mean, that day in the cafeteria. With the fork . . ." Heald clears his throat. "That was part of it, why the guards didn't shoot him. They believed the bullets wouldn't hurt him. He always said he already knew how he would die, and until that day nothing could hurt him. And after watching him stab himself in the throat and walk away unscathed, it's hard for a man not to wonder."

Courtney raises an eyebrow.

"Did he say how he'd die?" he asks.

The warden cracks a sad smile.

"He loved fried food. Always said that would be the end of him. Heart failure, I suppose. In fact, some of the prisoners who were closest to him, told me Oliver knew how his entire life would play out. That was one of the things he wrote about. Documenting his entire life, down to the minute. Everything that had already happened, and everything that had yet to happen. Do you . . ." Heald clears his throat. "Do you know where his books are? Did he get them back? I know he was handing them off to a visitor because of the volume limits on offenders' personal possessions."

I clench my jaw. Courtney sniffs.

Heald crosses his arms and turns away from the window to glare at me through his thick glasses.

"Have I not been forthcoming with you two?" he asks.

I lock eyes with Courtney. It's hard to read exactly what my partner is trying to convey with this particular brand of frown. I think it's skepticism.

"They have come up in the course of the investigation," says Courtney.

Heald's lips twitch.

"You don't understand what they are, do you?" Heald asks.

Courtney studies the warden's face.

"Do you?"

"I asked a simple question," Heald says. "Do you know where they are?"

"I'm sorry," Courtney says. "We can't discuss that."

"I'm trying to help you. Help all of us," Heald says. "Talk to me."

"I'm sorry," Courtney repeats.

The warden smiles strangely at Courtney.

"I understand now," he says, an unmistakable frost in his voice. "*You're* the chess player. Very well. I suppose we're done here."

He returns to his desk, opens a drawer, and pulls out one business card. Returns and hands it to me, totally ignoring Courtney. "Detective Donovan, here's my direct line—my cell—as well as my email. If you have any further questions, don't hesitate to call. I'm happy to assist in any way I can."

"Thanks for your time," I say.

"Pleasure," he says, and shows us to the door. He gives a cursory, ice-cold nod to Courtney. To me he says: "Detective, I meant it when I said I would love to play backgammon with you sometime. Best of luck with everything."

OUR DRIVE FROM prison back to civilization is pretty quiet, both playing back details of the visit in our heads before comparing notes—a practice that ensures greater accuracy. Truth is, each time I think through everything Heald said, the more disturbed I become.

The fork in his throat . . .

Without consulting Courtney, I follow the highway signs back to Denver, and pull into the parking lot of a Whole Foods. Haven't been inside of one since going expat five years ago, and am craving the comfort of overpriced goat milk yogurt and horseshit homeopathy.

And it turns out there's no Whole Foods like a Colorado Whole Foods. These folks aren't gonna buy their kale chips just anywhere. Many of the men here have bushy lumberjack beards and pierced ears. Some women have dreadlocks, and all look like they routinely give birth squatting in the forest.

I get a large coffee, muffin and cup of water and sit down across from Courtney, who filled up a bowl with leaves from the salad bar, and took an apple and a mango for dessert. He joylessly wolfs down his dry mesclun mix, then quarters the apple with a plastic knife—no small feat—and carefully carves away the skin.

"Well," I say, slurping down some black acid. The coffee here is nice and strong. "I'm pretty sure if the books were in that prison, Heald would know. And he wouldn't have gotten upset that we didn't give him any info about them."

"Mmhmm," Courtney says, concentrating on picking the seeds from the core of the apple with the tongs of a plastic fork.

I pluck a brown recycled Whole Foods napkin from the holder, pour my water on it and dab my filthy face.

"I feel kinda bad for that guy, to be honest."

Courtney is only half listening. Far more interested in sectioning his mango.

I pull the business card the warden gave me from my pocket and enter his number into Courtney's phone: Warden Nathan Heald.

Courtney slides a piece of mango between his teeth and squeezes the juice out with his mandible.

"Frank," Courtney says. "What kind of person could unite an entire prison? *Talk* his way out of a *maximum security* facility?"

I take a bit of muffin.

"You're buying all that?"

Courtney frowns. "Two days ago I wouldn't have. But . . ." He shrugs. "Oliver Vicks isn't in prison. He was in the red house last night. So you tell me how he got out."

"I know, Court. But that just doesn't seem possible. I don't care how charismatic you are . . . Selling used cars or something, fine. But nobody can charm their way out of prison."

Courtney shakes his head.

"This is well beyond charisma. Those demonstrations for one thing—they must have been pretty serious illusions. Because if you think a few thousand hardened offenders are going to become believers based on a few parlor tricks, well."

"What are you suggesting?" I say.

Courtney shrugs, taps on the tabletop.

"I'm not *suggesting* anything, but was just thinking. What if you lived in the time of Jesus. And for the sake of argument, let's say he was really walking on water and so on. To be precise, Christianity wasn't really founded until several decades after his death—but clearly this man had such a huge impact on people that, even several decades later, his memory was enough to start a world-changing religion. Why do you think he was so impactful? Was it the tricks? That's part of it. But it was also *him*. The way he behaved."

"I hope you're not comparing Jesus to a deranged serial killer," I say.

Courtney grimaces.

"I suppose I am. But only in the sense that they're able to influence large groups of people. I mean, have you ever met a politician face-to-face, Frank?"

"Sampson."

Courtney waves me off.

"No, I mean a real one. I was in the same room as Bill Clinton once. Some kind of fund-raiser—no, I didn't pay. It was part of a job—and I watched him, the way he talked to people. Every time he met someone he focused exclusively on them for like twenty seconds. You could tell he made them feel like they were the center of his world for that moment. And every single person turned away glowing, beaming from ear to ear. It was like, there was an energy in the room, radiating from wherever he was."

"You think Bill Clinton could talk his way out of SCF?"

"No I do not. Which means we're dealing with someone. . . Honestly I can't really imagine what he must be like."

I take a dry swallow of banana muffin. I don't like this line of thinking . . . we're putting him on a pedestal.

"I'm thinking about what Rico did," I say, changing the subject. "He thought we knew more about Oliver than we did. He thought we'd pretty immediately know what he was talking about when he said the books are where they belong, where Oliver will never go. Ya."

"What?"

"Ya. He ended with that."

I take out the phone and show Courtney the text again.

Left Boks wher they belong, where Soph never goes. Ya

"Didn't notice that," Courtney admits. "Maybe he was starting to spell another word? What starts with 'ya'? What about yak?"

I squint at him.

"Yeah, Courtney. I'll bet he was trying to tell us that he hid them inside of a yak."

"Yakitori?"

I roll my eyes.

"Forget it."

Courtney leans his head back.

"So far we've gotten some pretty unreliable eyewitness

accounts . . . Everyone seems to have some skin in this game—"
Courtney immediately winces at his poor choice of words. "But
there are one or two other people who have talked to Oliver, who
we haven't spoken to yet."

"Who?"

"The people from the restaurant in Colorado Springs where he
called the police on himself."

"That was twenty years ago . . ."

"Yeah," says Courtney, "but it sounds like he was kind of a reg-
ular there. Maybe we track down some people who used to work
there and interact with him. Especially that waitress. Maybe she
can help us understand who this guy is . . . his motivation."

He types a few things into his phone.

"It's about seventy minutes south of here. We can be there by
three."

I raise a skeptical eyebrow.

"That's a time suck. We only have two more days before Sampson drops the hammer on us. Think it's worth it?"

Courtney clicks his tongue.

"I don't like how little we know."

I nod. Every case or job has elements of uncertainty. You learn
to live with not knowing all the answers, maybe even long after
the job is done. If you let yourself get frustrated and caught up
in the myriad pieces that seem like they're not even made of the
same material as the rest of the puzzle, then you'll never get anywhere. You develop an intuition that tells you which threads to
follow; which ones will eventually lead you to the end, and which
lead nowhere.

This feels different though. Even though I've been off the job
a few years, I don't think I feel this way because I'm out of prac-

tice. Rather . . . it's not like a hard backgammon position, where you're simply not smart or practiced enough to solve it . . . more like being shown a position of a board game from some alien planet. Can't even tell which bits are the pieces, which bits are the board, or if it's even a board game at all.

"Ninety-nine percent of murders, no matter how gruesome they are, or how mentally ill the criminal is, are motivated by one of three very simple emotions," Courtney says. "Love, fear or shame."

"What about hate?" I ask. "What about greed?"

"Ah." Courtney smiles knowingly. "Common misconceptions. Hate and greed are secondary emotions that develop as a result of one of the other three. You hate someone because you love them and can't have them, or because you're scared of them, or they've made you feel ashamed. But you don't just *hate*. And greed is usually motivated by shame. You want something because you feel inadequate."

I mull this. *Love, fear, shame.*

"So which one are we dealing with here?" I ask.

"I don't know," Courtney says. "That's the problem. We don't understand why he did what he did, so we don't understand what or who we're looking for. We don't understand the books, and we certainly don't understand the man who created them. So let's go see the place where this started. Where Oliver Vicks sat and started writing. One thing we do know: The man is intimately attuned to his physical surroundings. If he chose this place to begin the execution of a twenty-year plan, he probably had a very good reason."

ARCHITECTURALLY, THE ROCKY Mountain Bar and Grill is about as unimpressive as it gets. Squat one-story building that looks like someone just stirred some generic building materials together and poured them into giant cookie-cutter mold. Only the green lettering and little mountain logo out front tells you it's not a chain restaurant like IHOP or Ruby Tuesday. We're one of three cars in a parking lot that could fit forty. It's midafternoon, not exactly peak hours, but still I'd be shocked if this place ever fills up.

We leave the windows down—the small-town vibe makes you feel like you can do that—and trot over the hot pavement to the entrance. In addition to steps, they have a ramp for wheelchairs leading up to the front door.

Maybe they have a lot of elderly customers?

There's a little rug to wipe your feet on, and the rest of the floor is white tile that perhaps sparkled sometime in the early seventies, but has been worn brown by years of repeated muddying and subsequent cleaning cycles. There's a long bar, and maybe fifteen empty bar stools with green upholstery in varying states of ruin. The vibe they're going for is family-friendly. They have some bottles of booze behind the bar, but I get the sense they're rarely used. Smells like fried food and Windex.

There's a man behind the bar whose broad tie-dye-clad back is to us. Doesn't seem to have heard us come in. We stand in the entrance waiting for him to turn around and seat us. I clear my throat. Nothing. Courtney says:

"Excuse me? Sir?"

We're answered by a round, tired-looking woman emerging from two saloon-style swinging doors on the far side of the restaurant.

"Kitchen's closed till five, sweeties," she says. "Sorry."

The man looks back at her, still apparently unaware we're here.

She makes an elaborate hand gesture to him. He turns and sees us for the first time, points apologetically to his ear.

Deaf.

Courtney responds by signing something to him, and a broad grin instantly spreads over the man's scruffy face. Beaming, he then turns back to the woman and paints some words in the air.

"If you two want to stay for coffee though, you're welcome. On the house," she says. "Not too often my husband finds someone new to chat with."

Courtney and I oblige, sitting down at the bar. Him and the now-giddy barman already appear deep in manual conversation.

"Two coffees?" she asks. "Milk and sugar?"

"Actually," Courtney says, turning to her, "Could I trouble you for a tea?" His face is creased, horribly apologetic, like he's demanding she name her first son after him.

"Of course."

I sit there with a stupid, uncomfortable smirk on my face while Courtney and the deaf barman commune.

"What's he saying? And how do you know sign language?" I ask. Courtney waves me off and doesn't answer.

"Fine," I say. Pick up a menu next to me on the counter to keep myself occupied. Pretty standard American fare: grilled meats and fried starches. Only outstanding feature of the laminated menus is that they have each item written out in Braille beneath the English. Wheelchair ramp, Braille, guess because he's deaf they're sensitive to disabilities here. I think of the raised Braille-like writing in the books.

Wonder if Oliver was inspired by this?

"Courtney," I say, "check it out."

My partner holds up an apologetic index finger to the barman and turns to me.

"Frank, make yourself useful. I'll speak to him, you speak to her. And try to look around."

The matronly waitress returns with two mugs, both emblazoned with the same green mountain logo.

"Just let me know if you want refills."

"Thanks." I smile.

"Pleasure," she says. She's probably late fifties, face creased. Her arms and hands are thick and strong. Beneath her green, standard-issue canvas waitress skirt, I see bulbous calves, terminating in a pair of expensive running shoes. I guess if there's one thing worth investing in as a waitress, it's shoes. The skin on her face is splotchy and uneven.

"Ma'am," I say, as she's turning back to the kitchen, Courtney still occupied with her husband. "If you don't mind me asking, how long have you been working here?"

She smiles sadly.

"Since the start, dear. It's a family business. We own it."

I proceed as if conducting verbal surgery.

"So then . . . you were here around twenty years ago?"

Her face darkens suddenly. She realizes what this is about.

"I was."

"So the two of us, we're private investigators. Would you mind if I asked you a few questions about Oliver Vicks?"

Her face goes rigid, and she snaps her fingers to get her husband's attention. They have a furious exchange; it's like their hands are playing some incredibly complex invisible musical instruments. By reading their body language and guessing, she isn't super enthusiastic about answering any questions, while he's a little more laid-back, maybe asking her what harm it will do.

Courtney intervenes with a raised hand and silently chimes in. Whatever he says seems to have quite an effect on both of them. They both nod, wide-eyed while he gesticulates. Finally she says to me:

"It's true? He just walked right out the front of the prison?"

I glance at Courtney, who shoots me a look like *I had to.* I get it. Sometimes to get people to confide in you, you have to make the first concession.

"Yes," I answer, leading her to a booth where we can talk without Courtney and her husband. Who knows how fluent Courtney's sign language is—I want to get as much as I can from her in good old English. To my great relief, she sits down across from me.

"So he's going to hurt more people, you think?" she asks me, voice surprisingly tender for someone whose exterior looks so well worn. A decaying jar filled with fresh honey.

"He already has, I'm afraid."

"*Dios mío . . .*" Her head hangs mournfully. "Well. I doubt I can help you. But I'm happy to try."

"You were here sometimes, when he was here?" I ask.

She nods.

"What was he like? How did he behave when he was here?"

She sits back in the booth.

"Pretty quiet. Just sat here, in that booth there—" She points to a booth closer to the kitchen. "Five hours every evening. During Becky's shift. Started at five on the dot, ended at ten. Ate something first, usually steak and French fries. He loved French fries. Then he drew in his notebooks. He was very exact. He arranged all his tools carefully before he started working. He didn't talk to me much. Didn't have much interest. But he talked to the girl, you know. Becky."

"What did they talk about?"

"It was mostly him doing the talking, to be honest. Weird stuff, the bits I overheard. I always thought he was trying to impress her by sounding smart or something. But I guess it worked."

"She was impressed by him?" I ask.

"Yes."

"Did they ever meet outside of here you think?"

She looks at her nails.

"I don't think so."

This woman has a lot to say, but needs to be asked the right questions.

"Who started coming here first? Oliver or Becky?"

Elaine thinks for a moment.

"Oliver, I think."

"So what did he do before Becky had shifts here? He still came at the same time? Or that started only once Becky was hired?"

Elaine rubs her wrist.

"I can't be sure, but . . . I think maybe he only started coming a lot once Becky was hired."

"And the drawing? He did that all along? Or only once he met Becky?"

Elaine frowns. She's never been asked this before.

"You know . . ." She exhales. "Yeah. I remember I waited on him a few times. And so that must have been before Becky came. And he wasn't working. You're right. He started this stuff once I hired Becky. It's all my fault, in a way. If I'd never hired her, you know . . ."

Her eyes mist over and she makes a steeple with her rough hands.

"So just to confirm," I say softly, "he started coming a lot, daily, only once Becky started having daily shifts?"

Elaine nods uncertainly.

"Pretty sure."

"What does he look like?" I ask, realizing the only picture we have is the grainy photo that was in the paper, and a mug shot when he was processed.

"Average height, dark hair, thin . . . the thing I remember most is his eyes. The centers seemed too dark, and the whites too white." She shudders. "It's like they were made of bright plastic. You couldn't miss those eyes."

"You said he was drawing?" I ask. "Did you ever catch a glimpse?"

"Couple times I looked as I walked past. Just looked like lines and colors. I knew something was wrong just from that," she says seriously. "Who just sits there every day and draws lines?"

I force a smile and nod that I hope engender empathy.

"You were here that night?" I ask.

She nods reluctantly.

"So then you must be . . ." I consult my notepad. "Elaine Rodriguez?" When she flinches, I try to reassure her: "I read the *Gazette* article you were quoted in."

She crosses her arms as if it's cold in here. But in fact the AC is doing little to counteract the greenhouse effect from the big glass windows.

"Yes. That's me."

"So . . . that night?" I ask, trying not to sound like I'm pleading.

"I already told everything to the cops," she says. "He asked for Becky. I went back outside where she was and told her not to go talk to him. I could feel something nasty in the air. But I guess it wouldn't have made much of a difference anyways . . ." She looks out the window, over my shoulder, like to avoid eye contact while she talks. "I didn't hear everything he said. But he showed that screwdriver and said he, you know, told her what he'd done . . . After that I don't remember a whole lot. The sirens and lights. They took him away."

"What about Becky?" I ask. "Did she keep working here?"

Elaine shakes her head adamantly.

"Oh no no. Once it was time to talk about that, she said she couldn't come back to this place again. And I understood, of course."

"Do you think Oliver wanted Becky? You know, sexually?" I ask.

Elaine shrugs.

"Probably. She was a beautiful girl. I figure to myself, you know, that's probably why he killed them. Some sick try to get her attention, you know? These head-cases think stuff like that will work."

"Did he ever say anything like that though? Did you ever see him really proposition her? Maybe she rejected him and he was upset or something?"

"No . . . nothing like that really . . ." Elaine says.

"Then why do you think that was his motivation? If you never saw any evidence?" I'm badgering her a little. It's a risky maneuver, could make her clam up, but gotta break some eggs . . .

"I . . . Well, I can't be sure, but there was one thing he said I think. I can't remember when it was. That night or not, or if I just made it up . . . he said something about her being his queen."

"His queen?" I ask.

Elaine nods.

"Yes."

I bite my lip.

"Anything else you might remember?"

"He said . . ." She squints, like the cloudy memory is hovering in front of her face. "Well, she was always curious about what he was drawing in his books too. And I think he said that night . . . he said she'd be his queen and he'd show her what was in the books."

I raise an eyebrow.

"So, when would this happen? When would she be his 'queen' and he'd show her what was in the books?"

Important not to feed her the answer and tamper with her memory . . . Want her to say it.

Elaine frowns, like she's confused herself.

"I guess . . . Well I guess he meant after prison. Because he knew the police were coming then."

Although this was the answer I was expecting, it also makes my head feel light.

But surely he knew that he'd be getting a life sentence, for multiple premeditated homicides. Which means that, if she's remembering correctly, he'd already planned his escape from prison. Sixteen years before.

I lower my head into my palms.

"How is that possible?" I groan loud enough to distract Courtney from his own silent conversation. He looks over at me from his bar stool like, *everything okay?* I wave him off: *Don't interrupt this.*

"Elaine," I say, massaging my temples. "This might sound like an insensitive question, in light of everything, but I'm only asking it because I want to understand the situation. You said before that you warned Becky not to speak to Oliver, but she did anyway. Do you think the attraction was mutual? Do you think she also liked him?"

Elaine rubs her bare bicep with a worn hand.

"Could be. She was young, you know."

"I ask," I say delicately, "because it's now sounding pretty likely that Oliver sought her out after leaving prison. That he did exactly what he said he would do. And maybe, just maybe, Becky wouldn't have told anybody that she saw him. She might have even helped him."

Elaine's face melts into disgust. She shakes her head.

"No. No."

"Elaine." I try to make my face look as kind as I can, but lean in a little to apply the emotional pressure. "When was the last time you spoke to Becky? Do you two keep in touch? Maybe you know how we could reach her?"

She blanches.

"I . . . I don't know. . . I . . ."

"Think about it, we could be helping her."

Instead of responding, she waves her hand in the air to get her husband's attention. He breaks off from his conversation with Courtney and they flash a series of impossibly elaborate signals to each other. She points to me once or twice, and I catch a gesture that looks like an inmate clinging to cell bars which I imagine is the sign for *prison*. They only talk half a minute—I consider that maybe sign language is more efficient than speaking.

When Elaine turns back to me her face is steel.

"She moved and changed her last name. She didn't want people knowing she was that girl. Last I heard she lives in Pueblo."

"How do you know that?" I ask, assuming Elaine did a little curiosity stalking, but trying to keep any accusation out of my voice.

"She came here to the diner a few years back," Elaine says, grimacing. "Asking me for money. She was definitely in a bad place. She talked about how much everything messed her up you know. Couldn't keep a job or anything. Then she emailed me a bunch after that, for a few months, to ask for more."

"Did you give her money?" Courtney asks, from his bar stool perch.

"When she came in in person I couldn't say no. But I ignored the emails . . . I . . . I was pretty sure she was on drugs."

I nod.

"So any way you could check that email?" I ask. "Tell us her last name?"

Elaine sighs and pulls out her phone.

"Who knows if I still have it . . ." she says, scrolling. "You're lucky I never delete emails . . . let's see. Carlson. Becky Carlson. That's her new last name. Don't have any info besides that. But at least a few years ago she lived in Pueblo, about an hour drive south of here."

I exhale with relief. Feel like a dentist after a successful extraction.

"Thanks so much for your time." I stand up and tap Courtney on the shoulder. "Let's go, we got what we need," I tell him.

Courtney waves good-bye.

"Thanks to both of you for your time."

"Help her if you can," Elaine says, still sitting. "But please be gentle. She's already been in more pain than I can imagine."

COURTNEY DRIVES WHILE I search for Becky Carlson on his phone. We've done this drive before, five years ago. Drove straight from Denver International Airport through Colorado Springs, through Pueblo, right to Beulah—a nothing town with under a thousand people. The landscape outside seems unfamiliar though; whether that's because I was drinking so heavily last time, or because last time it was winter. Guess I could down a couple Miller Lites as an experiment, see if that brings things into focus.

"Sampson keeps calling," I tell Courtney. "Not as frequently, but twelve times today already."

"If you accidentally pick up, theoretically he could track us by cell tower pings. Text him to stop calling us. That we agreed to bring them to him by four on Friday."

I send the text.

Please stop calling. We agreed to bring books by four on Friday. We'll call you if anything changes.

That seems to work, for the moment. According to the white pages site there are three Carlsons that live in Pueblo: R, Sam and L. Only Sam has an address listed.

"R could be Rebecca . . ." I say out loud. "Or Sam could be her husband."

"Try calling R first," Courtney orders.

"Call? And say what? Just wondering if you're the girl whose whole family was murdered twenty years ago? Wanna grab a soft serve? Let's check out the one with the address first. Maybe Sam is her husband."

"I don't want to waste time," he says. "I want to drive back to the red house after this. See if Oliver's been back there since."

I reach into Courtney's bag and pull out the GPS tracker. The chip hasn't moved.

"Pretty sure if he'd been there he would have taken Rico."

"If you have a better lead, I'm open to suggestions."

Pueblo starts looking vaguely familiar once we pull off the highway. It's a blue-collar city, built around a now-defunct steel mill. Lot of foreclosed homes, trailer parks, fast food drive-throughs, as well as a disproportionate number of gun stores and marijuana dispensaries.

Without explicitly admitting that Courtney's right, I dial the number for R Carlson. Rings six times.

"Hello . . . ?"

I'm almost sure it's her immediately. The surprise in her voice tells me this phone rarely rings: few relatives and friends. And I think Elaine was right: hoarseness, exhaustion, long drawn out syllables likely indicative of drug use.

I summon my gentlest, least threatening voice and decide to say everything like it's a question. To more perceptive people, it's an annoying conversational tic, but the subliminal uncertainty you project often puts unstable personalities at ease.

"Hello? Becky?"

"Who . . . is this?"

I give Courtney a thumbs-up. If her name wasn't Becky she would have said so.

"My name is Andrew? I'm calling from FedEx in Colorado Springs? We have a package here addressed for Becky Carlson, with a phone number, but what must be the wrong address, because we've had three failed deliveries. We'll hold it for you for a week if you want to come pick it up. Otherwise we'll have to return to sender?"

Short pause.

"Package?"

"Looks like a warehouse—probably something you ordered from Amazon or something, and just mistyped your address. Anyway like I said, you can come pick it up from our central office in Colorado Springs? We're on 53 East—"

"I actually live in Pueblo now . . . I must have put in an old address . . . without thinking."

I feel guilty. This is too easy.

This poor girl.

"Ohhh," I say. "Wow, yeah that's quite a drive. Listen, I can probably get another delivery attempt sent out tomorrow. What's your new address?"

"Um. 157 Mesa Road, apartment 4J. 80241."

"157 Mesa," I repeat, as I jot it down. "4J. 80241. Got it. I'll get that sent out to you ASAP. Have a great day."

"Okay."

I hang up and immediately type the address into Google maps. We're only seventeen minutes away.

"Stop at a bakery on the way," I say. "Gonna have to be delicate with this one."

157 MESA ROAD is part of a huge low-income apartment complex. Dozens of identical white stucco buildings that must contain at least 300 units. This colony makes me only slightly less sad than the prison we were in this morning. We drive around the winding parking lot for ten minutes before finding 157. That phone number was her landline—could tell by the sound of her picking up the receiver—and every lost minute makes me nervous that Becky has left home. As soon as Courtney parks, I grab the pink

paper bag filled with baked goods and we slam the doors shut, start up the outdoor staircase.

"I don't want to lie to her about who we are, or what we want," Courtney says. "It's too dirty."

"Just hope she doesn't slam the door in our face," I say, huffing as we climb.

"If she does, she does," he says.

I have a fresh sheen of sweat on my forehead by the time we reach 4J, on the fourth-floor landing. I take a deep breath, and ring the bell. Hear a chime go off inside. Nothing. I'm about to ring again, but Courtney stills my hand.

"Don't look desperate," he says. Runs a hand back through his buzzed hair, which leaves it unchanged.

Slow footsteps inside. Peephole goes dark, but I pretend like I don't notice. Just stand there, hands clasped in front of me, trying to look as uncreepy as possible.

Door opens in, but she keeps the chain on. It's pretty dark inside, can't see much besides a single wary eye and a pale, extremely thin arm.

"Yeah?" she asks. She has the voice of someone who smokes a few packs a day, but it could also just be exhaustion.

Most people would make the connection between our sudden arrival and the FedEx call a half hour ago—but she's obviously not super with it.

"I'm Frank," I say, "And this is Courtney. We . . ." I sigh, it's a sudden relief to not have to lie anymore. "We need your help, Becky."

"Who . . . are you?"

I blink. Think of the best way to answer that.

"Oliver Vicks escaped from Saddleback Correctional Facility. We're private investigators who are looking for him, and need your help."

I'm not sure what effect I expected that name to have on her. Maybe to faint, or cry . . . instead she makes a sound that's like a whimper, but more primal. A yelp almost, like a dog might make if you stepped on his paw. But she doesn't budge from her post at the door. If I had to guess, based on the dilation of her single eye and the way her weight suddenly shifts, pushing the door halfway closed, I'd say she is unable to even formulate a response verbally.

"I'm sure you don't want to think about anything related to this," I say. "But if we could just come in and talk to you for even ten minutes, it could really help us in tracking him down."

She's so overwhelmed, I think, that she can't even process what's happening. We have to appeal to her on some kind of very primitive level. Luckily I anticipated this.

"We brought you something to eat," I say, and hold up the pink bag. "Carrot cake, croissants and muffins."

She makes a sound like "Mfgh" . . . Her voice is horribly dry.

The door suddenly slams shut. I bite my lip. Then hear the chain clink, slide, and then the door pulls open to reveal Becky Carlson.

It takes all my willpower to force a smile, and not to stare. The skin of her face is chalk-white and flaky. Reminds me of an ancient piece of limestone left out and exposed to the elements for a thousand years. Blond hair is so thin and splotchy that you can see her white scalp in several places. She has loose skin around her neck, the kind you find on eighty-year-old women; it's so wrinkled and saggy that it's almost like a chicken wattle. It's sickening to think she's younger than me. She's so thin that even her extra small T-shirt is swimming on her.

But despite all this, I can believe that she used to be beautiful. Her eyes are still a rich blue, and if you squint—imagine her with okay skin—you can form a rough picture of what she must have looked like at seventeen, when she smiled as she took your order.

"C'mon," she rasps and gestures for us to enter. As I step across the threshold I'm physically jarred by the smell. Something like rotten meat or rancid cabbage . . . layer upon layer of odor. A pastiche of the worst kind of smells that combine to form an unequivocal note of decay.

The lights are all off, curtains drawn shut. We follow her across wall-to-wall carpeting littered with orange peels, empty Chinese food containers, clothes, magazines, soda cans, to a blue futon that, judging by the way she collapses onto it—less sits on than allows herself to be swallowed—is a central figure in her life. The only other place to sit is on a low glass table cluttered with cigarette butts and food stains. I clear enough space to sit down on the table, Courtney takes one look at it and remains standing. His hands are jammed as deep into his pockets as they'll go, and he's struggling, and failing, to keep the discomfort off his face.

There's an open kitchen to our right. A mountain of dirty dishes in the sink, and the faucet dripping slowly. Two interior doors, both open. One to the bathroom—which I pray I won't have to visit—and one to a bedroom with a bare mattress on the floor. There's an ancient, bulky TV on the floor facing the futon, a cathode ray tube—haven't seen a TV like this for at least fifteen years. *Jeopardy* is on, at low volume.

I put the bag from the bakery at the feet of Becky's futon, and she leans forward, picks a croissant out and devours it in a frenzy that makes the hairs on the back of my neck tingle.

When she finishes, I say: "So Becky, we were hoping we could ask you some questions."

"Okay," she says. She opens her mouth for a stilted inhalation, and I catch a glance of her teeth for the first time. Many are missing. That and the strips of charred foil littered on the floor make a pretty convincing case for heroin smoking.

I think, with a horrible twinge of guilt, *She actually might be more responsive if we encouraged her to smoke now . . .*

"So that night. If you can—"

"I knew you'd come," she says abruptly. "I knew you'd come looking for Sophnot."

Courtney goes rigid. I crack my knuckles.

"What do you mean?" I ask.

"He told me."

I swallow.

"Oliver Vicks told you? You've seen him? Has he come here?"

Her pale blue eyes narrow. "No . . ." she says. "Maybe it was a dream. Is he dead?"

My head is swimming a little from the smell. It's entirely conceivable, I think, that she could be mistaking dreams and reality. It's hard to know exactly which of her bizarre threads to follow . . . Oliver is clearly not dead, but better to let her keep talking than correct her.

"What else—whether it was a dream, or what—what else did he tell you?"

"Lots of things."

Without looking, she reaches a ghostly thin hand back into the pink bag and extracts a second croissant.

"Can you just tell us one thing?" Courtney says, the first time he's spoken since we came in here.

"Mmm . . ." She thinks for a moment as she tears apart the croissant like a hyena digging into an antelope. "About triangles," she says. "About Pythagoras . . . what did he say about triangles?"

Courtney raises an eyebrow. I lean in, figure I must have misheard, but Courtney—still standing—halts me with a hand on my shoulder.

"That if one angle is ninety degrees," he says, "then the length of the hypotenuse squared is equal to the squared sums of the other two shorter sides."

"That's right," she says, nodding, encouraged. Through a mouthful of mangled white pastry she adds: "Always—right?"

"Yes," responds Courtney. "Always."

"So . . ." She's suddenly energized, whether from the calories or the topic I can't say, but I find her change in demeanor frightening. Reminds me of a limp marionette being manipulated, jerked around by an unsteady hand, or a corpse suddenly sitting upright during his own funeral and grinning. "Can God create a right triangle that doesn't obey that law?"

I'm overcome with a sense of unreality. I'm getting a bit used to the smell, and the darkness. I imagine that this apartment is all that exists in the world, and that beyond these walls is an utter void which I remember only as some distant dream.

"I don't know," replies Courtney. "Yes, I guess. He's God. He can do anything."

"Wrong." Becky laughs, a raspy sound that makes me shudder. "He could, but it would require a complete undoing of this world. God restricted himself in order to create the world—this is a simple example. He said, 'In this world, there can be no right triangles that don't follow this rule.' It was a fact long before Pythagoras discovered it."

I'm not sure I'm entirely following, but Courtney seems to be. This is not what I expected from this interview . . .

"But Sophnot," she says. "He drew a triangle that didn't follow the rule."

"But you just said—" I start.

"And the triangle was empty. Really empty. There was no God in this triangle. It was outside his creation. Sophnot trapped God. Caught him in a contradiction."

She finishes her second croissant. I wonder when the last time she ate was.

"You call him Sophnot," I say slowly. "Did he call himself that when you knew him in the restaurant?"

This question takes the wind out of her sails. Her hands drop to her sides, and she falls backwards into the welcoming cushions of the blue futon.

"I, um . . ." she says, as she closes her eyes and nestles into the pillow.

"So only in the 'dreams'," I venture. "That's the only time you heard the name Sophnot?"

"Mmm . . ." She opens her eyes, but they're now looking somewhere far away. I don't know why—maybe it's the blue in her eyes—but I imagine she's picturing herself on a sailboat, floating in the middle of a quiet sea. And for the first time since entering, I remember this is a real, breathing, living person, and my heart breaks for this victim, and fills with rage for the man who for twenty years has somehow been slowly torturing her, destroying her, until all that remains is this sallow husk.

"I'm sure it's very painful to think about, but do you have any idea why he did what he did?" I ask.

"Did what?" she responds faintly.

Courtney and I exchange a quick glance.

This is definitely the right girl . . . right?

"You used to work at the Rocky Mountain Bar and Grill in Colorado Springs, right?"

"In another life," she sighs. Her shoulder twitches.

Courtney squats down on his haunches, puts his face close enough to her to engage, but not to threaten.

"Becky," he says. "Can you remember him ever telling you anything about his plans about the future? Maybe what he'd do after he got out of prison?"

"No," she says flatly.

"Did he ever contact you, after the restaurant?" Courtney says. "Maybe in the last few years?"

She doesn't respond.

"Do you remember him ever saying anything about you being his queen?" I ask.

The last word has a physical impact on her. She flinches like I made to slap her in the face. But then she closes her eyes again and, pulls her knees up onto the futon and tucks them to her chest.

"Stop," she says.

"Becky . . ." I say. "I know we're asking something very difficult of you, but if you could just search your memory . . . maybe he said something about the books?"

She doesn't respond, instead starts breathing fast, then her chest starts heaving. Her eyes go wide and she retches, spilling forward out of the futon onto the shag carpeting. She's on her elbows, sticks her forehead into the filthy carpet and clasps her palms over the back of her head.

"Becky?"

Courtney tries to brush her shoulder and she recoils from his touch.

"Don't touch me!" she screams, looking up at him. "No, no . . ."

Courtney gives me a helpless look. She buries her face back in the carpet and groans.

Courtney points to the door. "Let's go," he whispers. "We're just upsetting her."

I'm torn. Don't want to upset her further, but also don't feel like we've gotten anything concrete yet.

"Becky—" I start.

"Yes. He said I'd be his queen," she says, her voice low and lucid. "He said he'd make me a palace. And that my brother . . . my little brother. Every week I have dreams where he shows me my brother again. He's still there. He's still alive."

I wince, thinking of the evidence we found contrary to this in the red house. Take a deep breath, and instantly regret it.

"Becky, simple yes or no: Have you seen Oliver Vicks—in real life, not in a dream—since that night in the restaurant?"

"I don't know . . ." she whines, still crouched on the carpet. "I can't tell what's a dream and what's real . . ."

Time to push it.

"Well, we spoke to him on the phone last night," I say. "He's definitely not dead."

She locks eyes with me for a moment, as if trying to discern whether I'm telling the truth or not. And, if I'm reading this right, once she decides that wasn't a lie, she crumples. Her elbows fall away. She drops flat onto the carpet and screams into the filthy shag. The muffled cry of anguish makes me shudder. Courtney can't take it anymore—goes to the door and rushes out.

I stand up, trying to ignore how sticky the ass of my pants is.

Before following him out, I write down our cell phone number on a piece of my notepad and leave it for her on her glass table. She's sobbing and pounding her fists against the floor. It's difficult to watch.

"Call if you want to talk," I say.

I duck outside, but keep the door propped open with my boot. Courtney is a little white around the mouth, and the sweat on his brow has nothing to do with the heat.

"We can't just leave her like that, can we?" he asks me softly.

"What choice do we have?" I ask.

Courtney looks like he's about to say something, but then closes his mouth, stares at me, his entire face seeming to quiver. I close the door gently behind me.

"Man," I say.

Courtney just nods and then wordlessly lopes down the stairs. He sits down cross legged on the curb next to the Honda. I squat beside him.

"I'm fine," he says. "Just give me a second."

"Take your time," I say. "When you're ready you need to call Mindy and ask her some questions."

Courtney looks at me, shielding his eyes from the afternoon sun with a pale hand.

"Why?" he asks.

"I just started thinking in there, when she was talking about her brother, that we might have been thinking about these books wrong the whole time. We assumed that, like most books, what's written on the pages is the most important part. And the bindings are just there to protect the pages."

Courtney raises an eyebrow.

"What do you mean . . . ?" he says.

"What if, I mean, look if you're an architect, what's more important, the interior layout of the house or the way it looks from the outside?"

Courtney's eyes go wide and the faintest smile escapes his lips.

"Neither. They go hand in hand. They're one and the same."

"Right." I nod. "And the same could be said for a human body. Which is more important, all the stuff inside, the organs—or the exterior? The *skin*?"

Courtney nods as he stands up.

"So, if that's the case, then it's not as if Oliver is just binding these haphazardly, with whoever he happens to feel like killing," Courtney says. "The first book was *meant* to be bound with her brother—"

"And the most recent was meant for Rico," I say. "Why wouldn't he be as patient and deliberate with these victims as he is with everything else?"

Courtney scratches at his neck like he has fleas. He's excited.

"Why Rico?"

"No idea. Why Becky's brother? Why any of these people? That's why we have to talk to Mindy."

Courtney shakes his head.

"Don't follow."

"There were twenty-four drawers in the file cabinet in the red house," I say. "Rico's picture was in the twenty-second. He was meant for the twenty-second book. Which means there's two left. And if Mindy knows what's written in those last two books—maybe she has some photocopies or something she can read—maybe she can figure out who he has planned for them."

Courtney chews on his thumbnail.

"Maybe Rico knew who Oliver was planning to kill. And that's where Rico thinks the books belong? With them?"

I shake my head.

"That's a stretch. I was just thinking, if we know who he's planning to kill next, maybe we can find him, turn him in, and get the money back. Which may not be a bad idea, because I'm not super optimistic about us finding those books in the next two days."

"That's good Frank," he says. "Real good. I knew it was worth getting you from Budapest."

I snort.

"Yeah, thanks for that."

"Just to be clear, we're not telling Mindy *anything*, right?" I say. Courtney's got his penlight out in the passenger seat, examining the heretic's fork collar from the red house, probing with a pair of tweezers and his lock picks, carefully avoiding the razor-sharp prongs on the front of the device. Mindy refused to talk shop over the phone. Insisted that if we wanted any info to come talk to her in her hotel in Denver. Honestly, I probably would have done the same in her position.

I let my sneaker sink down on the gas. The highways between Denver, Colorado Springs and Pueblo are remarkably straight. I'm so tired that part of me feels like I could just fall asleep on the steering wheel and have Courtney nudge me awake in a half hour.

"Mmhmm," he murmurs.

"Not that we have all this figured out. We're still clearly missing some basic facts . . ." I say. "Still don't understand why anyone would *want* to go to prison for sixteen years. If he just wanted money from Sampson, is this really the most efficient way to do it?"

"Well," Courtney says, as he toys with the device, "I think we're pretty sure at this point that the books are more than just a lure for Sampson's money. Man, how the hell do you *open* this thing?"

Something snaps. Courtney yelps and I jump in my seat.

"What the hell was that?"

Courtney shows me the thin line of blood in his palm. Two previously retracted blades have shot out into the interior of the collar. I don't even want to think about what someone's neck would look like after this thing activated. Porous.

"Are you okay?" I say.

"I'm fine," Courtney replies, wrapping his palm with a bandage from his red bag. "This device is astoundingly complex."

"Yeah? Seems pretty simple to me."

"No I mean, the lock mechanism. There are two kinda weirdly shaped circular holes on either side of it. Each one has about thirty pins in it at varying depths . . . some are meant to be depressed, some aren't. To unlock this you need two *very* precise tubular keys to be entered simultaneously. Otherwise—"

"You're having a new ventilation system installed."

"Yes," Courtney says, and nods. "The metalwork is pretty staggering. I know locks, Frank. I've never seen anything like this. He made this himself. These must take him a month apiece to make. And there were at least seven of them just in that one room."

We're both silent for a moment, contemplating who we're dealing with. Someone manipulative enough to talk his way out of a prison, and compulsive enough to handcraft instruments of torture.

"Here's the million-dollar question," I say, struggling to keep my eyes open. "These people he manipulates: Sampson, Becky, all the followers he allegedly had in prison, sure seems like *they* believe his hogwash. But does *he?* Or is it all just a ruse to get whatever it is he wants?"

Courtney is quiet for a moment. Just when I think maybe he's nodded off he says:

"Are we sure it's hogwash?"

I grit my teeth. I know where this is going. The same place it did five years ago, our last job together.

"What are you suggesting, Courtney?" I ask, knowing exactly what he's suggesting.

"Well just . . ." He strokes his cheek. "The way he somehow knew Sampson's dream, the way he knew he'd get out of prison sixteen years in advance, the way he's apparently appearing in *Becky's* dreams—"

"Becky is a heroin addict."

"I'm just saying. As you pointed out, it also seems possible that he had his string of twenty-four victims planned out decades in advance. There was what Heald said about knowing every moment of his life, past and future. What if he really has some sort of actual methodology to, I don't know, do something?"

I don't respond.

"You know," Courtney continues. "Like manipulate things. The universe or God, or whatever you want to call it."

I chew on my lip.

"I didn't know you believed in God," I say.

"Well, I still haven't ruled it out," he says. I can tell he's picking his words carefully. "Still in information-gathering mode, you know. Waiting to make an informed decision." He clears his throat. "What about you, Frank?"

I stay silent, focus on the taillights of the sixteen-wheeler in the distance. I know what he's getting at. I've been expecting this since we met in the Ritz in Budapest.

"Frank," he says softly. "I know you have the tape."

I inhale sharply.

"What do you mean?" I ask, maybe accelerating a little out of anxiety.

"You brought it with you up to that hotel room, killed Greta, and then left. The tape wasn't found at the crime scene—it took me forever to confirm that, but I did. Which means you have it. I hope it's somewhere safe. There are people who would pay a pretty penny for that thing."

My first instinct is to lie. Tell Courtney he's wrong. But he wouldn't believe me, and at the moment I just don't have the mental energy to think of a plausible lie.

"It's somewhere safe," I say.

"And what it says . . . Did you listen?"

"I heard a bit, in the hotel room. Didn't listen since then though. Haven't heard it all."

Courtney is trying not to sound too eager. He's like a little kid pretending he could live without a bag of candy.

"And what . . . ?" Courtney says.

"I do believe that there are things we can't see," I say. "I'm not saying God, and I'm not convinced there's life after death, but there are things going on. I don't claim to understand them, but . . ." I clear my throat. "Let's just leave it at that."

"When we get out of this," Courtney says delicately, "Maybe you could take me to where you've stashed the tape?"

I look over at him. His fingers are interlocked, shoulders tense, eyes trained on me. Bandage on his hand looks to have done the job—cut wasn't too deep.

"You know, I probably trust you more than I trust myself," I say. "But you'll just have to believe me when I say I'm doing you a major favor by not letting you ever see or listen to that tape."

"That's a no?" he asks.

"That's a no," I confirm.

Courtney goes quiet, probably mulling whether it's worth it or not to keep prodding me. Seems to decide against it.

I watch miles of identical road melt in front of us and think about the tape, tucked into a tiny deposit box in a bank in Paris. I paid the fees for them to keep the box for me, sixty years, up front. In cash. Long ago decided that if I don't go back for it myself, I don't want anybody to. Best case, sixty years from now, some French bank manager opens the box, sees that thing, and tosses it in the trash.

IT'S ONLY TEN at night by the time we pull into the parking garage beside Mindy's hotel, but it feels like five in the morning. I keep seeing dark things flitting at the edge of my vision, little laughing faces that disappear as soon as I focus on them. I'm tired.

Mindy is staying at a very nice hotel. I'm shocked this kind of class exists in Denver, but apparently there's quite a big tourism industry here. The lobby is all crystal, black and white marble floors, bellboys in humiliating outfits. But the lobby is nothing compared to the hotel proper: All thirty stories are visible from the ground floor atrium. It's like they hollowed out the core of the whole building. Every floor has a balcony, from which you can see all the way down to the café on the ground floor. All four elevators are encased in transparent shafts, and you can see the guests inside ascending dizzyingly up to their rooms.

It reminds me a bit of Sampson's house, but way less creepy. In fact, the openness—total lack of shadow, unbelievable illumination that's filling what's essentially one massive room—is very peaceful somehow.

Nobody hassles us in the lobby. Hotels are some of the easiest places to snoop around, because you're just assumed to be a guest, and if you just act the part, most of the staff are too scared to incorrectly accost you.

We take the elevator up to the seventeenth floor. In the compact space, I get a real strong whiff of Courtney. He—like me— hasn't bathed since leaving Sampson's. Hopefully Mindy won't object to us using her shower.

We knock on 1719. See the peephole go dark for a second, and then Mindy lets us in. Slams the door behind us and bolts it.

"Don't touch anything," she says before we can even sit down.

She's wearing flannel pajamas and wrinkled white tank top. Her hair is out of control and her glasses are so dusty that they're almost cloudy. Her mousey cheeks are bright pink, as if with fever.

The room is nice. Or, it *was* nice. Mindy has done a real number on it. I'm not sure I could soil a hotel room this much in twenty-four hours if I tried. She's been ashing her joints directly onto the carpet. The surface of the only table in the room is buried beneath a mountain of papers, many stained with peanut butter. The room smells rank enough that I lose any self-consciousness I may have had about my current hygienic state.

She and Becky should hang out.

She sees me staring at the ash in the carpet. "It's on Sampson's card," she says. "I figured since he's already out forty-eight million, he won't notice the cleaning fee."

"So," Courtney says, sitting on the edge of one of two twin beds. I pull a chair from the desk and sit down myself. "We had some questions for you."

Mindy guffaws. Lights up a joint and doesn't bother to open the window to the balcony.

"You two must be at wit's end if you're coming to old *Mindy* for help. For some reason, Sampson seems to think you have the books. But if you did, I'm quite sure you wouldn't be here."

I lean forward in my chair to read one of the papers on top of the heap and Mindy instantly jumps to snatch it away.

"That's private research," she snaps, and then realizes that her laptop is open on her bed and rushes to close it, but not before I recognize the Expedia logo on the screen.

"Looks like you're at wit's end yourself," I say, "if you're planning on flying. Where are you going? London? Along with your hand-copied pages?"

She glares at me, seems to consider lying for a moment, then shrugs.

"What else am I going to do?" she says. "I'll never see the books again, and Sampson certainly isn't going to let me continue staying in his guesthouse after the aquarium incident."

"We might be able to find them," Courtney says. "We have some information."

I stare at him: *Don't tell her anything!*

He lowers his chin and shoots me a serious look: *Let me handle this.*

"What kind of information?" Mindy says.

"A text from Rico," Courtney says. "He stashed the books somewhere before he died. Sophnot killed him."

I feel blood rush to my cheeks. I shake my head at him: *What are you doing?*

"Patience, Frank," he says out loud, as if that ever made anybody more patient.

"What do you mean, Sophnot killed Rico?" she asks.

Courtney removes his camera from his acrylic satchel and

shows her pictures of the crime scene. She slaps a hand over her mouth.

"Oh my god," she gasps, and looks away. "I never . . . I thought he took the skin from the morgue or something."

"C'mon," I say. "He was in prison for murder. You never put two and two together?"

"It crossed my mind that he was killing other prisoners for this," she admits, looking quite ill. "But . . . I *knew* Rico . . . We saw him yesterday."

She takes a long draw, as though to medicate away the grisly image.

"So what was the text?"

"Done mourning already?" I ask.

She makes a face like she's sucking on a lemon.

"Just show me the goddamn phone, yeah?"

Courtney looks ready to just hand her the iPhone.

"Hold on," I say. "Let's talk more about these bindings."

Mindy folds her arms over her chest.

"What do you want to know?"

"What . . . I mean, what does it mean? Why do you think Oliver cares about binding them like this?"

Mindy throws her nearly finished joint to the carpet and grinds it out under her sock.

"I have a contact at Stanford, who has a lot of experience with this kind of thing. I spoke to her a few times about the bindings."

"Wait," I say. "How is this a common enough thing that there's an *expert* in this field at Stanford?"

Mindy sighs, like she's just now recalling how tedious it is to explain things to a slug like me.

"It's not common anymore, obviously. I mean, it was never

common. But there are a few dozen examples of this through-out history. The most recent documented binding of this sort was more than two hundred years ago. A doctor, for reasons I'm not entirely clear on, decided to bind a book he wrote on illnesses with the skin of a patient who died on his operating table. There was also one story of a guy who requested that a book be bound in *his own* skin after he died, and given to one of his pals. Any-ways, it's not like this is the only thing this woman studies, but there are a few such books in the Stanford library, and she's familiar with them."

"The other examples . . ." Courtney asks. "When else has this technique been used?"

Mindy nods, the topic obviously exciting her, the way I've seen gambler's eyes light up at just the mention of poker. The books are the only thing I've ever heard her talk about at length.

"So, the thing I found most interesting was—well, it's not con-firmed exactly, but there's a theory that several manuscripts from ancient Egypt—papyruses—were bound in human skin. They've mostly disintegrated—the leather wasn't well preserved—but that's one thing the woman at Stanford is looking into now."

I shift in my chair.

"What kind of manuscripts?" I ask, thinking about the story Heald told us about Joseph going down to Egypt.

Mindy shakes her head.

"I don't know—I don't think she even knows. I sense her re-search is at a fairly early stage. But still, I thought it was worth mentioning. Pertinent."

Courtney nods.

"Very interesting," he says softly.

"So I had a thought," I say. "Rico was supposed to be the

twenty-second book. That's twenty-two in twenty years, starting with the waitress's brother. Pretty deliberate. No doubt Oliver could have gone faster if he wanted to. Do you think there's like . . . is it possible he wants certain victims for certain volumes?"

Mindy's eyes open a little wider. "Hmm."

Courtney smiles at me, beaming like a proud parent.

I rub my fresh stubble and again regret shaving off my conversational comfort blanket. "And if so, do you think it could be possible to determine from the content of an unbound volume whose skin he wants for it?"

Mindy licks her chapped lips. I find her eagerness a bit revolting, given the context.

"It's an exciting idea. And I can't rule it out."

"Can you look in the copies you have, see if you can find something?"

She snorts.

"Maybe if I had four months to kill. And even then, I only have about twenty hand-copied pages total, each from a different volume. As I've mentioned several times, there is a ton of cross-reference. Imagine trying to understand something fundamental about *Crime and Punishment* by just reading the first five pages. Now imagine those pages are in Russian, and you don't read Russian, or know anybody who does."

"Still, good thinking Frank," Courtney says, probably unaware of how patronizing it sounds. "The Egyptian thing intrigues me. Doesn't seem like a coincidence."

"Because of the hieroglyphic nature of his writing?" Mindy asks.

Courtney raises an eyebrow.

"You don't know what *Sophnot* means?"

"No . . ." she says. "What do you mean? I thought it was just a nickname he gave himself."

"It's from the Old Testament," he says. "It *is* a nickname—that the Egyptian Pharaoh used once for Joseph. It means something like *he who solves riddles*. At least that's what the guy at the prison told us."

"You went to the prison! So how did he get out? Did he escape?" Mindy's voice cracks. "Show me the fucking text from Rico!"

I clear my throat. Courtney looks to me. The phone is in my pocket, but I don't reach for it. He turns to Mindy.

"First we need to address the event in which Frank and I manage to retrieve those books. I know you would like to take them yourself. That's understandable. But the situation is pretty dire. Sampson thinks we have the books. He said if we don't get them to him by Friday, he'll call his friends in the FBI to track us down. He'll probably tell them we stole forty-eight million dollars from him. It won't be pretty."

Mindy takes off her cloudy glasses and rubs her tired eyes.

"So why not tell him the truth? That you screwed up the swap."

"I didn't *screw up* anything!" I snap. "I still don't think you've gotten through your head: The situation was fucked from the start. Besides, Sampson wouldn't even believe the truth at this point. The reason he thinks we have the books, and is giving us until Friday at all, is because Oliver Vicks told him to."

Mindy blinks. "How do you know that?"

"Because he told us," I sigh. "Oliver Vicks—I guess it was him, he was using that voice thing—called us last night to tell us as much. *Oliver* is under the impression that we have the books because of something Rico said, I suppose. So if we just tell Sampson we don't have them he certainly wouldn't believe us over his man-crush. And even if he did, he'd still send the feds after us out of spite, for losing them. 'I'll clutch at your ankles and drag you down with me into hell' were the words he used."

Mindy plays with a clump of her nappy hair. Licks her dry lips.

"Wow," she says. "You two are in trouble."

"Well," I say. "Don't think *your* ankles are so safe. I'm sorry to tell you, but you're in pretty deep, too, whether you like it or not. Oliver knows you were at the aquarium, too, and probably thinks you conspired with us to take his books. If we can't find the books, or lead the cops to Oliver, he'll surely encourage Sampson to have you arrested too. Or send those guys in khaki after us. I'm afraid you're in the same boat as us."

She puts her glasses back on and fiddles with her lighter.

"Okay," she says.

"Okay?" I peer at her. "So . . . you're fine with us returning the books to Sampson?"

She shrugs. "What do you want me to say? Okay. You made your case and I agree. Can I see the text now please?"

Courtney looks to me for approval. I turn my palms to the ceiling.

"Fuck it." I pull the iPhone from my pocket, unlock it and pull up Rico's text. "Lord knows we're not getting anything out of it. And unless we find those books, come Friday our lives are going to be one long cavity search—and that's if we're lucky and don't end up like Rico."

She eagerly takes the phone from me.

"Left books where Sophnot never goes . . . Where they belong," she reads thoughtfully. "Ya?"

"Could be a yak. Or a Yakitori restaurant . . ." Courtney starts. I roll my eyes.

"You make anything of it?" I ask.

"No clue," she says, shrugging.

Is she lying to us? Is she just gonna go straight there afterwards and pick them up herself?

"That's why we went to the prison," Courtney says. "First to confirm that he wasn't there, and then . . . well if Oliver escaped that might be the place he'd never return to. Maybe Rico made his way there before the guys from the aquarium caught up to him. There would have been enough time."

"And?"

Courtney shakes his head. "It was a stretch anyways. But no, if Rico knew what happened in that place, the prison is the *last* place he'd stash the books."

Mindy's brown eyebrows furrow.

"Why. What happened in that place?"

I sigh. Maybe it's because I'm too exhausted to think of clever lies, or because we basically have zero leads at this point, and nothing to lose, I explain everything Heald told us. About how Oliver just walked out the front gates four years ago. And then the visit to Becky.

Mindy listens patiently, growing increasingly perturbed.

"So if I understand this right," she says, "You still have absolutely no idea where Rico stashed the books."

I grimace.

"Right. So. Where does Sophnot never go? And why would the books belong there?"

I study Mindy's face closely as she thinks.

"Why would Rico send you a riddle?" Mindy asks. "Why not just tell you exactly where he put them?"

Courtney sits up a little straighter.

"I don't know," he says.

"No idea," I say.

"I mean . . ." Mindy scratches an eyebrow. "He must have been worried that Sophnot or those guys from the aquarium would see this text. And somehow, he thought this was a text that *you two* would understand, but those guys, or even Sophnot himself wouldn't."

"Or that it would at least give us a better chance at getting there first . . ." I say. "I think it's probable that Rico only texted us once those guys hunted him down. Maybe after he'd dropped off the books, while he was running. If he just texted us an address and Oliver or the goons confiscated his phone, they'd just head straight there."

"Of course, Rico wasn't exactly in his right mind," Courtney says slowly. "We think he'd been chained up in that room for years. He was malnourished, probably sleep deprived . . . frantic at the time of writing this. There's a decent possibility that it's not even sensical."

We all consider this unsettling possibility for a moment—that we're reading too much into Rico's message.

"I have something that might help us," she says. "Something I found a few years ago."

She grabs her laptop, beckoning us to come closer. We sit on either side of her on the bed. She smells even worse than Courtney.

She opens a document with a bunch of links to old news articles.

"I found this stuff a few years ago," she explains. "Was trying to learn more about Oliver himself. Almost everything online is just about the buildings he designed, articles about ribbon cuttings and so on."

I spot a professional headshot of him in one of the open windows. He's grinning, looks legitimately happy. And I shudder as I study his eyes. It's subtle, but I can see what Elaine was talking about at the diner: The whites are too white. Glossy, like waxed ping-pong balls.

Mindy continues: "But then I came upon something I vaguely recalled hearing a few years ago, or maybe even reading, but I just never gave it much thought. Probably because it seemed to make so much sense: He's not a properly licensed architect."

I peer into the screen to read the article, but Mindy insists on paraphrasing it herself.

"A few years before he was arrested, it was uncovered that Oliver Vicks was a fraud. He'd never gone to architecture school. Never even went to university. In fact, he may not even have made it all the way through high school. He was first hired by a firm in Denver with a phony diploma from a small school in England. This was way before the days of the internet . . . couldn't Google him. And by all accounts, he knew exactly what he was doing, so there was no reason to ever be suspicious. And once you're in the company, working, getting contracts . . . why would anybody ever look into your past?"

"How was he found out?"

Mindy smiles.

"His firm had a project designing a huge industrial barn. To house hundreds of cows comfortably, with good lighting and ventilation—unlike the rest of the industry."

"A dairy . . ." I swallow. "Sampson's farm?"

Mindy nods.

"Somebody on the architecture side made a mistake in the plans, and only when the barn was nearly done did someone realize it wasn't up to code. The firm claimed they weren't liable for the cost of bringing it up to code, because the dairy hadn't provided all the proper zoning documents or something. There was a civil case, for the damages. They were asking for a million and a half dollars for renovations. Everyone on the design team had to testify including Oliver. But during discovery by the dairy farm's lawyers they did a fairly standard background check on him, and everything came out. That was the end."

"What happened after?" Courtney asks. "Did he keep working?"

"No," she says. "Obviously not. You can't have an unlicensed architect designing buildings. It's not even *safe*."

"But everything he'd already designed . . ." I say.

"Was fine, correct." Mindy nods. "Still, when I first found out about this I got ahold of someone who worked with Oliver on one project, told him I was a reporter, and he told me it was quite a scandal. He was shunned. Totally blacklisted. If this happened today, it would be all over Buzzfeed. Instead, there are just very few records of what happened after that."

"Seriously?" I say. "Oliver blamed Sampson for outing him? It's hardly his fault."

Mindy shrugs.

"Don't ask me to explain how Oliver Vicks thinks."

"So," Courtney says slowly. "You realized years ago that this was all an elaborate revenge by Sophnot?"

"I don't think it's a revenge thing," Mindy says. "I figured Oliver just remembered James from the trial, spotted him in prison and saw an opportunity to get a US Senator in his pocket.

Obviously it sometimes took on a sadistic flavor . . . advising him to cut off his genitals and so forth, but I think those were just further steps to ensure James's future loyalty. Obviously I thought Oliver was still in prison. I never imagined that he'd somehow managed to get Rico to steal the books for him."

"Well," I say, spreading my hands. "I think it's pretty clear *now* that it's a revenge thing. He's extorted forty-eight million dollars from Sampson. My question is, why the hell wouldn't you tell Sampson this?"

"I did," Mindy replies. "He already knew. Sophnot told him before James and I ever met. He told him it was part of God's plan, that being stripped of his job as an architect forced him into the humility he needed. He *thanked* James for what happened."

I shake my head.

"Well, there goes that. Was hoping we'd able to prove to Sampson he's been had by showing him this."

Mindy lights up another joint.

"It's way too late for that," she says. "It's hard to imagine anything that could shake James's faith in Sophnot at this point."

"Shame," Courtney sighs. "I told Frank earlier today. The only real motivators of crime are shame, love and fear. It appears we're dealing with a man who is trying to rectify his public shaming." He sucks in his boney cheeks. "In some ways that's the worst. Insecure men are always the most dangerous."

MINDY AGREES TO let us sleep there. It takes all my remaining strength to stay upright in the shower for long enough to soap myself up, wash my hair. Don't bother to brush my teeth—my eyes are twitching and my vision is like a TV screen that's not getting great antenna reception.

I don't even ask Courtney and Mindy to turn out the light for me. My head hits the pillow and immediately I flit into a half-dream state, where I can still hear the two of them speaking quietly, laughing a little, but it feels like it's a million miles away. And then I slip down into blissful darkness.

I'm the kind of sleeper who's still aware of his surroundings—a part of me never goes off alert. I probably could have snoozed until noon the next morning if a soft, high-pitched sound didn't jerk me awake around three.

My eyes shoot open, and I'm about to sit up and grab my gun when I realize what's happening. Mindy is sighing.

Mindy. Courtney. One bed.

Would have preferred an axe murderer bursting through the door and slaughtering us all. A little rustle of bedsheets. A slippery sound like a wet suction cup that I pray is just them kissing.

There's no way Courtney made a move. It was her. Trying to buy a little book insurance?

I try to ignore it, fall back asleep, but this genie won't get stuffed back in the bottle.

I stay totally still. Don't want to let them know I can hear them. The awkwardness would just be unbearable. At least I'm facing away from them . . .

They know I'm right here, right!?

Indecipherable whispering.

Rhythmic creaking of bedsprings.

God. Dammit.

Heavy breathing. Mindy makes a *serious* little gasp. It's almost worse not seeing it, because I'm imagining it. Courtney's bare boney back, Mindy's face aglow in ecstasy, her hands squeezing his tiny ass, pulling him deeper . . .

Jesus, Frank. Don't make this worse than it has to be.

"C'mon," she whispers. Well, now I know I wasn't imagining all of this. They're really doing this. Mindy and Courtney are *fucking* three feet away from me.

Don't they realize how goddamn tired I am? How badly I need this sleep? Maybe she knows I can hear. Maybe that kooky bitch gets off on that shit.

"Hit me." Her voice is raw.

"What? What do you mean?" I hear Courtney whisper.

"Hit me. Hard."

I hear a pathetic slap.

"C'mon, hard. Be a fucking man. Hit me. Punish me."

Another slap.

"Like that? Sorry I've never really–"

"Harder. Punish me."

The creaking quickens. The hairs on the back of my neck stand up.

"Hit me. Punish me. Tear my skin. Rip it off," she groans. "Bind me."

Creaking comes to a sudden halt.

"Stop, stop," mutters Courtney. "Stop it."

Mindy doesn't respond. The bedsprings get a break for a moment, and I can't tell exactly what's happening in the other bed.

Then she says something softly that gets lost in the buzz of the air conditioner.

"It's okay," Courtney says softly.

"I'm so sorry. I'm sorry. It's the books." I think she's crying. "They change you."

A little chill shoots down my spine.

"It's fine."

A few minutes of silence. Then she murmurs:

"The language, the complexity, the challenge and epiphanies . . . it's so exciting. But it's like a drug. It rewires your brain."

"There's a lot there that you haven't told us about."

"Of course," she says. She can't keep the longing out of her voice. "You'd love them, Courtney."

One of them shifts in the bed.

"But they were written by a criminal. A *murderer*."

Mindy never responds to that. They go quiet. After about ten minutes I'm pretty sure both of them have dozed off.

But I'm completely wired. And their little bout of lust cost me another night of sleep—because I already know there's no chance I'll be able to settle down now. I go through the motions, close my eyes and sink deeper into the pillow but the projector in my mind's eye whirrs to life, playing a hideous loop: Becky's sunken face, Sampson's self-imposed mutilation, the deep scratch marks where the leather collar was anchored to the bronze wall, the twenty-two passport-sized photos in the file cabinet. And dancing in and out of each scene is a ghost in a white wax mask molded to Rico's face.

I toss around in bed, too hot, too cold. Four in the morning. Five. Air-conditioning starts and stops. Courtney snores intermittently.

I think about our visit to the grill, about our talk with Warden Heald, about the orgy at the red house . . .

Wonder how often that happens? Wonder if any of those kids have a clue what's going on downstairs there.

Five thirty in the morning, and sleep is a distant memory. My body is so tired it hurts. My jaw kills from the shot I took from the baby bouncer, and my ribs hurt from a hit I can't remember—maybe he punched me in the gut while trying to strangle me. Legs are sore from all the running.

I wonder where Oliver Vicks is at this moment. If we can't find the books, the next best thing would be to find him and either lead the cops to him or just put a bullet in his brain.

Or maybe we'll get lucky, and that heart attack he predicted will hit tomorrow.

Courtney is right. The guy isn't crazy, in any conventional sense. He just happens to have a pretty wild belief set.

Which we still don't understand . . .

I sit up. In the other bed, Mindy and Courtney are a tangle of limbs, with key junctures mercifully concealed by a stiff white sheet. I slide open the top drawer of the nightstand between our beds, and I feel around for the Gideon Bible I'd assumed would be there. Take it into the bathroom and flip the light on.

I sit down on the only chair in the room—mitigate the blasphemy by closing the lid first—and flip open the periwinkle cover. I immediately remember why I've never really tried to read this thing. Table of contents is words like *Leviticus, Matthew, Corinthians,* which I'm familiar with in name only. I leave the bathroom to get the iPhone and return to the holy throne. Google *Joseph Egypt in bible.* Genesis 37. It takes me about five minutes to locate these inscrutable coordinates. It starts:

Joseph, a young man of seventeen, was tending the flocks with his brothers, the sons of Bilhah and the sons of Zilpah, his father's wives, and he brought their father a bad report about them . . .

The story of Joseph is long, and hard to understand. I recognize a few things from what Heald told us: Joseph's brothers selling him to slavers who take him to Egypt, the place where Pharaoh calls Joseph "Sophnot" (Zaphenath-Paneah in this edition. Based on my extensive trove of biblical knowledge, I assume it's the same thing). But the language is dense and archaic and maybe it's because it's five-thirty in the goddamn morning, or maybe because the Bible is the kind of thing you need a teacher to help you decipher, but every couple sentences my eyes go unfocused, and the words become little black ants scurrying around the page.

This story though . . . these fifteen pages must be damn important to Oliver Vicks. Is it possible he checked himself into prison, just to be like Joseph?

I slam the Bible shut and go back into the bedroom, letting the bathroom door close loudly, half hoping it wakes the two lovebirds up, and gives me an excuse to scream at them for ruining my night. I flop back down into bed.

What was I hoping for? A little-known passage where Sophnot—né Joseph–decides to go on a killing spree, and use his victims' skin to bind his papyrus manuscripts, then gives the exact street address he hides out in?

Oliver Vicks. So fearless that he checked himself into prison, knowing he'd walk out when he was good and ready. Doesn't fear death because he knows how he'll die.

So would he really leave his precious skin hanging in the red house, because he was scared of us?

Doesn't make sense.

I sit up again, and use the flashlight on the phone to find Courtney's red acrylic bag on the floor. Rummage through his tools until I find the GPS scanner, and return to bed with it. Flip it on. It scans for three minutes and finds nothing. The chip is gone.

"Didn't sleep well, Frank?" Mindy asks, between big bites of pancake at the hotel café. 7:30 a.m. Spent the last couple hours staring at the ceiling thinking about two things: 1) what happened to the chip and 2) if it's a big mistake to bring Mindy with us to the red house to find out. I think her intentions might be alright—she certainly shared a lot with us yesterday. But after hearing her loopy pillow talk . . . She's clearly not in her right mind and we can't risk her doing something crazy. What if Oliver Vicks is there in the red house? Would she try to stop us from killing him because he wrote the books she loves? If she's desperate enough to bang Courtney, well.

"No. No I did not sleep well," I say.

"Sure looked like you went down pretty quickly," says Courtney, wrapping up an absolute decimation of his fruit salad. He's eating fast and avoiding Mindy's eyes.

"Yeah, it was quick," I say, as dryly as I can. "Quick, but not super satisfying."

Neither of them seem to catch it. They just keep eating. All I've got is coffee and a cake donut. I feel sick.

"You two seem to have pretty *healthy* appetites this morning," I say.

"Yeah well." Courtney slurps down some orange juice. "We'll need our strength today. It's time to get access to any private CCTVs from around the aquarium, try to find Rico, and trace his path. It's a shot in the dark—even if we can get some businesses to show us their footage, there are hundreds of angles to review. And there are only three of us, and we only have one day. But I think it's our best chance. You should try to eat more, Frank. I'll get you a bowl of oatmeal."

Before I can protest, Courtney shoots up from his chair—obviously relieved at the excuse to extricate himself from the awkwardness—and rushes to the breakfast buffet. I watch Mindy drench a piece of pancake in syrup then scarf it down. I can't tell whether I'm over-or underestimating her. Is she really trying to be cooperative? Or was her desperate performance last night a carefully calculated ruse, to convince Courtney to let her take the books to London with her if we find them.

You'd love them Courtney . . .

Courtney returns with a big bowl of oatmeal, garnished with strawberries.

"Try to force something down," he says, putting a hand on my shoulder.

"Thanks, champ," I growl, and devour a tasteless spoonful. "So you two then, you two slept well?"

Courtney stares at the bottom of his orange juice glass. "Yeah, pretty well," he says softly.

"Did you sleep on the floor or something, Courtney?" I ask lightly.

"No, I mean. Well not on the floor, exactly . . ." he says, sounding like he has something stuck in his throat, awkwardly prodding some pieces of fruit.

"I just thought maybe after you two banged," I say offhandedly, "she kicked you out of bed."

Courtney drops his fork and goes deep red. Mindy continues eating, unfazed.

"Frank . . ." Courtney starts.

I shrug.

"You two are adults. You can do whatever you want," I say.

"We thought you were asleep," he stammers.

"I mean, I *was* asleep," I say. "Before you started."

"I don't see why this is even any of your business, Frank," says Mindy.

I turn to her slowly, raise an eyebrow in disbelief.

"Because I was *next to you*," I say. "But hey, it's not a big deal, really. Don't worry about it. Next time I'll get up and help. I've got a nasty right hook."

"Stop, Frank." Courtney's face is burning.

"It's fine," Mindy says, seemingly unfazed. "I'm a big girl. I can take it."

I smile.

"I'll say. Courtney, come help me build a fruit salad, would you?" *This* disturbs Mindy. Courtney looks first to me, then to Mindy, tugging nervously on the early sprouts of a mustache.

I stand up, grab him by the elbow, and half drag him to the breakfast buffet, well out of her earshot. He pushes me off of him.

"What are you doing?" he asks, not angry—he doesn't really get *angry*—but irritated.

"Oliver was at the red house," I say. "I checked the GPS last night. The chip died."

Courtney's features sharpen.

"That doesn't make sense. If he took the skin, we should be able to track him. There's no way he found the chip."

"Do you know how you make leather?" I ask.

Courtney frowns.

"Vaguely."

"I didn't either, until I looked it up last night," I say. "But after you hang the skin, you have to soak it for a long time, in lime-water, so that it gets loose, and you can scrape off hair and shit."

He rubs his pads of his thumbs and forefinger together.

"So the chip is in one of those metal barrels," he says morosely. "Submerged, and surrounded by metal. I'll bet that limewater is particularly corrosive too."

"That's my guess."

"Alright," he says. "So we'll go there. Maybe he's still there? That's what you're thinking?"

I shrug.

"Seems likely he's been there in the past twelve hours or so. We have no idea where the books are. But if we can find him, arrest him, maybe get the money back for Sampson, that would sure be a close second best."

Courtney mulls this, nods to himself, then looks over his shoulder at Mindy, sitting alone finishing up her pancakes. Turns back to me looking troubled.

"And you don't want to bring her. You want to ditch her again."

"Your intuition is phenomenal."

"Frank . . ." he says. "What about all the help she gave us last night?"

I smirk.

"Yes, Courtney. All the *help* she gave us last night."

He blinks emptily at me, and then his features sharpen.

"Frank, if you're insinuating that . . . no. C'mon. That was personal. That has nothing to do with my professional inclinations."

I cock my head at him like *really?*

"I . . . I," he stammers, "we just *like* each other, okay? It's not as if . . . it wasn't some sort of elaborate *ploy*. I really think she'll be helpful—she knows a million times more about Oliver Vicks than us."

"Sampson, Becky, the dudes in khaki," I hiss. "They're not bad people. They all think they're doing the right thing, because they're up to their necks in this mythology. They're not thinking clearly anymore. Mindy . . . I'm not saying she's there yet, but after the things she said last night, I think she's getting there."

Courtney holds his gaze level. Doesn't say anything.

"This is classic cult behavior," I say. "Otherwise intelligent people going out of their gourds because of a charismatic dude with some crazy ideas about life. And honestly, you're susceptible to this kind of stuff. You get excited and carried away by this sort of mumbo jumbo. I don't want her around you. I want you cold and methodical. Because we have like thirty hours to either find those books or find their author, or things are going to get real fucking dark."

His lower lip curls inward. Still he says nothing.

"Be *objective*, Court. I'm not saying she's not brilliant. Hell, I think as far as she knows she *does* want to help. But what if we find Oliver and—"

"Mindy is coming with us," he says calmly. "She cooperated with us last night. And she knows far more about Sophnot and his writing than either of us."

I take a few deep breaths.

"You know I always trust you," I say. "But I really think you're not thinking clearly about this."

He puts a boney hand on my shoulder.

"I promise you this. If we don't find the books—or Oliver Vicks—it won't be because we let Mindy tag along."

I swallow a retort, and nod along. There won't be any talking him out of this, I can see that. Not worth pushing it. I'll just have to keep a very close eye on her.

"I suggest you worry about things pertinent to the task at hand," he says. "For instance, something that's been bothering me since what Mindy told us last night. We all agree that Oliver is incredibly smart, and personable. Surely he had good grades, and would have aced any interview. So why didn't he just go to architecture school?"

THE DRIVE BACK to the red house is tense. Mindy knows she's unwanted, and stays silent in the backseat. Courtney cleans our Magnums, while I drive. Three straight nights without real sleep. Little shapes, bats of light, seem to keep flying across the windshield. Courtney should probably be driving.

It's a bit past nine when I park a quarter mile away, and approach the house on foot, Courtney and I first, pistols drawn. It seems unlikely that Oliver is just hanging around the dome, given that he knows we've been there before. But it's a mistake to try to predict this guy's behavior.

The other night the place glowed, and seemed to be alive. I was sure in the daytime the red shingles would sparkle, like solar panels, powering this dazzling structure. But in the morning light, the place just looks like an inflatable tennis tarpaulin tent.

I'm not sure whether I'm more relieved or disappointed that there are no cars parked outside.

"He's not here," I say.

"Don't let your guard down," Courtney replies.

The front door is unlocked. Pistols out, we enter. Red velvet hallways totally empty, and look recently steam-cleaned. We wander through the halls for a while, trying to find the chamber again, gradually becoming more relaxed as it seems clear this place has been fumigated.

Don't feel any of the creepiness from the other night, when it was filled with coked up, gallivanting teens. In fact, I feel a little silly now for ever being freaked out by this space. In the sober light of day it's totally harmless. The red walls look lame, the floor that just the other night appeared to me as infinite blackness looks cheap and poorly crafted. It's like there was a spell when we were here last, and it's worn off.

"Oliver designed this place?" Mindy asks, behind us. "For what? It's not like you could live here."

"Tuesday night we saw one practical application," I say, without turning around.

I grip my gun a bit tighter as we find the descending staircase I'm pretty sure leads to the chamber. The flimsy pine door opens to the hallway where the foursome was embroiled on a mattress. The mattress is gone. At the end of the hallway, the blast door to the chamber is ajar.

I already know it must be empty, but my heart still speeds up as I burst in, pistol first, Courtney right behind me. The automatic lights flick on and indeed, the room is totally bare. No basin to wash your feet. No little stone on the floor for incense. Strong smell of disinfectant.

The tapestry that separated the room into two is gone—it's just one long space now—and the place Rico had been hanging is empty.

The drafting table is gone, as are the tools or masks. Only thing left is the stone worktable—must have been too bulky to move. Courtney inspects the surface; he announces it's been scrubbed completely clean. The only proof that the other night wasn't just a bad dream are the designs painted on the walls and ceiling.

"He even took the barrels," I say. My voice echoes sharply in the claustrophobic space.

"Didn't leave a trace," Courtney says.

"So let's go. It's still early. Have at least a few hours to try to get CCTV footage."

"Why didn't you tell me about these walls?"

I turn, and see that Mindy is still standing near the door, her back to us as she examines a maze of red, white and blue lines. I don't know how she can just stare at it—every time my eyes catch the design I feel that familiar dizziness, the start of a migraine.

"What is it?" Courtney calls.

Mindy doesn't respond. Jerks off her backpack, and pulls a folder out. Combs through it frantically, then returns her attention to the wall. Courtney looks at me like: *See? I told you bringing her was a good idea.*

I return a look like: *We'll see.*

Mindy is on her knees, fanning out papers on the floor. We approach her.

"What's going on?" I say, gesturing to the wall in front of her without staring. "Is this writing?"

"Of course," she mutters, half to herself. "You thought he did all this just for aesthetic purposes?"

Courtney squints at the wall in front of her, rubs the place where his mustache would be, finding only the facial hair equivalent of a sloppily trimmed lawn. I force myself to stare at the wall as well, ignore the wave of nausea accompanying it. I don't see how this could possibly be a language. It looks like a Jackson Pollock painting.

"What does it say?" I ask, finally looking down to the bronze floor.

Mindy snorts, and swivels around. Casts her hands out in front of her at the expanse of walls.

"Do you have any idea how much information is written here?"

I shake my head.

She turns and presses the tip of her pinky at a spot on the wall.

"Look," she says. "Watch my finger."

I fight the dizziness and watch as her pinky traces a path,

and when I really look closely I can see that it's following a white square that's suspended above the red-and-blue chaos around it.

"See the square?" she says.

"Yes," Courtney says quickly.

"Now how about this."

Her pinky makes vertical lines through the square, and it takes a moment to see that she's tracing black lines, negative space, through it. I realize that when I can see patterns in the madness, I feel less sick, because my eyes can focus just on the foreground.

"A white square with black vertical lines," she says. "That's a symbol I've seen several times."

"What does it mean?" I ask.

"What does it look like to you?" she asks.

"A cage," Courtney says.

Mindy smiles.

"Right. Depending on the context, it means either a cage, servitude, or prison."

I think about what Heald told us, about one interpretation of the books was that they were the entirety of Oliver Vicks's life.

"Is it the same text as the books?" Courtney says.

Mindy shakes her head at him in disbelief.

"I've had about two minutes so far to examine it, Courtney. Give me time. Let me see if I can make something of it."

"Sounds good," I say, and squat down on the brass floor, like a baseball catcher.

She scowls.

"I need to concentrate," she says, and juts her chin at the blast door. "I need a month. But give me a half hour. We'll take it from there."

Courtney and I dutifully retreat to the velvet hallway. I immediately sink to the floor, the same place I dozed off Tuesday night. Courtney paces the length of the hall, hands clasped behind his back.

"I wonder if any of the kids who were here the other night know anything," he says.

"Doubt it," I say. "I'll bet Vicks just likes having them around in case he screws up a skinning, and needs some fresh meat."

Courtney seems to deliberately not hear this comment.

"Where will Sophnot never go?" he asks. "Where do the books belong?"

I roll my eyes.

"Ask me another couple thousand times, would you?"

"It's likely somewhere within three or four miles of the aquarium. I doubt Rico got in a bus."

"He certainly could have taken a cab," I say. "I would have."

Courtney keeps pacing.

"Court, you realize at some point this evening we have to consider making a run for it."

He halts suddenly and looks at me.

"What do you mean?"

"I mean we're supposed to get the books to Sampson early afternoon tomorrow. If that's not going to happen, and we're not going to find Oliver and get that money back, the best thing we can do is give ourselves a head start getting the hell out of Colorado."

Courtney grimaces. He knows I'm right.

"Sampson has threatened to send the feds after us," I say. "Maybe, *maybe*, if we're already on a plane to Vietnam by tomorrow evening we'll be able to hide for a couple years."

Courtney's frown stretches toward the floor.

"What about Sadie?" he says.

I bite my lip.

"Nothing would bring me more anguish than missing out on the rest of her life," I say. "But if we don't find those books . . ." I shake my head. "Better to be in hiding again than prison. Or dead."

Courtney is still for a second. Can nearly hear the whirring of the calculator behind his eyes.

"Five in the morning," I continue. "That's when I say we give up. Drive to Denver International Airport. Can be on a plane by nine probably. We'll call Sampson right before and tell him we'll meet him in a few hours to buy us some time. By the time he realizes we're not showing up we'll be over the Atlantic."

He shakes his head slowly.

"I don't think I can leave," he says.

"Don't tell me this is because of *her*," I growl.

"No. If we leave, this thing will just keep going. Nobody will know that Oliver is on the loose. He'll just keep killing. If by tomorrow we have nothing, I'm going to the cops with everything. Pictures of Rico's corpse. I'll rat out Heald, they'll go to the prison and confirm Oliver is gone—"

"You realize how dangerous that is, right?" I say. "Even on the slim chance that they believe you enough to investigate—that, best case, they *find* Oliver and pin everything on him—Sampson's reputation will be ruined, and he'll destroy you. He'll try to say you stole the money from him, and will discredit you by bringing me into it. Will say you abetted an Interpol fugitive . . . I can't even imagine the fallout from that."

Courtney clenches his hands into sharp little fists.

"I know," he says softly. "But the alternative . . . At the very least Oliver intends to kill two more people to finish binding his books. And if we know that and don't do anything about it, we're morally culpable."

I rub my eyes.

"We didn't ask to find this out," I say. "We were just supposed to swap some cash for books."

"We didn't ask for it," Courtney agrees. "But here we are."

Mindy pulls in the blast door and walks out to join us in the hallway. There's a wild look in her eyes.

"I need more time," she says, "but this stuff is amazing."

"What is it?" Courtney asks, before I can.

Mindy shakes her head in something like disbelief.

"I think . . . I mean it's a lot of things. His writing always is. It's less sophisticated than the writing in the books, so I'm making headway pretty fast. If I had to guess, he wrote this *before* the books. While he was still developing the nuances of his language—"

"But what does it say?" I blurt.

Mindy rubs her hair up out of her face, rolls her eyes like *I can't believe I have to work with this guy.*

"It's not the same content as the books. It's some kind of story. Just one narrative." Her voice is quivering with excitement. "He's trying to figure the story out, but keeps reworking it. A lot of the characters and patterns repeat themselves, with slight variations—I think that's him refining his thoughts."

"What's the story?"

She laughs way too hard. Kooky.

"I don't think you understand how long it takes to decipher these things. So far I've spotted the prison symbol I showed you, that's how they all start. He talks about prison, the books, dreams, money . . . Some of his favorite motifs, as we all know."

"Can you show us?" I say.

Mindy nods, and we follow her back into the chamber.

"The pattern repeats itself over and over," she says, taking us to one of the walls. "Here's the prison symbol, I already showed you that." Courtney and I nod, following her finger. "And here's the books—" She points to a circle with lines shooting out from its circumference. Looks like a child's sketch of a sun emitting rays.

"That doesn't look like books," Courtney says.

"Count the lines," she says. "Twenty-four. With no beginning and no end. He uses this symbol sometimes in the books as a sort of hashtag equivalent, with one of the lines being longer to show that he's alluding to something in another certain volume."

Courtney's eyes are wide.

"Okay," he whispers. "What's next?"

"Then this. The symbol which usually means *dream*, beside the one for money."

I ignore the thumping in my temples and try to see what Mindy sees.

"I don't see what you're talking about," I say. "Show us those two symbols again?"

She seems agitated. Wants us to leave so she can get back to studying this on her own.

"This is *dream*," she says, tracing something that to me looks like a foot. "And here is *money*." This one is what I'm sure is an animal's head, with two horns protruding from either side.

"Whoa, whoa," I say. "This is a symbolic language. How the hell does an animal face mean money?"

"It's not all literal," she says, an edge to her voice. Sounds like she's regretting trying to explain anything to us. "Sometimes it does maintain the more literal meaning of *cow*, but sometimes it's figurative. Money. Like cash cow."

"And explain the dream?" Courtney says.

Mindy shakes her head.

"Honestly, I don't have a clue what that's supposed to be. But I've seen it several times before, and am pretty sure it means *dream*. In the books it's often close to *sleep* and something that I think means *imagine*." She steps back from the wall. "Give me four more hours here. I think I can get something more tangible about what he was trying to do here."

Courtney scratches his scalp. I check out the symbols again. Like one of those 3-D Magic Eye puzzles it takes me a while of staring before I spot the white and black symbols Mindy pointed out to us just a moment before.

Prison. Dream. Money/Cow.

My stomach drops.

"Mindy . . ." I swallow. "How sure are you he wrote this before the books? At least twenty years ago?"

"Not certain, of course, but as I said, this is much simpler than the content of the books. It really looks like a precursor."

I turn to face the two of them.

"I don't think that symbol means either *money* or *cow*."

Mindy raises an eyebrow.

"Perhaps you'd like to fact check my thesis as well?" she asks.

"I think the symbol represents Senator James Henry Sampson," I say. "Oliver's eventual money source, but also a dairy farmer."

Mindy is silent for a second. A little hiss of air from between Courtney's teeth.

"And the dream," I say. "It well could mean any old generic dream in other places. But what does it that picture like to you two?"

Mindy says nothing. She's staring again at the symbols behind me.

"A foot," Courtney says.

"A foot?" I say. "Or a heel."

Courtney's eyes go wide.

"Sampson's dream . . ." he whispers.

I nod.

"What if this isn't a fictional story? What if this was Oliver Vicks's whiteboard? His planning. His to-do list. What he's refining here is his plan. Mindy, does that make sense?"

She doesn't respond for a while. Retraces the symbols with her pinky. Her hand is shaking a little.

"What was Sampson's dream?" she says finally.

"It's the recurring dream he had that Oliver eventually interpreted for him," I say. "That someone was behind him, dragging him down into the water, by his heel. He never told you about that?"

She shakes her head slightly.

"No," she says softly.

"So what do you think about Frank's idea?" Courtney says. "Could these be his plans?"

"Can't rule it out," she replies distantly. "Give me more time. A few more hours at least and I'll be able to tell you."

Courtney turns to me.

"What do you say Frank?" he asks. "I'm not sure if we have any leads better than what's written on these walls."

In response I pull the Gideon Bible from the hotel out of my backpack. Didn't make it to the part about theft last night.

"I'm not sure about that," I say, turning to my earmarked page. "I was reading through this last night. About Joseph. It's increasingly clear to me just how obsessed Sophnot was with this story. I'd like to speak to a pastor or something. I know I'm missing all the nuance of this story. Maybe we can find someone while you're working on this, Mindy. We'll come back to pick you up after."

"Fine," she says, not seeming to care what we're doing, as long as she gets her solo time with the drawings. "Courtney, go with him. I need to work on this alone."

"We can't leave you alone here," he says. "He could come back at any time."

She snorts.

"Yeah, I'm just a helpless woman. What would I do without my two men here to protect me? Leave me a gun. I've got as much of a chance of killing him as you do."

"She's got a point, Courtney."

Courtney pulls his Magnum from his ankle holster and hands it to her.

"You know how to use this?" he asks.

"Not really," she asks. "Explain it to me. Where does the bullet come out?"

He actually starts to answer her. She rolls her eyes, snatches the gun from him and slides it into the back of her pants.

"I lived with a Republican Senator for seven years," she says. "It would be pretty pathetic if I hadn't learned to use a gun all that time."

Courtney nods.

"Call if you find anything, or need anything. And we'll be back to pick you up in four hours, right? So one this afternoon?"

"Make it two," she says.

"Okay."

They look like they might kiss, but then they both overthink it, and settle on a hug that's so awkward I have to turn away. As we walk to the door he even turns and seems to consider giving her another wave good-bye. I put my hand on his hip and push him out into the velvet-padded hallway.

"You were reading the Bible last night?" Courtney asks.

"Yeah. While you were lying naked in bed with a girl, out of wedlock."

Courtney sniffs.

"It was pretty dense," I continue. "But I picked out enough to realize what we're dealing with."

We're out the front door. The fresh air is a relief.

"What do you mean? I read the whole Bible myself, but it's been years."

"I mean, last night I kept thinking about how important that story must have been to Sophnot, but I didn't realize *how* important until just now. We saw the superficial similarities before: prison, dreams, his nickname, but *that* was a whole other level."

"What do you mean?" he says.

I savor his question. It's great to be one step ahead of him for once.

"The cow thing. I guess you haven't read the story in a while. Pharaoh's dream? Seven lean cows and seven fat cows came out of the Nile. That was the dream that Joseph was pulled out of prison to interpret. The cow/dream imagery drove it home. There's no doubt that Oliver Vicks is obsessed with this story. He sees himself as a kindred spirit of this biblical character. And now I think it's clear he might have even been planning things based on those passages."

Courtney sniffs.

"Interesting."

"So I thought if we could find a pastor or—"

"No," Courtney says. "Genesis is part of the Old Testament. It was originally written in Hebrew, as you know. If we want someone familiar with the original language, and I think we do, considering Oliver was a bit of a linguistic purist as well, we need a rabbi."

Anybody else would be lording this correction over me. Courtney is an impartial as a spellchecker.

"Fine," I say. "A rabbi. Anything else, hotshot?"

"I wasn't going to say anything, because I know you're tired," he says, "But if we're going to meet a Bible scholar, I feel obligated to tell you that your fly has been open since we left the hotel."

COURTNEY DRIVES WHILE I look up the numbers of synagogues in Denver. I'm surprised at how many Google results we get. The first five numbers don't answer, and then I call something called the Chabad of Denver—the guy answers on the first ring. I put the devil machine on speaker for Courtney.

"Chabad of Denver," he says. He's clearly on a cell phone, somewhere busy.

"Hi, um, my name is Ben . . . I'm in the Denver area and, this might sound like a weird request, but I had some very specific questions about the Old Testament."

The guy chuckles. "Why is that weird? Go ahead—what's on your mind?"

"I . . ." I pause. "Are you a rabbi?"

"I am."

"So could you explain the story of Joseph to me? Like, in serious detail?"

"That's my job."

"Listen, is there any way we could meet in person? I—we—will come wherever you want. It's just that this might get detailed. We're happy to pay or whatever. Not sure how it works."

Another chuckle. "Sure. How's next Tuesday? I'm free from two to four in the afternoon."

I grind my teeth.

"It's actually somewhat urgent. If there was any way we could *possibly* meet now that would be . . ."

"Say no more. Um . . . yeah today is pretty crazy but if you want to come to my house right now I can speak."

I raise an eyebrow at Courtney. *This dude is inviting two strangers to his house?*

"Perfect. Where is it?"

"32 Madcock. When can you be here?"

"Um." I put it into Google maps.

"Twenty minutes, okay?" I say. "We'll drive as fast as we can."

"No need for that. See you in twenty. Looking forward."

THE BRICK HOUSE is modest. One story. Tiny, token yard. Minivan parked in the driveway, alongside a tricycle. Netless basketball hoop.

I ring the bell and the door opens inward almost immediately to reveal a sixty-something man who's positively beaming. His beard is reddish, with a lot of white. He has a black velvet skullcap and side locks. Wearing a white button-down tucked into black slacks. White strings—the kind I've seen before on religious Jews, but don't understand—are emerging from a few spots on his black leather belt. Source unknown.

"Rabbi Yisroel Lieberman," he says, smiling, and shoots out a pale white hand. "Call me Yisroel."

"I'm Ben," I say, "and this is my friend Lenny."

Lenny sounds more Jewish than Leonard, right?

These names seem to please him immensely.

"Wonderful. Come on in."

"Should we take off our shoes?" Courtney asks.

"No, no, don't worry about it."

We're in a small living room that's attached to a dining room. Something is cooking in the kitchen that smells like stew. The floor is littered with kids' toys. Besides that, there's a ratty green couch, and books. So many books. Every wall, from floor to ceiling, is bookcases. I take a closer look at one and realize that almost none of them are in English.

"Take a seat." Yisroel gestures to the couch. We sit. "You want anything to drink? Tea?"

"No thanks," I demur. I turn to Courtney, assuming he's about to take the rabbi up on his offer. But am shocked when he declines:

"No, thank you," he says. "Let's get right to the business."

"Of course." Yisroel plops down across from us. "So . . . *Yoseph?*"

"Beg your pardon?" I ask.

Just then a door closes and a woman walks out of somewhere. Must be his wife. About the same age. Thick glasses, no skin visible below the neck besides her hands.

"Hi," she says. "Can I get you something to eat or drink? Tea?"

"I already offered, Rivka," Yisroel says.

But this time Courtney can't resist:

"Actually, tea would be wonderful," Courtney says.

"I'm fine." I smile at her.

She steps into the kitchen.

"Sorry, *Yoseph* is the ancient Hebrew pronunciation of

'Joseph,'" Yisroel explains. "Or really, I should say that *Joseph* is the English equivalent of the real way of saying it."

"Ah." Courtney nods. "The Y often turns into J right? Like Jehovah?"

The rabbi winces.

"Exactly. We don't use that word, actually, but you're right. Anyways. What about the story can I help you with? And, if you don't mind me asking, why do you so urgently need to understand this Bible story? Thesis due tomorrow?"

I smile.

"Nothing like that. I . . ." I struggle for a moment to come up with a plausible lie. Then realize at this point, might as well just tell him the truth. "We're detectives. Private investigators. And we're searching for someone who seems to have taken a great interest in the story of Joseph. He even insists on being called *Sophnot*. You're familiar with that name?"

Yisroel's face darkens a little bit. He nods slowly.

"'Tsaphnat' is how I'd pronounce it. Tsaphnat-Paneah. It's a bit of an obscure term. The nickname Pharaoh gave to Joseph. It's only mentioned once or twice."

"It means *he who solves riddles,* right? Because he interpreted dreams?"

Yisroel frowns.

"Yes, that's if you think it was written in ancient Egyptian. Which most commentators do. Though, worth noting that if you read it as if it's Hebrew, it translates more literally to *concealer of faces.*"

I think of the wax mask of Rico's face and a little shiver shoots down my spine. Just in time, his wife carries in a cup of brown tea, stuffed with sprigs of fresh mint. She brings a chair with her, too, from the kitchen, because there's no coffee table in here. Puts the tea down on the chair.

"Let it cool a moment," she advises him, as if he's experiencing hot beverages for the first time.

"Thanks." Courtney smiles. Then Rivka leaves.

"Why would Pharaoh nickname him that?" I ask the rabbi.

"Great question," he says, and smiles. "And for that, we need to go back to the start of the story. Do you know the basics, or—"

"Assume we know nothing," I say. "I tried reading it last night, but it felt like reading Shakespeare. Missed a lot."

"Okay." He nods. "I'll do the standing-on-one-foot version of what may be the most interesting—and most difficult to understand—story in the Old Testament. Maybe anywhere, if you ask me. Joseph was Jacob's son. Jacob, his four wives, and their twelve sons—and an unclear number of daughters—lived in Canaan—somewhere in modern-day Israel. Joseph, despite not being the oldest, was Jacob's favorite son. He even gave him a coat of many colors as a present. That sounds familiar, right?"

We nod.

"So, this favoritism was an issue. If anyone should have been the favorite, it should have been the oldest brothers. Joseph parading around in his father's coat made his brothers jealous. But then it gets worse. Joseph starts having dreams. He tells his family that he had a dream: The sun, moon and twelve stars were bowing to him, Joseph. The sun was clearly his father, the moon his mother. In other words, he was prophesying that all his family would bow to him. As you can imagine, this didn't go over well. The brothers, out of jealousy, decided to kill Joseph—the dreamer. They threw him in a well and left him for dead. He was then picked up by a group of traders, who brought him down to Egypt as their slave. He was sold as a slave to a member of Pharaoh's guard, and then for reasons we probably don't have time for, arrested and thrown into prison."

"No, wait," Courtney says, sipping on his tea. "That could be important to us. Why was he arrested?"

Yisroel checks his watch.

"The owner's wife tried to seduce Joseph. When he refused her advance, she was so upset that she claimed that he assaulted her."

Courtney scratches his cheek and looks at me.

"A refused advance . . ."

I nod grimly. *Becky.*

"Okay. Let's keep going. What happened when he was in prison?"

Yisroel grins. I think he's happy to have such attentive students.

"Nothing much happened in prison for a while, until one of his cellmates, a wine steward told him about a dream he'd had. Joseph correctly interpreted the dream: that it meant his cellmate would be taken from prison and returned to his former post, as Pharaoh's cup bearer. Well, sure enough, the wine steward was taken out and exonerated. A few years later, Pharaoh himself had a series of dreams he didn't understand—"

"About the cows," I say. "Sorry, I remembered that bit."

"Yes." Yisroel nods. "Two dreams. One about cows coming from the Nile, one about stalks of grain. Nobody could interpret them to his satisfaction. Until this wine steward told him about Joseph, the boy who had interpreted his so accurately."

I cross my legs. Think about Sampson, who was continually dissatisfied with his dream interpreters, until Oliver came along . . . from prison . . .

"Joseph indeed interpreted Pharaoh's dream to his satisfaction: There would be seven years of grain surplus in Egypt, followed by seven years of famine. Joseph even advised the king to start saving grain now, so that they'd be the only people in the region with food when the famine hit. Pharaoh was so impressed by this young Hebrew that he instantly pulled him from jail, and made him his second in command over all Egypt."

"And that's when he gave him the nickname?" I asked.

"Yes." The rabbi nods.

"So it's about how he interpreted the dreams? How he solved the riddles of what the dreams meant?"

The rabbi tugs on his beard and meditates on this for a moment.

"Well, if you're going to interpret it as meaning *revealer,* then yes. As I mentioned if you read it in Hebrew it has an almost opposite meaning. As a concealer of something—faces. And so, following the Hebrew translation, I believe the nickname is an allusion to what happened *next* in the story."

Courtney leans forward in his seat, like an eager little puppy. Glad this is taking his mind off Mindy.

"What happens next?" Courtney asks.

Yisroel smiles.

"Sure enough, as Joseph predicted, the next seven years were great for crops. And the Egyptians were able to save a lot of leftover food for a rainy day. They accumulated huge storehouses of grain, all under Joseph's supervision. And then the famine hit. People came to Egypt from all over the region, because their leaders hadn't had the foresight to save up food. And to Pharaoh's great delight, Egypt was making a fortune selling away some of their extra food. And then . . . then ten boys showed up at Pharaoh's palace. Ten Hebrews who themselves were starving, and needed food to bring back for their parents."

"Joseph's brothers . . ." I murmur. "The ones who threw him in the pit and left him for dead."

Yisroel nods.

"Yes. An interesting twist, isn't it?"

"Coming full circle." I nod.

"Here the story becomes a bit difficult to understand. There would seem to be two obvious routes to take here right?" Yisroel asks.

I nod, without really knowing for sure what he's talking about.

"Yes," says Courtney.

"And those are?" Yisroel asks, grinning.

"Well." Courtney sips on his tea. "Either laugh in their face. Tell them the tables have turned, and now they're going to get their just deserts. *Or* to show he's the bigger man, and forgive them. Give them the food."

Yisroel nods.

"But Joseph, strangely, takes the middle ground. See—the thing is, it's been so long, and he's wearing Egyptian clothes . . . he recognizes his brothers, but they don't recognize *him*. It makes sense, really. Even if they thought this Egyptian viceroy bore a resemblance to their brother . . . it *couldn't* be him . . . second in command over Egypt? So Joseph, well for lack of a better word, toys with them. First he accuses them of stealing from him, makes them terrified that he's going to kill them. And then he insists on keeping one of them as a hostage until they go back to Canaan and bring their father and youngest brother, Benjamin down too. This whole sequence of events, this elaborate toying, I confess has always been difficult for me to understand. But finally, after all these games, Joseph can take it no more. Sobbing, he reveals himself: 'It is me, Joseph! Is my father still alive?' And the brothers embrace.

And instead of sending food back to Canaan, he invites the whole family down to Egypt, and sets them up in a good spot. The family flourishes for many years in Egypt, until eventually a new Pharaoh arises, and since he has no debt to Joseph, he has no problem enslaving the Israelites. And that is more or less the story of Joseph."

Courtney finishes his tea.

"So that's how the Jews got down to Egypt," I say. "You hear all the time about them being slave to the Egyptians, but not about how they got there in the first place."

Yisroel nods.

"Yes. It's quite a tale, isn't it?"

I nod silently, mind frantically trying to connect all of this to Oliver Vicks.

"Wait a second," Courtney says. "Forget the toying . . . I don't understand. If Joseph was so powerful, and had apparently forgiven his brothers, why didn't he contact them earlier? His poor parents thought he was dead . . . he could have helped them right away! Why did he let this drag on for years and years?"

Yisroel breaks into the widest grin of the day and slaps Courtney on the shoulder.

"We have a natural scholar here! That, my friends, is *the* question."

"And the answer?" I say.

He shrugs.

"Many people have tried to answer that. Some answers are more satisfactory than others."

"Is there an answer that you like?" asks Courtney.

Yisroel is silent for a moment, then nods slowly.

"The most common answer, which I confess I still find difficult, is that he let time languish this long in order to fulfill his prophetic dream. His brothers really *did* bow down to him, fulfilling his prophecy. Had he contacted them earlier, this wouldn't have come to fruition."

"And is that what you believe?" I ask, sensing that it's not.

"I . . . I have another thought. Though it doesn't cast Joseph—normally thought of as a hero—in the best light."

I raise an eyebrow.

"Yes?"

"I think, simply, that Joseph had a flair for the dramatic. A *very* serious flair. He understood what a pivotal point this was in the history of the Jewish people. And he understood that the longer he waited to reveal himself, the more shocking it would be . . . he wanted to make a story that would be told for generations and generations. And he succeeded."

"That's kind of cruel." I laugh. "Toying with people's emotions just for the sake of a grand, dramatic finale."

Yisroel nods. Then tugs on his beard, hesitates, and says:

"There's another thought I heard once at the *Shabbes* table . . . I haven't thought of it again until now but . . . I had a psychologist here as a guest, and he said, sort of as a joke, that if he had to diagnose the biblical character of Joseph objectively, based on this toying, his obsession with his prophecy coming true . . . well, it wouldn't be pretty—"

"Megalomaniacal," says Courtney. "Ruthless, lack of empathy . . . sociopathic maybe . . ."

Yisroel nods uncomfortably.

"But," I add, "he always seemed to believe, genuinely, that he was doing the right thing."

"And now you understand why so many people find this part of our canon so difficult." He checks his watch. "I have to teach a class across town in fifteen minutes. I'm so sorry, I would have loved to chat for longer. It was a pleasure."

We stand up and shake hands with him, thank him. He grabs his suit jacket, shows us to the door, and then follows us out.

"This man you're looking for," he asks us, outside. "He's done something horrible, hasn't he?"

I don't say anything. Courtney nods.

"I meet a lot of people," Yisroel explains. "Many are dealing with very nasty situations. I know the look."

He smiles at us, then rushes down to his minivan. Throws his briefcase into the front seat. He turns on the minivan, rolls down the window to wave good-bye again.

"How did Joseph die?" I suddenly shout after him.

Yisroel grins.

"Old age. Natural causes."

WE'RE FIVE MINUTES from the rabbi's house, trying to escape a suburban labyrinth, when Mindy calls. Courtney's driving, so I answer.

"We just finished at the rabbi. How's it—"

She cuts me off, breathless:

"What's Becky's number?"

"Becky?"

Courtney slams on the brakes right in the middle of the narrow street, seizes the phone from me and puts it on speaker.

"Mindy?" he shouts into the phone, as only someone unaccustomed to using them would. "Are you alright?"

"Fine. Left the red dome. Got a cab. I'm on the way to Pueblo." She's rattling off words like an auctioneer. It sounds like the window in her cab is rolled down and she's holding the phone out in the breeze. "I need to speak to Becky. I think I've figured something out."

Courtney pleads with his hands and eyes: *What's going on?*

"The books are at her apartment?" I ask.

"What? No. Just text me her number, yeah?"

Courtney picks up the phone and obliges.

"Why do you need to speak to Becky? What did you find?"

"Just, em, I'm not sure yet. I'll call you later okay?"

"No." I snatch the phone from Courtney. "Mindy, tell us what's—"

"I have to concentrate, buzz you later."

She hangs up.

"What was that?" Courtney asks, his eyes as wide as polished dinner plates.

I shake my head.

"I think your girlfriend just screwed us."

"What? What do you mean?"

"She knows something. She's keeping us in the dark."

Courtney snatches the phone from me and calls her back. His nostrils are flared in anticipation, and I can tell when it goes to answering machine because his face sours like a puppeteer just yanked the drawstring to pull the skin back tight over his bones. He hangs up and calls again. Same deal. He slowly places the phone in the cup holder.

I'm not sure how long the blue Saab has been behind us, honking angrily. *Middle America. In NYC we'd already have our windshield smashed.*

Courtney dutifully pulls us to the curb and lets the Saab pass.

"Well," he says quietly, and doesn't add anything.

Suppressing the *I told you so* reflex is surely my most noble gesture in recent memory.

"Yeah," I say.

"I mean," Courtney says. "She didn't *have* to call at all." He sounds like a guy trying to find the silver lining of his parachute not opening.

Hey, at least I'm more aerodynamic.

"Yes she did. For Becky's number."

"I guess we could drive down to Pueblo," he says. "Go to Becky's place."

"Why? What are we going to do, threaten her at gunpoint to tell us what she found? She obviously doesn't want to cooperate with us. She wants to find the books herself and take them to London . . . Just like she told us she wanted to on Tuesday."

"She wouldn't do that to us," Courtney says.

I can barely contain an eye roll.

You've known this girl for less than a week.

"Okay," I say. "Well, let's be pragmatic. That's what you always say. What now?"

Courtney seems to take a long time to wet his lips enough to speak again. Struggling to keep it together.

"I'm not sure this changes very much," he says. "We still need the books. Or Oliver. Barring those, there's also your suggestion to get as far away from this godforsaken flyover state as possible."

We sit in silence for a moment. Two kids bike past on training wheels, their mom in hot pursuit, snapping photos with her phone. A squirrel shoots up an oak tree. It feels strange that the world is continuing to operate as usual around us.

"Let's see where Sampson's head is," I say. "Haven't heard from him since I told him to stop calling."

Courtney nods in agreement, and hands me the phone.

I dial his cell phone, and am surprised by how long it rings. Last time we called him he picked up instantly.

"Frank! Courtney?" he gasps on speaker, like he just came up for air. "Where are you?"

"We're in Colorado," I say. "Not too far from you."

"Listen . . ." he says, forces softness into his voice. "Anything I said before, I apologize. I shouldn't have threatened you. I'm sure you two are in a tough spot. I appreciate that. Maybe you're thinking I didn't offer you enough money for this job, you're thinking about holding onto the books until I shell out a bit more. Come on by and let's talk about it. I'm one hundred percent open to paying you fellas more. But you just *have* to bring me those books by tomorrow."

I shrug at Courtney: *Not a bad idea, actually.*

He looks at me like I'm an idiot and mouths: *We don't have them.*

"I'll give you whatever you want." Sampson is still talking. Negotiating against himself. "*Anything.* I'll give you a million dollars. But I need them by tomorrow afternoon. If I don't get the books back to Sophnot by sunset, I . . . I don't know what he'll do."

"Is everything okay?" Courtney asks.

I swallow a bitter laugh.

Yeah, everything's just dandy.

"It's fine, it's fine," Sampson says, a little too adamantly. "It's just, well, I mean I spoke to Sophnot. He called me yesterday from prison. And it's the first time, well, I mean I have to confess, I'm a bit concerned about what he will do if he doesn't get them back in time. I don't claim to understand his methods, of course, I don't know how he could do anything since he's in SCF but . . . Just bring them to me. Tomorrow."

"What did he say, exactly?" I ask.

"He . . ." Sampson sounds like he's on the verge of tears. "He knows about Mindy, somehow. About me showing her the books. I wasn't supposed to do that. I knew that. I knew I was sinning, but I thought maybe Father would understand I had the purest intentions . . . Anyways he's not *upset*, exactly. He does understand. But he's talking now as if *I* have the books and am holding out on him. As if he doesn't trust *me*. I just want to make this all right. He has so much love, so much love . . ."

I rub my temples.

"James," I say. "You have to understand. Oliver Vicks is not your friend. He's trying to make your life miserable. And as we tried to explain to you the other night, he hasn't been in prison for years."

"*You're* not my friend!" he screams so suddenly into the phone I feel like my eardrum shatters. "Don't try to play games with me! Bring me the books by four tomorrow afternoon or so help me, I swear in his holy name I'll make you two beg me for your lives! I swear it!"

"Of course. Tomorrow at four," I say, and quickly hang up. "Christ," I say, rubbing my sweaty forehead. "What if we told him we don't have them?"

"He wouldn't believe us," Courtney says. "Remember, Oliver told him that the swap went through. So obviously he'd just assume that we'd taken them for ourselves."

I roll down the window and gulp down a few mouthfuls of hot air.

"How did this happen?" My throat is raw. "How did we get in this mess? We didn't do anything wrong. We don't deserve this. This has nothing to fucking *do* with us!" I punch the dashboard of the shitty rental car. "*Goddammit*, Courtney. Sampson's going to ruin our lives. I didn't *ask* for this shit. I signed up to swap a bag for another bag. That's *it*. And now we're stuck in the most unimaginable storm of steaming shit I just . . . I just . . ."

Courtney puts his hand on my shoulder.

"Take some deep breaths," he says in a soothing deep voice. "Just think about that. Slow, easy, deep breaths."

I try to obey.

In. Out.

"Now listen," he says. "Here's what I always tell myself when I'm tracking something, and it seems impossible: The books are *somewhere*. Okay? They didn't just evaporate into thin air. Rico put them *somewhere* and they're probably still there. We have a full twenty-six hours before we're supposed to give them to Sampson. And we're two very smart guys. This isn't over."

I look down in my lap and realize my hands are shaking horribly.

"I can't think," I say. "I'm exhausted. I need to sleep, even if it's just an hour."

"Sure," Courtney says, pulling the Honda back onto the road. "Let's find somewhere for you to sleep for an hour or two."

"I'm sorry about Mindy," I say. "I can tell you really liked her."

He keeps his eyes on the road. Doesn't reply.

"But Court, if she gets those books before us and leaves for London with them . . ." I'm too drained to describe the vivid image of strangling her with my bare hands, her eyes bulging out of her head.

"She'll call us if she finds anything," he says, mostly to himself. "She just needed to concentrate."

I shake my head.

"I'll bet you were one of those kids who bought dime bags of oregano in high school and couldn't tell the difference."

Courtney frowns.

"What do you mean?"

Exactly.

WE STOP AT Walgreens and buy three maps of downtown Denver, snacks and bottled coffee. It's two in the afternoon when we check into a $39/night motel in Aurora.

Courtney throws our bags on one of the two twin beds: He doesn't expect to use his.

He sits down cross-legged on the filthy carpet, pulls out his notebook, and tears the pages out—arranging them so he can see them all at once. Then spreads out the maps and circles the aquarium on all of them. He wants to chart logical paths Rico could have taken after fleeing.

I collapse on my bed. Desperately want to sleep, but it will take me a little while to wind down.

"Wanna talk anything over?" I ask.

He doesn't respond for a second, then sits back up and licks his lips.

"Sure," he says.

That's bad. If he wants to talk things over with me, it means he doesn't have anything.

"We start with the questions, Frank," he says, in a tone that's a little bit lecturey. I let it slide. "First the questions, then the answers."

"Okay," I say.

"What are the questions? If you had a genie right now and could ask him three questions, what would they be?"

I bury my nose in the pillow.

"Never mind. You just do your thing."

"Just—"

"Fine, fine," I say, turning back to face him. "Um, first. Where did Rico put the books?"

"Wrong," Courtney says.

"Wrong?" I say. "What do you mean?"

"That's not the right question. The question is: *Where are the books now?* Now, granted, the answer to both is probably the same. But we can't discount the possibility that someone else has found them already."

I roll my eyes. Think he's grandstanding a little, but whatever.

"Fine."

"Now let's call that question one," Courtney says. "In order to answer question one, we need to answer at least one of a few subquestions. Namely—"

"Where would have been the most convenient place for Rico to leave the books? Where would Sophnot 'never go'?"

Courtney nods, satisfied.

"Good."

I clench my jaw. *He doesn't have any more idea about this than I do.*

"Okay," Courtney says. "What's the second question you'd ask the genie?"

"Uhhhh." I tap my chin. "Where is Oliver Vicks at this exact moment?"

"Yes. And the subquestions?"

I sigh.

"There's a million. Why did he write these books in the first place? Why did he kill Becky's family—was it unrequited love?

Why does he need forty-eight million dollars . . ." I stop. Expounding all the things we don't know is making me feel a little sick, and even farther away from sleep.

"Yeah," Courtney says softly. "Right. All of that."

He slowly lowers his head to his notes, and his face reverts to his default frown, which means his brain is cranking up to full operating capacity.

"Courtney," I say. His head shoots up. "What did we decide about skipping town. If it's five, six in the morning and we've got nothing . . ."

Courtney's face goes a little stony.

"We'll discuss that later," he says. "I don't like planning on failure."

"We have to be reasonable though," I say. "I mean—"

"Later," he snaps, and returns to his notes. It's not angry exactly, but I nearly jump at the sudden force in his voice. He's obviously more upset about Mindy than he's letting on, just swallowing it until this is over. Poor guy. Poor Courtney . . .

"Frank. I have an idea."

Courtney is shaking me. I shoot up in bed and check my watch. I slept for seven hours, and it's nine in the evening. Pitch black outside. I don't feel the least bit refreshed. Was having nightmares, and I feel like I've been clenching myself into a ball and grinding my teeth.

"Why did you let me sleep?" I snap.

"I don't know," he says. "You just . . . you were so exhausted."

I stand up and rub my eyes. Grab for a bottle of coffee.

"Have you just been staring at that thing for seven hours?" I ask.

In response, Courtney shows me a map of Denver, now covered in a web of pen marks.

"Rogers and Stern Partners is only three and a half miles from the aquarium. It's where Oliver used to work, as an architect."

I blink at him.

"I don't get it."

"Oliver would never go back to that place—he'd be too ashamed. But more importantly, he'd be *recognized*. So that's why Rico left them there. Oliver couldn't walk in there to get the books, even if he knew they were there. But we can."

I mull this over.

"How would Rico know where Oliver used to work?" I ask

"I don't know," Courtney admits. "But same as me, I guess. An hour of Googling."

I rub my bicep.

"The office is definitely closed now," I say. "We'll have to wait till morning."

Courtney winces.

"Actually," he says, "it's a big office space. They have eighty employees. That's a lot to search so . . . I thought it would be better to go in now. When it's closed."

"Ugh, shit." I rub my temples. "Breaking into an office?"

"I don't think we'll have to break in, exactly," Courtney says. "It's on the twenty-third floor of a huge office building downtown. There should be a guard downstairs around the clock, even though the front doors will be locked, and a few people will be working late throughout the building. We should just be able to talk our way in."

"Talk our way in?"

Courtney nods.

"This isn't Manhattan, Frank. People here trust each other."

I eye him.

"You really think there's a decent chance the books are there?"

He squirms a little under my gaze.

"It's the only thing I can think of," he says—conveniently dodging the question.

"Guess we don't have a huge amount to lose," I sigh and grab the Honda keys off the dresser. "Let's take all our stuff with us," I say.

"So we can go to the airport after if the books aren't there?" Courtney asks, clearly challenging me.

I pat his stubbly cheek. He seems jarred by the physical contact. Or maybe he just noticed how grimy my hands are.

"I guess a little sleep helped me think more clearly. I realized that if we flee, Sampson will cancel my passport immediately. And they'll arrest me as soon as I come off the plane in Jakarta." I smile grimly. "I think we'll be in Colorado come Friday night, one way or another."

THERE'S A WALMART Supercenter a seven-minute drive from the motel that doesn't close until ten thirty. We stop there and buy cheap suits—for Plan A. Then duct tape, women's stockings and syringes (Courtney carries a few doses of injectable Propofol in his bag)—for the somewhat kinkier Plan B.

The traffic as we get closer to the office building is absurd. Doesn't take long to realize there's a Rockies game tonight, and our building isn't too far from Coors Field.

"Shit," I mutter, taking a sip of what will undoubtedly not be my last Red Bull of the evening. "Rockies game. Just our luck."

"I don't know how people can watch football . . ." Courtney says. I don't bother to correct him.

It's a quarter to eleven by the time we pass the building that contains the architecture firm. Problem is there's no parking. Every lot is open and catering to people here for the baseball game. But the game must have started a while ago, because the lots are all full. And you can forget about parking on the street.

Traffic is more or less gridlocked. Whether the game just ended, or these are people coming late to it, I don't know. It's taking almost four minutes to make it the length of a single block.

"This isn't gonna work," I growl.

"Keep looking, maybe we'll find something."

"What? Courtney—there's *nowhere* to park."

"Hold on, turn left here—we haven't been down this road yet."

I start obeying, then slam on the brakes as I realize there's only one lane on this road, and all the parked cars are facing toward me.

"It's a one-way road."

I reverse to get back into the "flow" of traffic—someone honks at me. I flip him off. Think about how unfortunate it would be if we get pulled over by the cops now.

"We're not gonna be able to park," I say. "Not in any conventional sense."

"What do you—"

I pull out of the traffic, and steer into a spot at the mouth of one of the full lots—in effect trapping several hundred cars inside the garage. Turn off the ignition.

"Frank . . ." Courtney seems roughly as horrified by this parking violation as he did by Rico's flayed carcass. "This will get towed in minutes."

"So we'll get a new rental. On Sampson's card." I grin. "Take all your shit."

I grab my duffel from the backseat. Courtney takes his attaché and red acrylic tool bag. We're already wearing the suits. Glad we packed light.

People stare in disbelief as we leave the Honda there. Some people seem furious, but one guy actually rolls down his window and gives us a grinning thumbs-up.

Courtney tries again Mindy on the way to the office building. Shakes his head in frustration.

We're the only people even remotely dressed up—everyone's wearing jerseys or T-shirts of Denver sports teams. Lotta college-aged kids. See some DU and CU gear. Most of these people appear extremely drunk. I wonder if Thursday nights are always this crazy—or if a sporting event in the vicinity is excuse enough, even if you're not attending.

Our destination is one of the taller buildings. A soaring rectangular prism of glass. The whole lobby floor is a Wells Fargo, and the rest is offices. Didn't have time to do much due diligence beyond that. Hopefully it won't matter.

"No guns," Courtney murmurs to me, as we stand shoulder to shoulder across the street. "There are literally thousands of cameras in there. You pull out a gun, and the cops are swarming within minutes."

"I know," I say. "Let me talk to him, okay?"

"Sure, sure." Courtney nods. "Honey, not vinegar, right?"

I restrain myself from mentioning that *he's* the one whose face always looks like he just swallowed a mouthful of balsamic.

"I know."

We cross the street, climb the exterior steps up to the revolving glass doors at the main entrance to the lobby. Inside, as Courtney guessed, the reception desk is still manned despite the hour. But there are two guys there, not one.

I breathe in deep, and then force a wide smile and rap on the glass of the locked revolving door. One of the guys looks up at me and points to a door to our right, then to the key card he's wearing around his neck:

To get in when the building is closed, you have to use your key card.

The guy looks back down to whatever he's watching behind the desk.

I knock again, and he looks up, now annoyed.

I spread my hands helplessly and pantomime: *no card.*

He looks at me blankly.

I wave him over. He looks at me like I'm crazy, and exchanges a look and a few words with his partner. They both look over at me. I smile and wave them over like, *I'll explain everything.*

Both of them wearily stand up and trot over to the revolving door. One is probably in his sixties, pink faced, probably a retired cop. The other is young and looks like a punk—I'm thinking he was a troubled juvenile who's cleaned up, and is super grateful to get this gig.

Stupid. They shouldn't have both left their post.

The old one unlocks the side door, the one you'd use your card to get in through. We rush over. The two of them are standing in the entrance.

"Sorry sir, you need your card to get in after six thirty," says the younger guy, clearly savoring his role as The Man.

Six thirty. . . we left the aquarium around what, four on Tuesday? He definitely could have just waltzed in.

"I know," I say, with genuine exasperation. "Thing is, we rushed off to a dinner meeting that, as you can see, went late. And we left all our stuff in the office including our cards. Need those materials tonight—have a huge presentation tomorrow."

The young guy crosses his arms, trying to look tough, and looks up at the older guy.

"You got ID?" Older guy asks. "Company ID or something?"

"Left it all upstairs." I shrug meekly. "Dumb, I know."

Old guy rolls his eyes, like *what morons.*

"What office?" he asks.

"Rogers and Stern, twenty-third floor."

The young guy just stands there with his arms folded. If it was up to him, he'd turn us away, I think. He's too scared to fuck up and lose this job. The older guy's just doing this job to keep busy in retirement; doesn't really give a shit.

"Alright. Come on in," the old guy sighs and limps back to the check-in desk. "Lemme check the rosters. What are your names?"

I bite my tongue.

Gig's up.

I make a move to retreat but Courtney puts a reassuring hand on my shoulder.

"Gregory White and Paul Buffet."

He clicks through something, breathing loudly through his nose.

"Rogers and Stern, right?" he confirms.

"Yes."

He frowns as he looks at the screen, then up at us.

"I had to shave my beard." Courtney smiles. "Wife wasn't having it."

The old guy mulls this for a second, then sinks into his rotating chair, relief on his face evident.

"Justin—take them up to the office and let them get their stuff."
Justin nods.

"I'll wait down here," Courtney says. "We don't both need to go up."

What the hell?

Our eyes meet for a second, and Courtney's eyes flit to the older guy. I get it, *if we both go up, we have no control over the old guy. If the old guy sees anything fishy on the CCTV, he raises the alarm.*

Maybe Courtney plans to just talk this guy's ear off. Try to convince him to go vegan. He's got hours of material in that bag.

"Okay," I tell him. "Be back in a few."

"Come on," says Justin, impatiently. I grab my duffel bag and follow him through the empty lobby to the elevators, the clicking of our footsteps echoing against the glass doors. He hits the up button, and smiles to me perfunctorily as we step into one of the six elevators.

"What floor, sir?" he asks.

"Twenty-three," I say. There's a magnetic reader on the elevator for cards, presumably needs to be used after hours. When the elevator doors don't close, I smile at Justin. "We forgot our cards, remember?"

"Oh, right." He nods, and beeps his. Elevator doors slide shut. Justin has his hands folded over his crotch. I wonder if he realizes what a classic gesture of fear that is.

That's not good. He shouldn't be afraid of me.

"You know what the score to the Rockies game is?" I ask, smiling. He shrugs.

"I'm from Arizona. Hate the Rockies."

My gaze zips to the mirrored camera discreetly tucked in

the corner of the elevator. There are cameras everywhere in the public spaces: elevators and hallways. Only once we're in the offices should the CCTV lose sight of us. Bulge in the right side of Justin's tan suit jacket. Gun. Doubt night guards at office buildings keep them loaded, but you never know. They *are* right in front of a bank.

"No kidding!" I say. "I used to live in Arizona myself. Whereabouts?"

"Tucson," he responds blandly.

"Beautiful city," I say.

"I hated it."

Strike two . . .

Doors open onto the twenty-third floor. Justin steps out first, waiting for me to lead the way.

Fuck. Fuck.

I choose right. Justin lets me walk ahead of him. I don't like that, him padding along behind me at a safe distance. I think he might be more perceptive than I gave him credit for.

"Law office, right?" he says, behind me.

I turn back and grin, stopping in my tracks to see if I can spot the name of the firm on any of the doors behind him.

"Nah, architecture firm."

Justin nods.

We don't pass the architecture office. I have to take another right, and then another. If we end up back at the elevator bank, the gig might be up.

Only thing going for me is this guy is young, doesn't want to screw up this job.

My heart drops. I see the glass entrance to Rogers and Stern now, but we're almost back at the elevators . . . it obviously would have been faster if I'd just turned left initially.

Just ignore it. Own it.

I stride purposefully to the glass double doors of Roger and Stern, as if I'd known my destination all along. Stop at the place for the card key, and turn and grin at Justin.

"You know, I don't think I remember seeing you guys around before," Justin says, little tremolo in his voice.

My stomach knots, and I turn back to the door so my face doesn't give anything away to him.

"Yeah, that's cuz you work nights," I say, forcing some humor into my voice. "I'm usually outta here at four."

"Right, right."

A little more reluctantly than I would have liked, Justin bends down and touches his key card to the lock. I hear a little magnetic click, and immediately push in the door to the firm and enter. Lights flick on automatically.

It's a beautiful waiting room. Stylish white leather couches, some interesting potted trees trimmed into perfect spheres. The wall across from the entrance is all glass, offering a stunning view of the Denver skyline. But as soon as I step in, my heart sinks. I know there's no way pallid Rico could have weaseled his way into this classy office unnoticed and just left a bag somewhere.

Never second-guess yourself in the heat of battle . . . I think . . . Maybe I'm just trying to convince myself to bail, because I'm scared.

I act like I've seen this waiting room a million times before. Turn left past the reception desk, to where the offices will be.

Oh boy.

It's a *really* big space—will take a while to thoroughly search.

The good news is that it's an open-office type layout, looks like employees work a lot at big library-style communal tables—so I won't have to break into many offices. Bad news is there are hundreds of file cabinets, and some of the tables even have built-in cabinets. No single cabinet could hold the duffel bag, but if someone took the books out, they could easily file them one at a time . . .

But who would put them in a file cabinet? Not Rico . . . not with those guys close behind me. I'd buzz into the office, hand the duffel bag to the receptionist, then scram.

I grind my teeth. I'm being overtaken by a feeling of futility. Can't really blame Courtney, the idea had a certain amount of logic, but we acted pretty impulsively. Would Rico realistically have entrusted the books to a total stranger?

Maybe he dropped them off with a note . . . saying this is for someone in particular. Maybe it is in someone's office or file cabinet.

I haven't even scoped the entire office yet. There appears to be a communal space—maybe a kitchen and break room—on the far side—and who knows, maybe more offices. Even if this is all though, it would take me at least a half hour just to do a cursory search.

I hear Justin shift behind me.

Fuck.

"You just gonna stand there, man?" he asks, finally growing annoyed. "Get your stuff and let's go."

I turn back to him. I wonder how aware he is that—being in a private office space—we're no longer being observed by his partner's CCTV. I glance down quickly at the walkie-talkie clipped to the pocket of his suit jacket.

Old model. Won't sound too crisp.

"Yeah, sorry, just had a few drinks at dinner," I say. "Actually I'm just gonna use the restroom a second, sorry."

I have no clue if there's even a bathroom in this office, or if they use a communal one in the halls. Doesn't matter. I rush around the edge of the maze of cubicles, toward the break room.

Justin comes after me.

"Sir, please. This isn't my job." He's half pleading, half losing his patience. "I need to get back downstairs. I'm not even supposed to leave the desk during my shift."

I speed up, dash around a large pillar and drop my duffel bag and pull out my ceramic knife. As soon as he rounds it after me I go straight for his right arm—the one that would grab his gun. Pull it behind his back, then wrap my right foot around his right calf and push him forwards. He face plants on the crisp white floor with an ugly smack. I fall down on top of him, keeping his arm pinned back.

"What the *fuck*," he cries . . . One hard tug back and I'd break his arm in about four places. Instead I reach inside his jacket, pull out his gun and toss it away, then turn him over onto his back and tickle his neck with the tip of my knife.

"Justin," I say softly. "I'm honestly very sorry about this."

His arm is pinned beneath him, obviously causing him great distress. He makes a sound like a dying animal. I put the sleeve of my suit jacket in his mouth.

"Listen, kid," I say slowly, seriously. "You're going to be fine. I won't cut you up unless you do something stupid. I'm just gonna lock you in an office. You'll probably be there until morning, okay? But you'll be fine. Okay?"

After a moment, he gives an unenthusiastic nod.

"I mean, I could break your arm if you want," I say. "Would

probably get you a few months of workplace leave. You want me to?"

His eyes go wide and he shakes his head frantically.

"Alright." I shrug. "Just trying to be helpful."

Keeping the blade nuzzled against his neck like a tender lover, I pull my duffel open with my other hand and remove my roll of duct tape.

I stand up. "Roll over," I command.

"Don't kill me, man," he says, rolling over onto his stomach. I bind his hands behind his back with duct tape. Tie his legs together, then put the knife down and roll him back over onto his back.

"What's your friend's name? The old guy?"

"Fuck you," he says.

I crouch down next to him.

"Look," I say, looking into his terrified eyes. "Tell me the old guy's name and you're going to wake up tomorrow morning in one piece, alright? We both know this is way above your pay grade."

"Fu—" he starts.

"Justin," I say. "If the next word out of your mouth isn't a name, I'm going to have to cut—"

"Ed," he says.

"Smart boy." I smile and pat his cheek. Then I gag him with duct tape and pull his walkie-talkie from his pocket.

"Ed?" I say into it, trying to imitate Justin's mild Latino accent, slightly high-pitched tough-guy voice.

"Yeah." Ed's tired voice comes back, as staticky as I'd hoped. Doubt he'll be able to tell I'm not Justin.

"This guy got sick up here. Throwing up. Drank too much. We'll be a little while."

"What? Sick?" he responds, sounds inconvenienced, but not in disbelief. "Goddammit. You gotta get down here. Can't be alone at the desk for longer than a bathroom break."

"Yeah, I know, but this guy is puking his guts out. Be back when we can."

A pause.

"Everything okay up there? You want me to call this in?"

"No, it's fine. He's just puking. Needs a few minutes."

"Goddammit."

"Sorry, Ed."

I take off my suit jacket and throw it over Justin's face so he can't see what's about to go down. Grab his legs and drag him into the break room. I hear a grunt as I clip his head against the door frame.

"Sorry."

I drop his legs, take a second to catch my breath. Then go out into the hall to do a lap. Figure out the best way to go about this methodically. Past the break room are four locked offices: Partner, Partner, Accounts, HR, two conference rooms and . . . a dark library. My heart speeds up.

If they were anywhere, they'd be here.

Lights in here aren't automatic. I find the switch and an enclosed domed light fixture on the ceiling flips on. It's a round room paneled in cherrywood bookcases. Reading tables, loungey hyper-trendy bean bag chairs, glazed wood floor.

Good news is this space is so uncluttered that I'd be able to spot them pretty easily. I do a slow lap around the perimeter of the room, scanning up and down each bookcase for unmarked spines of that sickly shade of yellow leather. Don't spot them. Do it a second time, to make sure, then leave the library.

"Justin?" It's the voice on the walkie-talkie. "What the hell is going on up there?"

Shit.

"Hey Ed," I say. "Sorry will be just a few more minutes. This guy is really sick."

"This is not okay."

"I know, I know."

I probably have fifteen more minutes, maybe twenty, until Ed realizes something is seriously wrong. Wonder if Courtney would risk drugging him with all those cameras around . . . ?

"Can I talk to Greg?" It's Courtney's voice.

"Yeah . . ." I say in Justin's voice. Then, in my own, I croak: "Hey man. Sorry, just, those martinis hit me all of a sudden."

"How long you going to be, man? We're supposed to be at Hannah's in fifteen."

He's telling me to hurry up. Doesn't think he can hold off Ed for much longer.

"Okay. We'll be down in ten," I say.

I run back through the communal work room, to the reception area. Dive behind it, and search frantically for anything resembling the duffel bag. Nada.

I comb the work area, looking under every table. Will just have to leave the file cabinets—unlikely someone would have taken each book out and filed it individually anyways.

No bag.

Where Sophnot will never go. Where they belong.

My face is bathed in sweat. I undo a couple buttons on my suit jacket.

I check my watch. 11:19. We have sixteen hours until we're

supposed to get the books to Sampson. I don't think they're here.

Wait.

Maybe there's something else that can help.

I rush back to the hallway with the four locked doors and try the one to HR.

It's locked, obviously. I peer into the lock. Courtney could pick it in five minutes, or I could bust through with my electric torch, but that makes a mess and is likely to set off the smoke alarms. The rest of the office, however, is a glass wall. Closed curtains.

Rush back to the break room, where poor Justin is writhing on the ground. I pull my suit jacket from his eyes. He glares up in terror.

"Don't worry, just needed this."

I snatch up my duffel bag and rush back to the HR office. Unzip my bag and find my hammer. Wrap my suit jacket around fist and hammer and bring it down as hard as I can on the glass.

The first blow cracks it. Second goes through smooth, making a head-sized hole. Takes me about two minutes to clear enough out for me to enter the office.

Automatic lights inside come to life.

There are four file cabinets. Something of a relief, actually, considering how many HRs keep their files exclusively digital these days. I rip open one at random and grin.

Personnel files.

Takes me about three minutes to move through alphabetically until I find Oliver Vicks.

Nice and fat.

I grab the walkie-talkie.

"Greg is heading down now, I'm gonna stay up here and clean up for a sec. He made a real mess," I say.

"What?" Ed is furious. "No, you get your ass down here *now* goddammit!"

I turn off the walkie-talkie, damming up Ed's stream of curses. Head back through the work room, reception office, back into the hallway. Take the elevator down using Justin's card, and shoot out into the lobby.

Both Courtney and Ed are staring at me in shock.

Realize I left my suit jacket upstairs, the top few buttons of my shirt are undone, and I'm absolutely dripping in sweat.

"Oh wow," Ed says. "You *do* look sick."

"Yeah." I smile weakly. "Justin will be down in a sec."

He notes the personnel file in my hand.

"That was what you needed?"

I nod.

"Yep. Have a good night, Ed."

Courtney and I rush out of the Wells Fargo lobby before Ed has a chance to question us any longer. Once we turn the corner, I toss the muted walkie-talkie in the trash and collapse onto a park bench. Don't realize how badly my hands are shaking.

Courtney sinks down beside me.

"No books?" he asks.

I look at him.

"Very perceptive."

"How thorough—"

"As thorough as I could be in twenty fucking minutes," I snap. I hand him Oliver Vicks's file. "I got this, but it's small consolation."

Courtney wordlessly snatches it from my hands, and opens it.

"You're welcome," I say.

He doesn't respond.

"Alright," I say. "We need to get out of here. Ed's gonna figure out pretty quickly that Justin's indisposed."

Courtney stands up.

"Which way did you leave the car?" he asks.

I can't tell if he's serious.

"I thought you understood," I say. "I left the car blocking in thousands of sports fans in downtown Denver, during a Rockies game. I'd say the odds of it still being there are—"

"Like a mouse completing a game of solitaire on the surface of the sun?" Courtney raises an eyebrow, an almost smile.

"Right, right . . ." I say, suddenly dying for a drink. "Don't expect a miracle every night though, champ."

MY SKULL MIGHT as well be filled with porridge. I'm trying to read the contents of Oliver Vicks's file, but the words refuse to cooperate; swimming around on the page like little fish.

We're sitting in a Starbucks inside the Denver Health Medical Center. Mostly because it's open 24/7, and nobody will hassle you for loitering. I think a sick part of me also wanted to be around people who have it even worse than us—just to keep things in perspective. To this end, I also picked up a half liter of the cheapest whiskey I could find. It's absolutely vile. Or at least, it was vile when I cracked it open. Four glugs later I'm starting to warm up to it.

We've been sitting here for hours. It's already nearly four in the morning. I've "read" the whole file myself, but have processed perhaps a dozen words—none of them consecutive.

"Got anything?" I ask Courtney, as I have every ten minutes for the last few hours, with largely disappointing results. Initially when he doesn't respond I assume he's in The Zone. Then I realize his eyes are nearly shut and there's a thin thread of drool oozing from the corner of his mouth. "Courtney?" I snap my fingers in front of his face and he calmly opens his eyes.

"Interesting. Mmh. Yes," he says slowly, rubbing his eyes. "Yes. Just saw some interesting things . . ."

Courtney's right eyelid starts twitching and he seems to be staring intently at something on the chest of my shirt. His head droops. I snap my fingers in front of his eyes again and he perks up, smiles in confusion.

"Hey," he says.

"Courtney? What was interesting?"

"Right, right . . ."

"Have another Red Bull," I say.

"No." He lazily swats away at nothing. "I'm good. Um, what I was going to say . . . oh, his first interview. He faked recommendation letters from real people. But there was no reason to doubt him, because of his portfolio." Courtney yawns and continues. "Listen to this note the interviewer jotted after looking through Oliver's portfolio: *Absolutely world class. Never seen such simultaneously brilliant detail kept in context of big picture. Clearly genius.*"

"Okay . . ." I say. "That's not really surprising though is it?"

"No," says Courtney. "But in the *first interview*, Oliver already made demands. One demand specifically: He wasn't going to do paperwork of any kind. No letters to clients or the city, no tenders . . . he said this stuff bogged him down. He said all he did was design. I think that kind of chutzpah would normally be a nonstarter, but because of the quality of his work in his portfolio, and the sample assignment they gave him, they hired him."

I scratch my chin.

"So now we know, that's probably because he had no clue about the bureaucratic process relating to buildings, eh? He was a prodigy at these sorts of designs, but had no idea about the logistics because he skipped school."

Courtney nods slowly, which I initially take as assent, but then realize it's his head bobbing to keep from going smack into the tabletop.

We have so many papers. In just a few days, Courtney has taken hundreds of pages of incredibly detailed notes, on everything from Sampson's story, what Mindy told us about the books, details from the scene of Rico's murder, the interview with the warden, the story of Joseph . . . Now we have Oliver's personnel file. So much data, but my data processing unit just won't function. And not only is my once potent Red Bull/coffee/whiskey tandem failing to jack me up, I think it's tearing apart my stomach lining.

Wait a second . . .

I reach down and scramble through my duffel bag.

"Where is it . . ." I mutter, scared maybe I tossed it at some point . . . No. My hands close on it. The Advil bottle I confiscated at the red house. I open it, take out a blue pill and place it on the tabletop between us. Courtney frowns.

"What is that?" he asks.

"No clue. Took it off some kids who seemed to be enjoying it at the red house."

Courtney picks it up and holds it to the light, reading the identifying numbers on it. Then types it into his phone.

"Dextroamphetamine," he says.

"What's that mean?" I ask.

"It's a particularly potent amphetamine. Used to treat ADD. You may know it by its brand name: Adderall."

"Perfect," I say. Courtney's face falls.

I snatch his phone and scan the article from the FDA website: *Oral or intranasal use produces euphoria or high. Snorting dextroamphetamine will lead to effects within 3 to 5 minutes, whereas oral ingestion takes 15 to 20 minutes, with less potent effects.*

I grab my hammer from my duffel, pour six blue pills in the middle of the table and delicately tap them into powder with the hammerhead.

"Frank!" Courtney scans around the Starbucks like a paranoid prairie dog, then back to me. "What the hell are you doing!?"

"I think it's pretty obvious that I'm grinding this into a snortable powder."

"In *here?*" he asks.

I glance around the Starbucks. It's mostly empty, and the only other occupants—a pair of nurses in lavender scrubs, a clearly distraught set of parents—appear to be dealing with their own shit. I shrug, then tear up a page from one of Oliver Vicks's professional evaluations, roll it up to make a little snorting tube. Use another bit of the paper to form four bright blue lines.

"Frank, this is not safe. I think that's a huge dose. And you've been drinking—"

"Correct." I grin. "This isn't for me."

Courtney's eyebrows fly up so high that for a second they look like two little hairy worms crawling along his forehead.

"I don't think so," he says.

"You're the one who can fit this stuff together," I say. "I'll supervise. Don't discount the stress of being in the managerial role."

"I'm not touching that stuff," Courtney says.

"I've snorted it before," I lie. "It's not a big deal. You just feel more awake."

Courtney shakes his head adamantly, like a little kid refusing his Brussels sprouts.

"Come on, man, it was prescribed by a doctor. It's safe. What is there to lose? You're so tired you can't see straight."

Courtney stares at the blue lines, frowning intensely.

"You do one first."

"One of us needs to stay sober."

Courtney crosses his arms defiantly.

"I think that's a pretty compelling argument for *me* to assume the supervisory role."

"Courtney," I sigh. "I don't claim to understand how your brain works. But I've seen you make connections that I never would have made in a million years. If we don't figure out where those books are, I'm probably going to spend the rest of my life in jail. If this stuff can help you think . . ."

He closes his eyes for a moment, then opens them, wordlessly takes the tube from me and—for quite obviously the first time in his life—snorts a line.

Leans back into his chair, and his eyes go a little cross-eyed as the stimulant trickles down the back of his throat.

"Good stuff, right?" I say, knowing full well there's no way he feels anything yet.

"I guess," he replies. "It's definitely subtle. Just feel a bit more energy."

"Yeah, that's because you only did one," I say. "Take another."

He raises an eyebrow.

"I don't know, Frank."

"If you really fuck up, the emergency room is upstairs. Hell, maybe we should just check ourselves in anyways. There are worse places to hide from Sampson and Oliver."

Courtney obligingly snorts down his second line. Coughs a little. Then taps on the table.

"I'm still tired," he says.

"Give it a minute . . ." I glance around the Starbucks again. Even if somebody had seen what we're doing, I doubt they'd give much of a shit. I take the file back from Courtney and try to read it again. The words still seem to be moving around on the page. I'd take some, too, but I meant what I said: One of us needs to keep his wits about him, be the arbiter of reason.

I close my eyes and try to concentrate.

Oliver Vicks. Oliver Vicks.

Fakes his architecture credentials, refuses to do paperwork, but gets hired anyway and is very successful until he gets found out at the hearing and shamed, starts writing these books, kills Becky's family, goes to prison, walks right out, sends Rico to steal the books, kills Rico . . .

I feel something on my wrist. My eyes snap open—I fell asleep. It's Courtney's hand. His pupils are huge and he's blinking extremely rapidly.

"I think I feel it," he says. "I can feel like, my heart, inside my chest. I can feel each palpitation against my ribs. My heart feels like, really really *big.*"

"Uh huh," I say.

"Yeah, like, my heart is so *powerful,*" Courtney says. "But okay, let's work."

He snatches the file back from me and starts combing through pages rapidly, muttering to himself. "Yeah, good medicine, Frank.

I think you were right. I'm gonna figure this stuff out. Shoulda used this before. Shoulda used this stuff *years* ago . . ."

I close my eyes again. Enter that nether zone between sleep and real life. The flickering lights of the Starbucks flash on the insides of my eyelids.

Fakes credentials, failed school, genius, megalomaniac . . . Thinks he's Joseph . . .

"Frank." Courtney is tapping on my wrist again, this time a bit more urgently.

"Figure it out?" I ask.

His head less shakes than spasms back and forth.

"My mouth is dry." He opens his mouth wide and massages his left jaw. Then closes it, cracks his knuckles in rapid succession, then starts doing what I can only describe as a sitting salsa dance—like a single move that's all clenched fists and elbows running on a loop. "My mouth is dry," he repeats.

"That's normal," I guess.

"Okay." He nods. "Okay. Good. I'm not worried, just checking."

"Okay," I say. "So. What do you think? Why would he—"

"The questions first," he says, reaching a finger into his mouth to poke at the inside of his cheek. "First we need to organize all the questions. We'll make a list. A . . . A very organized list. Then we'll just check off the answers one by one. That's our problem is we're not *organized*."

"No, our problem is we keep going in circles. We keep gathering information without *understanding* it."

"Because we're not being *organized*." Courtney leans in close. "We're not being *thoughtful* and *patient* enough. We're not paying attention to *subtlety*."

"Dude, those are just words. We don't understand jack shit. Putting this in a spreadsheet isn't suddenly gonna change that."

"Okay, okay." He nods. "So we'll just read through *everything*. *Carefully*. Start to finish. Should only take like four hours if we go fast. So that takes us to the morning—"

I tune out Courtney. Something's dawning on me, but it's elusive. Not a fact, but a feeling, a common thread winding its way through everything we know about Oliver Vicks.

Drops out of school, fakes his degree, writes the books in his own language, writes his own notes on the wall in his own language . . .

"I'll read each page, then you'll read it, then we'll summarize it—"

"Courtney," I snap. "Stop talking. Let me think."

I think about Oliver in the cellar of the red house, writing on the walls, developing his language.

Why? Why not just write in English? Or Ancient Hebrew? Or Latin?

So that nobody but him could understand it?

As sophisticated as Mindy claimed the language was, it sure looked kind of childish to me. Maybe the meaning is complex, but the drawing of the cow reminded me of the drawings Sadie used to bring home from kindergarten . . .

I sit up straight.

I think I know where the books are.

"Let me see the phone," I say.

Courtney eyes me, as if suspicious of this request, but he slides it across the table to me. I go to our text message records. Most recent is Sampson, then Mindy, then the phone Rico used to text us from the aquarium. That's all. The recent calls history is entirely consumed by Sampson . . .

"There was a phone number Oliver called us on, when we were at Sampson's," I say. "He used the voice transformer, and we thought it was Rico."

Courtney nods.

"I don't remember, but I think that's the same number he called us from when we were at Wendy's. It doesn't matter actually. My point is that he never texted us. He wanted the pictures of the bonds *faxed* to him instead of just good old text. Why?"

"Maybe because he was in prison so long he was unfamiliar with cell phones. When he was locked up fax machines were all the rage."

"Fine, could be," I respond. "But Becky's restaurant. The Rocky Mountain Bar and Grill. Did you happen to look at their menus? I did."

Courtney squints.

"Uh, maybe glanced at one. Why?"

"The deaf owner . . . He wanted to make sure the place was handicapped-friendly. Wheelchair ramps. And Braille on the menu."

Courtney nods ever so slightly.

"Okay . . ."

I grin broadly.

"That's why he didn't go to architecture school. That's why he writes in his own language. Courtney," I say. "I think Oliver Vicks can't read."

Courtney's frown turns to stone as he considers this.

"He's dyslexic," I say. "I remember there were a few weeks when they thought Sadie might be dyslexic, because she was really slow starting to read. Turned out she just needed a little more time to get started, but at the time I was really worried and spent like a month reading all about dyslexia. There are studies where dyslexic people can read Braille far more effectively than written language. I think that's why Oliver was at the grill before Becky ever started working there—it was the only place he could read the menu."

"Dyslexic . . ." Courtney's eyes are narrow, his shoulders clenched expectantly, breathing hard—he looks almost predatory.

"That's why he wrote in his own made-up language that's pictographic—he's really uncomfortable writing in English. Or maybe he can't at all."

Courtney taps his fingertips on the table like he's a stenographer taking notes on an invisible typewriter.

"Okay. I'm with you," he says. "Because even if maybe he can read a little bit, slowly, he's sensitive about this. Ashamed. He avoids any forum where he could possibly humiliate himself by making a mistake. Like text message. Or university."

"Right," I say. "And at this point, of course, he's far more comfortable writing in his own language."

He stops tapping his fingers.

"But so what?" he says. "Fine. Oliver can't read. That doesn't help us figure out where he is, or where the books are."

I lean in closer.

"Oh, I disagree."

Courtney fidgets.

"What. Tell me."

"Rico was locked up in that room for years right? He didn't have anything to do with himself but claw at his chain and look at the walls, and observe Oliver Vicks. Now even if he wasn't the sharpest guy, I think it's a reasonable assumption that after *years* in there he came to the same conclusion I just did. That Oliver Vicks just wasn't comfortable with written English. So he's running away from the aquarium wanting to stash the duffel somewhere, somewhere Oliver Vicks would never stumble upon them." I smile. "Somewhere where *books* belong."

Courtney lunges for his briefcase, combs through it frantically, until removing a map of Downtown Denver. Lays it flat on the table. Scans it desperately, until jabbing an index finger at a spot just a few blocks from the aquarium.

Something magical spreads across his features, bathing each one in turn in a shimmering glow. He forms a little *O* with his mouth and makes a sound that's disturbingly similar to one I heard last night.

"There it is Frank. The Denver Public Library," he whispers. "The public freaking library."

Part Four

Friday

Genesis 11:4
Come, let us build ourselves a city, with a tower that reaches to the heavens, so that we may make a name for ourselves; otherwise we will be scattered over the face of the whole earth.

THE DENVER PUBLIC Library doesn't open until ten. We sit down on a bench outside and wait. I wonder who designed this place . . . the exterior is like fifteen differently shaped and colored towers, from fifteen different eras, all sewn together into one architectural Frankenstein monster. I think maybe it's supposed to look industrial, a sort of parody of a massive, multitiered brick factory.

In the courtyard in front of the building are all kinds of weird sculptures; some sort of obelisks that are like enormous stone tentacles protruding from the ground, an amalgam of thick red pipes that might be fun for kids to play with during the day, but at this predawn witching hour it looks more like a trap, a web of blood-stained pipes and distended shadows.

What is with this city?

Staring at the building, my eyelids grow heavy, and I manage to doze off for a few hours.

Wrapped up in a jacket—it actually gets cool in the early hours before dawn—I have nonsense dreams. Sadie is in many of them, and even from inside of the dream I'm disturbed by how hard it is to picture what she looks like now. There's a moment where I'm walking side by side down a red velvet hallway next to Oliver Vicks, who's wearing the wax mask of Rico's face.

Concealer of faces.

I reach for his mask, take it off his face, and beneath there's a smiling headshot—that twenty-five-year-old photo that Mindy found on the internet. One of only two pictures I've ever seen of his real face.

The alarm on Courtney's phone jars me awake. Not him—he's out cold, lying flat beside me on the bench, his knees tucked into his chest, and everything enveloped by a flannel shirt. I'll bet he crashed pretty hard from that upper. I shake his spindly leg.

"C'mon Court," I say. "Library's open."

We're not the only ones waiting for the library to open. Lots of kids. Summer vacation. Some are with parents, some are in daycare-type groups. When the guards open the doors, kids swarm toward the opening, like they're worried the place is gonna run out of books.

The front doors open into a long, open hallway. An American flag and a Colorado state flag hang prominently from the ceiling, three stories up. Around the second floor stretches a panorama depicting the Denver skyline and Rocky Mountains. Archways along the length of the hallway have signs that indicate the Western Legacy collection, African-American Research Library, exhibition spaces, a place to research your genealogy . . .

Then there's the book listings: computer science & information, philosophy and psychology, religion, social sciences, language, literature.

"This place is enormous," Courtney says. "We could spend days looking through here. There are a million places he could have stashed those books."

"Let me see the text again," I say.

Courtney raises an eyebrow.

"You don't know it verbatim yet, Frank?"

I reach into the pocket of his jeans and pull his phone out. Scroll until I find it:

Left Boks wher they belong, where Soph never goes. Ya

"Ugh. 'Hey, I left the needle in the haystack for you guys.'"

"I think we're in the right place though," says Courtney.

"Me too . . ." I say, looking around to absorb the immensity of this building. "Where do the books 'belong'? Religion?"

"Sure."

We shuffle through a few rooms: galleries of Western land-scapes, empty this early in the morning, until we get to the religion stacks. Countless rows of books.

"Would he just slip them into the stacks?" I ask.

"I don't think so," Courtney replies. "They don't have stickers on them. They'd be found out pretty quickly."

"So then what the hell are we looking for?"

Courtney doesn't say anything.

"We don't have time," I say. "It's ten fifteen. Sampson is expect-ing the books at four. It would take us a week to search this whole building. At least."

Courtney licks his lips.

"Let's go to the information desk," he says. "And show them the text. Maybe there's something we're missing."

"There's nothing we're *missing*," I hiss. "It's like fifteen words. And the librarians don't know who 'Soph' is."

"What if he's talking about a different Soph . . ." Courtney says. "Sophocles . . . Should we check philosophy?"

"That's ridiculous. Fine, let's go to the desk."

The woman at the info desk is in her forties, and plump and butchy.

"Hi," I say, sidling up and smiling. "I was wondering if you could help us. Our friend wants us to find a book somewhere in here—kind of a scavenger hunt type thing."

"Alright." The librarian's face betrays no signs of comprehension.

"He sent us this kind of cryptic text. Was hoping you could make something of it."

I hold the phone out to show her. She slides a pair of reading glasses out from behind the counter—dunno why she doesn't just keep those on constantly, seeing as how she works in a library—and takes an inordinate amount of time to read the text.

"I think *Boks* is a misspelling of *Books*," she says finally.

I swallow the biggest eye roll of my life.

"We guessed the same," I say. "Anything else jump out at you? Any library lingo we might have missed?"

"What's *Soph*," she asks.

"Our illiterate friend," I say. "It's sort of a cruel joke. So where wouldn't an illiterate person go?"

She shrugs.

"Dunno."

I can feel my heart actively sinking in my breast.

"So, nada?" I ask.

"Why did he say ya at the end?" she said. "Did you ask him a question before that he's saying 'yes' to?"

"We thought it might mean yaki—" Courtney starts.

"We're not sure," I say. "Does that mean anything to you? Ya?"

She shrugs.

"Could mean the book is in the Young Adult section," she says.

Courtney's hand grabs my shoulder from behind and squeezes wicked hard. I turn to him. His eyes are blazing. I grin.

"Thanks so much," I say, turning back to the butchy librarian.

"Just doing my job," she says dispassionately. "Young Adult is on the third floor."

We must make it to the Young Adult section in under twenty seconds, scrambling up the stairs on all fours like hungry wolves.

There are kids in here. Kids around thirteen reading graphic novels while reclining in bean bags, playing some card game on a circular table, most on their laptops . . . We get a judgmental glare from the bow-tie-clad male librarian behind the info desk in here, ignore it. Scan the area.

"Okay, okay . . ." I say. Off to the right are traditional stacks of books, nine shelves high, at least ten feet tall. Computer booths . . . only place to stash them would be under the desks, but they'd be found almost instantly. Then there are the shelves meant for younger kids. These only go up to neck level and are stuffed with brightly colored volumes.

"You're Rico . . ." I mutter to myself. "You rush into this library, looking for someplace to stash these."

I look around again. The guy in the bow tie is still staring intently at us. I can't say I really blame him—I wouldn't want my kids hanging around us either. Especially Courtney. I always thought he could have had a killer acting career being typecast as a pedophile.

The guy straightens his bow tie and coughs a little conspicuously.

"You go look around those tall stacks," I whisper to Courtney. "I'll see if this guy saw anything on Tuesday."

I pad across the carpet to him. Try my best to smile. He's in his thirties—way too young to make a red bow tie acceptable. But, I do begrudgingly admit, it displays his status as an employee as surely as any name tag would.

I put my elbows on the desk and grin.

"Hi, I'm wondering if you can help me."

The guy smiles in a way I find singularly unpleasant.

"Sure. What are you looking for?"

"Were you by any chance working here last Tuesday? Late afternoon?"

He furrows his brow.

"I'm sorry, are you looking for a book?"

I flash my phony FBI badge.

"I don't want to alarm you." I lower my voice. "But we think someone may have left a bag in this section of library this past Tuesday."

He doesn't even bother looking at the badge.

"I'm sorry I didn't see anything."

"So you were working on Tuesday afternoon?"

He smiles again, too widely. And suddenly I get it:

He thinks I'm a paranoid vagrant. This is a public library after all . . .

"I don't work then," he says kindly. "Feel free to look around, the library is for *everyone*. But maybe this area isn't the best choice. This is exclusively for *children*, or their legal guardians."

"We're just going to have a quick look around." I smile at him and retreat from the desk. He smiles back, but doesn't take his eyes off me.

Shit.

I join Courtney in the Young Adult stacks.

"Hurry. The librarian thinks we're deviants."

Courtney throws up his hands.

"What the hell is wrong with you?"

"We should have worn the suits, and shaved. Just hurry. You

look through the stacks. I'm going to see if there's anywhere around here he could have just thrown the whole bag."

The YA/kids section is extensive. I weave past computer stations, kids sitting at tables reading magazines and laughing. There are other adults: parents and babysitters trying to instill in their wards a love of the written word. I glance under all the tables, behind a few bookcases that have a few inches between them and the wall.

Anybody seen a bag of books bound in human skin?

I look over at the bow-tied librarian. His eyes are locked on me from across the room. I pretend I don't notice.

The far end of this section opens into an area which an arched sign over the entrance proclaims to be *the reading garden.* A sign being held by a plastic gnome adorably insists *no shoes!* And then, double underlined, as if there's been problems enforcing this in the past, that this area is *kids only!*

The reading garden is half low-impact jungle gym, half reading nook. The floor is covered in carpeting thick enough to protect kids from themselves, like a psych ward. There are indentations in the walls where kids can cuddle up with a good book, tables covered with Legos, and something called the monkey house, which is a double-decker structure made of wood which kids can climb around in. And to my left, just inside the entrance, there's a closet where kids can kick off their shoes, hang up their coats, and drop off their *backpacks.* It's too dark for me to tell if it's there, but there's certainly room for a duffel bag in the bottom of that closet.

That's where I'd leave it. 100%.

I again peer back at the librarian. He's observing me with something that might be longing, like he's just daring me to make his day.

I gotta check that closet.

I cross under the threshold, into the reading garden. The librarian immediately picks up his phone and covers the mouthpiece, staring intently at me all the time.

I'm guessing this isn't because I'm wearing shoes.

There are only three kids in here, all playing quietly at the Lego table. I dash to the closet and my heart sinks as I see it's basically empty. No jackets, because it's summer. And no bags. It's early in the day.

And they might clear it out every night anyways . . . put everything in lost and found.

As long as I'm here, I scope out the whole perimeter of the area. The bag isn't small, and the books are a pretty distinct color. It takes one lap for me to be pretty sure they're not here. I stick my head in the window on the second floor of the monkey house. It's a room of dark wood, just high enough for a kid to crouch in. There are some stuffed monkeys in one corner, but not enough to conceal a whole bag.

"Hi."

I nearly jump out of my pants. Swivel to the left to see a young girl—probably eight—sitting against the wall. She has a big book open in her lap. My heart shoots to my throat.

It's bound in yellow leather.

Where are the rest of them?

"Hi," I say, and a high-pitched ringing whines in my right ear. "What are you reading?"

I jerk my head out quickly to check the status of the book Nazi. He's been joined at the desk by another colleague, a woman, and there's little doubt that they're discussing me. Plunge my head back into the darkness.

"What?" she says.

"I said, what are you reading there?"

"A cool book," she says.

"Looks like a picture book," I say.

She shakes her head adamantly.

"No. It's a grown-up book."

I bite my lip so hard I taste blood.

"Where did you find it?"

"Secret place. I found it yesterday."

"Could you show me?" I ask. "Please?"

"Why?"

"Because I want to read those books too."

"What's your name?"

"Frank."

"I'm Lina."

"Hi Lina." I try to smile. "Where are your parents?"

"My mom leaves me here when she works."

"Please, can you show me where you found that book? It's very important."

"You won't like this book. You won't understand."

I bite my lip so hard I taste blood.

"Do *you* understand?"

She nods wordlessly.

"What do you understand?" I say. "What's it about?"

"It's not *about* anything, she says. "It's just pretty and fun. Like Legos," she says, pointing through the wall to the Lego table behind me.

"Please." I try not to sound too desperate. "Please show me where you found that."

"If you promise," she says.

"Of course," I say. "Promise what?"

"Not to take them."

"I promise not to take them," I lie.

She nods, satisfied, then closes the book and crawls down the ladder to the first floor of the monkey house. Comes out to join me, clutching the yellow book to her chest. As soon as he sees the girl, the librarian's eyebrows shoot to the ceiling and he's back on the phone.

This time he must be calling security.

"Here," she says, leading me to one of the indents in the wall, a ledge where someone under four feet could lie down and read. She lifts up the bench to reveal a storage space underneath. I look inside and there's the green duffel bag, unzipped.

I pull it out and quickly count the books.

Please, please, please let them all be here.

They are. Twenty-three. Two of them are unbound, just held together by twine. She's holding the twenty-fourth.

I sling the bag over my shoulder, then kneel to look her in the eyes. Over her shoulder I see a rotund security guard making his way over.

"Listen, Lina," I say. "I'm very sorry, but I misled you. I have to take these books or else people are going to get hurt. Including the one you're holding."

She stares straight into my eyes, still hugging the book to her chest.

"Sir?" The security guard is at the entrance to the reading garden. "Sir, please come over here. This area is for children only."

"Please, Lina," I whisper. "If I don't have that I'm in big trouble."

She considers this for a second.

"Okay," she says, reluctantly handing me the book. "But you shouldn't read them before you sleep. They gave me weird dreams."

I throw it in the bag, zip it up and rush out to the security guard.

"I'm leaving," I say. "Sorry."

"That area is for children only," he says. I can tell he's trying to figure out whether he should let me go, or hold onto me and call the real cops. In other words, whether I'm a threat, or just a bit nutty.

"I'm a child," I say, and grin. "How do you know I'm not a child?"

"I'm going to have to ask you to leave the library," he says. "Come on, I'll escort you out."

"Alright," I say, and follow him out of the young adult section. The bow-tied librarian is so relieved to have us gone that he doesn't inquire about the green duffel bag tucked under my arm.

I SUCK DOWN my second refill of black coffee at a veggie restaurant a few blocks from the library. We ordered a red pepper hummus and chickpea fries to share, both taking tentative turns forcing some food down. I was chummy with a few murder detectives back when I was a cop. Best I could tell, there were only two types: Those who lost weight during nasty cases, and those who stress-ate and gained it. I'm glad Courtney is also in my camp—I have a grotesque memory of a colleague stuffing his face in the HQ break room while examining full-glossies of a double homicide.

The duffel bag holding the books is beside me in the booth. I thought maybe I'd feel relieved to have them in hand. But instead I feel only dread at what's yet to come today, one way or another. It's a few minutes after noon. I call Sampson on speakerphone. It takes him several rings to pick up.

"Hi," he says. I raise an eyebrow. Sampson sounds tired or

resigned. Courtney dunks a chickpea fry in some kind of vegan sauce, and then takes a tiny mouselike nibble.

"We're in Denver," I say. "Heading up soon. Should be there in an hour and a half with the books. Okay?"

A long pause.

"Okay," he says. He sounds like a sad little boy. "'Bye."

I place the phone back on the table, look at Courtney in confusion.

"What the hell?"

Courtney frowns at the phone, like he doesn't trust it after that exchange.

"Worrisome," he says. "Very worrisome."

"Finish eating and let's get up there ASAP."

"Okay," he says, then takes the phone and starts dialing.

"Who are you calling?" I ask.

"Mindy again. I'm going to tell her we have them. Don't worry, we're going straight to Sampson with them."

He eyes me warily, like waiting to see if I oppose the idea. Instead I swallow a spoonful of dry hummus. "Send my regards."

Courtney dials Mindy. Surreptitiously takes it off speakerphone. He holds his breath for a moment, then sets the phone back down and exhales despondently.

"Her phone is still off," he says. "It didn't even ring."

"Mmm," I say. "Maybe she decided to go to London."

"You'd think she'd want to stay in touch with us."

"Maybe the battery just died, Court," I say. "Or she was hit by a car. One of the two."

Courtney's face distends and I quickly add: "I'm kidding. I'm sure she has her charger with her. Listen, let's go get paid, get my passport, and take it from there."

I wave my hand in the air to get the check for our processed plants. Pay with my dwindling bankroll, and head out into the sun-drenched afternoon, my personal duffel on one shoulder, forty-eight million dollars' worth of books tucked into my sweaty armpit. At the first intersection we come to I hail a cab and poke my head into the passenger side window.

"Can you take us somewhere in Aspen?" I lean in and ask the cabbie. He laughs.

"You serious?"

I nod.

"That's three hours at least," he says. "Will cost you five hundred."

"We'll give you a thousand," I say.

He shrugs. "Fine by me. Pay up front though."

I wince.

"We're going to see Senator James Sampson," I say. "He'll write you a check when we get there."

The cabbie chortles. "Sure, pal." He starts rolling up the window. "Find another sucker."

"Wait," I say. Show him Sampson's credit card, then my phony Ben Donovan FBI ID. "I'm telling the truth. And we're federal agents—it's against the law to refuse us service."

He looks at the documents, confused, then finally buys the lie. We hop in the back of the taxi.

"You shaft me on this, I'm gonna tell whoever you work for. The gas alone—"

"We'll take care of you," I promise the cabbie.

Beside me, Courtney has formed a nervous steeple with his long fingers.

"I'm sure she's fine, champ," I say, putting a hand on his flannel-clad scapula.

He looks at me.

"You think I'm worried about Mindy?" he says. "I'm worried about what happens now."

"Huh?"

"We have to follow Sampson to the swap point, and bring in Oliver Vicks. If we don't find him first, he'll find us. He's not going to let us just walk away, not after seeing what he did to Rico in the red house."

I hiss. I kind of forgot that we'd discussed that. My face must betray me.

"You don't have to come, Frank," he says. "I'm the one who got you into this. You've done more than enough. I'll go myself."

I STEP OUT of the taxi and press the gate buzzer for at least ten minutes before Sampson's weary voice crackles through.

"Yeah?"

"It's Frank and Courtney."

A pause.

"Door's unlocked. In my office."

Then a buzz and the gate retreats.

"This really where Senator Sampson lives?" the driver asks, taking in the nude statues, manicured grass and of course, the glass monstrosity that seems to be swallowing the harsh afternoon sun and spitting it back out violently in our faces.

"It is," I respond.

"Always knew he was a weirdo." He looks back over his shoulder at us as he pulls into the driveway. "You two are feds . . . is he in trouble?"

I don't respond. Courtney says: "We're all in trouble."

I tell the cabbie to keep the car running while I dash in to get

Sampson and his checkbook. Courtney stays back. Hairs standing up on the back of my neck as I step in through the unlocked door. Three days ago, Sampson would have chopped off the baby-maker all over again to get those books back. And now he can't even be bothered to meet us on the front porch?

Something is very wrong.

The transparent rooms induce a wave of nausea . . . evoke that night I saw Sampson whipping himself. I make my way as fast as I can to his office, in the Spine. Big wooden door is ajar, as is the one leading into his office. Takes my eyes a moment to adjust to the darkness, realize Sampson is sitting hunched on his brown leather couch in a bathrobe.

"Senator," I say, stepping in.

"Hi," he says, without even looking in my direction.

"We need you to write a check. We took a cab here."

Soft exhale.

"Checkbook is on my desk. Sign it yourself."

I steal a glance at him as I rush to his desk. He doesn't even notice. This is the first time I've seen him without his hair perfectly combed. The skin on his face is pinched and pale. At his feet are perhaps forty empty Diet Pepsi cans.

The phones on his desk are dark, and I see that their cords have been ripped from the wall.

I wonder how long a Senator can call in sick, before the press gets wind . . .

"Are you alright?" I ask, the answer already pretty damn self-evident.

"I can't go out there," he mutters, waving vaguely in the air.

"Where?" I ask.

"It, it . . ." he says. "It's driving me *crazy*," he snaps bitterly.

I decide to clarify this later. I find his checkbook and rush out of the office, through a few glass rooms, and back to Courtney—who has the books slung over his shoulder—and the cabbie. Write him a check for $1,200 and sign it myself.

"Thanks, man." The cabbie grins.

"The extra two hundred is to not tell anyone about any of this," I say. We wait till the driver leaves, then Courtney turns to me.

"What's he like?" he asks.

"Bad," I say. "Really bad." I bite my lip. "I just realized, he didn't even ask me about the books."

Courtney frowns, then follows me back into the house.

Back into the office. Sampson doesn't look to have budged an inch. We sit down across from him, in the same chairs we were sitting in when he showed us his stump, and throw the duffel bag on the coffee table. Courtney unzips it, pulls one out and displays it to Sampson.

"Here they are," Courtney says. Sampson doesn't even glance up. Just takes a long, sad slurp of soda.

"Thank you," he says emptily.

"So," I say, leaning in, "I know it took a few extra days, but the job has been done, as you liked. So there's the matter of—"

"I can't pay you," Sampson says. "I have nothing left. Take whatever you want from me. Take the cars before they're seized. Some of my furniture is worth something. I have some watches . . . whatever. Take whatever you want. I'm sorry."

I swallow.

"And my passport . . . my identity . . ."

"Fine. All the papers are in the top drawer of my desk. Take them. What do I care." Sampson finishes his Diet Pepsi and drops the empty can, letting it join the growing pile at his feet with a clatter. "He took my money. Not Rico. Him. Sophnot."

I hear Courtney's sharp inhale beside me. I bite my lip.

"Half of the other eight million were phony," he says. "I couldn't get more than four. Sophnot tried to liquidate them, and called me . . ." Sampson's voice is trembling, and he's staring at the space between us. Then he reaches into the bag and pulls out a book. Studies it with something like disgust, and drops it back in. Neither Courtney nor I say anything.

"I know I can't understand everything he does, but I don't know what I did to deserve *this*." Sampson shakes his head slowly. "He's taken everything from me."

Courtney clears his throat.

"Well we still have these. We know they're worth *something*. Mindy . . ." Courtney trails off, not wanting to incriminate her. Sampson hardly seems to have heard him, in any case.

His drink shakes along with his usually steady hand. And then he drops the still-full can onto the carpet, and collapses, slipping off the couch into his pile of empties, clutching his sides and sobbing.

"Oh god," he moans into the carpet. "Oh sweet, sweet Lord. Please, *please* . . ." A chill shoots down my spine. "Please help me. I've made so many mistakes. I deserve nothing, I know . . ."

What *has* he done?

We let him cry for a while, awful choking sobs, sounds like a cat being strangled. Finally, Courtney can take it no more.

"What are you talking about?" Courtney asks. "What did Oliver do?"

Amidst his cries, Sampson manages to gesture to the fax machine beside his desk.

Courtney and I are there in a second. There's two dozen pages in the tray; received faxes. Courtney grabs them before I can.

"Cover page says these were sent today at nine-thirty this morning," he says, then tosses the cover page aside. The first page is a picture of Sampson, posing naked, looks like for a timed camera. His face looks younger, but it's post-surgery. In fact, it looks like the point of this photo is to display his new anatomy.

"Where's this from?" Courtney demands.

"I sent it to him," Sampson whimpers. "A lot of pictures. As proof that I did as he instructed."

Once it's clear that they're all in the same vein, Courtney combs through them pretty quickly, until arriving at a second cover sheet.

"Sent at ten this morning," says Courtney. He lets this page fall to the floor, and then stops breathing.

The next group of pictures is all Mindy. She's sitting on a wooden stool, a copy of this morning's newspaper on her lap. Around her neck is a thick leather collar.

Courtney drops the pictures onto the wood floor, puts his head in his hands.

"Oh god," I say. "Court—" I try to put a hand on his shoulder, but he slaps it away. Wordlessly walks back to Sampson and sits down on the couch, over his writhing form.

"What happened, James?" he says, with terrible calm.

"I don't know!" Sampson howls. "Yesterday he started to threaten me, what would happen if he didn't get the books. I told him he would! I told him it was all going to be fine, but then he sent those pictures. Of me. And then he took *Mindy*. I don't know how. And he says if he doesn't get his books he'll slaughter her and send those pictures to the press."

Courtney breathes fast.

"Alright," he says, voice wavering. "So we'll just go give him the books now and everything will be fine."

"But it doesn't matter. *He* took my money! It was all some kind of *game*. He took everything from me." He gestures to his groin. *"Everything."*

Courtney rises a few inches out of his chair.

"Call him," Courtney says softly, voice trembling. "Tell him you have the books and ask where to bring them."

Sampson rolls onto his side and vomits, violently retching through his cries, his whole body heaving in anguish.

"I can't call him," he whispers. "I can't talk to him. I'm so ashamed."

Courtney shoots to his feet, upends the glass coffee table which Sampson is cowering under, and lets it crash off to the side. He bends over Sampson and grabs him by the hair, jerks his head up until it's even with his.

"Call him!" Courtney roars. "Call him!"

Sampson looks up at Courtney with eyes more dead than alive, and then sullenly pulls his cell phone from his pocket. Puts it on speaker as it rings. The Darth-Vader voice answers immediately.

"Yes?"

"I, I . . . I have the books, Father." Some horrible mix of saliva and vomit dribbles down Sampson's chin. "Where shall I bring them?"

"Bring them to me in the prison, and we will study and celebrate the Sabbath together."

Courtney wrenches Sampson up a few inches by his hair and whispers in his ear.

"Father . . ." the Senator says into the phone. "What about the girl. What about Mindy?"

A short pause.

"She's learned to read the holy writings meant only for my eyes. The punishment for that is death. She will be sacrificed this Sabbath."

"But the pic . . . the pictures?" wheezes Sampson.

"Bring me my holy writings, and I will deal with you as if you were my own son. With nothing but love and compassion."

"Okay," Sampson gasps. "Okay."

Courtney hangs up the phone.

"How could he bring her into the prison?" Courtney grabs Sampson's neck and lifts the much larger man up until their eyes are nearly level. He's choking him a little.

"Courtney, easy," I say. My partner doesn't seem to hear me.

"How could he bring a girl into that prison?" Courtney demands. "Is he a prisoner or not!?"

"I don't know any more than you!" Sampson cries. "You heard him. He wants the books delivered to the prison."

Their noses are nearly touching.

"We're going now to fix your mistakes." Courtney shakes his head like a doll. "You understand that right?"

"Yyyes. Yes."

"Frank, check that your papers are in the desk."

I move to the desk and slide open the top drawer. There's a passport, a Social Security card, a birth certificate and a driver's license. My new name is Grant McRoberts.

"They look good, Court," I say, flipping through the heavy pages of the passport.

"All of Frank's new information is in the system?" Courtney demands from Sampson. "All those documents are legit?"

"I . . . Yes. It's all in the system."

Courtney lets Sampson drop, and the Senator lacks either the will or the strength to prevent his limp body from smacking back against the ground. Courtney zips the duffel bag back up and slings it over his shoulder. Stands over Sampson, glowering at him with revulsion.

"You should never have gotten us into this mess," Courtney says.

"I'm sorry," Sampson wheezes. "I'm so sorry."

"Give me the keys to the Hummer," Courtney says.

"On my desk."

"You're not a bad person," Courtney says. "I mean that."

Sampson looks up from the floor, face ashen, a bleak kind of hopefulness in his eyes.

"You're just weak," Courtney says, and for a second I think he's going to spit on the Senator. "Horribly, horribly weak."

He turns to me.

"If you leave now, I won't hold it against you."

I wince. Look down at my feet at a picture of Mindy, gasping for air through the thick collar.

I was never her biggest fan, but nobody deserves that.

And even if she did, there's simply no way I can let Courtney go meet Oliver Vicks alone.

"You drive."

COURTNEY'S KNUCKLES ARE white on the steering wheel. Since pulling out of Sampson's estate, he's been gripping it feverishly with both hands, like he's trying to strangle the life out of the Senator by proxy with his vehicle.

"Is Oliver Vicks coming and going from prison as he likes?" I ask. "Is that possible?"

"All we know about what happened there is based on what the warden told us," Courtney says. "Either he's remarkably unaware of what's happening right under his nose, or he lied to us."

"Why?" I say.

"Think about it," Courtney says, eyes pinned to the dotted yellow line on the highway; he's going so fast it appears solid. "He thought we were from the FBI. Instead of admitting that he *still* doesn't have control of his own prison, he made it sound like the problem was all resolved. And it worked. We left him alone."

I breathe through my teeth. Courtney takes the exit for Golden. According to the GPS, we're twenty minutes from the prison. It's about five thirty, but it's a long summer day. Still no trace of dusk.

"Let me see your phone," I say. Courtney pulls it out of the front pocket of his ratty jeans and hands it to me. "I'll call him."

"Speakerphone," Courtney insists.

He picks up after one ring.

"Nathan Heald," he says.

"Hi, Nathan, it's Ben Donovan. Me and my partner visited you a few days ago to discuss Oliver Vicks."

"Hi Ben," he says. "What can I do for you?"

"We have reason to believe Oliver Vicks is still in your facility."

Heald pauses a moment.

"I told you what happened. He hasn't been here for years."

"I know what you told us. I'm suggesting that it may not have been accurate. Is there a chance that he's continued to operate from your prison, without your knowledge? That some of your officers are loyal to him?"

Heald laughs.

"If a mouse moves in this prison, I know about it."

"Oliver Vicks is in your prison," Courtney shouts into the phone. "And he has a woman with him."

Heald sighs.

"You're welcome to come inspect my prison, but I think you'll both be sorely disappointed."

"We'll take you up on that," Courtney snaps, reaches over and ends the call. "He's bluffing. Lying to save his own ass."

There's a vein pulsing in Courtney's neck and the speedometer is ticking past 100. We rapidly advance on a red Chrysler. Courtney accelerates to pass it so abruptly that I think I can feel the g-force pinning me to my seat. The countryside is blurring into a sage-colored soup.

"Courtney," I say, "slow down. Pull over."

He doesn't seem to hear me.

"Pull the fuck over!" I yell in his ear.

He slams on the brakes and jerks the Hummer onto the shoulder.

"What?" he snaps, breathing hard. "Every minute we wait it becomes more likely he'll kill her."

"Courtney," I say as calmly as I can. "Something very wrong is going on there. Either because he's an idiot, or because he's complicit, Heald is letting Oliver Vicks come and go as he pleases. It sounds like there's a guard at the front gate waiting for us. So . . . obviously we're not going to just bring the books in with us."

"What?" Courtney's eyes narrow.

"Let's not be rash. We'll stash the books outside, go in and see what's going on, see what he's done with Min—negotiate to get Mindy back, then we'll go get the books and bring them to him."

Courtney's cheeks are cherry-red, narrow face tight with concern.

"I don't want to negotiate with him."

"Look man, what's the most important thing to you. Getting Mindy back, right? Prison security is going to take our guns. So if we go in with the books like a couple of chumps, Oliver or his guy will just take them with a smile and then it's all over. But we go in *without* the books, we have a chance to draw things out. Negotiate."

Courtney is silent for a moment.

"Court, I know you're eager. But we can't be stupid about this. Gotta be thoughtful. Patient."

He smacks the steering wheel with a flat palm.

"Fine," he says. "Fine, fine, *fine*. Where you wanna put them?"

Outside the car window is nothing but gently sloping hills. Boulders as grey as bone, waving grain, trees that seem to be hunched, cowering as if hiding from the fierce sun. Beside the highway runs a little creek.

"C'mon," I say, stepping out, swapping leather upholstery for gravel and dust. Courtney gathers himself for a moment, then slams his door and comes out to join me.

I scan the landscape, looking for someplace that I know will stand out enough for us to identify later. About every twenty seconds a car zooms past, throwing up a little cloud of dust that stings my eyes.

"You want to leave them out here?" he says. "In the middle of nowhere? What if it rains? They'll be ruined."

"We're only a fifteen-minute drive from the prison," I say. "We'll go in, figure out what the fuck is going on in there, then come back and get them. It hasn't rained in weeks. It's not gonna rain in the next few hours."

Courtney bites his lip.

"What if he gets upset, Frank? And hurts—"

"We *want* him upset." I glare at Courtney. "Listen, I know you got a thing for Mindy, but you gotta get a grip here. He's in your head, man. Think about it, if you're scared about the books being damaged, think about how freaked out *he'll* be. That's called leverage."

Courtney shifts his weight uncomfortably.

"Okay," he says.

"We'll leave our guns in the bottom of the bag too. If someone brings us back here to collect them we can blast their brains out. And we can't bring them into the prison with us anyways."

I unholster my Magnum, give it a nostalgic once-over, and tuck it in the duffel bag.

"I gave mine to Mindy," he says. "At the red house."

I don't respond to that. I'm sure he's thinking the same thing I am:

Did she even get a shot in at whoever abducted her?

Wordlessly, we look around us for a place to stash the bag. A dry breeze flaps through my T-shirt.

"There," Courtney says, guiding my line of sight with his spindly finger. Perhaps fifty meters from where we're standing, the earth curves up into a modest hill, and halfway up there's a low tangle of bushes that contrasts a bit with the landscape, on account of their purplish blue color.

"Let's just bury them," I say.

"Digging a hole that big will take forever," he says. "C'mon."

We have to jump over a little wooden fence that runs parallel to the highway. I wonder if this is private property.

It's farther than it looks to the blue bushes. We step awkwardly through high grass, sharp rocks, avoid little bramble bushes that have prickly burrs that stick to your pants. Despite my best efforts, I have a million little brown husks wrapped around my ankles by the time we get to the bush. Try to pick one off and it pricks my finger.

The purple bush thicket is very dense, and covers as much area as a baseball diamond. I bend down to sniff a prickly blue pine branch. It smells fresh and springy.

"What is this, juniper?" I ask Courtney. Juniper, I think, is the only kind of bush I know.

"Some type of dwarf evergreen," Courtney says.

I scan across the canopy of needles. At some points it grows taller than me.

"How are we gonna remember where we put them exactly, Court?" I ask.

Courtney scratches his scalp, then roots around in his red bag, pulls out a small tube of black spray paint.

"Why do you have that?" I ask.

"For security cameras." Courtney looks up at me like I'm an idiot. "Obviously."

He squats at a little red boulder that rests on the dirt and sprays a *C* on the face of it. Then picks up another small boulder, sprays an *F*, and places it at the edge of the thicket.

"I don't think you'd notice these if you weren't looking for them," he says, content, "these two form a straight line into the bushes. You crawl in a couple meters and drop the bag."

"Me?" I say. "What the fuck."

He picks at his scalp.

"Too cramped in there, you know . . ."

I roll my eyes. Forgot about his claustrophobia.

I get down on my stomach next to the *F* boulder, put the duffel out in front of me to protect my face, and crawl ahead, soldier style. Pine needles and branches immediately claw at my body. I can hardly see anything; the branches above block out most of the light in here. It's kind of like being at the bottom of a deep swimming pool, the surface seeming miles away. I have to keep my eyes closed every time I move anyways, to avoid them being scraped and poked.

I push forward, having to really muscle the brambles out of my way, and once I'm pretty sure I'm at least a few body lengths deep, I release the bag.

It's going to be nearly impossible to rotate and go back head-first. Equally implausible is standing: The branches are so thick over my head that I don't think I could push through. They're just thin enough close to the ground to maneuver through.

"Courtney?" I yell.

No response. I guess the sound in here is really muffled by the foliage.

I push backwards, going feet first through the path in the bush I cleared on the way in, and am deeply relieved when I feel my feet break out. I scurry out backwards and pant for breath. I'm sweating very heavily and can feel scratches all over my face and arms.

I glare at Courtney as I stand up and try to brush the dirt off my shirt, pants and arms.

"These neuroses of yours sure do come in handy, don't they?"

We lope back down to the car, me not even bothering to avoid the stick burrs. My lower back is killing me from the crawl.

When we get back to the car, Courtney spray paints a crude X on the gravel shoulder. I climb into the passenger seat and close the door.

Courtney walks around the front of the car and sidles into the driver's seat, turns the key and cranks the AC.

"We're going to get fucked, you know," I say, panting. "We keep thinking we've figured everything out. But at every turn we get fucked."

"I disagree." He frowns. "At no point during this have I thought we had anything figured out."

Before pulling the car back onto the highway, Courtney rips open his red acrylic purse and riffles through it with trembling fingers. Finally removes two plastic tubes, each a little narrower than a drinking straw, sealed at both ends. He holds one up to the sun, squints.

"What the hell is that?" I ask.

"Blowgun," he says. "Loaded with a poison dart."

He peels off a layer from the outside, and I see the whole outside is sticky like tape.

"It goes between your gum and your cheeks," he explains, and hands one to me.

I take the lethal instrument from him with the pads of my fingers. I frown at the little tube.

"What if it pricks my gums? What if I swallow it!?"

"It's sealed. When you're ready you roll it with your tongue until it's just sticking out from between your lips. Then blow, and it will pierce the seal and fire."

I peel the tape off the tube and use the rearview mirror to slide it into my cheek. He tapes in his own, and then jerks the Hummer into gear and takes us back onto the highway. A blue vein is pulsing in his slender neck.

"How hard is it to aim?" I ask. "Easier or harder than blowing kisses?"

"Not hard," he says. "Aim for the chest, just like you're shooting a gun, but anywhere it pierces the skin will do the trick. There's enough Tetrodotoxin in here to kill a horse. A person, even a large man, should be paralyzed in under a minute. Death in three."

"Christ."

"If it's all the same to you," he says, "if it comes to it, I'd like to be the one to kill him."

Courtney's grip on the wheel is so tight, his shoulders so tense, that his sinewy biceps are quivering like frightened kittens. This man is vegan—doesn't even eat *eggs* because he thinks it's cruel. Oliver Vicks has filled my gentle friend with all-consuming blood-lust. In this sense, Oliver has already won.

As we approach Saddleback Correctional Facility, the highway straightens, and the earth flattens, like we're on Satan's private boulevard.

The vein in Courtney's slender neck bulges rhythmically with his pulse. It's just past six. The sun is closer to dipping behind the mountains than it is to hanging over our heads.

"Listen," I say. "Again. I appreciate the irony of me saying this to you, but try to stay calm and patient. You're more riled up than me. Let me talk."

Courtney doesn't respond. He's hunched forward against the wheel like he's urging the Hummer to gallop even faster. Watching Courtney, I have the fleeting sensation that the car is being propelled by his sheer willpower.

The prison walls rise in the horizon like they're growing from the earth in fast-motion. I realize my hands are shaking in my lap, and the chest of my T-shirt is soaked in sweat.

"Courtney," I repeat. "I'll do most of the talking, okay? And

I'm not blowing this thing until we're sure we have an escape route."

"If he . . ."

Courtney trails off limply. I suspect I know what he's thinking: If he's done the same to Mindy he did to Rico . . . cooler heads will not be prevailing.

We grind to a halt at the front gate to the prison. The first checkpoint. A dozen khaki-clad guards mill around a gate, a few sitting in booths behind bulletproof glass. I glance up at the guard towers resting along the tops of the walls garnished with barbed wire.

One of the COs, a slender man, approaches the car.

"Let him talk first," I mutter to Courtney.

Courtney has our phony IDs out before the officer sticks his head in the window. The CO's cheeks are thin and creased with worry, but his polarized sunglasses betray little else.

"Help you?" he says, disregarding the IDs. "Visiting hours are Monday, ten to two."

So how was Sampson supposed to get in?

"Warden Heald is expecting us."

The guard blinks.

"Just a sec," he says.

He walks a few meters away—out of earshot—and speaks into his walkie-talkie. Nods. All the other guards blankly assess us, as if we're just part of the dull landscape. My throat is suddenly terribly dry . . . can't remember the last time I drank anything. The guard returns.

"You two were here a few days ago right?"

Courtney nods.

We run through the same deal as we did a few days ago. Car

search, vigorous pat down . . . I don't recognize any of the guards from last time, but they all run through the procedures in almost identical, mechanical fashion. This time though, it's infinitely more discomfiting giving up our tools, knowing Oliver Vicks is somewhere in here.

Would I even know him if I saw him? Our photos of him are so old.

They don't search our mouths, and the blowguns don't set off the metal detector—that dart probably has less metal content than a filling. The only holdup is the iPhone.

"No phones or cameras," says the CO drearily.

Courtney narrows his eyes.

We might need this to call Oliver. Tell him we're here . . .

"We keep the phone," I say. "If you have a problem with that, call the warden."

The wormy guy conducting the search, who doesn't look accustomed to making tough calls, wilts, and hands the phone back.

"Keep it in your pocket," he says. "No pictures."

Sergeant Don is waiting again at the end of the tunnel. His slight hunch makes him look like a dog excited to see us. He's standing beside three big-chested COs, who all dwarf him.

"I knew you'd be back." He smiles, eyes shining. I can almost see my reflection on his sweaty head. Looks like polished obsidian. "Nobody can resist this place!"

"That's right," I say.

He leans forward and peers into my face.

"What have you seen since you were last here," he says, not as a question. And then he promptly turns and walks the same way we did last time, toward the admin building.

We don't even try to make small talk this time, as they lead us through the same door in a chain link fence as tall as three men, one of several nested interior barriers.

We walk along another chain link fence, toward the admin building. On the other side is the big dusty yard. This time it's filled with hundreds of prisoners in identical grey onesies. Weeds spring up through cracks in the basketball court cement. There's some cheap plastic lawn furniture in one corner, beside a bench press and smattering of dumbbells. At the edge of the yard, the tall white brick buildings that house the cell blocks seem to be taunting me with their innocence. They could just as easily be college dorms or low-income apartment buildings.

The inmates glare at us as we walk past, with some kind of revulsion.

To the west of the yard, behind another fence, the construction on the new tower looks to be done for the day, and the white tarps have been removed.

The bottom ten floors are fully finished, the others are partially outlined in scaffolding, I-beams, metal, and strange, colorful shapes that glimmer in the dying sunlight and are impossible to discern from down here on the ground. The exterior of the tower though does not look normal. From our distance, still two chain link fences away, the outside reminds me of the scales of a sand-colored crocodile.

Apart from the glimmering glass top, each windowless floor is demarcated by horizontal stripes. There's something horribly organic about the color and texture of the tower's exterior—like it's the finger of a subterranean giant pointing toward heaven, or a distended, dried-out earthworm.

As we continue on the dirt path toward the admin building, nearing the tower, I see that there's a raised wooden platform at its base. Last time we were here it was covered in tools and construction equipment, but now it's totally cleared off. And on three stools sit three forms, all burdened by glinting chains. Two in khaki CO uniforms.

The third is Mindy.

Courtney falls out of line, and presses his face into the chain link fence, stares in disbelief at the tower, the hundreds of unruly looking inmates milling around its shadow, and Mindy. The hot sun beats down on them mercilessly. It's hard to see from this distance, but it looks like Mindy is wearing some kind of sackcloth and tied up so tightly she can't move.

He turns to our escorts, eyes wide.

"Do you see this?" he gasps. "There's a woman there—what the fuck. Go get her!"

Two of the big COs manage to keep stiff poker faces. The third can't contain a grimace at the prospect of entering the yard.

Sergeant Don exhales slowly and rubs a palm over his slick head, like to make sure it's still well lubricated. Then he walks to Courtney and places the same palm on his shoulder.

"It's a delicate situation," he says. "We can't go in there. All will become clear."

Courtney rears up to his full height.

"Delicate?" He gestures helplessly. "You're corrections officers! You're the ones with the guns! Go unlock her!"

Sergeant Don nods patiently. He seems totally unperturbed by the scene on the other side of the yard.

"The warden will explain. Come on."

Don and the officers gesture for us to keep following them. Courtney stares at me in shock, mouth half agape.

"What . . ." he tries to muster.

"I don't know," I say, grab him around the waist to fall back in line. "I know. Something's fucked. Keep your head."

Courtney's eyes are glued on her as we near the admin building. She and the two chained officers are sitting totally still beside what must be the entrance to the tower: a yawning black hole as tall as two men.

The guards lead us to the same entrance of the administration building as last time. I have to grab Courtney by the elbow and pull him inside, so reluctant is he to let Mindy out of his sight.

We lock eyes for a moment in the white plastered hallway as we follow the officers through the lobby. His distraught face belongs in some black-and-white documentary about war atrocities.

"What's going on here?" he whispers.

"I don't know."

I subtly tap the cheek holding the dart.

We just have to get in to see Oliver. Then we can end this.

Courtney's eyelids are twitching real bad and his hands are bright pink. I've seen this before—on guys withdrawing from a serious substance, just before they snap and do something they regret.

The lobby is a loud buzz of inefficient, decades-old air conditioners, dispassionate employees in stiff short-sleeved white button-downs—all men. I shudder. They all know a woman is in the stocks a few hundred meters away, but seem to be going about their business as usual.

Oliver Vicks is close. I try not to believe in chakra or "vibes," but whether he's sitting in an office somewhere in this building, or in a cell across the yard from here, I'm suddenly positive he's somewhere inside of this facility. I feel it—a kind of vibrating in my chest, or tingling in my temples, like wherever he is, he's emitting a sort of awful electricity.

Like last time, only Sergeant Don squeezes into the old elevator with us. I force a smile as the elevator begins its creaky ascent. The withered man smiles back.

"When I'm scared," he says, "I like to pray."

"Why don't you just do something about it?" I ask. "Go into the yard and get her."

Sergeant Don laughs.

"I was making a suggestion for you two. I fear nothing. I walk in the footsteps of the Lord."

I taste bile in my throat.

Have we just walked into a trap?

I force myself to smile.

"Yes." I swallow. "Maybe we'll pray."

Courtney's arms are crossed across his shallow chest, and he's staring at the dirty elevator floor, trying to contain his shock and rage.

I rub my tongue over the sheath containing the dart, confirming I haven't swallowed it. Just have to convince the warden to get us in to see Oliver . . .

The elevator doors open into the drab waiting room. The warden's assistant—*Allen?*—looks up briefly from his computer when we walk in and says, "Take a seat."

Sergeant Don again takes a seat across from the two of us and sits gripping his veiny biceps. The AC is loud in here, as is Allen's percussive typing. I check my watch: a quarter to seven.

"It's late," I say to Sergeant Don. "When do you head home?"

He smiles like this is a joke.

"I'll rest when my work is done," he says.

I turn to Courtney, sitting with his knees together, hands clinched into fists on his lap, thin eyebrows knitted in anguish. He tugs nervously on the bristles of his burgeoning mustache. I want to talk to Courtney, but don't want Don to overhear. Want to talk it through with him:

So the warden is just letting these prisoners, and Oliver Vicks, do whatever the hell they want?

Courtney is doing something weird with his hands. Trying to signal me. He has two fingers outstretched on his left hand, four on his right.

He looks at me, then to his hands, his pupils are oscillating from side to side ever so slightly, like his eyes are marbles floating in a glass of unsteady water. His complexion is green.

I give him a look: *What?*

Look at my hands.

Two and four? Six?

Sergeant Don looks away for a moment, and Courtney mouths: *twenty-four,* and nods with his head in the direction of the elevator.

I look at him confused. *Twenty-four what?*

He mouths: *floors.*

Floors? He must be talking about the tower outside. The one Mindy is chained in front of. My stomach does a little somersault as I realize what Courtney is trying to convey. Twenty-four floors. Twenty-four books.

That is Oliver Vicks's tower. And the inmates are building it for him.

"You two can go in," says Allen.

He buzzes us through the first door, into the closet-sized hallway. I'm about to ask Courtney to clarify if I understood what he was saying correctly, when Nathan Heald pulls open the interior door to his office.

"Welcome back, detectives."

He's wearing a different, but equally unflattering Hawaiian shirt. Thick horizontal stripes of alternating hues of bright purples, set against silhouetted palm trees. The shirt seems purposely designed to display his paunch, like it's some kind of trophy.

"Come on in," he says.

Thanks to the western exposure, and translucent lime-green curtains, his office feels a little like we're on the inside of a kiwi. But maybe due to our collective mood the air feels dark and heavy in here. He sits down behind his desk with a little hiss of relief. Picks at his salt-and-pepper beard with agitation. Courtney glares at him with withering contempt.

"There's a woman chained up in your prison yard," he says as calmly as he can. "And you aren't doing anything about it. I think you better start explaining. We know you lied to us. Oliver Vicks is still here. And by the looks of it, you've lost control of this facility."

Heald remains remarkably poised.

"And what would you like me to do?" he asks.

Courtney leans forward in his seat.

"We're going to need to speak to Oliver directly," Courtney says. Heald shakes his head.

"No chance. None of my men will set foot in the yard."

"You lied to us." Courtney's face turns crimson. "You said he wasn't here. He's been coming and going for years, hasn't he?" Courtney shoots to his feet and points to the lime-colored window. "Do you know what is going on out there? What your prisoners are building?"

Heald stays completely still.

Courtney strides to the window and pulls back the curtain to reveal the tower.

"Do you understand what the books are?" he half yells at Heald.

The warden is silent for a moment, then gives the slightest nod of his balding head.

"Yes."

"They're blueprints, aren't they?" demands Courtney, who then jabs a finger out the window. "For that thing. And you're *letting them build it!*"

Heald lowers his forehead into his palms, then sits back up straight, his thick bifocals filled with pain.

"That's just how things work around here. Oliver has run things inside of that fence for a decade. There's nothing I can do about it."

"You could have reported it years ago," I say.

"By the time I realized what was happening it was too late," he says. "I didn't know which of my men were loyal to him . . . they would have killed me."

"Where is he," Courtney spits, his eyes twitching in rage. "Right now?"

Heald gestures helplessly in the direction of the prison yard.

"He'll never let you get close. I'm sorry."

"Order your men to go in there and get her *right now,*" Courtney says, "or we're calling this in."

"Call it in? To who, the FBI?" The warden leans forward and puts his elbows on his desk. "How stupid do you think I am? I know you two aren't from the FBI. I've been in law enforcement for forty years, and if you two are FBI agents, I'll eat my shirt. I figure you two are true crime junkies, investigative journalists or something, that got caught up in something way out of your depth. And it was all fun and games, but now you're realizing that somebody might get killed"— Heald gestures to the window—"because you poked your noses into something you shouldn't have. But I've got good news."

Courtney is still standing by the window, trying to hold a poker face together. My heart is beating so fast it feels like my head is going to explode from blood pressure.

"I don't want anyone to die today either. And if we keep Oliver happy, nobody will. I can get Oliver to let the woman go. I'm sure of it. You just need to give me the books you're holding onto—that's for him—and turn over any written or photographic evidence of *anything* you've seen or heard relating to what's happening in this prison—that's for me. Do that, and you two and the woman walk away."

Courtney starts to say something and Heald holds up his palm in protest.

"And think carefully about lying to me, telling me you don't have the books. I happen to be pretty sure that you do. That's the only reason I'm even talking to you right now. But if I'm wrong about that, well—" He again gestures to Mindy, outside the window. "Then my hands are tied."

I hope my chest isn't rising and falling as hard as it feels like it is.

Courtney slowly returns to his seat beside me and sinks in.

"You're Oliver Vicks's pawn," Courtney says.

Heald sniffs, and pushes his glasses up a bit higher on his nose.

"I keep this prison running smoothly," he says. "Oliver Vicks wants his books. Do you have them or not?"

My nails are digging into the armrests of my chair. I turn to Courtney, assuming we'll think about how to play this for a moment, but he hardly hesitates:

"We have them."

Heald nods, pleased and relieved.

"Where are they? I'll send Don to get them."

I put a hand on Courtney's wrist, to stop him from blurting anything out.

"Nobody is getting them but us," I say, "and not until we know we're getting out of this. We want Oliver Vicks standing out in front of the gates with Mindy. Just the two of them. Then we'll swap."

Heald takes off his glasses to rub his eyes with his wrist, then puts them back on and looks up at us.

"You're really not in a position to negotiate with me," he says. "But we all want the same thing here. Go. It only takes one of you to go show my officers where they are. The other one will stay here while we talk to Oliver."

My mouth is so dry I can hardly speak.

"You're keeping one of us hostage?" I say.

Heald looks annoyed.

"Call it what you want. I can't have you two taking my officers on a runaround. I need to get him those books before sunset."

"Why?" Courtney asks.

Heald ignores the question, picks up his telephone receiver and says: "Allen, arrange a car and an escort for one of our 'investigators.' Mmhmm. Have them meet him downstairs outside the elevator. Five minutes."

He sets down the phone and sighs. Shakes his head and smiles weakly.

"Believe me, I don't want to be in this situation either. But it will be fine. I've dealt with Oliver for years. He's frightening, but a man of his word. If he says he'll make this swap, he means it. You two want a drink?"

"I'd actually love one," I say.

Maybe this will be okay . . . just get the books and walk out of here, like he says. He is in a tough spot . . .

"It's been a long week," laughs Heald sadly. Stands up, snatches the same bottle of scotch we drank from a few days ago, and three tumblers. Pours three generous drinks, recorks the bottle, and sits back down. Raises his glass in a toast.

"Here's to the weekend," he says.

I raise my glass, ignore the glare from Courtney, and gulp down half my glass. Heald shoots his down and smacks the empty glass down on the tabletop. Courtney hasn't touched his.

"You're not going to waste that are you?" he says. "That's 15-year-old scotch. Don't make me drink it."

Something happens to Courtney. His grip on his armrest suddenly tightens, and the blood drains from his face. Heald can't see it, but Courtney's legs are shaking under the desk. "I'm trying to keep a clear head," Courtney says, voice cracking.

What's wrong with him?

Courtney turns to me, eyes narrow.

"Ben, you go get the books, I'll stay here." He's sweating, and looks like he might faint. He's talking slowly, trying to convey something. "The warden is right. Don't mess around. Go straight there. To the farm."

The farm?

I shoot him a look of confusion, hoping he'll elaborate.

"Go," he says coldly, and the look in his eyes is so horrible that I feel I'm physically thrust up out of my chair, toward the exit.

"Hurry," says Heald, buzzing the door open for me.

I rush out into the waiting room. Allen smiles cursorily at me.

"They're waiting for you on the ground floor outside the elevator," he says. Business as usual.

I step into the elevator, head buzzing.

The farm? That's the name of Sadie's boarding school. Is that what Courtney meant?

He doesn't want me to give these officers the books. He wants me to run.

On the ground floor I'm greeted outside the elevator by Sergeant Don, two guards I'm pretty sure I haven't seen before, and the guy who looks like a potato.

"Come on then," Don says, eyes sparkling. "Let's go get the books."

In a daze, I follow them back through the admin building two behind me, two ahead of me. I frantically replay our encounter with Heald.

Courtney realized something I didn't, which freaked him out even more than Heald admitting he was cooperating with Oliver Vicks.

When? There was a moment when Courtney suddenly tensed. It was when Heald gave us the whiskey.

No . . . It was after that, after he'd already drank his, and Courtney didn't and he said . . .

That's 15-year-old scotch. Something distant and awful flashes across my mind, for a second I think it's an impossible blue-sky lightning over the mountains.

I stop in my tracks, and one of the guards collides into me from behind.

"What's wrong with you?" he asks. "C'mon."

My legs resume, on autopilot, but I suddenly have zero awareness of my surroundings. Just thinking of what just happened upstairs.

It was a 12-year-old scotch. I saw that right on the bottle last time we were here.

The warden confused the 2 for a 5. Nathan Heald is dyslexic.

I haven't seen a picture of Oliver Vicks more recent than twenty years ago . . . he was skinny, he didn't have a beard . . .

The horror is compounding. My vision is getting a bit splotchy. I feel feverish, and close to fainting. Does this make sense?

Of course it does. Of course it's fucking him.

There's no standoff between the officers and the prisoners. Oliver Vicks converted every last person here. And now he sits in the warden's office.

And I just left Courtney alone with him.

WE CLAMBER INTO an old cop car that says *Security* on the side, me in the caged rear. On my right is Potato, and his huge ass spills over into my lap. On my left is a younger guy, who is clearly very nervous, and trying to hide it. Don is driving. They start the car up, and then Don turns to look into the backseat. He licks his lip.

"Where we going?" he asks, not angry, but pretty clearly not in the mood for any more humor.

What the hell do I do? What happens if Courtney shoots the dart at Oliver?

He didn't want me to bring back the books. He wanted me to try to escape.

Because he knows it's hopeless.

"Sir," Don repeats, focusing somewhere above my head. "Where are we going?"

"East on Highway 90," I hear myself mumble. "I'll tell you when to stop."

The car shoots out through the security checkpoints. I can't get Courtney's face out of my head, the look he gave me when he had it all figured out.

Straight to the farm.

He knew it was over for Mindy, and whoever hung back. He was waiting for me to leave for him to take his shot at Oliver. Just trying to give me a puncher's chance of escaping.

I've got to make sure I'm right about this.

"Any of you guys have a cigarette?" I ask. None of them respond. I keep pushing: "Don't tell me the warden doesn't let you guys smoke cigarettes on the job? That's wild. What a tight ass."

Neither of the guys in the front seat turn to look at me, and the two on either side of me suddenly seem super fascinated with the backs of the seats.

"Scary situation, eh?" I ask Potato on my right. "Having this guy Oliver around?"

Nada. Face as stiff and straight as a board.

I turn to the younger guy on my left, who is breathing a little too fast. "You ever seen Oliver Vicks yourself? In person?"

He pretends like he can't hear me.

On the other side, Potato says:

"Please be quiet."

I ignore him.

"He's full of shit, you know." I continue prodding the younger guy. "This schmuck, Oliver, just slaps on a mask, goes around doing magic tricks and suddenly he's Jesus 2.0, right? He's crazy. You know he convinced someone to cut off his—"

"Stop talking. How much longer?" Don interjects forcefully, from the front seat.

"C'mon Don, just talking a little theology," I say. "Sorry, didn't realize you and Oliver Vicks were fucking butt budd—"

Sergeant Don instantly slams on the brakes. Were it not for the seat belt around my waist I would have been propelled face-first into the grate. We come to a complete halt in the middle of the two-lane rural highway—he didn't even bother to pull onto the shoulder.

"Where are we going?" he asks.

I haven't figured that out yet.

"I told you, just keep going. I'll tell you when to turn."

Don rushes out of the front seat and rips open the back door on my left. I flinch, sure he's going to grab me, but instead he pulls the young officer out onto the pavement. The much larger young guy doesn't resist. The other two guards in the car sit horribly still.

"Strip," Don tells the officer, his eyes like glowing coals.

"Don, what are you doing?" I ask. He ignores me. "What's going on?" I ask Potato. No response. He's not even watching as the younger guard unbuckles his belt and drops his khaki pants. Don stands arms akimbo, watching with satisfaction. Then the young guy unbuttons his shirt, pulls off his undershirt, and then, slowly, drops underwear, until he's standing totally buck naked in the middle of the highway.

The younger officer drops to his bare knees on the asphalt. Don picks up his discarded belt and begins to snap lashes across his back. The kneeling guard remains totally still, only his mouth is moving, forming words that I recognize only because I've seen this before . . .

For Sophnot, my father my king . . .

My heart thumps in my chest. The crack of leather on skin, as rhythmic as a pendulum. After maybe twenty lashes Don stops and peers in through the open door at me.

"Where are we going?" he says.

The young guy is shaking badly. His back is a maze of red stripes, glinting in the afternoon sun. Then he keels forward, smacking stomach first onto the highway.

"We need to get him to a hospital," I say.

"Where, exactly, are we going?" asks Sergeant Don, his voice dead.

I need more time . . . I need to get away from these guys. I can't give them the books . . .

"Where," Don repeats. "Answer me."

"I'm not talking until we drop him off at a hospital."

Sergeant Don blinks emptily at me. Then in a flash he unholsters his pistol.

I hear a scream escape my throat as Don puts the muzzle to the back of the kid's skull and fires three times.

My stomach falls out from under me. I put my hand on the grate to brace myself.

"Oh my god," I whisper. "Oh my god."

Don peels the kid's corpse off the highway, like a piece of roadkill. Slings it over his shoulder like venison.

"Pop the trunk," he instructs the guy in front. I can't bear to watch. Just hear the sick thump of dead meat behind me. Don reappears, picks up the young officer's discarded clothes. I hear the trunk slam closed.

Don climbs back into the front seat and turns to me.

"Where are the books," he says calmly.

What else can I do?

"It's just past mile marker 419," I mutter. "There's a shoulder on the road with a spray-painted *X*. Drive slowly. I'll tell you when to pull over."

"No more talking."

Sergeant Don jerks back around and gives the car some gas. The other two just keep staring straight ahead, like nothing's happened. I'm horribly aware of the empty seat to my left.

My vision is swimming, and it takes me a moment to realize I'm crying. Not tears of sorrow, for Mindy, Rico, Sampson, this young kid . . . any of the dozens of Oliver's victims whose names I'll never know. These are angry tears.

Courtney didn't kill Oliver with that blow dart. If he had, one of these guys would surely have gotten a call by now.

My fists are so tight that my fingernails are drawing blood.

I can't run from this and leave Courtney there, but I also can't just give them the books. Once Oliver has what he wants, there's just no way he'll let us walk away.

A strange peace comes over me as I realize how simple my situation is. Tonight I'll either kill Oliver Vicks, or find out if I have an eternal soul. Were this a backgammon game, I'd forfeit. But I have to make a move now, even if it's a dubious one.

Zugzwang.

THE CAR CREEPS ahead, CO in the front passenger seat continuously looking at me for confirmation that we're getting close. Sergeant Don spots the *X* before I do. He pulls over and turns off the ignition. We climb out of the car into the withering afternoon. They watch me expectantly.

"Out here?" asks Potato. I scope the landscape, takes me a moment to recognize the mass of blue bushes on the hillside.

"Yeah. In those bushes." I gesture to an area a bit to the left of the true location.

"I'll keep the car running," says Don. "Take him to get them."

Don staying in the car. That could make this tricky. Or impossible.

I lead Potato and the other guy—a wolf-faced man with sad grey eyes—to the bushes, high grass and gravel crunching under my tennis shoes. I hear them huffing behind me. Wonder if they have their hands on their pistols. We're walking west, toward the mountains. The sun looks to have another ninety minutes before its base dips below their peaks.

At the edge of the bushes I stop and look around. Spot the marked rocks about five meters to my right.

"They're deep inside the bush," I say. "I think right around here," I lie. "Go in and see."

They glare at me, study the tangled web of foreboding branches. Raise skeptical eyebrows.

They take the bait.

"No, no, you crawl in," says Potato. "We'll wait right here."

I feign reluctance.

"You're the boss."

I crouch down, and dive into the web of brambles. Don't have the bag to push ahead this time. Just put my forearms out in front of me and let them get scratched and bloodied.

If that's the worst that happens to me today . . .

When I think I'm at least two meters deep I pull the phone out of my pocket, wince as I get scraped up pulling it to my face, and dial 911. A bored-sounding woman answers:

"Emergency Response."

"There is a riot in progress at the Saddleback Correctional

Facility," I whisper. "We need help. I'm requesting immediate backup."

"The prison?"

"Yes. Please hurry."

"Find anything?" It's the distant voice of Potato. Must have heard me stop ruffling around.

"I'm sorry, sir," asks the woman on the phone. "Who am I speaking to?"

"I'm a corrections officer," I whisper, doesn't take much creativity to sound like a panicked mess. "The prisoners have escaped. They're everywhere. They're going to kill me. There's fire and blood—"

"Okay, and you said your location is—"

"I'm at the *prison*, it's a fucking riot!" I hiss.

"Okay . . . Looks like I have a squad car about twenty minutes from your location. I'll send him to check up on you right away."

Fuck. She thinks I'm full of shit. Or an insane prisoner.

"No, you don't understand, it's a disaster. We need helicopters and the SWAT team—"

"I understand sir. Help is on the way. Stay calm. Can you describe what's happening in more detail please?"

"Hey," one of the guards is shouting. Any longer and he's going to follow me in here. "What are you doing in there?"

I let the call drop.

Pigfuck.

Best case, 911 sends a few squad cars who will get to the front gate, ask if there's a riot in progress, and get laughed at. More likely they'll call the admin building first and be reassured that everything is fine.

"Wrong spot!" I yell.

I scoot backwards. As soon as it emerges from the bush, the wolf-faced officer grabs my ankle and rips me out backwards. I just barely have time to shove the phone back in my pocket before I'm back under the blue sky, eye to eye with the barrel of Potato's pistol.

"What the heck are you doing?" he demands, face red. His hand is trembling. He's scared of what will happen to him if he doesn't get the books to Don. "You're messing with us."

"No, no." I show him my palms. "I'm sorry. I made a mistake. It's in these bushes, I swear."

Wolf grunts: "One more bush, then we're going to blow your nuts off."

I grin weakly.

"I hardly use the damn things anymore."

Now I have only one plausible move, and I don't like it. But I have to get back in the prison, and I have to do it without anyone knowing. The car is parked about forty meters away—far enough that even if Don is watching he probably can't see exactly what's going down over here. No point delaying this. Nothing good is happening to Courtney and Mindy back in the prison.

"Go," Potato says.

I sit up, push myself up to my feet. Then, hands raised over my head, crunch over dead stalks and dry sand to the spot marked by the spray-painted rocks.

I give them a thumbs-up, and wriggle into the bush with abandon, like diving into a swimming pool. Hardly feel the sharp tendrils scratching my face. Smells nice in here at least, like fresh herbal tea. Dig in a little deeper, struck by the odd impression that I'm trying to squeeze back into the womb. There *is* something weirdly comforting about the cool dark in here. Like the whole world back there doesn't exist . . . sort of like the feeling I got in the red house.

I spot the duffel. Hastily unzip it, plunge my hand in and grope until I find my Magnum. Then pull my phone back out of my pocket and call the only number I have memorized. Four rings.

Hi you've reached Sadie. Leave a message and I'll get back to you ASAP.

I can hardly speak for a moment, her tender voice paralyzing me, awakening some part of me that I forgot existed. My feet feel heavy, chest numb.

"Hhhiii, sweetie," I whisper. "It's Dad. Listen I . . ." I swallow. "I just, I'm about to get into something very dangerous in a moment. I can't give you too many details but . . . it looks like big trouble. So I just wanted to say, if you don't hear from me in the next couple days . . . Christ. I'm sorry—"

Beep. *If you're satisfied with your message, press one, or just hang—*

I hang up, well short of satisfied, but in a bit of a time crunch.

Zip back up the bag and yell:

"I got it, fellas!"

I squirm, manage to shove the gun into the back of my pants, pull my T-shirt down over the grip, and then back out of the bush.

Potato immediately snatches the bag from me, unzips it and peers inside. As soon as he recognizes them, his face twists into a kind of terrified awe. He quickly pulls out a walkie-talkie, keeping one eye on the books, as if he's scared they'll disappear.

"Sergeant. We have the books. Should we bring him back or sacrifice him ourselves?"

My jaw tightens and I reach for the butt of the pistol in my pants. Wolf is glaring at me. If the answer is the latter, I have no chance.

Potato nods and hangs up.

"You're to come back with us."

I exhale.

They've relaxed noticeably now that they have the books. They were worried about what Sophnot and Don would do to them. They're actually a bit giddy now.

"Let me see them?" Wolf asks Potato. He hesitates, then smiles, unzips the bag and they both lean in for a glance.

I rip the Magnum from my jeans and unload, the sound of each shot echoing seemingly across the whole landscape. I empty the whole round, six shots, trying to avoid anything lethal. I go for the roasted chicken spots: thighs and shoulders.

Both drop to the ground. Potato is cognizant enough to reach for his weapon, but I'm on top of him in a second, pistol whip him in the forehead, then snatch the gun from his holster and chuck it. Wolf's Glock, which still has a full clip, I keep. Look up to see what's happening with Don. The car is nickel-sized, hard to see exactly what's going on, but I hear the sound of a door slamming.

He heard the shots. Took the bait.

And now the hard part. I leave the bag beside Potato. Sprint downhill, at a diagonal that will take me about forty meters south of the parked car, staying low and taking a wide enough berth that Don won't spot me on his mad charge up to the bushes.

I dash like a madman, until I'm about two-thirds of the way to the road, then drop and crouch behind a boulder. Can hardly breathe, adrenaline pulsing in my skull. I spot Don's stooped form raging up to his fallen comrades, maybe two minutes away from reaching them.

He has to run uphill, I get to run downhill. I might actually have plenty of time.

I shove up and gallop down the last rocky slope, onto the highway. Look back up to the bush. I squint and am pretty sure I see Don holding the bag of books. I imagine he's overjoyed that I didn't take them, and figures I just ran off into the hills.

I stagger toward the car, trying to stay low, praying Don is too distracted to notice my shadow streaking across the road. My legs are absolutely screaming by the time I duck behind the vehicle and very quietly try the scorching handle to the driver's side door. He didn't bother to lock it, but he did take the keys with him.

I hit the button to pop the trunk, and then delicately close the driver's door and open the backseat and sneak back to the trunk. Peer over the lip of the rear windshield. Don appears to just be leaving the scene—on the phone—with the duffel bag slung over his shoulder. No sign of his pals.

I try not to think too much about what's about to happen, as I lift the trunk a quarter of the way up. I confirm that the young officer's crumpled uniform is back here—it's bunched up next to his head. I take a very, *very* deep breath, and then roll in, landing with a sickening squelch on top of what used to be the young guard.

I pull the trunk door down over us until the latch touches, but doesn't click shut. It's pitch black, very, very hot, and smells like a butcher shop. It's so cramped I'm basically spooning the corpse. A thought flashes in my head that I try to ignore:

This is probably the most action I've gotten in a year.

I keep Wolf's Glock pointed straight up, in case Don decides to put the books in the trunk. But I doubt he'd want to put those sacred texts next to a corpse.

Just gotta hope this old car doesn't have a super sensitive trunk ajar light . . .

My face and neck are completely bathed in sweat, and I'm still breathing very hard from the run. Kind of feels like my brain is an overheating computer. Try to pretend that the still-warm form next to me is anything besides what it actually is.

This is it. Nothing is worse than this. This is hell.

After what feels like an eternity, I hear what must be Don returning to the car. I hold my breath. I hear the front door slam, and he starts the ignition. I nearly lose my grip on the trunk door as he smashes the gas.

He left those guys out there.

I place the Glock between my knees and hold onto the trunk door for dear life, fingers already shaking as I alternately prevent it from flying up or clicking into place, locking me in. A little bump in the road sends my elbow into the dead man's ear.

"Sorry," I whisper to my companion. "If it makes you feel any better, I'm also having a really bad day."

THE CAR SLOWS and takes a few speed bumps that indicate a return to the prison. Three minutes after the car is parked, I hear a chorus of voices outside. I think the COs are clamoring for a peek at the books. Rising above the din is Sergeant Don's call for discipline.

I grip the latch as hard as I can, vaguely thinking if someone tries to open the trunk now for some reason I'll hold it closed . . . not sure what my endgame is there. Hard to think of anything besides the heat in here. Throat parched, and feel like I'm being baked alive.

Finally the voices of the corrections officers retreat. I allow myself a stiff inhale and immediately gag on the musk of fresh death.

I let the trunk open just enough to give me a sliver of light to work with. I wriggle out of my jeans, and pull on the young guard's pants. Can't button them—he has a little smaller waist than me. I pull his khaki shirt on over my T-shirt, snatch his sunglasses, belt and holster, then force myself to count up to a hundred. Every additional second of this heat absolute agony. At forty I can't take it anymore. Crack the trunk up a quarter inch and look around. Empty parking lot. Allow myself another quarter inch, until I can see the closest sentry tower. There's somebody up there, but he doesn't seem to be looking in my direction. Would probably be prudent to take another couple minutes of scoping, but the heat is unbearable. I shove up the trunk door halfway, leap out quickly, and then quietly close it. Scamper into the shade of a green industrial dumpster resting at the edge of the lot and collapse.

The relief of fresh air is so pleasant that for a moment I forget the urgency of my mission, and just savor the breeze against my cheeks. Some rancid smell from the dumpster snaps me out of my reverie.

Prison leftovers . . .

I peer around the edge of the dumpster. Behind the admin building, past a couple high chain fences, rises the tower. Thin, rigid, sand-colored layers separated by concentric rings, culminating in a shimmering glass tip. Without the white flaps, the spire is definitely a little phallic.

Maybe Vicks is insecure about more than just his reading level.

Beyond the tower, the bottom of the sun is flirting with the tops of the mountains. I put on the guard's sunglasses, then tuck the khakis into the waistline and fasten the belt. Hopefully nobody will notice that my pants are unbuttoned.

If that's the reason I don't get away with this, someone upstairs has a very sick sense of humor.

I holster my Glock, take a deep breath, and step out of the shade of the dumpster.

Act natural.

Telling yourself this, of course, is the best way of ensuring you act weird and stilted.

I cross the parking lot, forcing a smile to my face, then decide that's actually particularly weird. I haven't seen anybody smile in this place besides Sergeant Don, and the guy who turned out to be Oliver Vicks.

I do my best to avoid the front security checkpoint area, although there are only a couple guys left there. I stride down to the dirt path that leads into the side entrance of the admin building.

Just rush to the elevator, take it up. Kill Allen the secretary. Burst in and send Oliver Vicks to kingdom come.

That's not gonna happen. Dozens of officers and secretaries are streaming *out* of that side door. A veritable wave of khaki. I quickly whip off my sunglasses once I see that none of them are wearing theirs. And what's more, these guys *are* smiling. They're chatting, and joking with each other. It's like somebody just rang the dinner bell and all the miners just threw down their picks on the spot. Quitting time.

I get swept up in the horde, have no choice but to go along with everyone else. We're filing into the yard that contains the tower through an open door in the chain link fence. The officers are greeted convivially by grinning prisoners in jumpsuits. They slap each other on the back like old friends.

Prisoners and COs are streaming into this open space from all directions. Thousands of them milling around, talking a little. Some of them sit cross-legged on the ground like we're about to have the most surreal picnic in the world.

The offenders' politeness is astonishing. As is the fact that hundreds of guards are just *mingling* with them.

The whole yard is filled with the low murmur of friendly chit-chat. If you close your eyes it sounds like a cocktail party; the clink of handcuffs on officer's belts could be champagne flutes.

I'm so overwhelmed by the strangeness of it all that I don't immediately notice the new addition to the wooden platform in front of the tower. There are now four short stools on the platform. Mindy and the two other men have been joined by Courtney, who is shrouded in a matching brown sackcloth.

If anybody was paying attention to me, my face probably would have betrayed me in that moment. Courtney, Mindy and the other two have collars around their necks that look very similar to the ones we found in the red house. The four collars are attached by chains to what looks like very heavy metal balls resting in their laps. The stage faces west, straight into the heart of the merciless evening sun. But instead of shielding their eyes, all four prisoners are sitting upright, stiff, glaring in the light, as if they can see their fate on the horizon and are determined to accept it proudly.

Walking slowly enough to not attract attention, I weave my way through the crowd, toward the tower. As I get closer to the base I see that etched into the sandy stone coating of the tower are black murals of faces. Rudimentary ones, almost like charcoal cave drawings—dark eyes, black pits of mouths. As best I can tell, the bottom ten finished floors are windowless. The unfinished fourteen are open air scaffolding. The glass dome on the top reflects the sun, like it's just one big window.

I pull up short about fifteen yards from the stage, because that's where the edge of the crowd stops, as if there's some invisible barrier preventing them from getting any closer.

All four prisoners are positioned right in front of the entrance, a gaping hole in the tower's side that seems like it's swallowing and consuming the rays of the dying sun.

From this close I understand why they're all sitting so upright, chins in the air: Strapped against each prisoner's neck is a shiny instrument of death, the horrible mechanism that was attached to the collar that Courtney took from the red house.

Heretic's forks.

Two sharp prongs extend up from the collar to rest against their jugular veins, and two more pointed downwards scrape against their sternums. They all have to keep their heads peeled back. If they let them drop they'll pierce their own necks.

My legs threaten to collapse on me, and I sit down to try to compose myself. It's lucky I haven't eaten anything in a few hours.

It takes me about five minutes to catch Courtney's eyes. Just staring at him intently until he notices. He rotates his head ever so slightly, and when his eyes lock onto mine from across the stretch of yard, I feel like the blood is standing still in my veins. When he recognizes me, his eyes widen in horror: *Why are you here? Get out of here.*

I pantomime a gun with my thumb and index finger: *I'm going to kill him.*

Courtney's eyes are deep with sorrow. He actually smiles ever so slightly, as much as his neck clamp will allow: *No chance.*

I wish I could reach over and pat his shoulder. Mindy is sitting on his left. Her eyes are droopy, face eggplant purple, lips scorched and peeling—has she been chained up here all day? He looks back at me, face still rigid, but tears streaming down his cheeks. He's furious with me. With considerable effort, he mouths: *GO!*

Then he winces. I see a wet line of blood on his chest. He looks away from me, as if he can't even bear to see me there.

An expectant murmuring from the crowd diverts my attention from my partner. Something's happening on the other side of the yard. Those who were sitting rise to their feet, and I hastily join them, take a few steps back from the front row and let myself be absorbed by the anonymity of the mob. I turn and strain on tiptoe to see what's going on.

And then even the murmuring of the crowd stops. Silence descends, a silence so complete you can hear cars on the highway, and the buzz of the air conditioners from the dormitory buildings, even though they're on the other side of the yard.

As if prompted, everyone sits down on the ground, wherever they are. I sit down so fast I nearly stumble over. Recover, and look backwards, away from the tower, to where everybody else is gazing expectantly. Still can't immediately tell what's going on, because of the sun, but I perceive that there's a sort of processional happening. Prisoners walking in single file through a gap in the seated crowd, all holding identical pieces of wooden furniture that I initially take for high chairs. They march to the stairs and file up onto the stage, all wearing an expression of solemnity. Each in turn sets down his chair on the stage, then exits down a staircase on the opposite side and sits down in the front row.

They're arranging the chairs in a circle, like for a professional game of duck, duck goose.

They're not chairs. They're lecterns.

The last prisoner puts his lectern in the last slot, completing the circle.

A circle of twenty-four.

The sun is grazing the tips of the mountains, bathing the stage and the faces of the four condemned in red-tinged light. The silence from the prisoners in the audience is absolute. I swear I can hear Mindy's raspy breathing all the way from here. A warm breeze ruffles through the audience, kissing my cheeks, rustling through Courtney and Mindy's sackcloths, like a momentary mercy from God. And then the stillness returns. The sun hangs expectantly, like he's refusing to set until he, too, gets to see where this is all going. Were I wearing a watch, I'm sure the second hand would suddenly cease its relentless march around its cage, stretch and yawn after a long day of ticking, and slow to a meandering stroll around its eternal perimeter.

Maybe it's the very real specter of imminent death, or the fact that I can't remember the last time I really watched a sunset, but the moment is suddenly so peaceful . . .

A sound in the distance, at the entrance to the yard. Jingling of metal—like a tambourine—in rhythm of footsteps. A single upright form drifts through the prisoners, almost floating through the dusk. I squint. His gloved hands brush the heads of sitting prisoners as he passes them, each one jerking slightly as if his touch is electrifying. The jingle that comes with every step must be from the gold chest plate he's wearing, ornately carved and inlaid with bright polished stones.

He's wearing a white robe and nothing on his feet. A white hood is draped over his head. As he nears I see he's wearing a wax mask, and has a silk bag slung over his shoulder. My heart screams as he passes within a few meters of me. I put a hand over my cheek and look down. Thank God I'm not sitting on the edge of the aisle.

He slowly ascends the staircase, and his bare feet pad gently toward the circle of lecterns. His wax mask, I think, is fat-cheeked, cherubic. The face of a child.

The faces of the inmates on either side of me are stoic, rapt, as Sophnot unslings the silk bag from his shoulder and puts it down at his feet. I put my forearms on my knees and crouch behind them to hide my lower face.

Sophnot reaches in and removes a single book. Mounts it on one of the lecterns, and opens it to a page somewhere in the middle. The second book takes him a moment to place—like he's thinking about where to put it in relation to the first. One by one, he removes the books and deliberately places them on their appropriate lectern. Nobody speaks.

Finally, after what feels like silent hours, Sophnot drops the empty sack at his feet, and steps backwards into the middle of the circle. He raises one hand.

"Good Sabbath, my sons," he says. He's not yelling, but his voice is incredibly resonant—enough that I have no doubt that even the people in the farthest corner of the yard can hear him.

The sitting congregants reply as one:

"Good Sabbath, Father."

He steps toward one of the lecterns, flips through a few pages, studies something through the eye slits of his mask.

"I want to start this week on a page from the volume that corresponds to the fifth floor."

His voice is definitely Nathan Heald's. Although in his office he was clearly restraining the power of his voice. The projection of his voice, louder even than if he was speaking through a bullhorn, is mesmerizing.

"This is related to the concept of the circular river, which flows in a continuous loop, which I spoke about three Sabbaths prior. And you will recall the thought experiment of a computer program, whose lone function is to provide a platform upon which to replicate the program from scratch. The tricks the one we once called God used to spark the flame of consciousness. That primitive magic has outgrown its use."

Sophnot clears his throat, bends at the waist and peers into the book through his mask. Reads:

"A boy wanders until he comes to the entrance of a small village. The entrance is guarded by an oracle. 'May I enter?' the boy asks. The oracle says, 'Let me first consult with the heavens, to foresee if you'll bring good or evil upon the people of the village.' The oracle consults, and then returns to the boy. 'You may not enter. If you enter the village you will steal from—'"

Sophnot pauses for a moment. Appears to be thinking. "This approximately means 'someone who mends shoes'—a cobbler. The oracle says 'If you enter the village you will steal from the cobbler. Go, and never set foot here.' The boy leaves, grows old, and dies far far away from that village, never meeting the cobbler. Was what the oracle saw a lie?"

Sophnot steps back from the book, positions himself again in the exact center of the circle of books. He's silent for a moment. I look again at Courtney, who doesn't even notice. His eyes, like all those in the crowd, are fixed on the figure in white.

"One of you dreamt this last night," Sophnot says. "Which of you dreamt this?"

Deep silence. Then a faint voice, behind me, to my left.

"I dreamt this, Father."

I turn to look at the speaker. A slender man with wild grey hair. Sophnot nods knowingly.

"In the dream, you were the boy," he says, not as a question.

"Yes, Father."

"And who was the oracle?"

The man blinks.

"I don't know, Father."

Sophnot nods.

"Then let us learn."

Sophnot steps to the next lectern. Flips through the pages.

"The volume which corresponds to the sixth floor speaks of a room the color of a grey sea. This is understood to be an allusion to the human brain. When you are born you enter the room through a door. All the days of your life you sit in this room. When you die you leave through the same door." Sophnot looks up from the book. "Years ago I left the room through the door, yet here I stand. I have seen the oracle on the other side of the wall—the one we used to call 'God'—who whispers to us through thin paper, lies to us about what will be. But he cannot see us. For to see us would be to tear through the wall, and destroy the very idea of the room. The wall is made of the only substance on earth which insulates its contents from God's prying eyes." Sophnot points to his white hooded head. "Skin."

The sun is half hidden behind the mountains, his colors turning dark and angry. The horizon is a thick line of violet. In the low light you could almost imagine that Oliver's not wearing a mask—that he's assumed the face of whatever boy he took that mold from.

"This is the oracle's folly. He wrapped our minds in skin, castrating himself. He can only listen through the wall—never see. Outside our skin, though, he can see. And all out here—" Sophnot gestures toward the mountains, the congregation. "He sees us. Even now, he intrudes on our Sabbath. But only here," Sophnot says, pointing backwards at his tower, "here we finally have peace. Here is *my* domain. And soon we will complete the physical man-ifestation of our holy writ. My friends!" he shouts. "This week, as I foresaw, I secured for us the funding to finish our project!"

For the first time, noise from the prisoners. They applaud and cheer. Sophnot scans the crowd, basking in their praise. My chest freezes for a minute when I think maybe he's looking straight at me through his mask—I forget to keep hiding my face—but even-tually his gaze moves on.

"The oracle—the one we called 'God'—lies to us. But I am Sophnot. I see things he doesn't!"

The prisoners and officers now stand up and whoop. I stand up, but keep my head down. First time in my life I'm thankful I'm not that tall.

"The world is a circular river, my friends," Sophnot's voice booms. "To each of you, standing on the banks"—he turns and seems to direct this to his four prisoners—"you think you are moving forward. But I was always both directly behind you, and far in front of you, waiting, waiting for you to bring me exactly what I needed."

Cheers. One prisoner in the front row breaks into a frenetic dance, the kind you see from hippies tripping on acid at Coachella.

Sophnot raises both robed hands to the west, where the sun has all but disappeared behind the peaks.

"The Sabbath has nearly arrived, my sons. The week is nearly concluded. Shall the Sabbath once again be ushered in by our bride?"

The cheering becomes a chorus of ecstatic affirmations: *"Yes! Yes! It shall!"*

The prisoners and officers scream and leap around, like they're so excited they're trying to jump right out of their skins.

Some random inmate grips my biceps and forces me to join his insane dance. He kicks his bare feet up toward the sky. His eyes are wide in rapture, mouth hanging agape like he's experiencing a sustained orgasm.

"The *queen!*" he gasps. "The *queen* is here!"

He jumps up and down, jerking me along until I manage to shove him off of me. The unfazed leech quickly finds a new host, and the music-less dancing continues for a few minutes, rising in fervor and intensity, until Sophnot again raises his arm and his voice reverberates like thunder:

"She's here!" The voice of Sophnot immediately puts an end to the jubilation. Every prisoner falls to his knees.

I peek up and see that on the stage, Sophnot is forcing the four collared prisoners on stage to stand up off their stools, despite the leaden balls in their laps, and the spikes pressing up against their necks. When he puts his hands on Courtney's shoulders and lifts him out of his seat, my vision goes red, and it takes every ounce of restraint in my body not to simply unholster and fire. The four of them stand with their chins raised to the sky, all clearly struggling to cradle the heavy balls in their arms.

Sophnot raises his hands and points west, back to the entrance of the yard where he came in what feels like hours ago.

"Kneel for your queen!" he bellows, and everyone falls into a groveling position.

I have no choice but to lower my own forehead to the dusty cement, just like everyone else.

For a long time, I don't hear anything. The sun has all but set now, the thousands of us prostrating beneath a veil of darkness.

Delicate, padding footsteps, proceeding down the same aisle Sophnot did. I'm dying to look up, but don't dare—in my peripheral vision I can see the prone figures beside me are unflinching. Hollow echoes as the source of the footsteps reaches the stairs to the stage.

Oh man. Oh no . . .

Before I even look up, I know who's standing onstage with Oliver Vicks.

"The Sabbath Queen has arrived!" Everyone gradually unfolds themselves. Gets to their knees first, then their feet. I expected this, but it doesn't make it less sickening: Standing beside Sophnot in the center of the circle is Becky Carlson. His arm is curved around her waist, gripping a handful of her emaciated hip. The dead expression she wears betrays nothing. She's holding a big bouquet of white and yellow flowers.

I can hardly bring myself to look at her withered form, swimming inside a long-sleeved white gown, as Sophnot greedily runs his hand up and down her side, squeezing handfuls of flesh wherever he can find them. The sentry towers have trained their floodlights on the stage, making the whole thing resemble a sort of macabre theatre.

Then he drops his arm, turns, and makes a motion with his right hand.

My hand moves to my Glock.

If he's going to execute them now, I have no choice.

"Go to your Sabbath meal, my sons," Sophnot cries. "You will find delicate meats, fresh breads, rich wines. I bought these for you from this week's bounty—serve me by enjoying them! Meditate on my teachings. And after we eat, we will spill the blood of these heretics. Make an *Afikomen*—the dessert sacrifice—and show the one we used to call 'God' the weakness of his creations. Good Sabbath!"

"*Good Sabbath, Father Sophnot!*"

Sophnot stands still on stage for a moment, arm around Becky's waist, as the giddy men file out of the yard, toward the dormitories. Then he starts gathering the books himself and placing them back in his silk sack. In the dark, he looks like a rotund ghost, slipping lithely between his lecterns, closing and handling each book as delicately as one might an infant. Becky stands still, gripping her bouquet tightly, face blank.

I walk as slowly as I dare—don't want to stick out—worried that I'll have no choice but to follow the men into the dining hall. But then Sophnot finishes gathering his books, slings the bag over his shoulder, and leads Becky into the black hole in the front of the tower, leaving four shapes sitting stilly outside the tower entrance.

The sentries move the floodlights away from the platform, and I have my chance. I fall out of line, and stride toward the stage with great purpose, praying nobody questions my intentions. Knees quivering, I reach the edge of the stairs, and find a small gap between them and the exterior of the tower. Drop to my stomach and look around. Nobody has followed me. They're all too eager to get to their meal.

In minutes the yard is completely empty; guards and prisoners alike retreating into the low white buildings on the perimeter of the yard. And then the sentry lights shut off . . . suppose even the guards up there are going to the meal. The only sound is the shuffling of the four prisoners on their stools.

I wait a few more moments to be safe. A faint whirr from well over my head, like a helicopter.

Did the cops decide to check into my call??

No. It's an elevator rising up through the core of the unfinished floors over the tower, like passing through some enormous urethra. The elevator appears to stop just beneath the glowing top floor.

I take a few deep breaths and shove up, slink up the stairs to the wooden platform. The four forms are on their stools, deadly still. I cringe as my footsteps make the wood creak, but I can't help myself from rushing to Courtney and Mindy.

She looks to be in worse shape. Even in the darkness I can see her face is discolored from the sun, a few more hours of that and she might have started charring. Her breaths are shallow, neck straining to stay erect. Her arms are wrapped around the heavy lead ball in her lap, clinging to it like a life preserver.

I lean in close to her collar, study the tanned leather and intricate metallurgy to see how to unlock it.

"Don't . . . touch," Courtney gasps, to my left.

His watery green eyes come into focus. The collar isn't quite choking him, but every syllable is a horrible strain.

"Sensiti-ive," he whispers, and shows me his palm, where the collar cut his hand in the car a few nights ago.

"I'm not touching it," I say.

I inspect the heavy cuff around his neck. Two round holes on either side for the keys. And as Courtney discovered, if you enter the wrong keys, there are those two dormant interior blades ready to awaken.

"I can get you out of this maybe," I whisper. "Sophnot must have the keys."

"No." He closes his eyes and then slowly opens them. "Just go."

"Did you fire your dart?" I ask.

Courtney takes a deep, careful breath through his nose.

He wheezes, "Aimed for chest. Hit metal."

He must have been wearing that breastplate under his shirt.

I rub the top of his head. His scalp is cold under my trembling hands.

"Where does he keep the keys? In his robe?"

Courtney smiles mirthlessly. The sadness in his eyes makes my heart feel like ice. "Don't know . . . Didn't see them . . . Should be tubular. Two of them, almost identical, but not quite."

I close my eyes for a moment. I can feel Courtney's slow pulse in my fingertips, the hot night air on the back of my neck. Taste blood in my mouth, from biting my own gums. I'm terribly thirsty.

I help first Mindy, then Courtney off their stools, lowering the heavy balls gently to the ground, so they can at least lie down on the deck instead of having to support the weight of the ball in their lap. I do the same for the two chained up officers—both of whom look bewildered by my presence, but don't speak. Then I approach the gaping black entrance. Can't see anything on the other side, and a cool breeze is blowing out, as if the whole place is air conditioned.

"Easy job, eh?" I smile sadly at Courtney. "You know where there are surprisingly few death cults this time of year? Budapest."

I unholster my Glock and clench it tightly as I step in through the arched doorway.

THE FIRST THING I notice is the change in the air density. The atmosphere in here is thick and heavy, like a muggy Florida evening. Except it's actually slightly chilly.

My eyes slowly adjust to the dim light. I'm standing in a space so large I can't quite perceive where it stops in any direction. Just inches over my head, as if the tower was built for someone just my height, runs a network of red and blue pipes—I can't actually tell whether they are painted red and blue, or if they're transparent, and carrying red and blue fluid. To both my left and right are staircases that cling to the curved walls, rise along it, spiraling up.

But I think I'd rather take the elevator.

I take a step forward and stumble, catch my fall with my palms and just barely avoid smacking my chin on the dark wood floor. My head is pounding, and I'm getting that familiar pain in my skull that signals the beginning of a migraine. I slowly pick myself back up, squint at the dark floor, trying to figure out what I tripped over. Take another step forward, and nearly trip again, just barely catching myself.

The floor is at some kind of angle. It's like trying to walk on a ship deck during a storm. I rub sweat out of my eyes.

What the hell is this place?

I stoop to my knees and crawl forward slowly, constantly scanning for Sophnot. I hear nothing except my own breathing, the knees of my pants rubbing against the floor. The floor is some kind of wood, strangely warm to the touch, like from geothermal activity.

I stick my pistol back in my pants since I need both hands to crawl effectively. The light is dim and faintly purple, but I have no idea where it's coming from—I don't see any lamps or windows. There's a breeze, but the cool air carries neither the recycled scent of air conditioning nor the dryness of the Colorado night—it's like the air is blowing in from some other world.

The proportions of space in here are as absurd and arbitrary as a fever dream. The slant of the floor is making me so disoriented that I pull my wallet out, find a particularly flaccid business card, and start ripping off little pieces and dropping them on the floor as I proceed, forming a little bread crumb trail.

As I crawl further ahead, the maze of pipes over my head becomes denser, until it's a kind of ceiling, like a forest canopy. Up through the cracks in the web I see only darkness. I reach up to brush the pipes and recoil. They're wet and warm. I sniff my wet fingers and the smell reminds me of the fetal pig dissection we had to do in middle school.

Formaldehyde?

I crawl forward, still dropping business card pieces with trembling hands. A sharp breeze on my cheek draws my gaze upward. A few meters ahead there's a break in the web of pipes, and the glint of a solid metal shaft.

I crawl slowly to the elevator, starting to adjust somewhat to the weird slant of the floor. I use the holes in the birdcage shaft to pull myself up to my feet. Peering up through the grating I can see only darkness. It doesn't take me long to locate the call button. I smack it a couple times, thinking I'll take it up to the twenty-third floor, so I can surprise the bastard, but it doesn't seem to register. With a sinking heart, I then notice the keyhole beneath the button.

So it's either the stairs, or just wait down here for them to return.

But when they return, the yard will be filled again with prisoners. I have to get at him while he's alone with Becky.

I'm going to turn and follow my bread crumb trail back to the entrance when I hear something creak on the other side of the empty elevator shaft.

I instinctually go for my weapon, and nearly trip over my own feet. Catch myself and go still.

Could it be Oliver? I saw the elevator go up . . . maybe he sent Becky up by herself?

I stand still, focus on keeping my breaths quiet. The sound doesn't startle me the second time; it's too deep and heavy to be a person. It sounds more like the building is settling into its foundation, and groaning with relief.

Keeping one hand outstretched for balance, one still gripping the butt of my pistol, I slowly turn the corner of the elevator shaft and grope forward in the direction of the sound. It grows louder as I step away from the elevator. I drop a few pieces of torn business card and keep moving ahead, until reaching what seems to be a sort of stone archway, wide enough for two to enter side by side.

·The air blowing out of this tunnel is warmer, and I see the web of red and blue pipes over my head appear to be bulging, like high-pressured hoses. I keep walking ahead, keeping one hand on the wall of the path. It's not stone, feels more like lichen or moss, warm and damp to the touch.

The walkway opens into a circular room. The ceiling is violently pulsing red and blue tubes. Periodically I hear the groaning sound again . . . seems to be coming from the mossy walls of this room.

In the center of the room is a knee-height circle of polished stone. I grit my teeth. On the lip closest to me is the bouquet Becky was holding outside.

They stopped here before taking the elevator.

As I approach the flowers, I see the circle is a pool, filled with still black water. I lean over the pool and peer in, and am so horrified by what I see that I stumble backwards. On the surface of the pool is reflected a picture-perfect image of Becky's little brother, with his eyes closed.

Jesus Christ.

Pulse pounding in my temples. I force myself back to the pool, and look again. A still, peaceful child's face. For a few seconds it remains unmoving, and then the eyes and mouth open, and the groan reverberates inside my chest.

I feel faint. I step back from the pool and lean against a wall.

It's just some kind of illusion. He probably has a projector under the water. Or coming from above.

Turn up over my shoulder. No projector. Just the web of pipes.

I tear myself away from the disgusting ceiling. This isn't why I'm here.

Where is this bastard?

I turn and, keeping my arms out for balance, like I'm walking on a diving board, follow the white specks of paper back past the elevator shaft, to the entrance and the two staircases. I choose the one on the right and start climbing, grip my pistol tight in my shooting hand in case someone jumps out of the shadows.

The steps are very narrow. I hug the wall for fear of falling off. Keep one eye on the steps rising in front of me, the other scanning above me for signs of Sophnot and Becky. Etched into the rising walls are smiling, childlike faces, all crying what appears to be blood. I climb above the ceiling of pipes from the first floor. From the edge, the second floor looks much like the first, with an apparently identical ceiling of red and blue pipes.

I think I see the outline of another mossy entranceway, which I assume holds another pool.

Keep climbing. The air is so thick with moisture that it feels like it's resisting me at every step. Feels like I'm pushing through a swimming pool.

Pass three or four more floors. All the same. My legs are exhausted. I still haven't seen the source of the violet light that—

mercifully—is saving me from doing this climb in complete darkness.

The staircase I'm on periodically intersects with its counter-clockwise counterpart, which is snaking up in reverse. When it does, the stairs meet in a shared ledge. Then each starts again, with a foot of vertical space between it and the platform.

I stick with my clockwise stairs, and keep climbing, ignoring the mounting ache in my lower back, the fire in my chest.

Maybe if Sophnot took the stairs every day he wouldn't be so chunky.

After what I guess is ten floors, the wall on one side of me falls away. The rest of the floors are unfinished. The staircases continue spiraling upwards, but now without support on *either* side.

I stare up at fourteen floors of this winding tightrope walk. The stairs can't be more than two feet wide, and up this high the breeze is much stronger than on the ground . . . One strong gust and we could be looking at some Pollock-inspired splatter art.

Lamb: Study in red.

I wipe some cool sweat off my forehead with my already sat-urated khaki shirt. Clench my jaw, and keep climbing, praying the elevator overhead doesn't come to life and carry Oliver back downstairs to kill Courtney and Mindy.

There are no pipes or anything on these floors. Just unfinished wood flooring. No archways, no reflecting pools. I actually find this switch somewhat comforting. The spell of the bottom ten floors is broken. If I strain my neck, I can see the illuminated glass top up above, and what I think is the resting elevator. I have little doubt this is where Oliver and Becky are.

I wind around and around the periphery of the tower, now far above the dormant sentry towers. The only light is that of the just rising moon, a few stars. Good thing we're in Colorado. In NYC the haze would block most of this.

I stop thinking about the stairs. My body is pretty well used to the motion by now. Can climb pretty much on automatic. If one of them is misshapen, that's going to be a problem. My legs aren't in much pain anymore—or rather, they are but I can't feel it. The fresh air seems to have helped my head.

The key to the stairs is kind of tricking myself into being indifferent between falling and climbing. If I fall I'll cruise peacefully down through the night, dying instantly upon impact. If I make it to the top, I'll try to kill Oliver, likely fail, and then be strung up and butchered.

Floors nineteen, twenty, twenty-one. . . I think I hear a sound drifting from the top floor. Some kind of music I think, that I can't quite identify. In the middle of floor twenty-two the staircases meet for the last time, and I slip as I climb from the shared platform back onto my staircase. I grope frantically for something to hold onto and nearly lose my grip on the pistol.

I kneel on the platform, panting.

Reholster my pistol and resume my trek. As I ascend the final floors, the music grows louder and more distinct.

At the top of the final floor, the staircase winds into a cement enclosure. A narrow stairway that reminds me of those underground storage spaces every restaurant in NYC has. I sit down on a step and catch my breath for a moment. Or rather, try to catch my breath, but I'm exhausted. Totally spent. Light-headed from exertion.

I'll bet I'm the first person to ever take the stairs all the way up here.

I unbutton my khaki shirt and toss it off into the night. Watch it flutter in the breeze then disappear from sight.

I close my eyes. Breathe through my nose. I know the song seeping from the floor overhead. It's from the early nineties I think. Don't remember the name or artist, but recognize the overplayed chorus: *Where were they going without ever knowing the way?*

I can't wait any longer.

I follow the stairs up as they wind into a room.

I frown, confused. This is not what I expected.

I'm in a sort of cramped, cheap-looking space, filled with metal cabinets holding trays and dishes. Linoleum floor. Pans hang everywhere. An eight-burner stove, industrial-style compact oven. A huge grill.

A kitchen?

What the fuck?

The music is coming from the adjacent room. I wind past a second grill, a row of deep fryers, until I spot two swinging, saloon-style doors. Bright light leaks through the slats. I approach the doors slowly, then kneel and peer into the next room.

The scene before me takes the wind out of my body.

I'm looking at an exact replica of the Rocky Mountain Bar and Grill, where we interviewed Elaine. Where Becky Carlson used to work. The floor is checkered black and white tile, a bit shinier than I remembered. The upholstered bar stools are the same dark green. The glare from the lights the kind that will sober you up at any time of night. The music is coming from a CD deck resting on the bar. There's the cubby with all the board games, framed dollar bill behind the bar, same tall glasses for making old-school soda drinks. The only notable additions I can spot are a bunch of shiny instruments of torture, collars and whips, hanging on the coat rack near the entrance.

Oliver Vicks is seated in one of the booths next to the window. The front of his white cloak is open–the most lethal man in the state is wearing a purple paisley shirt while munching on greasy French fries. Standing over him is Becky Carlson, wearing a horrible, pleated green waitress uniform, with a name tag on the lapel. She's holding a yellow notepad in one hand and a pen in the other. Resting on the bar, I note, are a wax mask, white robe and the silk bag holding the books. In front of him on the table are writing implements and what must be some new literary undertaking. They're unaware of me watching. Over the next song that's come on—something by Christina Aguilera, Oliver is ordering:

"And I'd like sour cream on the side. As usual."

I turn away from the swinging doors and try to think. Without even realizing, I've un-holstered my gun and am gripping it like I'm hanging over an abyss.

Think, Frank. Think, you fucking dumbass.

I can't kill Oliver until I know how to unlock the collars on Mindy and Courtney.

So, what . . . burst in with the gun and demand he tell me?

Will never work. He knows the same thing I know—I have no bargaining power. I need to create leverage.

Slowly turn back to the scene on the other side of the wood slats.

Becky is finishing up the order, voice almost indiscernible in the shadow of Christina's powerful vocals: "Anything to drink?"

Oliver smiles.

"Just ice water."

"Okay."

"Thanks so much. I love you."

I think she hesitates ever so slightly.

"I love you too," she replies softly, tucks her notepad into her pocket and walks toward me. I scramble to hide, but there's no time. She gently pushes through the swinging doors, into the kitchen.

I quickly put a finger to my lips. But she doesn't even seem surprised to see me. Her eyes register only confusion. I don't think she recognizes me. I peek through the swinging doors, see that Oliver is preoccupied with writing.

"Hi," I whisper. "I'm Frank. Lamb. I was at your apartment . . . we brought you croissants and muffins."

This last bit seems to register with her. She nods slowly. She seems neither pleased or upset to see me, just totally disoriented by what's going on. Her breath is awful, like catnip and stale licorice.

Heroin smoke.

She's only half here.

"I can help you," I whisper. "I can get you out of this."

The skin on her face seems to tighten. She says nothing.

"Do you know where he keeps his keys?"

I take a step toward her and she flinches, like a dog that's used to getting kicked.

"Becky," I say, and spread my arms. "It's okay. I'm not going to hurt you."

Then I take another step toward her and again she recoils. Her body is silently quivering, like she's being lightly electrocuted.

"Becky, do you know where his keys are?"

"I've never . . ." she whispers. "I've never seen any keys."

I dash back to peek through the wooden slats on the swinging doors, see if Oliver has noticed anything awry. He still appears absorbed in his work.

I try to slow my breathing. A weak plan starts forming in my head.

"Do you have any papers in here?" I ask her. "Not the notepad. Like full-sized pages."

She blinks slowly at me, and shakes her head.

I scan the kitchen. Freezer, double sink for dishwashing, prep surfaces with storage space underneath, grill, deep fryer. Higher up on shelves are grilling utensils, oils . . .

The sink. Maybe.

I drop to the grimy tile floor and open the cabinet beneath the sink, part of the unit. It's totally empty, nobody bothered to replicate the contents of the actual Bar and Grill. Except . . . yes. Still taped to the top of the cabinet space, wrapped in plastic, is the user manual and warranty information. I tear it out and rip off the plastic.

The sink is made by something called Lincoln Manufacturing, and will have to do. At least the pages are clean and crisp.

"One more thing," I tell her. "Can I see that pad and pen for a second?"

She slowly hands them to me.

"I'm going to write you a note. If he kills me, bring this to Elaine, at the grill in Colorado Springs as soon as you leave here for the week. Alright?"

Her blue eyes tremble. She dutifully nods.

Elaine,

 This is from Frank. PI who visited a few days ago. Call the police and tell them that Nathan Heald, the warden at SCF, is Oliver Vicks's fake name. He killed Rico Suarez, Courtney Lavagnino, Mindy Craxton, and me, Frank Lamb.

 Please call my daughter, Sadie: (777) 418-2902 and explain what happened to me.

  F

I tear the note off the pad, fold it and give it to Becky.

Tuck my Glock into the back of my pants, take a deep breath, and walk into the ersatz Rocky Mountain Bar and Grill, carrying the user manual in my right hand.

Oliver Vicks looks up from his writing immediately.

"Son, why aren't you at the communal meal! You know you aren't permitted in here—" He doesn't immediately recognize me. But then he pushes his thick bifocals up onto his forehead to reveal the horrible whites of his eyes. Even from across the length of the restaurant they're jarringly pure, like polished ivory. "Frank!" he cries with something like delight. "Frankie Lamb. Wait, don't tell me you walked all those stairs . . . ?"

"I did," I say, voice cracking. "Every last fucking one of them."

He winces. "Don't use that language here, Frank. This is a sacred space." He gestures to the booth across from him. "Come on in. Sit down and we'll talk like civilized people."

I take two steps closer. A thin stream of bile rises in my throat. My hands are shaking as I ease myself into the booth across from Oliver Vicks.

Sophnot.

"Well." He smiles. "It doesn't take a lot of imagination to figure out why you're here."

I say nothing. Try to stare at his forehead. Bite my lip too hard and taste warm blood in my mouth. He keeps talking.

"Frank Lamb . . . Lamb of God, the sacrificial lamb. You had to know I wasn't likely to just agree to let you and the two prisoners downstairs walk out of here. You had to know that the second you walked in here I was likely to slice your throat."

He flicks the middle finger of his right hand, and a gleaming blade the length of a steak knife shoots out from the wrist of his white cloak. He has some contraption attached to his forearm, much like the ones on his collars.

"Do you have a dart in your cheek? Like Courtney?"

I blink. I nod my head slowly, then open my mouth, pull back my lips and peel the dart from my gum. Put it on the table between us.

He cocks his head at me and smiles. His eyes seem to whiten. They're the color of stars.

"Gun?" he asks, seeming genuinely curious.

"Yes," I say, pulling the Glock out and showing it to him. "But I'm not here to kill you."

He fixes his white eyes on me. They seem to be scanning me on a wavelength I can't perceive, like an MRI probing me for deceit.

"Of course you're not here to kill me. You're smart enough to see that's a waste of everyone's time. Becky!" he shouts to the kitchen. "I'm starving!"

He looks back at me.

"The service here is terrible," he says. Then he takes the blade protruding from his sleeve, clenches his bicep, and appears to stab himself in the heart. His paisley shirt tears, and I see the steel disappear into his flesh. He grimaces in mild discomfort, then swiftly pulls the knife back out and slams his hand back on the table. His shirt is torn where he stabbed, but no wound.

I can't feel my legs. Try to appear unimpressed, try to process the visual trickery I just witnessed, but my face must betray my shock.

"I have seen the day of my death, Frank." A toothy grin. He picks up one of his French fries and waggles it at me. "I've seen it. These little guys here, they'll be the end of me. Not a knife, not a gun . . . saturated fat." He tosses the fry in his mouth and gnashes it. "But until that day, I have nothing to fear. *You* on the other hand"—he spreads his palms helplessly—"I'm afraid this will be your last Sabbath here on earth. But you must have known that when you walked in here. Unless you really are as boneheaded as old James says. And, well, when *James* says someone is bone-headed I mean . . . you wouldn't believe how little he argued when I told him to cut off his balls. Would you believe—I didn't say anything about the pecker! He just took the initiative." Oliver shakes his head, chuckling, getting a little lost in thought.

I take a deep breath. I can feel my pulse in my neck. I set the pistol on the table, beside my dart. A gesture of good faith.

"I came up here to make a deal with you," I say.

He purses his lips.

"A deal? Okay. I like deals. What were you thinking?"

I glance outside the window to my left. Can see the dark outline of one of the prison dormitories and the admin building. Beyond, headlights of lone cars on the highway. Feels a bit like we're in the space needle, but Seattle has disappeared.

"Sampson gave you four million in fake unregistered stock certificates," I say. "I'm guessing you needed all forty-eight million for construction costs on this tower. So I suspect you'd be interested to know where the four million of actual certificates are. The ones he kept to himself."

I squeeze my thigh under the table to confirm it's still there. I'm sure that forty-eight number he asked for was no accident—he figured out that that was the maximum Sampson would be able to get for him. So it's certainly plausible that Sampson has another four lying around.

The black pupils of Oliver's eyes go still, trained on me. I toss the user manual onto the table.

"I have the other four million in certificates. I took them from Sampson. Here's one of the investor materials included when he bought them. Explains the legal limits of unregistered stocks, rights and so on, including how illegal it is to transfer or sell them. And there's a place where Sampson had to sign for reading all this info on page twenty. Clearly shows that he purchased the full eight million."

His eyes narrow. I slide the manual toward him: *Take a look.*

"Obviously I didn't bring the four million with me," I say, trying to stop my voice from wavering. "I'm not *that* much of a bonehead."

Becky interrupts, bursting through the swinging doors, bearing a heavy tray that I can't believe her wispy frame can support.

I welcome the distraction, but Oliver doesn't look away from me as she unloads a charred steak, an extremely healthy side of sour cream, and a refill of greasy fries.

Oliver doesn't touch the papers. Instead unrolls his green cloth napkin and tucks it into the collar of his paisley shirt, and smiles at Becky.

"It looks delicious, thank you," he says. "I love you."

Becky smiles and then bends over and pecks his cheek.

"I love you too," she whispers.

My stomach roils as he reaches up and strokes her wispy white hair.

"Did you forget something?" he asks.

"The ice water," she says softly. "Sorry."

"No problem, but hurry. It was *hot* out there. Especially when you're wearing as many layers as I was," he laughs.

Becky gives a cursory smile, then trudges back to the kitchen.

"Well, Frank," he says, as he takes a dollop of sour cream and swabs it over the top of his French fries. "Guilty as charged. I'd love nothing more than another four million dollars." He takes a nibble of steak, then a few more fries. "So?" he asks, as he repeatedly dunks a single french fry, until it's little more than a delivery mechanism for a huge glop of sour cream. "How am I going to get this money?"

"You let the three of us go. I'll go get the money and bring it back to you."

He rolls his eyes.

"That sounds a little dubious."

I force myself to stay silent. Wait for him to make a counter-offer.

Oliver focuses on his steak for a moment, cutting off a blackened bite, stabbing it with his fork, and rubbing it in gravy.

"Is it true?" he asks. I nearly lose control of my bladder. "Do you really play backgammon?'"

"I'm sorry?"

"When you were in my office on Wednesday, you said you were a backgammon player. Is that true?"

"Yes," I say. "I play."

"Me too," he says. "What I like so much about the game, unlike other gambling games like poker, is that there are no secrets. There are no hole cards. No informational disparity. Both players can see precisely what's happening. The skill is in how you perceive what's right in front of you." He cocks his head at me. "I'm a *very* good backgammon player," he says, and smiles. "And I'm not entirely sure I believe you."

My stomach goes cold.

"It wasn't hard to get them," I say, heart screaming. "I was staying in his house. He had them in his office."

"Mmmhmm . . ." He crams a handful of fries into his mouth and chews thoughtfully. "Yeah, I just can't shake the feeling that you're wasting my time here, Frank. I think we might be done here."

"I'm telling the truth," I say. And point over his shoulder to the homemade collars hanging on the coat rack. "Put one of those collars on me and send me out to get the money. I'll have to come back here for you to unlock me."

He raises a bushy eyebrow in surprise.

"Interesting," he says. Mulls this for a second. I hope he's thinking that he has nothing to lose. That I'm even dumber than he thought.

Maybe I am.

"Alright," he says.

He stands up from the booth and turns his back to me. He's wearing jean cutoffs under his unbuttoned robe. I search for the outline of a set of keys in his back pockets as he walks to the coat rack near the diner "entrance"–in this recreation the glass door leads only to the warm evening. Don't see any bulge in his pants. Off the rack, he picks up one of his homemade collars.

Returns to the table and plunks it down. It's a variant without the heretic's fork, but the lock mechanism appears to be the same as the ones Courtney and Mindy are wearing: those two holes on either side of the collar.

"There's no prongs," he explains. "Wouldn't want you to accidentally kill yourself before you get the money."

"And if somehow I don't get the money, Courtney and Mindy will end up like Rico?"

Oliver pauses for a moment, then shakes his head slowly.

"No, no, no . . ." he says. "They should be so lucky. What I did for Rico, that was an honor for him. He did more or less what I wanted. I immortalized Rico. He'll live on forever, on the twenty-second floor of this tower. Those people downstairs . . . their deaths will be strictly sacrificial. To show the one we once called God how delicate his creations are. To show that, without my great *kindness*—" He's starting to sound upset. "Without my *love* for you, death is a finality that the one we once called God cannot prevent." He licks some grease off his lips. "Put the collar on and go. You should hurry. It's only a matter of time before they simply won't be able to stop themselves from falling asleep, or their neck muscles spasm and give way. I'd give the girl another three or four hours."

I take a deep breath, maybe the last one for a while.

"Alright."

"Mmm . . ." he says. He does something with his mouth. Makes a weird kind of tic that attracts my eyes, and I realize the collar has been opened, and I missed how he did it. But he's holding the open collar in his delicate hands, and there are no keys in sight. Did he somehow put them back in his cloak already? Some sleight of hand?

"Here Frank," he says, offering the collar to me like a gift. "Put it on yourself."

The way he's holding it, in those tender little drawing hands of his, I see it. The pinky on his left hand is a little crooked. There are no keys. Those two holes are for his uniquely shaped, particularly small fifth fingers.

I take the collar, and hold it up to the harsh fluorescent light. Pretend to be deliberating.

I need his fingers. I don't need the rest of him.

"Frank?" he says gently. "Go ahead and put it on. It's alright."

I drop the collar and snatch up my Glock. Fire three times, straight at his forehead. All three miss to the left, shatter the window at the far end of the dining room. His face is untouched. Warm air gushes in through the hole in the glass.

He smiles strangely at me, like he feels a little sorry for me.

Blood pounding in my ears.

What I just saw is impossible. It must be some kind of illusion. He's using mirrors . . .

Hand trembling, I empty the chamber. Two more shots aimed straight at his chest. Both open up holes in the green upholstery of the faux-leather booth. Little puffs of insulation. He stares at me. The whites of his eyes are like so pure, so shiny. Like an untouched snow.

"So there's no money?" he says.

I drop the empty gun.

"How . . . ?" I say, struggling to find my voice.

"I did nothing," he says. "Maybe the gun is miscalibrated. Or, more likely, you subconsciously don't actually want to kill me. All I know is that I've seen the prophecy. And that's not how I die, no matter how hard you try."

He's messing with my head, somehow. Provoke him. Make him careless.

"My money is on a pill overdose," I say. "After misreading the instructions." I gesture to the papers on the table. "This is the user manual for the sink in the kitchen. I recommend *Hooked on Phonics*."

His face goes beet red, and in a snap second he's out of the booth. I swipe at him with the metal collar, but his speed is astounding for his roly-poly build. Before I can raise the collar for another parry he has both hands curled around my neck. He hurls me out of my seat and the shiny white tile rises to meet my cheek, jarring a tooth loose. I instinctively roll over onto my back so I can protect myself with my legs. He removes a dagger from the inside pocket of his cloak and holds it blade-down. I shove backwards just as he swipes at my groin. He misses the goods, but connects with my right thigh, tearing a strip out of the khaki pants and leaving a bright red gash. I don't feel the cut. Too much adrenaline. He stabs downward again. I catch his wrist with my right hand, and he kicks me in the head.

My vision goes black for a half second, but I keep my grip on his wrist. He kicks again, connecting with my temple, and then he abandons the knife, throws off his cloak—like it's time to get serious—and flips me over onto my stomach.

The white tile under my head smells of bleach. I hear a snap somewhere above me. Vicks has ripped his leather belt out of his jean shorts and fastened it around my neck. My face is pressed into the floor. I try to flip over and he kicks me in the back of the head while he tightens, choking the life out of me. I hear him grunting, both with exertion and satisfaction.

My vision goes bright, and then entirely white. I feel my limbs spasming of their own volition, flapping helplessly against the floor. Feels like my chest is being crushed by a piano, then like I'm at the bottom of the ocean.

The whole world is shrinking. Black creeping into the edges. A very nasty gurgling sound that I'm vaguely aware is coming from my own mouth. Can't feel anything past my elbows—

A sharp clank and the belt around my neck goes slack.

I flop over onto my back, wheezing, trying to gulp down air, can't get it down fast enough.

Oliver Vicks is on his knees beside me, stunned, Becky standing over both of us clutching an empty cast-iron pot.

The air I manage to suck in is so sweet that I gasp for more—

breathe in too quickly—and start to retch. Oliver recovers, shoots to his feet, and throws Becky to the floor.

"You whore!" he screams. "You goddamn whore!"

He kicks her in the gut and she whines.

"After all I've done for you!"

Knives in the kitchen.

I roll toward the kitchen on my belly like a writhing maggot, leaving a trail of blood from my thigh, laboring for breath. I'm just inside the swinging doors when he catches up with me. Grabs me from behind by my hair and throws me forward into a metal cabinet. Some sharp corner catches me in the side.

I fall forward onto my stomach, face-to-face with a drain in the middle of the kitchen floor.

He grabs my hair again, this time pulling me up, and then slamming me onto one of the prep tables, pushing my cheek into steel. A cutting board. In my peripheral I see him select a Chinese chef knife. See the glint of its edge. He pushes my skull in harder, to expose the back of my neck more. I'm a turkey on the log.

I flail, and kick backwards, catching something soft. His grip on my head loosens enough for me to flip around. For a moment we're eye to eye, his blade high over his shoulder, coming down, poised to embed itself in my sternum. I push off the table, move in closer to him to avoid the blade, and wrap my foot around his ankle to trip him backwards. The only move I remember from elementary school Judo. As his balance shifts away from me, I move into a half embrace, flip him around, and shove him forward, submerging his face in the oil in the deep fryer.

A massive sizzle, and flecks fly up and slap against my face.

The hand holding down the back of his head is burning just from proximity to the grease.

There's a horrible smell, burning hair mixed with falafel. His body convulses. My hand is burning so badly from the heat that I can't keep it there, and I have to release.

I stumble backwards as Oliver's hunched form rises from the fryer.

I behold him from behind as he emits a gurgle that's worse than any scream. He flails blindly and turns to face me. His shirt is quickly eroding, and his face and chest look like they're covered in purple boils the size of plump cherries. I see that burning flesh has congealed over his eyes. His words are stifled by a mouth nearly sealed shut.

"I can't see," he says.

I take another step back, out of the range of his groping hands. His face is slick with the oil that's still consuming his flesh. His lips are swollen and look like slabs of pink rubber.

He whines a sound that I think is "Becky."

She's here, at the swinging doors, watching. She emits a gasp of horror.

At the sound of her voice, Oliver Vicks goes into a frenzy, swinging his hands like he's swatting away a horde of invisible flies. He staggers toward Becky, navigating with something like sonar.

"My queen," he groans, through a mouth half-sealed by melted flesh. And then he reaches her and locks her in an embrace. Pushes her into the wall and grabs at her breast. "My queen . . ." I think he's sobbing.

I've lost a lot of blood from my thigh. I can hardly feel my hands, and my first attempt to push myself off the freezer, toward him, fails badly.

"Becky, my queen," he cries—his voice warbled and tremulous. He's pushing into her, like he's trying to absorb her into him. "Bind me! Bind me!"

I find my footing. I make the mistake of glancing down at my thigh wound. It's much worse than I initially thought.

"The last two books . . . They're for *us* Becky." His head is between her breasts, he's screaming into her chest. She's paralyzed by shock, as he grips varying parts of her with increasingly fervent desperation, like he knows it's the last time. "Bound together, *forever* on the top floors."

I cross the length of the kitchen, more tripping than running, propelling myself just by leaning forward, only pure rage keeping me on my feet.

I fall on Oliver from behind, grab his half-burned scalp and take him to the floor with me. I have him in a headlock with one arm. His face, deformed and shiny with oil, is like a nest of pink larvae, or sludge that will someday congeal into lunch meat. He doesn't resist as I tighten the chokehold, and he gradually, quietly, stops moving.

I drop his head and shove his body off of me. Staring up at the ceiling, trying to breathe. My hands are soaked in stuff I don't even want to think about.

Becky crouches next to his body, as if in disbelief. I'm so lightheaded.

Can't go to sleep.

I need to unlock Courtney and Mindy, and get myself to a hospital.

"Becky," I groan. "Help me."

She wraps her tiny hands around my chest and tries to pull me up.

I take the help, gripping her boney shoulder to stand up. I glance down at what used to be Oliver Vicks and wish I hadn't. There's messes and there's *messes*. Someone is gonna conduct the post-mortem from hell tonight.

"I need the sharpest knife in the kitchen," I tell her. "A cheese knife maybe. And ice." She hands me a cleaver. *Even better*. I kneel at the mess and—pretty damn near desensitized to gore at this point—chop off both his pinkies. Fold them into a bag of ice and push myself back to my feet.

The wound on my leg is deep and increasingly worrisome. I'm losing a lot of blood and am way past woozy. I pull off my shirt, and wrap it around the wound tightly to stop the blood loss and maybe help it start to clot.

"The stairs," I groan. "I can't make it down those stairs."

She shakes her head.

"There's an elevator." She takes my hand, and leads me through a door in the back of the kitchen, what in the original layout would have probably have led outside. This one, however, opens into a birdcage elevator. Twenty-four unmarked buttons. I hit the one on the bottom and nothing happens. Becky points to two circular holes beneath the panel of numbers.

I put the icepack on the elevator floor, unfold it and remove the fingers. She takes them from me—I guess she's seen how these work—straightens them out and plugs them into the two holes simultaneously. She's about to hit button for the ground floor—

"Wait," I say. Stumble back through the kitchen, past what's left of Sophnot, through the swinging doors into the dining room. Snatch the silk bag with the books off the bar, sling it over my shoulder, and return to the elevator.

"We might all be able to retire off of these babies," I say. "Let's go."

She hits the bottom button and we begin our grinding descent.

My throat is bruised, and my thigh is throbbing as the adrenaline reserves bottom out. The dry night air as we pass through the unfinished floors feels good. I blink down at my lower body and hardly recognize it beneath the biblical quantities of blood. I think at least the bleeding has slowed under the pressure of the makeshift bandage. Becky folds the fingers back into the ice-pack. Everything smells like grease.

There's a thud, which takes me a moment to realize is the elevator coming to a halt. I'm lying on the floor of the cage. I just want to sleep.

"Come on." Becky's ghostly face glows in the purple light. She's holding Oliver's white hooded robe and wax mask. She took them down with her. "Put these on. Come on."

She tries, feebly, to lift me to my feet. The blind leading the blind.

I crawl up the grated wall of the cage and let Becky slip the white robe on over my bare chest.

She opens the elevator door and takes my hand, leading me under the canopy of red and blue pipes. She has no trouble traversing the disorienting terrain, pulling me along like a sled dog. The space seems so much more ordinary than it did before. I wonder idly if I'd imagined the groaning, the stone pool . . .

At the exit, Becky slips something cold and stiff onto my face and secures it with an elastic band. The mask. She slings my arm

around her shoulder to support me—a knobby walking stick—
and then guides me out onto the platform.

The yard is still empty.

"Hurry," she says. "They're at their meal."

I limp over to one of the two officers. High stakes practice.

His eyes go wide as he sees me approach, clad in mask.

"Father," he gasps. "Please."

I ignore him. Unfold the ice bag to reveal the two pink fingers.
It's only been about fifteen minutes since I severed them—they
still look pretty vital. If they've withered too much, I suspect they
won't work. But surely Sophnot had to leave himself *some* margin
of error.

Oliver opened the collar with the neck facing me. Which
means his right pinky goes in the hole to the *left* of the center.

But which is which?

Fuck.

One looks slightly crooked. Which was his right hand. Right?

I take the two pinkies between my index and thumbs and
gently insert them on either side of the guard's collar. It springs
open easily and the collar drops at my feet.

He gasps, big disbelieving breaths. The relief that rushes over
his face is profound as he lets the weighted ball roll off his lap.

I can hear the faint hiss of breath through Mindy's nostrils.
I spring open her collar and she pitches forward onto her knees.

"Ohhh," she cries, drawing in deep gulps of air. "Ohhh."

Courtney's eyes regard my masked face with something between confusion and fear. Thinks I'm Oliver Vicks unlocking them.

"Should just be a day or two," I say, displaying the severed
pinkies. "Make a simple swap and collect our check, right? Easy
peasy."

I stick the fingers into his collar. It springs open harmlessly. The relief on my friend's features makes me forget my stinging thigh for a moment. He rubs his hands over his neck and throat, like to confirm they're still there.

He looks at the severed fingers I'm holding, tries to ask something, but lets it go.

I let Mindy and Courtney collect themselves while I unlock the second officer.

Becky is gazing at all of us, as if she still doesn't quite believe what's happening.

Courtney crawls over to Mindy and puts his arm over her shaking shoulders.

I limp over to them. "Hey," I say through the hole in the mask, "we have to leave right now." I point across the yard. A few inmates are milling around outside the cafeteria. I lift the robe to show them my gash. "They'll be back any minute. And I don't think I can pass as Oliver for long."

Courtney stands up and helps Mindy to her feet. Her face is badly sunburned, and there's a deep red stripe around her neck.

"Water," she says.

"Just hang on a little longer," I say. "Come on. Act like you're my prisoners."

I leave the two officers groaning on the ground. Guide Courtney, Mindy and Becky down the stairs on the edge of the wooden platform. We're a pathetic procession. Mindy is so weak she can hardly walk, Becky is still in a daze, and I'm limping badly. All three of them are barefoot.

"Hurry," I whisper.

Within ten minutes they'll turn the floodlights back on, and this place will be packed.

We make it to the gate in the chain link fence without being spotted.

"Parking lot," I say. "Hopefully they left the keys in our Hummer like last time."

We follow the dirt path that winds around the admin building toward the parking lot. There are lights on at the front entrance, and at least a few officers there on duty, missing out on the meal. We pass the row of Dumpsters, and spot the Hummer pretty quickly; not many visitors at this hour.

Courtney helps Mindy and Becky into the backseat.

I crawl into the driver's seat and am relieved to see the keys in the ignition. Courtney climbs in and closes the passenger door.

"Can you drive?" he asks. "Aren't you woozy?"

I pull the wax mask down over my face.

"I'll be fine."

Mindy coughs in the backseat.

I turn the car on, take a deep breath, and pull out of the parking lot, following the path toward the front gate.

"Nobody talk," I say, as I roll up at the inside of the closed gate. An officer strides over from the tollbooth, deeply confused by this development. I roll down the window, and when he sees my hood and mask, his face freezes.

"Father," he wheezes, and looks away, as he's terrified of even looking directly into my masked face.

The other officers on the scene approach us, to see what's going on.

"Get back!" bellows a voice I recognize. Sergeant Don pushes his way past the other officers, storms over to the car and pushes the stunned officer aside. But when he sees the mask his own wrinkled features contort into something between fear and disbelief.

"Father," he says, and hangs his head in deference, puts his hand over his eyes. "I'm sorry. We'll open the gate. We just weren't expecting you. I thought there would be another . . ." Slowly he looks back up and removes his hand, as he realizes who else is in the car with me. He still doesn't look at me, but his dark eyebrows arch in confusion as his gaze shifts from Courtney, to Becky, to Mindy. "Father," he says slowly. "These were meant to be sacrifices. I don't understand."

I take a deep breath, ignore the pulsing pain in my leg, and stick my hooded head halfway out the window.

"Don, my son," I growl, as low as I can manage. "I always planned to put you on the twenty-third floor. But if you keep me waiting one second longer, you'll be sacrificed along with these sinners."

My heart stops as Sergeant Don's face runs a gamut of emotions.

"Of course." He smiles and turns. "Open!" he yells.

The first and second security gates spread apart. We're ten meters from freedom.

"Good Sabbath," I say.

"Good Sabbath, Father," Don answers.

I let my foot fall onto the gas and burn metal through those two gates. Don't exhale until we're half a mile from the prison. I pull over to the shoulder, rip off the mask and throw it out the window. I'm hyperventilating.

"Oh god. Oh god," I cry.

"Change with me," Courtney says. "I'll drive. You're losing a lot of blood."

I open the driver's seat and tumble to the pavement. Courtney's pale face appears over me, a full, poorly shaved moon.

"Come on," he says, helping me up. I put my hand around his shoulders as he guides me to the passenger side door. He sniffs.

"Why do you smell like cooking oil?" he says.

"I was just in hell," I say, collapsing into the passenger seat. "You'll be surprised to know, hell looks a lot like a family restaurant."

I close my eyes as Courtney starts to drive. Mindy makes a horrible sound behind me.

"We're going straight to get you water," Courtney says, and his voice sounds far away. "And I can get you hooked up to an IV."

If Mindy responds, I don't catch it. My head is swimming.

I roll down the window and dry wind from the open window blasts my cheeks. The dark hills in the distance rise and fall like the earth beneath them is breathing. I hear a high voice, whether it's coming from Becky in the backseat, or the wind in my ears I can't tell.

"My father, my king."

I OPEN MY eyes and am looking at something I don't quite understand. Swirls of white and brown. For a few seconds I think I'm staring at some kind of amazing coffee cake. And then as my vision focuses I realize it's a water-stained ceiling. I turn my head to the left and suddenly everything hurts: jaws, neck, ribs, back, *thigh*. Feels like I got hit by a truck last night.

Courtney is sleeping in a bed beside me, snoring gently. Light streams in at the edges of the heavy curtains.

"Hey," I say, my voice hoarse. "Hey!"

Courtney sighs and rolls over. Blinks at me.

"Morning," he says. "How's your thigh?"

With great effort, I turn my gaze down to my lower body. I'm wearing a pair of bright white underwear that I don't recognize. My right thigh is swathed in a heavy bandage. I reach down, touch the cut and recoil.

"Hurts," I say.

"Yeah. It's pretty deep. But I cleaned it out really well last night. It's probably gonna hurt to put weight on it for at least two weeks."

"Where are we?" I say. "I don't remember coming here."

"Some motel on the way back to Denver," he says.

"Why didn't we go to the hospital?"

"They would have asked a lot of questions," he says. "And we don't know what the fallout of this is going to be. Besides, they couldn't have done more than I did, short of give you a blood transfusion. But you didn't need that. Mindy is next door on an IV. You can buy the fluid over the counter, you know."

"Becky?" My voice sounds weird in my ears.

"I left her in bed," Courtney says. "But this morning we'll either need to get her to a clinic, or find her some heroin."

I grimace. There aren't many worse things to watch than someone withdrawing from heroin.

I try to sit up in bed, and Courtney throws off his covers and rushes over to me. He's wearing a fresh white undershirt, straight out of the package.

"Whoa, whoa," he says. "Just rest today. You probably shouldn't walk."

I settle back into the lumpy mattress.

"Did you walk into a Walgreens last night wearing a sackcloth?" I ask.

"Walmart Supercenter," he says. "And you'd be surprised how well the cashier took it."

"Can you get me some coffee? And something to eat?"

He yawns and stretches to the ceiling, pulling his T-shirt up to display his convex midriff.

"Okay. I'll check on the girls and be back with coffee in a sec."

He pulls on a new pair of jeans, and sneakers and leaves me alone in the room. I inspect my torso. There's a nasty bruise that extends from my right hip all the way up my side. I poke it and groan in agony.

I rub my eyes and think about what happened last night. The face in the pool, the stairs, the diner . . .

Shooting him five times, point blank, and missing.

I wonder if Courtney tried calling the authorities last night, telling them about what's going on in SCF, maybe omitting some of the wilder details. Doubt anyone's going to believe that an inmate has been running that place for over a decade.

Still not sure I can believe it.

Courtney returns, way too quickly to have gone across the street.

"Where's my coffee?" I ask.

The door slams shut. It's not Courtney, it's Mindy. She looks awful. Face raw and peeling from the sunburn. I see the dried blood on her wrist from where she must have pulled out her IV herself.

"Mindy?" I try to sit up and regret it. "What are you doing. You should rest."

She ignores me, just starts tearing apart the room like a maniac. Flings the dresser drawers open, storms into the bathroom, then back out, and stares at me.

"Where are they?" she asks, voice so hoarse she sounds like the voice-changer Oliver used on the phone.

"Whoa, whoa. Sit down," I say, nodding to Courtney's bed. "You probably shouldn't be walking around. Courtney's bringing us some stuff from across the street."

She drops to her knees and gropes under Courtney's bed. I hear her grunt, and she pulls out the silk bag containing the books, and stands up. When she snatches the keys to the Hummer off the nightstand I grab her wrist.

"What the fuck are you doing?" I ask.

"Let go of me," she rasps.

"Give me the bag. I can't let you—"

With her other hand she picks up the bedside lamp, and brings the heavy base down on my left shoulder. I hear an awful crack, and I go light-headed for a second.

"Jesus!" I scream. My entire arm goes numb and I lose my grip on her. She drops the lamp and heads for the door. I try to roll out of bed, and the movement on my shoulder takes my breath away. It's broken.

"Mindy!" I yell. "Don't be stupid! You think we can't find you?"

She rushes out, slamming the door shut behind her.

Epilogue

"YOU SURE YOU don't want to call first?" Courtney asks, pulling our latest rental car into a metered parking place across from the boarding school.

"I want to surprise her," I say. I check my fresh shave in the rearview mirror. Rub a comb through my hair for the fiftieth time this morning. Rub some lint off of my shoulder sling.

"You look great," Courtney says. "Don't be nervous."

I step out of the car into the brisk air.

"I look like a public service announcement for unsafe working conditions," I say, gesturing with my free hand to my cast, and the cut over my right eye which, seven weeks later, still hasn't healed thanks to a secondary infection.

He locks the car and pulls his new flannel shirt tighter over his skeletal frame. We got enough cash from pawning Sampson's shit to justify a shopping trip at REI.

"What's the plan?" he asks.

"If anybody asks, we'll say we were invited to give a guest lecture on making the wrong life decisions."

We cross the street and walk straight into campus. Don't even have to hop a fence.

It's no Saddleback Correctional Facility.

Yet, I'm at least as nervous as if we were breaking back into the prison. Haven't seen Sadie face-to-face for five years, and since then we've probably only had three phone conversations that lasted longer than fifteen minutes.

Just chill. You're her dad. She loves you.

I think about the first ten years of her life, the two of us in that slummy apartment on the Lower East Side, me dropping her off at elementary school every morning then scrounging for freelance PI work. Can't believe *that* ended up being the golden age.

Courtney and I walk shoulder to shoulder across an immaculately groomed lawn, me trying to fight my limp, Court anxiously scanning his surroundings like this pristine campus is a war zone. We get a few looks from the uniformed kids rushing between classes, but nobody stops us.

It's eleven thirty, so we find a picnic table with a view of the cafeteria and wait for lunch.

"Beautiful facility," Courtney says, surveying the colonial red brick buildings, carefully trimmed hedges, expansive green lawns.

"Nice to know my money was footing the landscaping bill," I sigh. "Thanks for coming here with me."

"Well, you couldn't really drive across the country wearing that." He motions to my sling. "And it's not as if I had a lot of other pressing opportunities."

He taps his fingertips against the wooden tabletop and tries to smile. He's tried to hide it, stay upbeat, but he's nowhere close to forgetting about Mindy.

I pull the comb back out of my sling and brush the hair out of my eyes.

"You're fine," he reassures me.

At noon there's a campus-wide bell, and students pour from the buildings, laugh and shriek their way toward the cafeteria.

Courtney removes a pair of binoculars from his acrylic bag. I rip them away from him before he can use them.

"Are you nuts?" I say. "Are you *trying* to get on the sex offender registry?"

I look from face to face, a little part of me scared I won't even recognize her. They're all wearing the same navy blue, and from thirty feet away I'm not even sure about some of their genders.

But when I spot her, there's no doubt in my mind. I feel like I'm having the air squeezed out of me.

"That's her," I say, mostly to myself, and leap from the bench, bound across the lawn to her, ignoring the pain in my thigh. I push through the pubescent swamp, eyes focused only on the prize.

"Sadie!" I say. "Hey!"

I catch up to her right outside the cafeteria. She's with four friends, two girls and two guys. For a moment I can't talk, just gawk at her stupidly. When I left her she was a wide-eyed kid. Now she's halfway toward womanhood. She's only a head shorter than me, and she holds herself with a sort of confidence she definitely didn't learn from me. Her hair is darker than I remember, and short. A little curly. Her brown eyes though are exactly the same.

"Sadie," I say. "Hey. It's me."

Her friends look between me and her with confusion. She's quiet for a second, then—in that voice I know so well from her answering machine—"What happened?" she says, looking at my cast and the wound over my eye.

"Got into a little tussle," I grin. "But you should see the other guy. Did you get my messages?"

She nods quickly.

"Wait here, I'll be right back okay?"

"Sure," I say. "Sure."

I stand outside the cafeteria while laughing kids swarm past me, a few minutes pass, and then they're all swallowed by the dining hall. I wait outside, in the suddenly silent courtyard. Courtney is sitting at the same bench, observing. I give him a thumbs-up, as I anxiously shift my weight from foot to foot.

My heart leaps as I see someone leaving the cafeteria, and then drops when I see it's not Sadie, it's one of the boys she was with.

"Hi," he says, approaching me, clearly a little nervous. "Um, sorry, Sadie said she can't talk now."

I swallow.

"Should I come back later? After classes?"

"Um . . ." He clasps his hands behind his back. "No, I don't think so. Maybe just call her later or something."

I'm a little dizzy. I stare at him levelly.

"What did she say exactly, champ?"

"She . . ." He hesitates. "She said to tell you not to come visit her here. That's all."

I feel my face tightening. I force myself to nod.

"Are you her boyfriend?" I ask.

He shrugs.

"Yeah. Guess so."

"What's your name?"

"Russell."

"Alright Russell," I say. "Be nice to her."

I can't keep it together anymore. Turn and walk back to Courtney, vision blurry with tears. I collapse across from him at the picnic table, facedown on the wood tabletop.

"Frank . . ." He puts a hand on my shoulder. "I'm so sorry."

I stay facedown for a few long minutes, trying to hide from the world. Finally compose myself enough to sit up and face Courtney.

"I can't . . . ." I shake my head, sniffle. "I have nowhere to go."

He scratches his cheek.

"I know what you mean." Courtney frowns seriously. "It will be okay."

I can't bring myself to respond.

"I suppose what I meant to say is, well, to borrow a metaphor from Senator James Henry Sampson, it could well be that life is a complex, but intentional and perfect, oriental rug. But that pattern isn't visible when you're an ant right on the surface."

"Right," I croak. "Sure."

Courtney has the good sense to shut up for a bit. Folds his arms and stares off into the distance. I close my eyes, listen to the giggling coeds, hissing of sprinklers.

"I'm flying tonight," he says. "You're welcome to join."

I open my eyes.

"To where?"

"To look for work."

I shake my head.

"Sorry Court. I'm done with that shit."

He slowly rises from the picnic table, looks at me, eyes damp. Nods slowly, like he was expecting that answer.

"You looking for Mindy?"

For the first time I can remember, Courtney laughs.

"No, no . . ." He pulls a folded piece of paper, encased in plastic, out of his pocket. "I figure it's only a matter of time before *she* comes looking for *me*."

"What is that?"

"One page." He smiles. "She'll need it for the whole set."

"Guess you're not as dumb as I thought."

He extends a boney hand to me, and I clasp it.

"It was good working with you again, Frank."

"You too."

"If you change your mind," he says, "you know how to reach me."

Then he drops his hand, turns, and I watch his storklike form recede, until he disappears between a pair of red brick buildings.

Author's Note

I TOOK VERY few liberties when it came to discussing content from the Old Testament. There are, of course, subjective interpretations of Biblical events sprinkled in the book—for example, many would disagree that Joseph's character exhibited megalomaniacal traits. However, anything characterized as being textually based is, to the best of my knowledge and abilities, accurate. There is one notable exception: In the scene at the rabbi's house in Denver, Yisroel says that that *Sophnot-Paneah* (or: *Zaphenath-Paneah* as it's more commonly rendered) translates roughly to *concealer of faces* in Hebrew. Although the word *Paneah* is very close to the Hebrew word for face, *Zapehnath* (Sophnot) is an Egyptian word that doesn't translate to anything in Biblical Hebrew.

Acknowledgments

BIG THANKS TO:

My agent Elizabeth Copps—the most wonderful partner a writer could ask for. Additionally, everyone else at MCA including Maria Carvainis and Martha Guzman.

Everybody at Witness Impulse, especially my editor Chloe Moffett, who is always a pleasure to work with, and continues to astound me with her insightfulness.

I'm deeply indebted to everybody who read early drafts of this. I'm fortunate to be surrounded by a group of very talented readers and editors, who have no reservations about telling me when I've made mistakes:

My brother, Noah Rinsky
Maxx Loup
Eric Alterman
Daniel Millenson
Oliver Worth (No relation)
Rebecca Strapp

And a huge thanks to Mom and Dad, my biggest fans.

Want more of Frank Lamb and Courtney Lavagnino?
Keep reading for an excerpt from E.Z. Rinsky's
debut noir mystery:

PALINDROME

Available now wherever ebooks are sold!

Prelude

SAVANNAH AWOKE TO the sound of a faucet dripping somewhere over her head. She felt groggy and her mouth was dry. Couldn't quite remember where she was, and the thick darkness offered no clues.

Her butt was numb. She tried to shift around in the wooden chair she found herself sitting in. Frowned as she realized that she could hardly move. Fingers tingling, mind foggy. She felt drugged, detached from her body, like she was floating above her own head, looking down on herself below.

She took a deep, worried breath, and as the smell of the cellar rushed into her lungs—rank, like damp soil—her heart sank. She remembered where she was. A ninety-pound dumbbell bound to her ankles had kept her prisoner to this chair for what felt like weeks, submerged in the complete darkness of this basement, flitting between terrible dreams and this cold, stale reality.

But something had changed since she'd last been awake. Her face. The skin on her face was burning, like she'd had a harsh chemical peel.

Savannah reached a finger to her cheek to inspect the burns and recoiled in pain.

She gritted her teeth as she lightly brushed her face to inspect the damage. Unfamiliar grooves ran down her cold cheeks, over her forehead and chin. She bit her lip and shuddered as she traced the fresh lines with her fingertips, trying to figure out what had happened to her. She imagined her face looked like the surface of some lonely moon, covered in deep canals and craters.

She dropped her hand as a door slammed somewhere off in the distance—from the same direction as the faucet? Heavy footsteps clomped down stairs, then the door to the cellar groaned open, the ancient hinges protesting the intrusion.

"What happened to my face?" Savannah asked as her captor slammed the door closed. She was surprised at how weak and grainy her voice sounded. Her captor ignored her, was fiddling with what sounded like tools in a plastic bag. "Wait," Savannah realized. "Did you turn on a light? I can't see you. I can't see anything. I can't see."

"I know." A deep, rumbling voice from across the room that reminded Savannah of a lawn mower engine.

"I'm also very thirsty," Savannah said, her voice sounding small and pathetic coming from her parched lips.

Her captor dropped something on what sounded like a table-top. Clanking of metal on metal. More ruffling of what Savannah definitely recognized as plastic grocery bags. Heavy breathing.

"Can I please have something to drink?" Savannah said.

Her captor ignored her again, now occupied with what sounded like a socket wrench. A pipe gurgled over her head. This was the first time this person had lingered here, done anything but drop food or water on her lap. The first time that she recalled, anyways; it felt like her memories were buried in the bottom of a deep well, and every time she tried to summon one, the bucket came up empty.

"Are you feeling totally awake? Alert?" her captor finally asked.

"I . . . guess."

It sounded like items were being taken out of the plastic bag and dropped onto the tabletop. A cold draft from somewhere ran through her hair. Clicking, and the sound of metal on metal— a gun?

"Are you going to kill me?"

"Yes."

Savannah was surprised to find that this answer brought neither fear nor relief. It was simply a procedural footnote in the saga that had been the last few weeks—or months?

"Today?"

"In just a few moments."

"What did you do to my face?"

No response. She settled deeper into the damp wooden chair that she could hardly even feel beneath her anymore. She'd long since given up any hope of moving the dumbbell. Her captor muttered something that Savannah couldn't make out, then stepped close to her. She could feel warm, stale breath on her lacerated cheeks. She struggled to remember what this person looked like, wasn't sure if she'd ever actually seen their face.

"Okay."

There was an unmistakable anticipation in the voice today. Until now it had always been bland, cold, methodical: *Here is your water. Here is your food.* But today her captor sounded almost nervous.

"I need you to listen very closely to my instructions. If you don't pay attention, this will all be for nothing."

Savannah bit her lip so hard she tasted blood.

More heavy breathing. Her captor's breath smelled not unpleasant. Like cinnamon gum.

"I was able to locate your sister."

Savannah's heart fluttered to life for the first time in ages.

"I don't have a sister." The listless lie left her dry throat quivering.

"Her name is Greta. She lives in Manhattan. In a studio on 86th and Amsterdam. She is a financial analyst for a large bank and owns a German shepherd."

Savannah couldn't contain her whimper. The helplessness she'd felt the first days of her captivity—before she'd resigned herself to her fate—returned. She raised a weak hand in an attempt to slap or grasp the captor she couldn't see, but caught only air.

"Please don't hurt her," she gasped.

"I won't touch her if you follow my instructions. Do you agree to follow my instructions?"

Savannah inhaled sharply. "Yes."

"Do you swear to do exactly as I say?"

Savannah lowered her head. "Yes. I swear."

"Good."

Something shuffled near her feet, and again she heard the crinkle of a plastic bag. A wet sound of smacking lips right next to her ear, then a tender whisper:

"When a person dies, their soul departs their body instantly. At the moment their heart stops. They are here one moment and gone the next. But that isn't going to happen to you, Savannah."

It was the first time she'd ever heard this person say her name. It sickened her. The last syllable hung in the stale air between them for a moment. Her captor was panting in her ear like an expectant dog. The faucet in the distance continued to drip.

"Why isn't that going to happen to me?" Savannah finally asked.

"Because of what I've done."

A cold hand suddenly brushed the scars on her face. She could sense a sort of affection in the way her captor traced the lines around her eyes, down to her chin. "My guess is you will have three to five minutes in between."

Savannah's mouth was dry and sticky.

"I don't understand."

"I want to understand where we go after we die. You will die, but you will be tethered, anchored here in physicality. We can only fool them for a few minutes, but that should be more than enough."

Savannah's voice cracked.

"Enough for what?"

The voice seemed surprised. "For you to tell me what's happening."

She heard some fidgeting as the voice backed away from her ear and moved directly in front of her face. Savannah heard two clicks. "This is a tape recorder. Everything you say while your soul is tethered will be recorded. As soon as you see something, anything, start speaking. Describe it. Describe everything you see in as great a detail possible. This is the most important thing. Do you understand?"

Savannah shifted in her chair.

"Yes."

"And if you disobey me, if you intend to spite me by keeping silent, by keeping the secret to yourself, then I will find your sister and kill her also."

Satisfied, her captor rose and shuffled around. Savannah heard what sounded like the clink of glass.

"Please don't hurt my sister," she heard herself saying. "If I don't say anything, it's not because I'm not cooperating. It's because, maybe, because it's not working. Hurting her won't do any good."

No reply. The silence deepened as the faucet in the distance was finally turned off.

Her captor again moved in close and said, "I'm ready. Do you understand your instructions?"

"I . . ." Savannah was crying. She felt very strange. "Yes. I understand."

"Do you have any questions? If you do, please ask. It's important that you understand."

"I . . . Will it hurt? Dying?"

Her captor made a sound that was almost like a light chuckle.

A click as the tape recorder was switched on.

"You tell me."

Play

"LISTEN TO YOUR breath. Inhale all the way, fill your lungs, and then let it out, *Hmmmm*."

The wood-paneled studio is filled with the exhalations of two dozen spandex-clad students—nearly all women, all of whom are either younger than me or just immaculately preserved by years of "practice." The ten-year-old reason I'm here is crouching on the mat next to mine, her eyes closed in fervent concentration, stick-thin arms stretching toward opposite walls in her miniature warrior. At least *she's* enjoying herself. My white V-neck is soaked in sweat, my knees and butt are screaming in pain, and—as anticipated—I feel way more stressed than I did a half hour ago.

". . . down into the tabletop position, and then you're going to slowly touch your left knee to your right elbow."

The instructor folds herself up into a pretzel like it's the most natural thing in the world. The blond woman next to me is a fucking contortionist; they'd burn you at the stake in the Middle Ages for moving like this. I try to jerk my knee up to my chest, forcing it, gritting my teeth, and instead of any sort of profound insight, I'm rewarded with a shooting pain up my back.

Sadie has no problem with any of the poses. Little kids' bodies are like putty, plus they don't really have any awful realities lingering in the back of their skulls while they're trying to stretch: unpaid utilities bills, looming root canals, sexual dry spells.

I'm more or less collapsed now on my mat, wheezing like the little engine who couldn't, almost certainly the person in this room who needs this the most and is enjoying it the least.

". . . We're going to bring it back to downward dog now. Bend your knees if you need, and remember we all have different levels of flexibility and strength . . ."

I'm sure the instructor is addressing this directly at me, but I'm too ashamed to meet her gaze. Instead I focus my attention on my daughter, effortlessly arching her lower back, swanlike. It seems impossible that we share genetic material.

As something snaps in my lower back, I curse the parents of her school friends. Who introduces their kids to yoga in fourth grade? Last week when I picked Sadie up from school she started begging me to take her to a yoga class because all her friends are into it. So I gotta choose between being the stick-in-the-mud single dad who they whisper about at PTA meetings, the one whose poor daughter is missing out on all the opportunities afforded by your conventional healthy-as-fuck nuclear family, or exposing her to this indoctrinating witchcraft bullshit—smug, slender women who think they're the only people on the planet who know how to breathe.

Finally we're doing the only position my creaky body is qualified for: lying flat on your back, chilling. But even now, as we're supposed to be clearing our minds of karmic toxins, I'm thinking about last night, combing through the jacket pockets of a corpse someone threw in a Dumpster behind a Chinatown deli. Hoisting 180 pounds of deadweight onto my shoulders and tossing him facedown onto the cold cement, cutting a line down the back of his sweatshirt with my ceramic knife, other hand clasped over my nose to keep out the smell. Pulling back the fabric with a gloved hand to reveal the end of a two-week-long investigation: a splotchy brown birthmark the shape of a ketchup bottle. Snapping a few pictures to erase any doubt in the widow's mind, then flipping him over onto his back, writing his name, address and phone number on an index card. I call the cops from a pay phone, tell them where they can find the guy, then head over to his widow's house both to deliver the bad news and collect my fee—*I promised to find your husband, sweetheart, didn't say anything about what condition he'd be in.*

Not my fault that he was a bad high-stakes mahjong player but didn't know it. Or at least didn't figure it out till he owed enough to buy a small house in the Poconos.

"Dad, come on. It's over."

Sadie is standing over my heaving form, her pink face expressing both gratitude and sympathy. I sit up with a grunt. Around us, flushed coeds roll up their mats and talk about which juice bar to go to.

"Did you like it?" she asks as I follow her to a wall of wood cubbies and squeeze between a skinny woman who's positively glowing and a sweaty man in a wifebeater to retrieve our clothes.

"It was alright," I tell Sadie as I hand her her coat. Before handing Sadie her backpack, I covertly remove my Magnum from the side pocket and tuck it into my waist. Was starting to feel naked without it. "A lot of it hurt, to be honest."

"That means you need it!" she says seriously as we get in line to exit. No way to avoid the instructor, who is standing by the door with a tissue box for donations. I force a smile and drop in a five—if I just think of these classes as a self-serve S&M dungeon, I guess it's sort of a bargain.

I hold Sadie's hand as we walk down the staircase, past a flurry of glistening women too young for me to even think about in a sexual way. At this point it's just painful. They do smile at Sadie though and even grin at me when they realize the nature of to-day's masochism session. I'm no longer a creepy, groaning, forty-five-year-old guy in their eyes. I'm a daddy.

"Can we get ice cream?" Sadie asks as soon we burst out into the brisk January afternoon. St. Marks Place is momentarily jar-ring after the calm of the studio: teens loitering in front of head shops and tattoo parlors, impatient taxi drivers honking to no avail, tourists taking pictures of storefronts I've never even both-ered looking at.

"It's too cold for ice cream," I protest, even as Sadie's tiny gloved hand pulls me toward an admittedly enticing dessert spot across the street. The line extends all the way outside. Better be good.

"How can it be too cold for ice cream if I want it?" she replies.

I drop her hand to inspect the dwindling contents of my wallet and curse to myself. Costs twenty dollars just to leave your apart-ment in this city, triple that if you have a kid. I have only four bucks left after that gouging at the yoga studio. They better take cards. I look up, and Sadie's already sprinted across the street and gotten in line.

"Sadie!" I say and barrel after her, squeezing between the bum-pers of two taxis. I wedge beside her in line, ignoring a dirty look from the orange-faced guy behind her. I grab her shoulders and stare into her wide eyes. "You can't do that. There's too many people around here. I could lose you."

She shrugs and looks away, cranes her neck trying to get an advance view of the selection of artisanal flavors.

"I can't see," she complains. "Pick me up."

I grip her skinny hips through her puffy green coat and, with a grunt, heave her up onto my shoulders so she can see over the line. My first involuntary thought: how light she is compared to last night's dumpster corpse. I try to push that from my mind.

"See anything good?" I moan, my shoulders and arms still shaky from the yoga.

"I don't know. I don't know what they taste like by just looking."

I roll my eyes and lower her to the ground. Within moments, Sadie is rocking back and forth impatiently. The line is moving glacially, each client appearing to take at least six or seven samples, nodding seriously as they taste, mulling each one over, discussing the flavors with their companions like they're philosophy dissertations. Sadie looks tormented.

"How was school today?" I ask, trying to distract her.

"Fine," she shrugs, not taking her eyes off the distant dessert counter. To her it must seem we're an eternity away. Everything is so black and white at her age. Right now she's in hell—is there anything worse than waiting in a stagnant line? And once she gets the ice cream: total, unadulterated bliss. Maybe it's silly, but I envy that feast-or-famine mind-set. Certainly better than middling in the neutral nether-zone. If my life were a food, it would be bland grey pudding, sweetened only by a touch of Sadie and the rare occasion when a client pays me on time.

"Fine? Did you learn anything cool? Besides what all your friends are doing?"

"Nah."

The line inches forward as a satisfied young couple peels off from the cashier and leaves the shop, sharing a grotesque mound of chocolate ice cream piled tenuously atop a waffle cone. Another man a few spots ahead of us throws his hands up in exasperation and storms off, giving up.

"What are you gonna get, Dad?" Sadie asks, jumping out of her skin.

"Nothing. I told you, it's too cold for ice cream."

"I think when you see the ice cream up there you will change your mind," she says.

"Nope."

"You don't know. You don't know what you'll feel like when you see the ice cream."

"Yes I do," I say. "I've been around ice cream before."

Sadie rolls her eyes and sighs, like *I'm* the child.

"You think you know everything, Dad. You know a lot, but not everything."

I'm probably not supposed to let my daughter speak to me like that, but then, I probably won't be winning any parenting medals anytime soon either.

It takes fifteen minutes to reach the pearly gates. Saint Peter is a slightly overweight redheaded boy wearing his corporate baseball cap backwards. His pitiful rebellion. He stands slouched behind his array of gourmet offerings, his vacant eyes not exactly conveying pride in his work.

"Next customer," he grunts wearily.

Sadie takes a moment to scan the brightly colored flavors until she fixates on a bucket of pink.

"Can I taste the strawberry oatmeal cookie?" Sadie nearly shrieks.

Glassy eyed, the boy diligently scoops a tiny sample onto a plastic spoon and hands it to her. Her eyes go wide when she sticks it in her mouth.

"I want that!" she declares.

"Are you sure you don't wanna try anything else?" I say. "We waited so long."

"Nope. I like that. That's what I want."

"You heard the lady," I instruct the employee. "A small strawberry oatmeal cookie in a cup."

"Cone!" insists Sadie.

"No. You'll drip it all over yourself. Cup," I assure him.

I stare at Sadie's exuberant face as the boy readies her dessert. She looks like she's gonna burst.

"This is the best part," I tell her. "The anticipation. It's always better than the actual thing."

"No it's not."

"Six bucks," says the boy, the cup of pink ice cream visible beside him behind the glass display.

"You take cards?"

"Cash only."

"Jesus," I mutter to myself and open my wallet, pantomiming surprise when I discover my four pathetic singles. How the hell is that not enough for a small cup of ice cream? I summon an exasperated look—it doesn't take much—and hold out the four pitiful bills.

"I have four," I say. "I'm sorry. Is that alright? I'll come back later and bring you another two."

The boy looks confused. "It's six," he states.

"I understand. But I only have four. I'm sorry. I'll come back later with another two."

Sadie is wearing a mask of horror as the possible implications of the situation become clear to her.

"There's an ATM across the street," he says.

"Alright. Can we just have the ice cream now though? I don't want to wait in line again. Then I'll run across the street and get the cash."

"Uhhhh . . ." The boy's mouth is open slightly; this sort of decision tree analysis is way beyond his job description. "Sorry, it's six bucks."

Sadie's upper lip is trembling. Jesus. I bite my lip and lean in close to him. My daughter is not leaving here without her ice cream.

"Listen to me carefully, you shit stain," I whisper. "I want you to look down, through the glass, at my waist."

Confused, he obliges, and first squints, then recoils when he understands. The silver butt of a .38 Magnum is protruding from my belt line.

The color drains from his face.

"W-w-what the fuck, man?"

He nearly shoves the cup of ice cream at me.

"Take it, man. Fucking *nut job*."

I smile and hand him the four dollars.

"Thanks, we'll be back in a second." I give the cup and a plastic spoon to Sadie and watch her face light up as she takes a monstrous bite. The boy is still staring blankly at me, terrified.

"That's fucked up, man," I hear him mutter.

Maybe I should write a parenting book.

I take Sadie by the hand and pull her out of the ice cream shop into the busy sidewalk before the kid can gather his wits. It occurs to me that while I fully intended to bring him his money at the time, it would be really awkward at this point.

We walk to Washington Square Park and find a park bench where Sadie can plow through her ice cream with abandon. I can't help feeling a little satisfied.

The case of Frank Lamb and the overpriced artisanal ice cream: closed.

My phone starts vibrating. Must be the widow. Probably can't accept the finality of last night's revelation and wants me to play therapist.

Nope. Blocked number.

"Hello?"

"Is this Frank Lamb?" It's a woman's voice, but not the widow. Deep and silky.

"Last time I checked."

"I'd like to hire you," she says as Sadie scrapes the bottom of the cup.

"Let's talk. You're in the city?"

"Yes."

I try to imagine what the woman on the other end looks like and have a hard time even getting started.

"Whereabouts? I could swing by your office or home or whatever."

"I'll come to you."

I sigh. "That's fine. I should caution you though, I work out of my apartment. But I assure you I'm the consummate professional when it comes to—"

"I'm actually calling because I hear you have a tendency to be unprofessional."

Oh boy.

"Alright. 247 East Broadway. I can be back there by five. That work?"

She's already hung up.

***

I'm a private investigator, but that's vague. My job is getting things for people. It never fails to surprise me how many people want things: A woman wants a gold watch—an heirloom—back from her estranged brother. An insurance company wants evidence of fraud. A dirtbag wants the money another dirtbag owes him, plus maybe the dirtbag himself. A lawyer wants a reason to disqualify a juror. A half-senile man realizes he threw out papers with his Social Security information, pays me three grand to follow the trash, protecting an identity that's not worth stealing.

I never ask why they want it; I just get it for them and collect my bounty. This has nothing to do with professionalism. I'm simply not interested. I have my life with Sadie and my job as a retriever, crawling through the grease that lubricates the gears of society to recover ideas, objects, evidence, people. I usually loathe my clients, but it's a loathing born of fear—that if I crawl around in this muck too long, I'll be absorbed by it, dragging Sadie down with me.

I used to think more about how I ended up here—examining Dumpster corpses, snapping pictures of adulterous trysts, manipulating the truth out of low-ranking drug mules—but it's proven to be an exercise in masochism. Looking back, it feels like I never had a choice, like the river of fate just pushed me here and I never bothered resisting the current until I was in too deep. I went to law school because people always told me I'd be a good lawyer, but I took leave after a year and a half, when my mom got sick, and never went back. Worked as a bartender for a few years until someone offered me an entry-level marketing job. Was promptly fired after deciding I was smarter than my boss and explaining my reasoning to her, sprinkling in some admittedly unnecessary commentary on her appearance for flavor. Went back to bartending and started taking night classes at cop academy, figuring at least I wouldn't have to work in an office. I figured wrong and spent a miserable four years filling out paperwork and biting my tongue in the 21st Precinct. Then Sadie fell into my lap, and I saw an opportunity to make a move: private sector. Be my own boss, work my own hours, make a name for myself.

It took three months before I got my first job, a referral from a detective I was friendly with. An insurance fraud investigation, fairly basic PI stuff. A Wall Street quant's Upper West Side town house burned down two months after he took out a well-above-market policy on it. Smart guys think they can get away with anything.

It didn't take long for things to get ugly. Turned out he stopped showing up at work shortly after the "accident," and not even his wife knew where he went. Comes out he had a real bad coke problem. Burned through a six-figure salary, then started buying blow on margin. Give the guy credit—he had the foresight to see where this was headed, and the patience to wait two months before torching his home and ditching his wife and three kids.

Took me a week to discover that the quant was still in touch with one of his coworkers, a weak-willed man who broke down as soon as I asked if he knew about the fraud before it happened, which would make him complicit.

I found the poor quant in a motel room upstate, shades drawn, shaking under the covers, thin streams of blood pouring from his nose. Just waiting for someone like me to put my shoulder through the door.

When I told him I was a PI, he knew the gig was up. Blew his brains out, coating the still life behind the bed with what looked like Bolognese sauce. First time I'd seen anything like that. I fainted.

That's when I got the first inkling of what I'd gotten myself into. It was going to be an ugly life; that would be the price I'd pay for self-employment. Didn't have the prescience to just get out then. Insurance company recovered the claim and offered me another job, paying me double. I didn't like snooping, but apparently I was pretty good at it.

Most of the time—assuming *someone* knows the location of the mark—my job is comprised of two easy steps: Find the person who knows where it is, and then make them tell you. Sometimes they can't wait to get it off their chest, and sometimes you gotta beat the piñata to get the candy. Every person holds their knowledge behind a combination lock, and in eight years of this shit, I have yet to meet a combo that doesn't consist of some mix of fear, trust and greed.

***

The downstairs buzzer goes off before I can get my place anywhere close to clean. The kitchen is strewn with evidence of last night's culinary fiasco—a "Mexican casserole" I whipped up after paying the babysitter, which Sadie correctly diagnosed as nothing but salsa, canned beans and cheddar poured over corn tortillas and microwaved.

"It's so bad that you're not even eating it!" the little empress said, noting my untouched plate. I just shrugged, didn't explain that the smell of trash-soaked flesh was still in my nose, on my jacket and gloves.

I buzz in my prospective client, then race to my room, rip off an ancient Rolling Stones T-shirt and slap on a wrinkled blue button-down. In the living room, Sadie is on the couch, swimming in one of my old wifebeaters, reading a library book and drinking instant hot cocoa. I should probably be more concerned about her sugar intake.

"Sadie, could you read in your room? I'm sorry, but I'm gonna have a meeting in the kitchen."

"Okay," she says, popping up. "How long? Are you working tonight?"

"I don't think so," I say, straightening my collar. "No open cases. We'll watch a movie or something, alright? Your pick."

"Okay," she says, ducking into her room: a section of the living room I paid someone to wall off a few years ago. She's got enough room for a twin mattress and a dresser, that's about it, but she probably won't mind for a couple more years at least.

A firm knock on the door. My guest scaled those steps pretty damn fast. I quickly assess the apartment as a prospective client might: the mess in the kitchen, clothes coating the carpeted living room floor, Sadie's schoolwork all over the dinner table. If she wants unprofessional, she's come to the right place.

I begin my apology before the door is even open.

"I'm sorry about the mess. Fridays are cleaning day, I swear we have a system—"

My sheepish grin freezes as I pull the door back to reveal a jarringly beautiful woman. I'm rendered momentarily speechless as

I drink her in. Just south of six feet—about two inches taller than me. Auburn hair trimmed to a length that only truly beautiful women can pull off. Wide green eyes, flawless, sharp cheeks. A body with the gentle hills and valleys of a rolling Scottish countryside, evident beneath a tight black turtleneck. She's wearing black leather gloves and red silk pants that hug a breathtaking pair of hips. Her rigid expression reveals nothing more than the fact that she's likely impervious to stupid flirtation, *so don't even try, hotshot.*

"Frank Lamb?" she says, her low voice immediately recognizable as the one I heard on the phone.

"That's what it says on the buzzer." *Jesus, Frank. Stupid, stupid.* "Please come in. You don't have a coat?"

She ignores the question. I beckon her to the dinner table and bid her to sit down in the most comfortable chair I own: a plush art deco number that Sadie and I found on 5th Street. She sits stiffly upright as I sweep Sadie's math homework to the side. There's something almost robotic about this woman. If she notices the mess, she's doing a great job of hiding it.

"Hi." Sadie has come out of her room to size up our visitor.

"Sadie." I turn and force some oomph into my voice. "I asked you to stay in your room and read until we're done."

"It's okay, she doesn't mind, right?" Sadie beams a grin at our guest, the one that usually charms any woman within fifteen years of birthing age, but this target's icy exterior is surprisingly impenetrable.

"Actually, I think it's best if I meet with Mr. Lamb in private," she says.

I give Sadie a glare like *sorry, but you're gonna have to scram, kid*, and she reluctantly retreats back into her room.

"Sorry," I say. "That's my daughter. Like I said, I don't usually meet clients here."

"I love children," she says emptily. "You're married?"

"No."

"Where's her mother?" The question catches me off guard.

"Not in the picture."

"Not in the picture?" Only her sharp gaze tells me it's a question.

"This is getting pretty personal, considering you haven't even told me your name yet."

She frowns, as if she's displeased with herself, like this is a mistake she makes often and is working to correct.

"Of course. That was rude. My name is Greta Kanter."

She doesn't offer me her hand. Her gloves are still on. She's not showing a sliver of flesh below where the crest of her tight black turtleneck hugs her neck. I'm thinking, if she's a leper, then sign me up for leprosy.

"Nice to meet you, Greta. Well, first things first. If you don't mind, I must insist on seeing some photo ID and knowing who gave you my name. Both are kind of standard."

She purses a pair of creamy lips and wordlessly plucks a green leather wallet from some fold of her pants, hands me a driver's license. I copy down the info—taking a little longer than I have to so I can admire a DMV photo that could pass for a glamour shot.

She says, "I got your name from Orange."

Ugh.

I was hired about eight months ago by a Columbia linguistics professor to gather proof that her loser husband was having an affair. She was all but sure he'd been cheating on her and didn't want to give him a penny when she divorced him. It only took two days to figure out that whatever he was doing, he was doing it behind an incredibly sketchy-looking metal grated door on West 59th Street, nestled between an old Polish restaurant and Laundromat. The husband stops a couple times a week in the early evening, buzzes in, then leaves four or five hours later. I figure, too much time for sex, plus I never see women coming or going. Must be drugs or gambling. Finally, after watching this guy for a week, I buzz in myself and wave to the little CC camera. A voice tells me to wait, and thirty seconds later a grotesque fat man in a tan suit materializes from the darkness, huffing from what must be some steep steps, followed by two dudes in sweatshirts, each about two heads taller than me and looking straight out of a Ukrainian mail-order meathead catalogue.

The fat guy is pale, with black eyes sunk deep into his rubbery face. He's built like a 350-pound teapot, and his face bulges and bloats in all the worst places. Gives me a greasy handshake, introduces himself as Matty Julius, but everyone calls him Orange. He's doused in expensive cologne, and I catch the monogram on his silk pocket square. I think he puts in a lot of effort to draw attention from the parts of his appearance he can't change. I also think he might be wearing a toupee.

He explains he's seen me out here taking pictures of his facade over the last few nights, and if I'd be so kind as to turn those photos over to him, he'd be happy to offer double whatever my current employer is paying me. I casually note the size of the rocks on his stubby fingers, think I could probably ask for triple and he wouldn't blink, but explain that I already signed a contract—I'm an investigator, not a mercenary. But he needn't worry; the pictures will never be seen by anyone but my client.

He nods, satisfied, impressed even. I can tell he's one of these guys who takes a lot of pride in being a man of his word. Unbelievable how many dirtbags consider themselves men of honor. He's about to sidle back into his nether-lair when he stops and asks if I have a card, says he's actually in need of a snooper. Especially one he knows won't sell him down the river to a higher bidder.

Matty "Orange" Julius calls me two weeks later. He and his goons pick me up in a black Escalade and drive me around town while he describes the job. He wants me to hunt down a pair of Italians who sold him what he claims is a fake Rembrandt. I say I don't know jack about art, and he replies all I have to know is how to track down shitbags. Cuts me a check for the down payment right there in the car, catches my smirk when I see *Midtown Fitness, DBA* in the upper left-hand corner, and then I'm off, Orange never clueing me in to the precise nature of his apparently very well-decorated subterranean operation.

It was two months before I busted in on the Italians in their recently acquired Miami penthouse, brandishing my Magnum and screaming to drop the prosecco and kiss the fucking carpet. Finding them had required less blurring than straight-up mauling of certain laws. Notably: those against breaking and entering, aggressive interrogation techniques, and whichever amendment preserves an immigrant's right to not be knocked unconscious, bound with duct tape, and hauled back to Manhattan in the trunk of a rented Hyundai with very bad shocks.

"Look," I tell Greta, handing her back her license, "you should know that's not my usual purview. I got caught a little deep in that mess and ended up doing some things I'm not proud of. If you're looking to hurt someone, I'm not your guy. Hurting happens incidentally, but I try to avoid it. And if you want someone *killed*, I'm going to advise you to just turn around, as I'd be legally obliged to report that."

In the silence that follows, I find myself desperately hoping she doesn't take my advice. I really need the work. I try to keep my gaze level with hers, but it's like looking into the sun.

Finally she licks her lips. It's subtle and quick but doesn't escape my attention.

"Nothing like that, Mr. Lamb." She interlocks her gloved hands in front of her on the table, still sitting straight as a flagpole. Maybe she does yoga. "I want you to find something for me. And Orange Julius spoke very highly of your tracking abilities. As for the legality of the methods you employ, I couldn't care less. I care only about results."

I swallow hard. I've never met a woman like this. She's beyond gorgeous, sure, but something about her unnerves me. Her skin is *too* perfect, her wide, unblinking green eyes coldly calculating. It's like aliens created a flawless synthetic human from silicone. She's like a parody of beauty.

"Alright," I say. "I'm listening."

She reaches a gloved hand into her black leather handbag and removes a thick folder. She's about to open it but seems to think better of it and looks at me. The dying January day seeps in from the window behind me, casting half her face in pale, orange light. Her eyes are locked in a subtle—but fierce—glare that, with a little imagination, could be construed as sexual. I try to force that thought out of my head; I've seen guys crush on their clients, and it never ends well. Sure, Sadie could use a mom, but Greta doesn't quite strike me as the nurturing type.

"The first and most important thing to understand, Mr.

Lamb, is that I value discretion. Nothing I tell you can be mentioned to anyone, even if you don't decide to accept my case. Is that clear?"

I've already lost control of this situation. Usually I'm the one laying down the ground rules, telling the flustered client how it's gonna be.

"That's actually very standard with PIs," I say, trying to sound authoritative. "If you'd like me to sign some type of nondisclosure though, I'd be happy to."

"That won't be necessary," she says, then reaches back into her purse and pulls out five crisp hundred-dollar bills. She drops them on the table and slides them toward me, her tightly gloved hand dragging sensuously across my shitty Ikea tabletop. "But I'd like you to have this in advance, as a way of thanking you for not sharing this with anyone."

I can feel my forehead crinkling of its own volition. Five hundred bucks just to keep this quiet? Must be plenty more where that came from.

But I slide the bills back to her.

"I haven't agreed to work for you yet, Greta. But I assure you that nothing you say to me leaves this room." With a smile, I add, "Again, unless you ask me to kill someone."

She frowns but leaves the bills out in plain sight, as if to remind me that they're there if I want them. Then she hands me the folder, grimacing like she's giving up her child for adoption. It's a police report, at least three hundred pages thick, stuffed with typed memos, glossy pictures and court documents.

The front page says simply, *Savannah Kanter. Homicide. 7/21/08.*

"Your . . ."

"Sister," she says. I shift in my chair. Before I can express my condolences, she clarifies: "I'm not asking you to investigate a murder. The case was closed two weeks after her death. The murderer turned himself in and has been incarcerated ever since."

"Okay." I make a triangle with my fingertips and try to ignore the way her chest slowly expands and contracts beneath that tight turtleneck. It's weird that she has a copy of the police report. Detectives' offices will usually give relatives a copy eventually if they ask for it, but the last thing most families want is to dwell on the grisly details. "Then . . . ?"

"I need you to find a by-product of the murder."

By-product?

"Let's start at the beginning," I say. It feels like a feeble attempt to take control of this dialogue. Her unblinking eyes, low breathing, rigid posture . . . She's like a magnet, sending my usually trusty compass spinning. I've never met a person who carries themselves like she does. "What happened to your sister?"

She hesitates, like she's summoning the strength for whatever's about to come out of her mouth next. She's so fucking beautiful. I'm trying to not imagine kissing her but can't help myself. Imagine sliding my hands down her hips, the weight of her heaving form on top of me—

"My family was on vacation. Me, Savannah and our parents. We rented a beach house a few miles south of Bangor. Maine. I was twenty-eight, Savannah was twenty-four—"

This was five years ago, so she's only thirty-three now? I had her pegged for early forties.

"We'd been there for three days, the four of us just relaxing. Swimming and lounging on the beach during the day. Playing cards and drinking at night. We hadn't been together for a while.

My father's job requires constant travel, and he and my mother are always in Europe, Asia—"

"What does he do exactly?"

"Journalist. Writes international news for an English periodical. On day four of our trip we went into town. We got ice cream on the boardwalk and sat down on a picnic bench. Savannah handed me her cone and said she was going to run to the bathroom. She never came back."

She pauses and gazes at the back of her gloved hand. I make a mental note to mention this to Sadie as a cautionary tale—*this is why you always hold Daddy's hand in public.*

"Are you alright?" I ask. "Would you like a glass of water?"

Yeah, that will fix everything. Idiot.

She ignores me anyways:

"For twelve days, nothing. It still seems impossible, given the scope of the search, that we didn't find her. Every hotel in the state was emailed her picture. Police barricades on all major highways stopped cars at random. My father got on the local news and offered a half-million-dollar reward." She smiles emptily. "My parents had money. The police took it very seriously. They found some of Savannah's hairs in a parking lot about a hundred fifty feet from where we were sitting. There must have been a struggle while she was forced into a car. That was all they had to go on."

I'm struck by how impassively she describes all this; the same detached tone in which one might read a dense legal document or narrate a documentary on indigenous Indians. It's been years, so maybe she's just recited this so many times that it's become rote, devoid of emotion, the facts no longer resonant of the horror she must have gone through.

"No eyewitnesses saw her being shoved in the car?" I ask.

"No."

"Identifiable tire tracks near the hair?" I ask. "Anything caught on camera?"

"No," she shakes her head. "Gravel parking lot. Too vague. And we're talking about rural Maine. Not cameras on every corner, like here."

"Okay, so then?"

"Twelve days later a man approached a traffic cop in Portland and said he killed Savannah. He showed him a Polaroid of her corpse and told him where he could find the body. It was there. In the cellar of a cabin seven miles south of the boardwalk."

"Just a second," I say and quickly jump from my chair to stick my head into the living room, making sure that Sadie isn't eavesdropping on this. Kids should learn about murder the right way: on television, when their parents aren't around. I return to my seat. Greta's face is unwavering.

"Why her?" I ask, figuring the answer is that she was as beautiful as her sister.

"The police thought it was because she was small, much shorter than me, and skinnier. She weighed around a hundred pounds. She would have been relatively easy to drag back to the car." She pauses, and then, as if anticipating my next question, adds, "She wasn't raped."

"I don't have much experience with homicide, but I imagine that's unusual."

Greta's nostrils flare. "That is perhaps the least unusual part of the whole thing. She was asphyxiated," she continues. "In court, he explained that he tied a plastic bag around her head until she stopped breathing."

I'm suddenly seized by an overpowering desire for a drink.

There's a bottle of rye on the bookcase, visible over Greta's right shoulder, but it's not even dark out yet, and I'm pretty sure that day drinking isn't the kind of unprofessionalism she had in mind. From the window behind me I hear somebody on East Broadway screaming in Spanish and what sounds like the clattering of a metal trashcan.

"I don't understand what you want me to do," I say, imagining an iced double shot burning its way down my throat.

"You're not very patient, are you?" she asks, without the slightest hint of flirtation in her voice. She speaks slowly and deliberately, mechanically, like someone keeps pulling a drawstring on her back to trigger prerecorded phrases. Images of her in the throes of passion keep trying to burrow in through my ear and nest in my brain, and I keep mentally swatting them away like mosquitoes.

"No, I'm not," I say. "I seriously might have ADD. I hope that's not a deal breaker."

Again, she ignores my pathetic attempt at humor. This reminds me of every bad first date I've ever been on.

Greta grabs the folder back from me. She flips through it for half a minute—I desperately want to ask her about the gloves but resist—and finds a photocopy of an article from a local Maine newspaper. I scan the first paragraph.

"Silas Graham. Even sounds like a murderer. He pleaded insanity?"

"Yes. And it held up."

"Because he turned himself in?"

"There's more. He also confessed to killing his parents twenty-two years before and told them where they could find *those* bodies. Their decomposed bodies were buried in a scrap yard in rural Alabama, identifiable only by dental records. But indeed, it didn't take long to discover that the two of them were declared missing when Silas was around eleven. Silas was taken into foster care shortly thereafter. It took less than two weeks of court time to determine that he was likely a paranoid schizophrenic, and he was committed to an institution for the criminally insane."

That bottle is looking better and better. I'm no prude, but this kind of shit—kidnapped and murdered girls—isn't exactly my wheelhouse.

"I was on the force for a few years before going solo," I say. "In my very limited experience with this sort of thing, the 'criminally insane' verdict is usually indicative of little more than an expensive team of lawyers."

She smirks ever so slightly and flips a few pages deeper into the folder. "Not this time. Look at his face."

I inspect the grainy black-and-white photo she's pointing at for a moment, then recoil.

"Oh my god." I have to look away, the picture is making me a little ill. "Are those burns?"

"Tattoos. All over his face."

Greta continues flipping through the folder and stops at a full glossy. She stares at it a moment, taking in slowly what must be a picture of her sister. She breathes deeply, then rotates it in my direction. What I see makes my stomach tingle with cold. Savannah lying faceup on a coroner's slab. Her face has the exact same tattoos as her killer.

"Jesus," I gasp.

Greta nods and mercifully flips to another page.

"What the fuck?" I ask. "Why would he do that to her, then kill her?"

Her green eyes seem to be staring at something very far away. A siren screams down East Broadway and then fades.

"I've long since given up trying to understand," she says, her words sounding weighed down. "But here's the important thing." She flips to another article about Silas's trial and points to a circled paragraph. "Read," she says.

. . . next to the body was found a Sony tape recorder, a model discontinued in 1992. Throughout the brief trial, Mr. Graham displayed an exceptional willingness to cooperate. The only exception being when asked about the purpose of this device, to which Mr. Graham repeated only, "I made a tape. I made a tape of her dying." When pressed as to the nature of this tape, Graham showed uncharacteristic reticence, shaking his head and occasionally appearing close to tears . . .

I look up into Greta's glowing eyes.

"I want you to find the tape," she says.

I can't contain a snort. "The guy was nuts. He probably didn't even know what he was saying."

She stares past me, out the living room window. Not much of a view beyond the brick co-op towers across the street.

"He knew," she says.

What little willpower I have evaporates. I shoot out of my chair, return with two lowballs and the bottle of rye. Pour myself four fingers.

"Want any?" I ask.

She purses her lips. "No."

I shoot down half of it. Instantly I'm hit with a little hazy relief, and lean back in my chair.

"Alright, so let's pretend you're right. It exists. What do you want with this alleged cassette tape?"

She doesn't respond. Stares unblinking over my right shoulder.

"Greta, if you want me to find this—"

"On the last day of the trial the verdict was read," she starts. "Life in an institution for the criminally insane. I remember his face when this was announced. He seemed relieved—or pleased perhaps. Don't ask me why. As they were leading him down the aisle, out of the courtroom, he stopped at the front row, where I was sitting with my parents, and leaned in close to me. He was so close I could smell his breath—his teeth were rotting brown, and it smelled like he hadn't brushed them for years." The first traces of emotion I've heard from Greta so far. Voice wavering slightly in anger. "And his tattoos . . . he didn't even seem human. His voice was so awful. Throaty and raw."

She stops and looks at me for a painfully long moment. I shiver involuntarily. She seems to be deliberating whether or not to continue.

She says, "He leaned in close and whispered, '*It was worth it. I got what I wanted.*'"

I polish off my rye and have to tuck my fingers under my thighs to resist a refill.

I say, "Like I said, he's crazy."

"He made a tape of her dying, Lamb. That's what he said."

I raise an eyebrow. Greta's face is cracking slightly with emotion. Yet there's something about the way she's telling this story that doesn't quite ring true with me. It seems rehearsed, though that could just be because she's gone through this so many times. But I can't shake the feeling that she's omitting crucial details. And why hasn't she taken off those gloves?

As the light fades outside, Greta's pale skin seems to turn luminescent, glowing like a jack-o'-lantern filled with blue ice.

"Sure you don't want a drink?" I ask, my left leg fidgeting uncontrollably.

Greta doesn't seem to have heard the question. I suddenly remember poor Sadie, sitting alone in her room all this time. She probably doesn't even mind. I got her a bunch of good stuff from the library last week. But she'll probably guilt the hell out of me once Greta leaves.

"So . . ." I finally say, leaning in closer. I can smell her expensive perfume and minty breath.

Greta purses her lips, like she's swishing her next words around in her cheek; tasting them before releasing them.

"I told all this to the detectives on the case. They didn't care. They found the killer, that's all that mattered to them. Why should they care about some cassette tape?"

I shake my head slowly, mulling over the implications of what Greta is telling me. "But . . ." I swallow a laugh of disbelief. "I mean, surely you have to agree the most likely scenario is that it simply doesn't—"

"It exists, Lamb," she spits. Then she suddenly starts rubbing viciously at her upper cheeks, rubbing until I understand that she's scraping away a thick layer of makeup to reveal dark blue circles hanging beneath her eyes. "It's all I can think about. It's out there somewhere. Savannah's last words. And I can't make peace with this until I have it back. The thought of some sicko out there listening to her . . . I haven't really *slept* for five years."

Another long, empty pause. Another siren screams down East Broadway.

"Isn't it possible you misheard?"

"No," she growls, and the sudden shift in her voice makes me jump slightly out of my seat, then try to compose myself. She's growing heated, her face starting to glow pink. "And either he still has it, or he stashed it somewhere before he was arrested. It's mine, Lamb, you understand? He has my sister's voice. Her dying words. Nobody should have that but me."

I'm not quite sure I *do* understand.

"Okay. So suppose I agree to try to find this—"

"You'll start by talking to Silas. He's housed in the Berkley Clinic—a mental institution a hundred miles north of the cabin where my sister was murdered. I'll give you ten thousand up front. And three hundred thousand when the tape is in my hands. Cash. And I'll be able to tell if it's the real thing, because it will be Savannah's voice."

A three-hundred-thousand-dollar bounty for something other than a briefcase filled with five hundred thousand in cash is nearly unheard of. This is it. The holy grail of snooping. This is the stuff PIs dream of. But I summon my best poker face, act unimpressed by her offer.

"I'm guessing Silas isn't going to be thrilled with the prospect of cooperating."

"That's where your unprofessionalism comes in," she says.

"There are guards, no? Loony bins are basically prisons."

"For three hundred thousand dollars, I suspect you could get creative."

This is a lot to process. While my gears are still turning, she sits back in her chair and conveys something with the slightest upturn of her lip that may be flirtatious but reads more likely as disgust. Her smudged makeup does nothing to mar her beauty. On the contrary, the imperfection gives her the slightest air of vulnerability. She glowers at me and lowers her voice.

"And once I have the tape," she says, "you will have me. However you want."

Her face is completely deadpan. Betrays no hint that this is something she would enjoy in any way. It's just another part of the generous compensation she's offering. My poker face is wilting, my heart screaming, pushing blood to every corner of my body. Controlling myself is taking every inch of concentration. Both legs are shaking. She frightens me.

"Ten thousand up front, but another five for expenses," I practically squeak. "And make it three fifty. Only half of that is for me. I'm going to need help."

She weighs this for a moment. "Who?"

My mouth is dry. I can't tell if this thing seizing me is lust or terror. Either way, I suddenly want her out of my apartment, away from Sadie. I clear my throat.

"I had help on the Orange case, never could have done it alone. Courtney Lavagnino is the best tracker I've ever worked with. Honestly, he's a genius."

"Courtney?" She spits his name out like it's bitter. I catch a glimmer of fiery orange in her eyes. "That's a man?"

"He was the brains behind finding the forgers," I gush, eager to change the topic. "He's brilliant. Speaks like seven languages. He once found a ninety-year-old Nazi hiding out in New Zealand, based only on a water-damaged black-and-white photo of him from the war. He worked briefly for the DEA, gathering evidence against drug moguls, but quit because he needed to work at his own speed. He was hired by a hot sauce manufacturer to find a pepper seed—a single fucking *seed*—rumored to grow into the hottest pepper known to man. He found it. If you're serious about getting this tape back, you'll pay for both of us."

She runs a gloved hand through her hair. I want to say she's calming herself down, but really she never actually flipped out. Did she ever even raise her voice? She's able to project this terror just with her eyes.

"Then give me his information. It sounds like he's the one I need, not you."

I shake my head. "If you want to find a truffle, you can't just hire the pig."

She raises an eyebrow. I clarify: "For Courtney, it's all an intellectual exercise. He's a pure tracker—not always a man of action. If you want someone to locate the tape, hire Courtney. If you want someone to *get* the tape, you need both of us."

Greta mulls this over. I sense the additional fifty grand is inconsequential to her if it means a higher chance of her holding the tape in her hands.

"Where was the seed?" she asks.

"In the safe-deposit box of a South American dictator. Courtney wouldn't tell me which one. He was apparently a connoisseur and collector of peppers, bought it on the black market for millions. As I said—he *found* it. I believe he was working with someone like myself, who figured out how to actually steal the thing."

If I'm underselling Courtney's competence in the field a bit, it's more than offset by failing to mention his occasional interpersonal gaffes. He almost derailed our search for the forgers by growing impatient with what turned out to be a key witness, pointing out inconsistencies in that poor, confused girl's story with the callous logic of a poacher doing his taxes. Nearly broke her, and it took me hours of comfort and coaxing to finally extract what we needed out of her.

Greta reaches into her purse and removes a large wad of hun-dreds. Counts them out and plops them on the table.

"Well this time, locating it is not sufficient. I want you to hand it to me. Here is ten thousand up front, plus five for expenses. After three days call me on this number"—she scribbles it down on a page in the police report— "and report your progress."

"Don't you want to sign—"

"No contracts. Just get me the tape. Call me sooner if you discover anything important."

I can hardly stand up to let her out. My legs are trembling, and the tips of my fingers are numb. By the time I manage to pull myself up, she's already out the door, the click of her black boots receding down the staircase. I stare at the pile of money on the table and try to remember if I ever actually agreed to this.

About the Author

E.Z. RINSKY has worked as a statistics professor, copywriter and—for one misguided year—a street musician. He is the author of *Palindrome,* and currently lives in Tel Aviv. More at ezrinsky.com.

Discover great authors, exclusive offers, and more at hc.com.